Her Males

INVI WRIGHT

COMPLETED WORKS

STANDALONES

The Nanny | A Nanny/Single Father Romance
Lord of Dread | An Arranged Marriage Historical Romance
Aine | A Dark Shifter Romance

THE FEMALE SERIES

The Female is a why choose demon romance with a dark dystopian setting, declining fertility rates, captured women, and three irresistible men.

The Female
Her Males
Their War
Chev's Mate
Queens

THE CURSED KINGDOM SERIES

The Cursed Kingdom is a slow burning, why choose romance with a mystical faerie realm, two infuriatingly attractive princes, and high conflict between the faerie and shifter kingdoms.

The Cursed Kingdom
The Shattered Kingdom

TRIGGER WARNINGS CAN BE FOUND ON:
inviwright.com

UPCOMING WORKS

STANDALONES

His Assignment | A Bodyguard Mafia Romance (Coming 2026)
The Dragon's Agreement | A Dragon Fantasy Romance (Release Date TBD)

LAND OF WOLVES DUOLOGY

Land of Wolves is a high intensity shifter romance with fated mates, government indoctrination that leads to painful betrayal, and impending war between the shifters and humans.
Land of Wolves | Part One (Coming 2026)
Land of Wolves | Part Two (Release Date TBD)

ONGOING SERIES

Fates | Book Six of *The Female* Series (Release Date TBD)
The Hidden Kingdom | Book Three of *The Cursed Kingdom* Series (Release date TBD)

STAY CONNECTED

SOCIAL MEDIA

Follow Invi Wright on social media to stay up to date on her newest releases, listen to her gab about romance & fantasy books, get regular book recs, and join a fun community of romance lovers!

TikTok & Instagram: @inviwright

EXCLUSIVE CONTENT & CHARACTER ART

Subscribe to **@inviwright** on Patreon for:

- Exclusive access to ongoing novellas
- Exclusive audio chapters
- SFW and NSFW character art
- Partake in polls (help decide what book she'll write next!)
- A free ebook copy of every book she publishes

THANK YOU

The largest thank you possible to my husband. You gave me the confidence and support to pursue writing, and none of this would be possible without you.

Also, to my Patreon subscribers: Inesha Thompson, Ashleigh Drew, Bhavini, Gigielle, OrangeyOranges, Melissa Childs, Sharon Hartsoe, Maria Anderson, Leilani S., Vanessa Turpin, Verity K, Patience I, Jack Lewis Landsmen, Lone Hornbech Bünger, Dakota Lane, Kimberly Belbot. Your support is the sole reason I'm able to do this, and I can't properly convey in words just how much you mean to me. I hope you enjoy this story!

COPYRIGHT

Editing by: Amy McNulty

Chapter One

CHARLOTTE

I'M IN WAY over my head.

Aziel pushes his dark hair out of his face before grabbing his drink and leaning back in his chair. It's been a few days since he last shaved, and I eye the stubble along his jaw with a frown.

What's he been doing since he parted ways with Gray?

Aziel's black eyes meet mine as he brings the glass to his lips, and I look away as he begins to drink. He never returned home after his fight with Gray, and his absence has most definitely *not* made my heart grow fonder.

Gray sits on my right, and a thin bead of water trails down his neck from where his hair still drips. He'd just gotten out of the shower when Aziel called, and the curly black strands are yet to completely dry. They drip into the collar of his navy-blue shirt before disappearing underneath the fabric, but he hardly seems to notice as he rolls his sleeves up his muscular forearms and glances at Silas.

The Fate is on my left, his thigh pressing against mine, and he's the only one of the three who looks entirely composed. He always does, though, and I swallow past the lump in my throat as his black eyes meet mine. It takes everything on me not to look at the full lips that were on me just yesterday.

Silas shoots me a sly smile, and I mindlessly fiddle with the hem of my shirt before pushing my messy brown hair over my shoulder and turning away.

I tap my foot against the ground and look around the stuffy boardroom we're currently sitting in, my anxiety making me fidgety. I'm not used to leaving the house, and I had no time to mentally prepare for this last-minute meeting.

It's probably not accidental that Aziel waited until the last minute to inform us about it.

Aziel was radio silent for almost twenty-four hours after Gray returned and told us Aziel was going to Envy to speak to Levia, and he didn't reach out until late in the night to tell Gray and Silas to meet him in Envy within the hour.

He said nothing about bringing me, but I'm glad Gray woke me up and let me come along.

I want to be included in this.

Gray drops a hand to my thigh, his touch comforting. He must smell my unease, and I bring my hand to his and squeeze around his fingers as I sneak a glance at Levia.

He's already watching me, and I don't like the look of his cocky smirk as he mindlessly flips through the pages of the female report. It's thinner than the one I found in Gray's office, and I assume Aziel removed anything too incriminating.

Levia shoots me a sickly-sweet smile as he drops his elbows to the table and rests his chin in his hand. His black eyes narrow just slightly as he looks between Gray and me. This is the first time Gray's ever shown me public affection, and I'm sure Levia's heard rumors about our relationship.

Aziel clears his throat.

"Well?" he asks.

Levia continues to stare at me. I'm not sure what I imagined the King of Envy would look like, but this isn't it. He's got the typical black hair and black eyes all the demons seem to share, but Levia is thin and borderline gangly, whereas most of the others I've met have been full of muscle.

He also has this air of awkwardness that's impossible not to notice.

I fight the urge to look to Silas for direction. Our close contact felt awkward at first, considering we still haven't addressed what happened between us, but now I'm grateful.

"Look away from Charlie." Aziel's voice is full of poorly restrained tension. "My female is of no interest to you."

That catches Levia's attention, and my shoulders relax as he finally looks away.

"*Your* female?" he asks, chuckling slightly. "There's no need to continue that lie in here. I have no interest in outing Gray's relationship to Asmod."

His words are met with silence, and the unbearable tension in the room grows.

"Besides, I know you intend to bond with my niece," he continues. "Shay's quite excited."

I grind my teeth as Aziel gives a noncommittal hum and takes another sip of his drink.

"We've long since been allies, Levia, and we'd like your help in taking over the Seekers' facilities and enforcing new regulations across all the realms," Aziel says.

Levia raises a brow and flicks through the pages of the report. He's hardly looked at it, let alone read any detail, and I struggle to understand where his air of nonchalance is coming from. Why go through the effort of setting up this meeting if he's so uninterested?

"Do I look like a fool, Aziel? Do you think my people don't

visit your kingdom and come back with stories of your *regulations*? The ones that have been in effect for the past forty years." Levia spits the word *regulations* like it's burned him. "If you come out with this report, I give it days before word spreads and there's the threat of war against your kingdom. The ogres are looking for any excuse to take you out."

Levia turns to me and leans in. "They hate the Wraths. Always have, always will."

My pulse races as I give a jerky nod. I have a feeling he's only speaking to me to make Aziel mad.

"That's why we've come to you," Aziel argues. "You're close with Mammon, and with both the Envy and Greed kingdoms backing us, there isn't a risk of war. Nobody would willingly enter a fight against the three of us."

Levia sucks on his teeth.

"My people have been suffering, Aziel, and this level of involvement will be draining. Many species will fight back when we try telling them how to behave. If my men each have a wife of their own and a young female on the way, I'm sure they'll feel much more motivated to join your cause. My people need something tangible to fight for, not just an idea."

Gray squeezes my thigh, and Silas places his hand on my other one. This is the first contact Silas and I have had since our encounter in the library, and I fight with everything I have not to react as his fingers dig into my flesh.

"Are you suggesting I give you my women?" Aziel asks.

He sounds pissed, and I fear he's about to lose control as the glass in his hand shatters. Nobody reacts to it, and a shadow smoothly moves forward and begins cleaning up the mess.

"You have more than enough of them."

Aziel waves away the shadow. "My women are not for sale."

I'm relieved to hear that. Aziel may be one of the world's

biggest assholes, but at least he seems to care about his people.

Levia takes a moment to consider Aziel's words, and I bounce my knee as I wait. This conversation isn't going how I hoped. I'm not sure what I thought would happen, but it wasn't Levia suggesting Aziel give away the Wrath women like they're trading cards.

"Very well," Levia concedes. "Give me a few years to get things moving in Envy. Once I see your information is true and we have an uptick in female births, I will help."

Years? With so many already on the brink of extinction, we don't have the luxury of time.

Aziel pinches the bridge of his nose, and I watch him with mild interest. He's more composed than I thought he'd be.

Silas chimes in. "Let us discuss this privately and get back to you."

There's nothing to discuss. If Levia doesn't want to help, we will keep searching until we find someone willing. Men have grown callous around the topic and treatment of females over the years, but I'm sure there are many leaders out there who care.

"Nothing is stopping me from creating a drug that simulates the oxytocin women need," Levia threatens.

I stiffen.

That's precisely why we're here. We don't need help spreading the information—we need help controlling how it's handled. Anybody could, in theory, drug women with the required oxytocin and rape them until they're pregnant with a female. It's what we're trying to avoid, and my blood runs cold as Levia threatens to do exactly that.

"Why don't you go ahead and give it a try?" Aziel's threat is poorly veiled.

I take pleasure in how Levia's throat bobs. He's scared of Aziel, and I like seeing it. Demons are one of the strongest species, and Wraths are the deadliest among them.

"I want five years to begin the rehabilitation process within Envy," Levia says.

Over my dead body.

Gray nudges my shoulder, capturing my attention, and gestures for me to stand. Silas removes his hand from my thigh as I do so, and he turns to say something to Levia as Gray teleports me back to the manor.

My body feels heavy and disorientated as the front sitting room materializes around us, and I squeeze Gray's arms as I struggle to regain my footing. He holds my waist until I'm steady, and I glare at the floor as I try to collect my thoughts.

Gray's patient, and he silently pulls up a chair for me to sit in.

I plop down with a huff before dropping my head into my hands. His feet inch forward before he crouches and peers up at me from between my fingers.

"We'll work on a compromise," he whispers, grabbing my hands and pulling them away from my face. "I promise."

I refuse to meet his eye. Prior to being captured by the Seekers, I'd never been confronted with such intense emotions. My life was nothing more than a series of monotonous days.

I woke up every morning knowing I would eat breakfast in the kitchen, help clean the house, read a book or stare at a wall until dinner, then go to bed. Occasionally, I'd hide in my hole, but even that became monotonous after a while.

Gray runs his hands up and down my thighs. He continues even when Silas and Aziel materialize in the room. Aziel stands in the corner, watching, while Silas crouches beside Gray. My eyes practically bulge out of my head when Silas leans forward and kisses my knee over the material of my jeans. I look at Gray, trying to read his reaction, but he barely has one.

"What's going on between the three of you?" Aziel asks.

Silas stands and turns toward the Wrath. "Charlie's my female," he says. That's news to me. We've hardly spoken since he went down on me the other day, and our few interactions since then have been painfully formal.

Silas takes a step closer to Aziel.

"And where the fuck have you been?" he asks, gesturing around the room. "We're supposed to be a unit, and pulling us into a meeting with Levia with no prep is a fucking *ambush*, Aziel."

Aziel looks confused for about half a second before his stern gaze lands on Gray. "I told Gray I was going to Envy."

Gray stands and turns so quickly that I'm surprised he doesn't give himself whiplash. "You told me you were going to Envy, but you said nothing about not coming home afterward!"

Aziel only shrugs.

"We don't have *years* to wait," I say, eager to discuss that part of the meeting. None of my males pushed back on the prospect of waiting years, and to say I'm pissed would be an understatement.

"We have no intention of waiting five years, my love," Gray comforts, his voice soft. He's speaking to me like I'm a child, and I'm not a fan.

I stand, frustrated, before sitting back down. I don't know how to handle this, and I'm overwhelmed.

"Let's go upstairs and rest. It's late," Gray says, shooting Aziel another pointed glare. "We can discuss this tomorrow morning."

I don't want to postpone this conversation any longer, but I have to admit that it will likely go smoother when emotions aren't so high—especially on my end.

Despite my doubts, I let Gray take my hand and lead me upstairs.

Chapter Two

CHARLOTTE

MY BACK HURTS, and I twist side to side to try to crack my lower spine before crawling out of bed.

It's early, but I'm eager to continue discussing last night's meeting with Gray and Silas.

I'm still pissed by their lack of response when they found out what the issue with the female births is, but I'm willing to put that behind me. It seems like they're genuinely trying to fix things, and I can't be of any help if I'm avoiding them.

I grab a change of clothes from my closet before entering my bathroom.

A small part of me wants to peer into Gray's bedroom to see if he's awake, but I avoid the temptation. I'm scared if he gets me alone, he will bombard me with questions about Silas.

He gets an inch and takes a mile.

I do have to admit he's been good about giving me space these past few days, though. I half-expected him to hammer me with questions about what happened between Silas and me the first chance he got, but he hasn't pried. I'm grateful, and I have no idea how to tackle that situation.

I can't believe I called Silas *my male*, and I'm still shocked that he reciprocated.

After all this time, I thoroughly convinced myself it wouldn't happen between us. Silas made it clear he had no interest in being in a relationship with me, and I'm struggling to understand what's changed his mind.

Fuck, I mean, he's never once treated me as anything other than a slightly annoying roommate. He even rejected me when I first tried to deepen things between us.

My mind continues to race as I step in the shower and wash yesterday's grime off my body. It makes me feel significantly better, and by the time I finally make my way downstairs, I feel about half ready for this conversation.

I head into the dining room, expecting to see them eating breakfast, but the space is empty. Gray usually insists that everybody eats meals together, but I suppose there's enough going on that he's not pushing it.

"Gray?" I call out, making my way to his office.

Silas pops his head out of Aziel's doorway and gestures for me to enter. My palms grow clammy, and I wipe them on my pants as I enter Aziel's office.

Aziel is sitting behind his desk, and I'm glad there's a physical object between us as I go to the couch Gray's currently occupying. He moves over so I have room to sit, and I lower myself onto the cushion before awkwardly clearing my throat.

The room looks the same as it always does, and I'm happy to note that Shay's nowhere to be found. I haven't seen her since before Gray and Aziel got into their fight, but I'm not going to complain.

She makes me uncomfortable.

Silas shuts the office door and sits in one of the chairs directly across from Aziel's desk.

"We haven't spoken about anything important," Gray says.

I nod, happy to hear it.

Aziel is the first to speak. "We need Levia as an ally. Wraths are strong, but we don't have the resources to support this ourselves. Most species tolerate the Seekers because they're a neutral organization, but they won't like having us on their land. I can guarantee the ogres and dragons will see this as an act of war."

"The humans will probably fight back, too. They don't like you," I add.

Aziel shakes his head and grabs a pen off his desk. He fiddles with it while Gray turns to look me in the eye, and I can't help but find myself annoyed by Aziel's lack of interest in what I have to say.

"The humans will complain, but they don't have the means to fight us," Gray says. "There are only a few species that pose a threat. The other demon kingdoms are our biggest concern, hence why we want to get Levia on our side before going public. My dad is notoriously neutral, so he's not a worry, but Mammon could be a problem. She's the Queen of Greed, and she's been looking for an excuse to wage war with Aziel for centuries. Having Levia on our side would mitigate that risk. She doesn't have the means for a fight against both Wrath and Envy.

"We're also worried about the ogres," Gray continues to explain. "They don't compete with us in strength, but they outnumber us four to one."

I nod. Good to know.

"There are also the shifters and the elves, but they're notably kind to females, so we're not worried about them fighting against any regulations we put in place," Silas adds.

I've heard of the shifters and elves. They're blessed breeds, born with fated mates they spend their lives searching for. Rumor has it they've never had much of an issue with females, which I suppose makes sense, considering they cherish mates so deeply.

"Five years is too long," I say.

Aziel stands and paces the length of the room. He looks stressed, and I'm beginning to understand why he hesitated to tackle this problem. I'm sure it was easy to make changes within his kingdom, but doing so at this scale is more politics than anybody wants to deal with.

He's infringing on territory and laws that aren't his, and I'm sure people aren't going to take kindly to that. Demons are already feared because of their strength and power, and this isn't going to make it any better.

"Five years is not long for us," Aziel says. "You are young, but when you live for thousands of years, it's nothing. Envies and Wraths have gotten along for decades, and what Levia asked for reflects that. He would have demanded triple the time if it were anybody else."

I lean forward and rest my forehead on my knees. Gray rubs my back, his hand sliding from the base of my neck to the bottom of my spine. It feels good, and he does it again as I groan into my legs.

"Silas?" I ask, wanting confirmation from somebody other than Aziel.

Aziel scoffs.

"I agree with him," Silas says. "We can try to get it down to a year or two, but I don't think five is unreasonable."

This isn't what I want to hear, but I have to admit I don't have the experience they do.

"I'll set another meeting with Levia later this week to discuss," Aziel decides.

I don't know what more there is to discuss, but I don't ask.

It kills me to know that, at this very moment, millions upon millions of females are either stuck in facilities or being abused by males. It will take years to see any meaningful change, but the sooner we start, the sooner we can help them.

Maybe it's fate that Aziel purchased me. I doubt they'd be doing this if I hadn't found the report and made such a big deal about it.

I'd ask Silas, but I know he won't answer. He's elusive regarding what he does and doesn't know.

Gray taps my spine, and I take that as my cue to get up. Silas is waiting by the door, and I mindlessly follow him into the hallway.

"Is now a good time to speak about us?" Silas asks, turning to me.

No. But I nod, and Gray practically glues himself to my back as Silas leads us to the library. It smells like books, the scent calming as we make our way to the small sitting area in the back corner.

I knew this conversation was going to happen eventually.

Silas sits in one of the leather chairs, and Gray follows suit and fills the other. That leaves me with the small couch, and I clear my throat before nervously lowering myself onto it. *Here goes nothing.*

"You and Silas were intimate," Gray starts.

I give a jerky nod. Fuck, this is embarrassing.

"Do you have feelings for Silas?" Gray continues.

My eyes dart toward Silas. He's got his hands laced together in his lap, the man the picture of nonchalance. I wish I knew what he was thinking, and I nervously pick at the skin of my fingers as I try to read him.

He said he wants to be my male, but I'm scared that was said in the heat of the moment. He's been distant since then, his actions not backing up his words. Gray never leaves me alone, and he has no problems making his affections known.

Silas is more reserved, and it makes him hard to read.

I turn to Gray. "Are you upset I was with Silas while you were gone?"

Gray barks out a laugh and shakes his head, the action so violent that it whips his hair around his face. "Of course not. I've told you before: I like when you lust after Silas and Aziel."

I struggle to believe that after seeing him and Aziel fight.

Gray must see my hesitation as he huffs and runs a hand through his hair, and before I can understand what he's doing, he's jumping out of his chair and straddling Silas's lap.

Silas's hands instinctively move to Gray's hips as the incubus brings their lips together. Gray twists so I can see, and I watch with wide eyes as Silas opens his mouth and lets Gray in. Their kiss is surprisingly passionate, and Silas buries his fingers into Gray's hips with a low moan.

Should this upset me?

Gray groans, and I clench my thighs together. Distress is most definitely not the emotion I'm feeling. A second later, Gray pulls away, and a sinful smirk spreads across his lips as he climbs off Silas's lap.

Silas wipes at his bottom lip.

"What was that, Gray?"

Gray is practically vibrating with excitement, and his eyes dart between Silas and me before settling on Silas.

"I'm making a point," he says.

Silas lets out a quiet laugh. "Are you? Or are you just trying to find an excuse to kiss me?" Silas's words sound harsh, but he says them with a smile.

Gray rolls his eyes and moves toward me. I bounce my foot on the ground, my pulse racing as he sits on the couch to my right. I'm all too aware that he and Silas are watching my every move, and I shove my hands under my thighs so nobody sees them shaking.

"You're overthinking things, Charlie. I love you, and I want whatever will make you happy." Gray pauses and gives me a moment to absorb those words, his smile growing as I flush. I suppose I knew he loved me, but it's nice hearing the words said out loud. "You're my female, and I like that you're Silas's, too. Were you upset to see me kiss him? Jealous? Angry?"

I shake my head, but I don't elaborate. I'm sure they both can smell my arousal.

Gray reaches forward and gently pries my hands out from underneath my thighs. He ignores my clammy palms as he holds my hands within his.

"That's how I feel when you and Silas are together," Gray continues. "I'm not jealous, and I'm not angry. It makes me happy."

Does it?

Silas leaves his chair and kneels in front of me. My face feels warm as he slowly takes my hands from Gray and clasps them between his. I hope he can't feel just how sweaty they've gotten. I've been dreading having this conversation.

Silas's lips twitch before he leans in. He moves slowly, giving me ample time to pull away, before pressing his mouth to mine. The kiss is slow, and I don't put up a fight when Silas tilts his head to the side and deepens it.

Unlike our prior kisses, this one is unhurried. I don't try to pull his hair as I've done in the past, and Silas doesn't make any attempts to slide his hands up my shirt or into my pants. It's nice, and Gray runs a comforting hand down my back to show his support.

Silas pulls away after a few seconds, but he doesn't go far. He continues to kneel between my thighs, and I rest my hands on his shoulders as I wait to hear what he has to say.

"I'll use the human terms," he decides. "I want you to be my girlfriend, Charlie, and I want both Gray and me to be your boyfriends."

Gray brings his hands together with a loud clap, and I can't help but crack a cheesy smile. He truly isn't upset by this?

"There's obviously a lot we'll need to figure out, but I'm excited to see where we go," Gray says, pulling me into his lap.

His chest presses against my back, and he hugs me tight as he peppers my cheek and neck with kisses.

Silas chimes in. "We'll tell you if anything you ever do makes us upset. Don't worry."

Gray makes an odd noise in the back of his throat as he gets a strand of my hair in his mouth, and Silas chuckles as he reaches forward and pushes my hair aside. Being between the two of them is intimidating, and I don't know what to do with my hands as Silas leans in and connects his lips to the side of my neck where Gray was just mindlessly kissing.

Fuck.

I shiver and drop my head against Gray's chest. This is not how I anticipated this conversation going, but I'm not complaining.

A second pair of lips find my neck, and I clench my thighs together.

Gray and Silas kiss my skin, and I instinctively jerk my hips when I feel their lips meet. They kiss, using me as an excuse, and I let out a quiet moan as Silas drops a hand to my thigh. His fingers twitch against my skin before he pulls away, and I take great pleasure in seeing just how frazzled he looks.

For once, the poised, in-control fate is out of his element.

"Do you want to be my girlfriend, Charlie?" Silas asks.

Warmth pools in my lower belly as I give a jerky nod.

Silas squeezes my waist. "Then it's settled."

What?

"That's it? I'm your girlfriend now?" This was too easy. "And what about you and Gray?"

Silas glances at Gray, but neither jumps in to answer. I once asked Silas if he intended to bond with Gray and Aziel when they found their female, and he skirted around the question. It seems to be a point of contention between the two, but I figure now's a good time to ask.

The silence stretches, and after a few seconds, Gray reaches around me and cups Silas's cheek. Silas licks his lips, and I resist the urge to laugh as Gray takes that as an invitation to run his thumb across them.

"What about me?" Gray asks, his voice low.

His hold on Silas's cheek is intimate, and Silas seems to melt under it as he gulps and tilts his head back. He's struggling for an answer, but Gray doesn't push.

"We can take it slow," Gray promises.

Silas nods. "Slow," he repeats.

I climb off Gray's lap and sit on the other side of the couch, and Silas stares at Gray for a moment longer before returning to his chair.

"I'm glad we have that settled!" Gray says, his eyes flickering excitedly between Silas and me. "I would like all three of us to share a bed. Starting tonight."

Silas snorts.

It's not the most enthusiastic response, but Gray doesn't seem to care. I do have to admit I like the idea of all three of us sleeping together. I've grown comfortable with having Gray by my side, and I enjoyed the one night I shared a bed with Silas.

"What happened between you and Aziel?" Silas asks the incubus.

Gray's been avoiding the topic, and he seems to shrink in on himself before abruptly stiffening and returning to his relaxed posture. His initial reaction has already given him away, though, and I can't help but feel concerned.

I bring my finger to my mouth, ready to chew at the skin, before dropping it into my lap when Silas snaps his head toward me with a subtle shake. He turns back to Gray a moment later, still waiting for an answer.

Gray's throat bobs as he gulps. "We've agreed to part ways," he finally says.

I still.

What does he mean they decided to *part ways*? They're already bonded, and from what I've been told, that means they're going to be connected for the rest of their lives.

"I don't understand," I admit.

Gray sighs and glances at the small coffee table between us. It's bare, but he stares at it like it's the most interesting thing in the world.

"We'll always be bonded, but we aren't going to honor it. We won't share," he explains, his eyes moistening. "I want you, Charlie."

My bottom lip wobbles, and I bite it to keep it steady as I absorb that information. I hate being the reason for this wedge between them, but I can't lie and say I'm not relieved.

The thought of someday being bonded with Gray is surreal, filling my stomach with butterflies.

"I love you," I say.

Gray lunges, and I dissolve into a fit of laughter as he tries and fails to tickle me. Even Silas seems to enjoy watching Gray jab his fingers into my ribcage, and it takes a good five minutes before I'm able to pry the prodding fingers away and make an escape.

Chapter Three

CHARLOTTE

I MAKE IT only two steps into my bedroom before my door flies open and Gray saunters inside. He looks awfully proud of himself as he struts into my space, and I raise a brow before turning and heading into my closet.

"Can I sleep with you tonight?" he asks.

I resist the urge to laugh.

"I believe you already declared your plans to sleep with Silas and me tonight."

My lips purse as I peer at my pajama options. What should I wear to bed? I've taken to wearing the slinky outfits Gray purchased, but they feel inappropriate if Silas is joining us. I don't want to send the wrong message—not that I know exactly what message I want to send in the first place.

I'm not against being intimate with the two, but I don't want them to think I expect it. They both kissed me this afternoon, but for all I know, that may be as far as they wish to go. *Fuck.* Silas technically didn't even agree to sleep with us.

He didn't argue when Gray made his announcement, but that doesn't mean he intends to join us.

I sink my teeth into my bottom lip, suddenly anxious. I hope he comes. I've been thinking about it all day, and I'm sure even my tutor, Rock, could tell my mind wasn't on my studies.

Everything he said went in one ear and out the other.

I stare into my pajama drawer for a long moment before pulling out one of Gray's shirts. It falls to my mid-thigh, and it's both comfortable and appropriate. My underwear is next, and I grab a cheeky black pair and slip them on.

They're comfortable but cute enough that I won't be embarrassed if Silas sees them.

Gray's leaning against my bathroom door, waiting, and he doesn't bother hiding his appreciation for my outfit as I walk into his room.

He's got the largest bed, so it only makes sense we sleep in there.

Silas strolls into Gray's bedroom the moment I reach the bed. He's wearing only a pair of underwear, and I can't seem to look away from his muscular chest as he points to my bedroom door.

"I'll sleep in Charlie's bed, but I'm not going anywhere near Gray's," he says.

What's his problem with Gray's bed?

"Gray's bed is bigger," I argue. "And he just got new sheets."

I helped pick them out, and I'm pretty fond of the soft cotton. They're much better than the silk he had before, and I no longer feel like I'm going to slip off the bed. Silas approaches as Gray disappears, and it takes everything in me not to stare at his nearly naked body.

I'm sure he wouldn't mind, but I don't want to be rude.

There's also the tiny voice in my head that whispers that Gray will get upset, but I do my best to ignore it. I have to trust that Gray and Silas will be upfront and tell me if I do something either of them doesn't like.

"I've been living with Gray for a long time, Charlie, and that mattress will forever be tainted in my eyes," Silas says, cupping my cheeks. "Besides, your bed is smaller, so we'll be forced to cuddle. I thought you'd like that."

He runs his thumbs over my cheekbones, the touch distracting.

"I like my space, actually," I say, shooting my arms out to my sides. "So I can sprawl."

Silas snorts and pulls me into his arms. My pulse races as he tosses me over his shoulder, and I glare at his back as he carries me into my room. Both his hands rest on the backs of my thighs, his fingers dangerously close to my butt.

I wonder if he knows I'm not wearing shorts under my shirt. Probably. Not much gets past these men.

Silas drops me onto my bed, and I land with a squawk beside Gray. He's already made himself comfortable under my sheets, and he looks mighty proud of himself as he lifts them and urges me to get under. I do so quickly, my heart beating out of my chest.

I'm about to sleep in the same bed as Gray and Silas.

Silas turns off my bedroom light before climbing in on my other side. He rarely goes to bed at the same time as us, and I wonder if he's purposefully doing so tonight. The silence between us feels deafening once Silas finally gets adjusted.

What now? I stare at the ceiling and rub my feet together.

"I'm hungry." Gray is the first to break the silence.

He rolls over, and a second later, I feel his fingers trail up my arm. His touch is light, and I hold my breath as Silas turns toward me. I clench my hands into tight fists by my sides. I want this, want them, but I don't know where to start.

Gray finds his way to the bottom of my shirt, and Silas joins in to help him pull it up my thighs.

"Is this okay?" Silas asks.

I give a jerky nod. "Yes."

Gray props himself up on his elbow and leans over me, and I can just barely make out his silhouette in the dark as he brings his mouth to mine. A small amount of his lust pours out as he kisses me, and I moan against his lips as his fingers find the waistband of my underwear.

"Spread your legs," Silas says.

The sheets shift as Silas moves down my body, his lips grazing my thighs. He settles himself between them, and I drop a hand to the top of his head as he begins kissing my sensitive skin. Heat coils in my lower abdomen, and I roll my hips in a desperate search for friction.

He's quick to provide it, and I smash my jaw shut as he pulls my underwear to the side and licks up the length of my slit. It feels good, and I arch my back as Gray slides down to join him.

The two settle comfortably between my thighs, and I wish I could see them in the dark room as I run my fingers through their hair.

"Lick her," Gray whispers.

A tongue, I assume Silas's, is on me a second later. He moans as he pleasures me, and after a few seconds, he backs away so Gray can have a turn. Gray's a bit rougher than Silas, and he eases a finger inside me as he sucks on my clit.

My thighs begin to shake, and the two continue taking turns until I tense up and find my release. I'm unsure who's licking me as I cum, but they continue until I shiver and push both heads away.

Gray chuckles and rises to his knees, and Silas quickly follows.

My eyes are finally starting to adjust to the dark, letting me see Gray lean in and kiss Silas. He trails his hand down Silas's chest, feeling the muscular skin.

"Can I touch you?" Gray asks.

Silas gives a jerky nod, and Gray smiles before turning to me.

I pant, also nodding. "Please."

Gray pushes Silas onto his back next to me, and I roll onto my side to better watch.

"You've never let me touch you before," Gray says, kissing his stomach. Silas moans, his eyes flashing to me as I kneel on the bed.

Gray grabs my hips and guides me so I'm kneeling between Silas's spread thighs. His back presses against my front, and I shiver as his warm breath ghosts over my ear.

"Why don't you touch him with your hand? The way you did to me before," Gray suggests.

My pulse races as I inch my hands up Silas's thighs. I'm not the most experienced, and I don't want Silas to feel disappointed. Even if Gray doesn't necessarily love what I'm doing, he can at least feed on it.

Licking my lips, I glance anxiously at Silas. He smiles and brushes some hair off my forehead, and I gulp before lowering my gaze back to his covered erection.

Even if I'm not great at pleasuring him, refusing to try isn't going to make me any better.

I try to hide the slight tremor in my hands as I reach forward and toy with the waistband of his underwear, but he seems to notice it anyway and grabs my wrists to stop me.

"I'm not interested in doing something you aren't one hundred percent sure about," Silas says.

Gray rubs reassuring circles into the skin of my belly, but he doesn't interfere.

"I just..." I stammer, clearing my throat as my face grows warm. "Just don't expect a lot from me."

Silas stills. "Is that what this is about?" He lets out a dry laugh and relaxes into the mattress. "You don't have to worry about that. I'll enjoy whatever you do."

I lick my lips and pull his underwear down his thighs. He's hard, and I can't help but gasp as I take him in my hand. Silas's dick is thick, and I twist my fist as I try to close my fingers around his girth.

"Do you like it?" Gray chuckles as I press my thumb into the vein running up the underside.

Silas grunts and jerks his hips, his fists moving to his thighs. He grips the muscle tightly, his fingertips digging into his skin.

"Fuck," he exhales. "That feels good."

Gray leans over me to grab something from my bedside table, and I just about die of embarrassment when he returns with the bottle of lube he keeps hidden in there. He pops open the top and squirts some onto Silas.

Silas watches with heavy-lidded eyes, his chest rising as he pants into the air between us.

The lube helps smooth out my strokes as I tentatively slide my hand up and down his shaft. Silas's hips twitch into my fist, and his stomach muscles flex with each movement.

Gray inhales loudly, probably feeding, before he wraps his arm around me and takes hold of Silas. My excitement grows as we both stroke the fate, and after a minute, I let go and move aside.

Silas's eyes dart to me, concern written all over his face, but I shoot him a smile to show I'm not upset. Gray speeds up, twisting his fist every time he reaches the tip, and Silas arches his back with a low moan.

I continue moving away.

"Where do you think you're disappearing to, Charlie?" Gray asks.

Instead of answering, I grab Silas's hand and bring it to Gray. I want to see them together. Gray shoves his underwear down his thighs and moves closer to Silas, filling the space I once occupied as Silas curls his hand around Gray's length.

"Oh," I breathe.

Gray and Silas hold one another, each moving with a fluidity only a demon can possess.

"Have you ever been with a man?" Gray asks, thrusting into Silas's hand.

Silas visibly gulps before shaking his head. The answer makes Gray smile, and a second later, he pushes Silas's thighs apart.

Silas groans. "You're not fucking me."

Gray ignores him and slides into the open space he just created. Their hips touch, and Gray curls a hand around both his cock and Silas's and begins to stroke them at the same time. I gasp, and Silas throws his head back with a strangled moan.

If this is how Gray feels when he sees me with Silas, I understand why he pushed so hard for us to be together.

I love this.

"Look away for a moment, Charlie," Gray says.

What? Gray moves to cover my eyes, and I shove his hand away with a huff.

"What're you doing?"

"There's friction, and incubi can produce their own form of lube," Silas explains. "Gray's embarrassed about his—always has been—and he doesn't want you to see it."

Why would he be embarrassed about that?

"I want to see it," I say.

Gray gives Silas a pointed glare as he takes hold of himself and squeezes. To my complete surprise, a clear fluid begins to seep out of his tip. It looks eerily similar to cum, and Gray slowly strokes himself until it's dripping down his fist.

I don't understand why he's shy about it, but I don't question it as Gray curls his hands back around both cocks. Silas moans as

Gray works them, his hips rocking upward with each stroke.

The sound of wetness fills the room, and Silas's moans grow throaty as his orgasm builds. His muscles tense as he cums, and Gray doesn't seem far behind.

Gray releases Silas and focuses on himself, and Silas and I watch as he throws his head back and finishes on the fate.

"Fuck," Gray curses.

Silas runs a hand through his hair as Gray cums on him, and I can't help but let out a tiny giggle as the two collapse into a heap of limbs.

"This was a good icebreaker," I say.

Gray seems to be taking advantage of post-orgasm Silas as he pins the fate to the bed with his naked body. Silas peers at me over Gray's head, his lips curled into a smile.

"I suppose it was," Silas agrees.

He lets Gray lie on him for a while before making his way into the bathroom to clean himself. The light turns on a moment before the door is quietly shut, and I lie back on the bed with a shiver.

I didn't think I'd like seeing them together as much as I did.

Gray rolls over and reaches for me, seemingly intent on rubbing my cheek, before he remembers his hand is dirty and pulls away.

"I'll be right back," he says, climbing off the bed and making his way to the bathroom.

Silas mumbles something as Gray pushes open the door, but I'm too far away to make out the individual words. I assume it's about Gray's lack of knocking. The incubus isn't exactly known for his privacy.

I fix the crumpled bedsheets and climb back under them while I wait for Gray and Silas to return. Seeing them together has helped calm a lot of my worries. They're at ease with one another, and there's no tension between us.

I cause all the awkwardness, and I hope that goes away with time.

I'm comfortable around Gray, but Silas will take some getting used to. He and I have always gotten along, but there's always been a clear line drawn between us. The intimacy is new, and while I like it, it feels foreign.

"I'll sleep in the middle so you don't get too hot," Gray offers, stepping into the room.

Silas isn't far behind, and I happily scooch to the edge of the bed and make room for the two. I assumed I'd be in the middle since I'm the smallest, but I'm sure not going to complain if Gray wants it. The incubus loves attention, and I love having my own space.

It's a win-win.

I grunt and shove at the body actively rolling on top of me. Heavy limbs weigh me down onto the mattress, making me feel suffocated and trapped. Why am I in the middle?

"Gray!" I huff, annoyed.

Gray lets out a low groan and swats at my hands. He still doesn't move, though, and in my angry, grumpy state, I slam my palms into his chest with more force. The body, which I'm pretty sure belongs to Gray, finally rolls over to give me some space, and I breathe a sigh of relief.

"I'm hot," I say, frustrated with the warmth the two men produce.

An arm snakes around my stomach and tugs me into a chest, and I grunt before rearing back and donkey-kicking the person behind me. I'm tired of being grabbed, and I've gotten half the sleep I need tonight.

We should've just fucking slept in Gray's bed.

"Let me go!" I whine, pushing at the arm around my waist.

Instead of disappearing, it tightens, and before I know it, I'm being thrown over a chest and tossed out of the middle. I flail in a sad attempt to catch myself.

"Shut the fuck up, Charlie," Gray says, shoving me toward the edge of the bed.

His mean words go in one ear and out the other as I sigh and sink into the mattress, enjoying the cool sheets. He can be angry all he wants, but if he wanted to get a good night's sleep, he should've stopped suffocating me.

Unable to resist, I peek at Gray through my lashes. He's fully awake and glaring at me, and I offer a weak smile before giving a slight shrug. Grumpy boy.

His eyes narrow in response to my smirk, and I hold in a laugh as he spins and reaches blindly for Silas. The blankets around his arms move as he tries to cuddle the fate, and a pained grunt slips from his lips as he jerks back.

It appears I'm not the only one looking for space.

Gray rolls onto his back with a huff, his arms crossed over his chest. Feeling slightly guilty that Silas and I have rejected him, I inch forward and wrap my arm around his waist.

Silas turns and props himself up on his elbow, his black eyes sliding down my figure before he drops back on the mattress.

"I don't think sharing a bed is going to work," he says, his voice thick with sleep.

"We just need to give it time," Gray urges.

Silas runs a hand down his face. "Can I go back to my room?"

Gray and I answer simultaneously.

"No."

Silas is silent for a long moment before he rolls away. I give Gray's waist a tight squeeze before tentatively slipping my hand into the waistband of his underwear.

Gray remains still as I curl my fingers around his length and hold him in my hand. It twitches, probably due to my cold fingers, but remains soft. I like that he's letting me hold arguably the most sensitive part of his body, and I give it a gentle squeeze before kissing his shoulder and relaxing.

It feels nice to explore when there's no expectation for me to make it feel good.

I take my time learning him as my eyelids grow heavy, gently tracing his length before poking at his balls. Gray chuckles at my curiosity, his hand loosely curling around my forearm as his thumb rubs gentle, comforting circles into my wrist.

He falls asleep before I do, his breathing evening out and his grip gradually slipping away. It doesn't take me long to follow, my fingers stilling in his underwear as I drift off.

"Fuck off." Gray grunts, wiggling and kicking out his foot.

I'm in the middle again, but the top comforter has been removed so I don't get too hot.

I groan, frustrated, and reach up to feel the face of the man whose chest I'm resting on. The sharp cheekbones and shorter hair tell me it's Silas, and I curl further into his chest with a contented sigh.

Silas wraps his arm around my waist and buries his face against the top of my head, his breath tickling my scalp.

"Stop rubbing your toes on me," Silas says, I assume to Gray, before kicking out his foot and accidentally hitting me in the shin.

I clench my jaw shut and sit up. Gray and Silas go silent as I lean over and check the clock, the pair hopefully feeling guilty for waking me. It's around the time I usually get up and head downstairs to meet with Rock for tutoring, and I find myself relieved to climb out of bed.

Gray and Silas are getting on my last nerve.

They're quick to follow me out of bed, and Gray and Silas leave to get dressed while I remain in my room and get ready. We've settled into a nice routine while Aziel has been gone, and I pray the Wrath's return doesn't ruin it as I make my way downstairs.

I smell food before I see it, and my stomach grumbles as I step into the dining room. Aziel's already sitting at the head of the table, the man impossible to miss, but I'm relieved to see Silas and Gray are here already, too.

I'd hate to be alone with Aziel.

Gray and Silas sit on either side of him, and I tentatively lower myself next to Gray.

"It took you three long enough to join. The food's going to be cold," Aziel complains.

He refuses to look in my direction as the hazy, dark shadows move forward and begin placing serving platters on the table, their movements smooth and well-rehearsed. They made a demonic dish today, some rice and vegetable mixture.

We're silent as the shadows filter out of the room, the air between us awkward. Gray nervously clears his throat before grabbing my plate and filling it with food.

"Thanks," I mumble as he sets it before me.

He nods and does the same for Silas. The fate takes the plate with a smile, and Gray visibly hesitates before serving Aziel. He fills his plate last.

This is so uncomfortable.

Deciding to be the bigger person, I suck in a deep breath and turn to Aziel. He meets my gaze head-on.

"Did you sleep well?" I ask.

The words sound formal as they slip from my mouth, and I can't help but wince as they filter through my ears. Gray and Silas quietly begin eating as they glance between Aziel and me. I avoid looking at either of them, not wanting to lose my confidence.

Aziel doesn't respond right away, choosing instead to stare at me with his ever-angry expression.

I force a weak smile on my face. I want to help keep the peace between him and Gray, which means I need to be nice. I still think it's Aziel who should be apologizing to me, but I've come to realize he has no intention of doing that.

He's hundreds of years old, but leave it to me to have to be the bigger person.

"No, I didn't *sleep well*," Aziel finally answers. "I spent most of the night listening to you whore yourself out to my two best friends."

My smile falters, and I dip my chin before grabbing my fork and shoving some food in my mouth. At least it can't be said I didn't try.

"Aziel," Gray warns.

Silas stands and walks around the table, his sudden movements drawing our attention. Aziel frowns and sinks in his seat as the fate plops himself down on the other side of me.

"You're not a whore," he says.

I know that. The silence between us stretches as we begin to eat, and the rhythmic clanking and scraping of our silverware only makes things worse. Silas places his left hand on my thigh as he eats with his right, the touch subtle but soothing.

It's weird how smoothly he's transitioning into this boyfriend role, but I like it. Silas provides a softer intimacy, and his actions are a welcome change from the in-your-face affection Gray prefers.

My stomach expands as I eat, and I glance around to ensure nobody's looking before unbuttoning my jeans. It allows my full belly to jut out, and I'm careful to keep my pants hidden under the table as I set my fork down and lean back in my chair.

Aziel watches my every action, but I pretend not to notice. I don't know what I'm going to do about him. I've made my attempt to be friendly, and I'm not going to continue putting myself out there if he's going to be a dick.

Letting him ever touch me was a mistake. There's no denying he's attractive, but that doesn't make up for his lacking personality. He thrives off the chaos he creates.

Aziel clears his throat. "I slept fine. Thank you for asking."

I blink. What? I didn't realize Aziel could give a straightforward, borderline even polite answer without spontaneously combusting. It's also the complete opposite of what he said earlier, so clearly a lie.

Gray sinks his teeth into his bottom lip to hide a smile.

"That's good," I mumble, unsure what to say.

Nobody's ever accused me of being a great conversationalist.

"Are you full?" Gray asks, nodding toward my half-empty plate.

He served me more food than I'd ever be able to eat, but I think I made a decent dent.

Gray doesn't wait for my answer before grabbing the serving spoon. He drops a giant portion of food on my plate, and I can't help but laugh as I grab his wrist to stop him from grabbing more. Silas even lets out a quiet snicker, encouraging me as I pry the spoon out of Gray's hands and set it down.

"I'm full, I promise. I know where the kitchen is if I get hungry later."

"What's going on between you three?" Aziel asks.

Silas gives my thigh a gentle squeeze. The touch is comforting, and I turn just in time to see the tail end of his grin.

"We're together," he says.

"And you plan to bond with her as Gray does?"

Aziel's eyes dart toward Gray before settling on my neck.

There's nothing there, but I still resist the urge to scrunch up underneath his critical stare.

"We haven't discussed it," Silas says.

Aziel doesn't ask any further questions, and we sit in tense silence until he stands and leaves without an explanation a few minutes later.

"What're you and Rock working on today?" Gray asks, breaking the tension.

I shrug, unsure. I just show up and do what Rock tells me.

"Rock said you're doing well in most of the subjects!" Gray continues, sounding excited. "It seems like you're struggling a bit in math but doing great in history and language."

My eyes narrow. Has he been having secret meetings with Rock behind my back? Gray seems to realize his mistake as he grimaces and disappears into thin air.

Silas lets out an abrupt laugh, seemingly finding the entire thing hilarious, and I turn to him with a sharp glare. It's not funny. His eyes widen as he takes in my angered state, and I fight the urge to scream when he shoots me a broad smile and vanishes, too.

I tap my pencil eraser against the desk, impatient as I wait for Rock to finish grading my test. I usually like to watch as he does it, but all I can think about is how he and Gray have secret meetings to discuss my progress.

How long have they been meeting?

Gray does tend to be a bit nosy, but I didn't realize my intellectual achievements, or lack thereof, were of any interest to him.

Rock grimaces as he sets my test down and scribbles some

final notes in the margins. He's wearing his usual black robes, and his shirt sleeve slides down his shadowy hand with each movement of his arm.

I try to read as he writes, but he angles the paper away so I can't see. Tapping my pencil more aggressively, I crane my neck even harder.

"You're impatient." He slides the test in my direction, and I grimace as I take in the number of corrections. Holding back a sigh, I grab the sheet and scan his notes.

While I didn't do as badly as I anticipated, I by no means did well. History is one of my better subjects, too, but I've been distracted lately and have trouble paying attention to Rock's lessons. All I can think about are the females.

"Are you going to tell Gray about this?" I ask, unable to hide the bite to my words.

"Yes, and I'll probably also tell Silas and Aziel when they ask."

I freeze. Have all three men been pulling Rock aside for updates on my tutoring? I ball my hands into fists on my lap. It's one thing to have Gray and Silas eavesdrop on me, but I can't believe Aziel is doing it, too. Why does he even care?

Rock doesn't acknowledge my visible anger. I don't even know why it makes me so mad.

I enjoy my tutoring, but I have to admit it makes me feel dumb. I didn't realize how many things I didn't know until recently, and I'm embarrassed to have my males know, too. I don't want them to see the extent of my lack of education.

"How often are you meeting with them?" I ask.

Rock shrugs. "Frequently."

Everybody needs to get out of my business. Rock's my friend, and I don't appreciate them talking about me behind my back.

My thumbnail scratches at the thin paper as I flip the page and look over all the notes on the back. It amazes me how knowledgeable Rock is. He seems to know everything, and I wonder if it's because demons take education seriously or if he's smarter than average.

"Did you hear about our meeting with Levia earlier this week?" I ask, unable to keep my mind off it for longer than five minutes.

"The King of Envy?" Rock asks.

I nod, and after a brief hesitation, he dips his chin in confirmation.

"Silas mentioned it. He also said you're upset about the five-year waiting period."

Seriously? Is there anything they *don't* talk about?

"What are your thoughts?" I ask, eager to hear his opinion.

Rock hums and leans back in the chair, the robes around his hazy form shifting as he mulls over my question. I straighten my back as I wait, appreciating how he thinks through his responses before sharing them.

Aziel should try that.

"I'm conflicted," he finally says, his voice low. "I think Levia is a good ally, but one of the blessed breeds would be a better option. The elves are known for their technology and the shifters for their strength." Rock clears his throat before continuing. "I understand why Aziel wants to stick with a demon alliance, but this isn't a demon-exclusive problem."

I sit on the edge of my seat. "I thought the blessed breeds have become near-impossible to work with since the declines. They rarely leave their lands."

Rock contemplates my words.

"That's true, but I think they'd be willing to fight for this cause. They've got a soft spot for women," he says. "Most species don't love Wrath, primarily because of how Aziel's father chose to lead, but I think the shifters would fight for the females."

I suck in my cheeks as my excitement grows. Rock could get in trouble for openly speaking against Aziel, but what he says is beyond brilliant.

This is a fantastic idea.

I don't understand why my males haven't thought of this already. Aziel has set up another meeting with Levia for later this week, but maybe we can postpone it and meet with the shifters beforehand.

I'm sure Aziel has a way of getting in contact with them.

I practically bounce in my seat as I think over all the possibilities. Gray left to run some errands, but I think Silas is in his office. Rock chuckles as he sees my eyes flicker to my door. I've still got an hour left of tutoring.

"Go on," he says.

Was I that obvious? "Are you sure?"

Rock nods, and I look him over to ensure he's not upset before leaving and making my way down the hallway toward Gray's office. His door is cracked open, and I peer in to see him in the middle of a phone call. I'm unsure what he does for work, and I linger in the doorway until he notices me. He's speaking the demonic language, his words guttural and clipped, and he shoots me a friendly smile before turning away and continuing his conversation.

I attempt to eavesdrop before giving up and going to Silas's office. He's sitting behind his desk, and he shuts his computer and gestures to his lap as I push his door closed and approach.

"Yes?" he asks.

His hands settle on my hips as I get comfortable on his lap, and I gently push back his hair before scanning his chest for a nipple. It's cold in here, and the moment I spot the bump in his shirt, I'm grabbing and twisting. He gasps and shoves me away, his hands flying to cover his chest in shock.

"Stop asking Rock about me," I snap, needing to get that out before addressing the topic of the females.

Silas frowns and swats my hands away when I reach for his nipples again.

The muscle in his jaw twitches seconds before his power reaches my lungs. It's been a long time since he's let it out around me, and I feel its effects immediately.

It's unsettling, and I furrow my brow as I fight against it.

The power that seeps from Gray makes me aroused, but Silas's makes me want to curl up and hide. Silas doesn't seem to notice he's let it out, and a throaty chuckle bubbles up out of his throat as he grabs my wrists and pins my arms to my side.

His laugh dies out as he takes notice of my current state. I half-expect him to tuck it back in, but instead, he cups my cheeks and releases more.

"It's okay, Charlie," he says, smoothing his thumbs over my eyebrows to soften the muscles. "You're doing so good."

I manage to give a jerky nod.

It feels like trying to breathe underwater, and I shut my eyes as I try to focus on getting enough oxygen into my lungs. Silas continues to whisper assurances as I grab his forearms, and after a few minutes, my racing pulse begins to settle.

"I'm going to leave it here from now on," he says. "And we can slowly increase over time. I want you to learn to be comfortable around it. Around me."

I lick my lips and drop my head against his chest. Silas rubs my back, patiently waiting for me to collect my thoughts. My mouth feels dry when I finally work up the courage to face him again, and my cheeks are tinted red from embarrassment.

Objectively, I know it's not my fault I struggle around them, but the way it highlights our power imbalance is slightly humiliating. It draws attention to how weak I am.

"I talked to Rock," I say.

Silas hums. "Did you? My detached nipple and I couldn't tell."

I snort and shoot him a goofy grin. It's what he deserved. Besides, it's not like the demons have many weak spots, and pinching their nipples is the only way I've found that I can hurt them.

Although I'm sure it's more shocking than it is painful.

"You're familiar with the shifters?" I ask.

Silas raises a brow.

I flush. Of course he knows about them. The man's like a million years old, and I'm sure he knows everything I do and then some.

"Have you considered going to them with the findings instead of Levia?"

My fists curl into the fabric of his shirt, my excitement poorly contained. If the shifters care about females as much as they're rumored to, I doubt they'd ask for a waiting period.

Silas's lips twitch downward. Why doesn't he like that idea?

"The shifters don't like us. Levia was correct in saying that it won't take long for people to realize we sat on this information once it gets out. Many will be pissed, the shifters especially. I doubt they'll want to help us, and they'd probably take the information and run with it while simultaneously waging war against us."

He makes a good point. Levia put two and two together within minutes, and I assume it won't take long for others to come to the same conclusion. Many will be livid when they realize Aziel kept this information hidden.

The extinction of an entire gender is an issue too significant to use for personal gain, which is precisely what Aziel did.

Species began to partner up once the issue was detected, and many information-sharing-based alliances were established. The decline happened so suddenly and, for many species, was so immediately detrimental that funding for scientific studies was dropped rather quickly.

The human world, at least, fell into chaos within a matter of years. Warring countries began targeting females, and by the time the humans decided to come together as one, too much damage had been done.

I suspect something similar happened to many other species.

"You don't think you could come together for the sake of the females?" I ask. "You guys fucked up, but you're making a genuine effort to fix it now."

Silas doesn't look convinced.

"Can we at least try?" I practically beg.

The sound of Silas's office door opening captures my attention, and I turn just in time to see Gray come strolling inside. He grins as he takes in my position on Silas's lap, clearly pleased by it, before he drops onto the sofa.

I move to get up, but Silas tightens his hold on me so I can't leave.

"I don't think it would hurt to try," Gray offers, answering the question I asked Silas earlier. "Let's see if we can use that option as leverage during our talks with Levia first."

Silas frowns but doesn't immediately argue, which I take as a good sign.

Chapter Four

GRAY

SHOULD I TELL Charlie we can smell her fear? She adjusts on Silas's lap, and after a moment's hesitation, I decide against saying anything. It'll probably just make things worse.

We've been waiting inside Levia's conference room for almost five minutes now, a fact that's greatly pissed off Aziel, and there's been screaming coming from the doors behind it the entire time.

Silas wraps his arms around Charlie's waist and gives her a gentle squeeze, and I smile at the two before turning toward Aziel. He blatantly avoids looking in their direction, his lips curled into a permanent frown.

I'm sure he's not having fun watching me and Silas choose Charlie over him.

He went from thinking he'd have me, Silas, and a female as his bonded, to now only one female. Wraths generally prefer to be monogamous, but I know he cares more for Silas and me than he lets on.

Charlie shivers and grabs Silas's wrists as the screaming continues. I'm sure this is all a ploy by Levia, and I resist the urge to roll my eyes at the dramatization of it. He hopes to scare our female and gain the upper hand, but he fails to realize Aziel isn't affected by Charlie's fear.

I may have thought long ago that Aziel cared for her, but now I realize that what happened at the Lust party was a fluke. Aziel's too selfish to see how amazing Charlie is, and she deserves better than some male who needs to be *convinced* to care for her.

"What's going on in there?" she asks Silas, gesturing toward the door from which the screams are emerging.

Silas shrugs and presses a kiss to the back of her head.

"I don't know, but it's nothing for you to worry about," he assures her.

It's not what I would've said, but I don't correct him. I need to be better about letting them figure out their relationship on their own, which is admittedly more challenging than I initially anticipated.

Charlie makes it obvious she prefers me to Silas, which I can't blame her for. I've been with her for months while Silas only just admitted his interest, but I can tell it's upsetting the fate. I don't want to say anything and cause her to be even weirder around him, but I'm trying not to interrupt whenever they're alone.

Even though I desperately want to.

Charlie leans into his chest with a sigh, and her hands slide down his wrists before she slots her fingers between his. I beam as I watch. I'm happy they're together, and I'm even more pleased as Silas's arousal reaches my nose.

I can't remember the last time he was intimate with anybody, and now he's lusting twenty-four-seven around Charlie. She throws herself on his lap? He's horny. She holds his hand? He's horny. She sneezes? He's horny.

I fucking love it.

Charlie fed me well, but being able to take from somebody as strong as Silas has me at the next level of full. It feels good, and I'm pleasantly surprised by his openness to being intimate with me. I can count on one hand the number of times I've snuck into his dreams, but I've only ever been able to feed from him once.

A fate's mind is tricky, and it's next to impossible to sneak into, even for an incubus.

I learned not to try early on, and there's never been an opportunity to seduce him outside of his dreams. He's always made it clear he's not interested, and I feared it would ruin our friendship if I pushed too hard.

Charlie shifts in Silas's lap, and I resist the urge to feed off the lust he emits.

It's not enough to fill me, not even close, but it's an excellent mid-afternoon snack.

I wonder if I can get him to feed me later. Charlie wants our intimacy to be special, but Silas doesn't hold the same reservations. I'm grateful Charlie hasn't ever asked about his past, but Silas had his fair share of women before the declines.

My sister included.

I purse my lips and cross my arms over my chest.

He was with her before we all agreed to someday bond with the same female, and he hasn't looked in her direction since, but I'm still pissed. He was supposed to put me first.

Silas glances in my direction, his eyebrows pulled tight. I'm sure he can sense I'm upset, and I do my best to hide my physical reactions so Charlie doesn't catch on, too. She's already nervous about our meeting with Levia, and I don't want to make it worse.

She'll learn to conceal her emotions better with time, but I assume that won't be for a long while.

It's good that she has thousands of years to learn.

We haven't yet discussed it, but I fully intend to bond with her. I don't want to rush into anything, and I'll wait patiently until she's ready, but I'm sure she's who I want. Silas hasn't mentioned it, either, but I assume it's on his mind.

He doesn't do anything without thoroughly thinking it through, and I can't see him pursuing Charlie if he didn't see it as a long-term thing. He knows she's my female, and I know he wouldn't do that to her or me.

I can't wait.

It's a shame there aren't other human and demon pairings I can investigate for information. I'd love to know how a demon bond affects a human. Her kind doesn't have bonds as we do, and I'm interested in seeing how her body takes it.

There have been a few reports of bonds between species that have them and those that don't, and thankfully, none have resulted in injury. I don't know what I'd do if my bond had the potential to hurt Charlie.

I'm anxious enough about babies as it is.

Human infants are tiny compared to demon ones. Charlie's a very average human, and I fear my children will harm her, especially if she grows pregnant with twins. We'll have to have doctors monitoring her twenty-four-seven.

I clear my throat, drawing Charlie's attention.

"Do you want to have children?" I ask.

I can't believe I've never asked her this.

Charlie's cheeks grow impossibly red. "I do."

That's very good to hear. Silas gives her thighs a tight squeeze before he shoots me a confused look, but I ignore it and turn back to Charlie. We haven't had penetrative sex yet, a fact that goes against every fucking incubus gene in my body, but I look forward to the day I can fill her with myself.

I want to give her my children immediately, but I know that's not right.

When we have time alone, I'll ask if she'd like me to put her on human birth control. I have a feeling her answer will be yes, and I'll have one of our shadows ensure it gets taken properly so she doesn't fall pregnant with a baby she's not ready for.

I just need to figure out how to get human birth control. It was once popular, but it's rarely used nowadays. Males want their females to get pregnant.

"Fucking stop, Gray," Aziel snaps, turning to shoot me a glare.

Silas hides his laugh in Charlie's neck, and she looks between Aziel and me with apparent confusion.

"Gray is seeping lust," Silas whispers.

I'm sure it's all Aziel can smell right now. Good. Let him bask in it.

The door to Levia's conference room opens before I can comment. Aziel straightens up, and Charlie jumps off Silas's lap and slides into her own chair. Silas looks annoyed by her retreat, but he doesn't say anything about it.

I know he felt special when she chose to sit on his lap in the first place.

Her fear fills the room, and I lean over the table with a low hum.

"I want to watch you touch Silas tonight," I whisper.

Silas clears his throat, and I click my tongue against the roof of my mouth as I sit back down. I'm proud of myself as the scent of her fear diminishes.

Forcing any thoughts of sex away, I link my hands on the table and turn toward Levia. He watches us all with a smirk, the sneaky bastard undoubtedly trying to read our relationships. Aziel may have a long history with the King of Envy, but I don't trust him.

"Sorry to keep you waiting." His lips twitch upward as Charlie lets out an involuntary shiver.

Shay slips into the room and takes a seat, her presence more than a little annoying. Her dark hair is thrown back into a slick ponytail, and she wears a large pendant around her neck that draws attention to the low cut of her tight red dress. Her black eyes dart along the room before settling on me, but I pretend not to notice.

Charlie will never admit it, but I know she feels uncomfortable around the woman with whom Silas and I have been intimate.

If I could go back in time and warn myself to stay away from Shay, I would in a heartbeat. I rarely feel ashamed and regretful about the men and women I've been with, but Shay's managed to weasel herself into that category.

My fingers twitch as I'm overwhelmed with the urge to pull Charlie onto my lap and provide assurances that she's the only woman I want. She hates it when I do that, especially when we're in public, but I'll make sure to tell her later.

Levia continues to smirk. I want to grab the back of his head and slam his face into the table until it's gone. I'd probably try if Aziel weren't here. He gets too worked up whenever I fight. Our bond makes him eager to defend me, and his wrath makes it hard for him to stop.

He'd probably end up killing Levia, putting us back at square one.

We have a plan, and we need to stick with it.

"I hope you've had ample time to discuss my conditions." Levia is the first to speak.

Aziel nods and nudges a folder he brought with him across the table. He could have sent this over beforehand to give Levia time to look it over, but the whole point is to spring this information on him.

Levia says nothing as he reaches out and grabs it.

"We've considered it, but we aren't willing to wait five years," Aziel says. "Too many have already been lost, and we can't justify postponing any longer."

Levia scoffs. "Tell me again, how many years did you give yourself?"

"We're willing to give you six months," Silas adds, ignoring Levia's question.

Levia leans back in his chair. His eyes narrow as he looks over us, and I mentally cheer when Charlie straightens up instead of shrinking underneath his stare. I can only imagine how hard it must be for her to remain firm when she's being hit with the full extent of his power.

My female is so strong.

"No." Levia shakes his head with a laugh. "You want my help; I want five years."

I make brief eye contact with Charlie as Aziel shrugs and slides the documents back in his direction.

"That's fine," he says, the lie rolling smoothly off his tongue. "Thanks for your time."

Levia grinds his teeth, looking confused, while Shay laces her hands on the table and leans forward. She hardly looks in Aziel's direction, and I hope that means she's given up on her hope of being his female.

If he wants to take somebody other than Charlie, fine, but I at least want it to be with a woman we all like. If he brings a female into our home, I need her to get along with Charlie. Our human is weak and can't realistically defend herself against a demon, and I won't put her life in danger by keeping her near one who wants to see her dead.

It doesn't matter how many stone necklaces Silas gives her.

"You no longer want my help?" Levia laughs, like the matter doesn't affect him, but I can tell by his tight smile that he's upset.

He's the King of Envy for a reason, and he needs to feel included. He thrives off the praise, and being a part of the movement that saved the females is too much for him to pass up.

I lick my lips and turn to Charlie as Levia waves over a few shadows.

"Get us some drinks," he orders.

He can't handle being the odd man out, and his desperation not only to be included but also to be a key component makes him especially susceptible to our plan. At least, I hope it does.

"Come here," I say to Charlie.

She stands and walks around the table. She takes the long way to avoid Levia and Shay, a smart move, and I push back my chair to make room for her to sit on my lap.

"We've got a meeting set up with the shifters tomorrow, and I anticipate they'll be more than happy to help," Aziel says, grumbling as he pretends to struggle to get the zipper on his bag.

The snort that emerges from Charlie's throat is a bit louder than necessary, but it successfully distracts Levia and keeps him from thinking too deeply about what Aziel's saying. He watches Charlie grab the bag from Aziel and zip it up herself.

Her frantic, uncoordinated human movements are hard to block out.

"Shifters hate you," Levia says.

The shadows return and place full cups of demon alcohol in front of us. I ignore mine and move Charlie's out of the way. I doubt she intends to drink it, but I'd rather be safe than sorry. Envy alcohol is strong, and I want her to keep her wits about her.

I chime in. "They like the females more than they hate Aziel."

Shay bores holes into the side of my head as I wrap my arms around Charlie's waist. Levia does the same, and Silas clears his throat to draw their attention to him.

I bury my face in the back of Charlie's neck and let my lust out. She agreed to this plan, but I still feel bad as I allow it to fill the space around us. This might throw her into a frenzy, but I'll help alleviate the burn should it come to that.

Charlie slouches into me almost immediately, her legs spreading underneath the table as the smell of her arousal seeps through the room. She was so nervous about this part of the plan, and I try to get it over with as quickly as possible as I slip my hand between her thighs and sink two fingers into her.

The table hides the view, but the sound of her wet sex is audible to everybody.

I turn to hide my face from Levia and Shay as I angle my hand so it'll hurt Charlie if she tries to move. The plan is for her scent to distract everybody, but I'm not trying to give them a show. The best way we could think to prevent her rocking was to cause her just enough pain to overshadow the pleasure.

Charlie flinches as she jerks her hips and meets the sharp end of my thumb.

Levia doesn't know me well enough to realize how unusual this behavior is for me, and I hope he's willing to ignore the rumors he's heard and believe I'm just like any other incubus he's come across.

They do these things for fun, thriving off attention and lust.

Silas grunts and reaches for Charlie, but Aziel beats him to it and yanks her out of my arms. This is the other thing Charlie was worried about, but Aziel must be the person to hold her. Levia doesn't respect Silas or me enough to have this discussion without Aziel present, and needing to leave to take care of Charlie is the perfect excuse for Aziel to rush Levia for an answer.

"Fucking incubus," Aziel mumbles, setting Charlie on his lap.

She winces as he slips his hand between her legs and digs his fingers into the soft flesh of her thigh. She made me promise not to let him touch her intimately, and I listen and ensure he isn't copping a feel.

Shay meets my eye for a brief moment, her face tight. Her

calm expression tells me immediately that she sees through this charade. She knows me too well.

I expect her to call us out on it, but instead, she crosses her arms over her chest and presses her lips together. Typical. Shay works for herself and herself only. Whatever her plan is, it doesn't include stopping this deal from going through.

"I'm leaving," Aziel says, standing. He holds Charlie tightly at the waist so she can't wiggle against him. She still tries, and her unfocused eyes land on me with desperation. Her pupils are fully blown out, and I resist the urge to yank her out of Aziel's grubby hands.

"We aren't finished!" Levia snaps, his harsh glare turning to Charlie.

Aziel pushes the damp hair out of her face. If I didn't know any better, I'd say he seems genuinely concerned as he runs his thumb over her wrinkled forehead, smoothing the skin.

"There's nothing left to discuss," Aziel says. "You aren't willing to compromise, and I have a female to care for. Silas can stay and speak on my behalf if you wish to discuss this further. Gray is coming with me."

Charlie's panting slows as she gradually begins to overcome my lust, my strong female slowly learning to block it out. I know she still burns, though, and that pain won't disappear until I've touched her.

"The shifters aren't worth your time. Their armies are nothing compared to mine," Levia argues, playing perfectly into our plan.

Aziel clenches his jaw. "I'm leaving in ten seconds. Either you agree to six months or I'm going to the shifters," he says.

Levia slams his fists on the table, and a wave of his power flows through the room. I turn to Charlie in a panic, fearful of how overwhelmed it will make her, but I'm relieved to see Aziel snarl and step back.

He hardly seems to be paying attention to what he's doing as he grabs the hem of his shirt and raises it to Charlie's mouth. She fights against him, confused, as he pushes the fabric against her face to create a barrier.

"One year?" Levia relents. "That's the lowest I'll go."

"Fine. I'll send somebody around with paperwork tomorrow," Aziel responds, continuing to fight with Charlie as he vanishes.

I don't hesitate to follow, not trusting them alone together. The last time Aziel was alone with Charlie in her frenzied state, he was stupid and tried to soothe her himself.

A thousand-year-old virginal demon with a weak, sex-crazed human is not a good combination.

Charlie is clinging to Aziel when I arrive, her hips rocking hopelessly against his hip as he tries to put her on the couch.

"Charlie."

She throws herself at me the moment I say her name, her legs kicking off Aziel's shins for leverage. He grunts and releases her, and Silas emerges with a cold, wet rag.

"Here," Silas says, handing it over.

I take it from him as Charlie pulls me into her arms, and I rush to shove her hair out of the way and press the cloth against the back of her neck. My lust isn't as intense as my dad's, and it won't get her nearly as high.

This should be enough to calm her down.

Aziel steps back and watches as I slide the cloth over the back of Charlie's neck. She clings to me, her mouth on my shoulder as I sit on the couch. Her fingers curl around my forearms as she straddles me, but she doesn't try rocking or moving as I slide the rag to the front of her neck and down into her shirt.

Silas must have dipped the cloth in ice water, and I feel a bit guilty as Charlie shivers and tries to pull away. It's too cold to be refreshing, but it does the job nonetheless.

"Is she okay?" Aziel asks.

He sounds concerned, and Silas takes it upon himself to explain how the cold shocks her system and overrides the high. I don't think Charlie's health is any of Aziel's business, but I keep my focus on Charlie.

Her heart rate gradually begins to slow, and I let out a relieved sigh when her pupils begin to shrink back to their usual size.

That's always a good sign.

After a few minutes, she lets out a nervous laugh and pushes my hand away. I let her.

"Did it work?" she asks.

I pull back and look down at her, eager to confirm she's no longer feeling the effects of my lust. I can smell that she's still aroused, but it's manageable. Charlie offers me a weak smile before turning and glancing at Aziel and Silas.

They linger on the other side of the room, Silas appearing relieved while Aziel stands around with a deep-set frown and furrowed brows. It's a dramatic shift from the concern he was showing only moments prior, and I have a feeling he's purposefully putting on a façade.

Why does he even care if Charlie sees his concern?

I'm sure he's still got his childish crush on her, but he's made it more than clear he has no intention of bonding with her.

"Well?" Charlie pries.

She mindlessly rubs her temples, and I can only imagine how nasty a headache she has right now. I'll have her drink some water and take a painkiller before bed.

"We got Levia to agree to a year," I say. "Aziel's going to send somebody over tomorrow morning to sign an agreement."

Charlie looks pleased. "And you're sure he won't change his mind before then?"

Aziel interjects. "No. Levia honors his agreements, even if

they're merely spoken."

I'm not the biggest fan of Levia, but I have to admit he's historically been true to his word. I think that's why he and Aziel have gotten along so well. The two aren't necessarily friends, but they don't hate one another and that's a big thing for Aziel.

Silas and I are the only people he gets along with. It's quite sad.

"And we're still meeting with the shifters tomorrow, right?" Charlie asks.

She glances at Aziel before sliding her gaze to Silas. The fate nods, but he doesn't look pleased. He doesn't have much faith in the shifters and has made his reservations about involving them quite clear, but I don't think it'll cause any harm.

It's not like we plan to tell them outright what we know. This is just to start a conversation and test the waters between us.

"Yes," I answer, confirming we still plan to meet with the shifters.

"You can't come," Aziel blurts out.

Charlie jolts. "And why not? You promised to let me participate, and now you want to go off and have secret meetings without me?"

She scrambles out of my lap and spins around to face Aziel head-on. He hardly seems intimidated by her stare.

"The shifters hate me, and I don't need them trying to steal you while we're in their territory," Aziel says, his words trailing off as he spins in search of something.

He clicks his tongue against the roof of his mouth as he approaches his desk and hunts through the drawers. What the fuck is he doing?

"Nobody's going to steal me," Charlie argues. "Besides, you said yourself that they're kind to females."

That's the problem.

"The Wrath kingdom has a horrible reputation, and I'm sure they've made many assumptions about our relationship," I say. "They very likely think we're abusing you, and they'll probably feel inclined to 'rescue' you."

I run my hands up and down Charlie's arms to try and curb some of her growing anger. It seems to work as she leans back against my chest.

Aziel continues rooting through his drawers, an action I think is simply because he feels uncomfortable and needs something to distract himself. Silas lowers himself into the chair opposite Aziel's desk.

"You can invite them here," Charlie suggests.

Aziel shakes his head, not even taking a moment to consider her suggestion. "No, Charlie."

He slams his desk drawer shut, and Charlie stands as anger erupts from her. She wavers on her feet before sitting back down with a huff.

I wish to speak up and argue for her, but I want her to have her own voice. I want her to feel at ease in this house, and a small part of me likes seeing her argue with Aziel. It's good that she feels comfortable enough to do so.

"It's *Charlotte* to you," she decides.

Silas drops his head and looks away to hide his laughter. Aziel's back stiffens as Charlie's words filter through him, and I can't help but let out a quiet snort. She's feisty.

"I'll be staying home with you," I say, reaching for her hands.

"We won't even be discussing the females," Aziel says. "This is just to open up a conversation and see if there's a possible relationship to build."

Charlie gulps and pulls her hands out of mine. "So you lied to me?"

What? I shake my head, confused, but Charlie moves to the

other end of the couch. We never lied to her. What is she talking about?

"I agreed to humiliate myself in front of Levia and Shay because I thought you would support my plan in return," she hisses. "I thought this was a give and take. I support your idea, you support mine."

We *are* supporting her idea. None of us is particularly excited about going to the shifters, but we're doing it because Charlie is adamant. Aziel clears his throat and leans against his desk while Silas and I exchange glances.

"Our meeting with the shifters was always intended to be just a conversation starter," Silas says. "It'd be dangerous to go in and share everything we know. We never intended for you to think otherwise."

He stands from his chair and attempts to approach, but Charlie shoots him a sharp glare until he sits back down.

"You led me to believe otherwise," she says.

I run a hand through my hair. It wasn't intentional. Charlie's young and inexperienced, but I thought this was obvious. The hurt on her face tells me otherwise, though.

"No, we didn't," Aziel snaps. "If you're unsure about things, you should ask instead of assuming."

I clear my throat and shake my head. He meets my eye before pursing his lips and turning away. Aziel's always been known for his brutal honesty, but he's taking it too far. Charlie's too sensitive about her intelligence for him to be commenting on it.

Charlie glances at the ceiling, her eyes growing wet.

Aziel deflates as he sees her tears, his hands clenching and unclenching at his sides. He looks painfully uncomfortable as she wipes her cheeks, and I raise a brow as I wait to see what he's going to do.

"Stop doing that," he eventually says.

I shut my eyes. I don't think I've ever met somebody as horrible at talking to women as Aziel. If it were a competition, he'd win a fucking trophy. He shifts his weight from foot to foot as she tries to hide her subtle crying, and I let out a low sigh before turning and pulling her into my side.

"I'm sorry," I whisper. "I should've taken care to make sure you understood exactly what was happening."

Silas approaches and kneels by her feet.

Aziel sucks in his cheeks as he watches us, but I don't pay him any attention. If he has a problem with Silas and me being intimate with Charlie, he needs to pull up his big boy panties and get over it. He made his decision, and now he has to live with it.

"Our intention was never to mislead you," Silas assures our female, sliding his hands up her thighs. He stops at her waist and gives it a tight squeeze.

Charlie lets out a puff of hot air and gives a jerky nod. She's embarrassed, but there's nothing to be embarrassed about. She's young and has spent most of her life in hiding. It's understandable she'd have trouble reading between the lines and understanding the intricate nuances of our decisions and plans.

We should have made sure she truly understood what she was agreeing to.

She's smart, and she just needs time to learn.

"If they're receptive, will you tell them about the females?" she asks Silas.

Silas's chest expands as he sucks in a breath, his head rocking back and forth as he thinks through an answer. I'm willing to bet the answer would be a firm *no* if he weren't trying to spare her feelings.

"If they're friendly, we'll mention that we have people working on it and are pursuing some exciting findings," he decides.

"No, we most definitely will not," Aziel says, shutting down the plan immediately.

Silas doesn't argue with him, but he shoots Charlie a wink before bending and kissing her knee.

Chapter Five

CHARLOTTE

I GROAN AND wrap my arms around Silas's chest, annoyed as he shifts below me. I can vaguely hear him chuckling, but I ignore it and burrow further into his armpit.

"Charlie," he teases, lifting his arm to look down at me.

I peer at him through my lashes and flush at the sight of his cheesy grin. His hair's messy from sleep, but it still looks good.

"Where's Gray?" I ask.

Silas's eyes dart to the empty bed behind me before he shrugs.

"He woke up early and left. I think he's in his office catching up on work."

"What exactly does Gray do for work?" I pry.

I've never really thought to ask, but I'm curious. He seems to have more free time than Silas and Aziel, but occasionally, he'll escape to his office for a few hours.

"Believe it or not, Gray helps manage our forest service. He has a strange fascination with agriculture and helps oversee the lands. We have a dedicated forest service team, and Gray inserted himself into it about sixty years ago." Silas's lips curl into a smile as he shares this information.

To say I'm shocked would be a complete understatement. I had absolutely no idea.

"And what do you do?" I ask.

Silas shrugs. "I help Aziel."

I imagine that's got to be a horrible job. Being the leader of Wrath is probably a lot of work, and I'm sure a significant portion of it has been falling to Silas whenever Aziel's been off in the pits.

I'd be pissed if I were Silas.

"So you're pretty much the de facto King of Wrath," I tease.

Silas looks pointedly uncomfortable as he shakes his head. "No. Fates aren't leaders. It's a conflict of interest and could get me punished. I help with the finances and offer suggestions, but I don't make decisions."

"Get you punished?" I ask. "By whom?"

I'd pay good money to understand Silas better. He's an enigma, and not knowing is driving me crazy.

"By Fate. I mess up, and suddenly, I find myself burning to death in a once-in-a-million-year sinkhole that I'm somehow unable to teleport out of." Silas laughs as he says this, but I have a feeling he's not joking.

The thought of Silas dying brings a shiver to my spine, and I press myself further against his side. He's only in his underwear, and I bury my face in his exposed chest as he wraps his arms around me and pulls me into a tight hug.

It feels nice, and I enjoy it for a moment before climbing on top of him. There's always a slight moment of fear that Silas will push me away when I do things like this, but instead, he brings his hands to my hips with a wide smile.

Without thinking, I lean forward and kiss him. His breath hitches, and I tilt my head to the side to deepen it. Silas is gentle as his tongue slides between my lips and brushes against mine, and I moan into his mouth before pulling away.

"What do you want me to do?" I ask, my shaky voice revealing my nerves. "You know, to you?"

Silas's eyebrows furrow, and I sink my teeth into my bottom lip as I wait for his response. It's no secret he likes women to dominate him, but I'm still confused about what that consists of.

I'm happy to do it. I just need to know what *it* is.

"You don't need to worry about that," Silas says, deflecting.

I frown as he tries again to connect his lips to mine, unhappy he isn't giving me the answers I want. Why is he avoiding it? I hope it isn't because he thinks I'm judging.

Silas ignores my annoyance as he brings his mouth to my neck. He licks the column of my throat before sucking on the skin where my shoulder meets my neck.

"Tell me." I gasp.

"No."

I grit my teeth as he gently bites my skin, and I shiver before pulling myself out of his mouth's reach and cupping his chin. He stares at me with wide eyes, looking wild. I take a moment to enjoy it before turning and shouting Gray's name.

My voice is loud, and Silas groans as I push his hair out of his face and beam down at him. It doesn't take long for Gray to come barreling into the room.

"You rang?"

I plant my hands against Silas's chest before peering at Gray.

"Silas won't tell me what he wants," I pout.

Gray's eyes dart between Silas and me, his smile growing.

"I'll be right back." Gray practically squeals as he rushes out of the room.

Silas shifts underneath me, and I feel a hardness pressing into my thigh. It makes me feel good to know I've turned him on, and I move so I'm sitting directly over his erection.

There's an excited glint in his eye as he stares up at me, and without thinking, I cup his face and rub my thumbs over his cheeks.

There's some slight stubble along his jaw, but his skin is otherwise soft.

Silas leans into my hand and kisses my palm as Gray returns. He's carrying some fabric in his hands, and I eye it as he approaches and sets it on the bed. I'm not familiar with sex objects, but Silas seems to recognize it as his hips twitch underneath mine.

Gray kisses my cheek before turning and doing the same to Silas.

"These are all brand new. Never been used on anybody else," he whispers in the fate's ear.

Silas seems relieved.

Gray grabs the fabric and hands it to me. It's surprisingly soft, and I slide my fingers over it with a low hum. Am I supposed to tie Silas up with it?

"It's enchanted, so it's stronger than it looks," Gray says before laughing and flicking Silas's shoulder. "Silas can still break through it, but it won't come apart if he accidentally jerks."

Silas pants as I grab his wrists and move them to the headboard, and he bites at his bottom lip as Gray helps me tie him up. This doesn't seem too hard. I climb off him, and Gray pulls Silas's underwear off before helping me tie his ankles.

"What's your safe word?" Gray asks Silas.

"Red."

"Where are you?"

"Obviously green," Silas says with a slight roll of his eyes.

Gray flicks his shoulder again. I've read about safe words in a few of my romance books, but I've never used them in real life. There's never been a need.

Silas lightly tugs at his ties, testing them out, while I turn to

Gray and wait for instruction. I'm not dumb, and I know they're starting me off with what they think is easy, but I'm determined to prove I'm not going to be scared away.

Gray gestures for me to sit between Silas's thighs. The fate is already hard, and I can't pull my eyes away from his length as I settle on the bed between his spread legs. His cock lies thick and heavy on his belly, and it twitches as I reach out and curl my fingers around the base.

"Fuck," Silas breathes.

Gray settles on the bed behind me.

"If you're up for it, I'm sure Silas would love to feel your mouth," he says, wrapping his arms around my waist.

His fingers tickle the exposed skin of my thighs before sliding up my long shirt and down into my underwear. My hand tightens around Silas as Gray circles his fingers around my clit. It feels good, and I bite back a moan before planting my hand on the bed beside Silas's hip and leaning down.

I understand the basics of a blowjob, and I look up and meet Silas's gaze for a brief second before running my tongue up the underside of his cock. He throws his head back with a moan, and I take that as encouragement and let him into my mouth.

He's warm against my tongue, and I take as much of him as I can before pulling back up. Silas's hips twitch, but he keeps them relatively still as I go down again. This isn't bad.

Gray works two fingers into me before bringing his other hand to Silas. He curls his fingers around mine and shows me how to stroke the length I can't fit into my mouth. Silas curses as Gray and I move together, both of us pleasuring the fate.

I love knowing I'm making him feel good, and I moan around his shaft as I speed up my motions.

"I'm—fuck, fuck," Silas hisses, his thighs tensing around me.

Gray rocks his fingers into me, pressing against all the right spots before he slows and pulls my mouth off Silas.

Silas cries and jerks against the mattress, his breaths choppy as his orgasm is stalled.

"This is called edging," he whispers, kissing my shoulder. "Silas loves to hate it."

Interesting. "How do you know so much about what Silas likes?"

Gray clears his throat. "Thin walls and good hearing."

Silas barely pays us any attention as he tugs on his restraints. Gray gives him a sharp pinch on his inner thigh in response, the action stilling the fate almost immediately. A dark bruise forms and heals before my very eyes.

Gray continues to pleasure me with my fingers, and once Silas has settled, the incubus removes one hand and brings it back to Silas. He curls his hand around the base and strokes while I take the fate into my mouth. I do my best to keep my teeth away, but Silas doesn't seem to mind the few times I accidentally graze them against him.

If anything, he seems to actively enjoy it. He twitches every time, and he practically convulses when I decide to test the waters and purposefully let my front teeth scrape his length. Gray encourages it, and we do this until Silas is practically in tears.

"Please, please, I'm sorry," Silas begs, his black eyes staring down at me.

His cock is achingly hard and leaking, but it's hard for me to feel bad when Gray is giving me the same treatment. He works me up, only to stop when I'm on the edge. It's driving me crazy.

"Charlie, please, baby, I'm so close," Silas chokes out when I slide my fingernail up the vein on the underside of his cock.

I take him in my mouth again, but I intend to see it through this time. Silas tugs on his restraints as he trembles beneath me, his hips twitching as he cries out. Gray kisses my shoulder and moans as Silas throws his head back.

His pained cry is the only warning I have that he's about to cum, and I continue to work my mouth over him until he stills and begins to fill it. I choke a bit at first, but I keep the tip of him between my lips until he's finished.

Silas slumps against the mattress, and I pull away and swallow what he released. It's bitter, but not bad.

"Thank you," Silas says.

He stares at me through heavy-lidded eyes, and I sink my teeth into my bottom lip before climbing on top of him. I want to have sex.

I notice Silas's eyes are wet as I lean over him, and I can't help but grin as I wipe one of the tears off his cheek. Good. This is what he deserves for underestimating me.

I bend and kiss him before reaching between us and taking hold of his dick. He's still hard.

"What're you doing?" Gray asks, moving to the side of Silas and me. His eyes crinkle as he watches me fumble around.

"Having sex?"

Silas twitches in my hand.

"No," Gray says, running a gentle hand down my spine. "There's something I want you to use first."

He's teleporting out of the room before I can ask what. Silas smiles at me, and his expression tells me he knows precisely what Gray's doing. They've clearly had discussions about this already, and I frown before tightening my grip on Silas and trying to put him inside me.

Silas grunts, his neck straining as I shove him against my entrance.

"Shit, Charlie! You're going to hurt yourself."

I ignore him, sinking my teeth into my bottom lip as I struggle to get him in. It was never this hard in the books.

"Just give me a second," I grunt, embarrassed as I miss my entrance and accidentally slam him against my hard pubic bone.

Silas hisses, and his eyes screw shut as he breathes harshly through his nose. He remains hard despite the pain, his length twitching as I make another attempt.

Gray returns before I find any success. I shoot him a sharp glare, but he only watches my attempt with kind eyes.

"It's not going to work, Charlie," he says. "Lie on Silas's chest."

I huff, but I do as he says.

He kneels on the bed and sets a silicone penis and a bottle of lube next to us. The toy is shorter and thinner than his and Silas's cocks, and I can't help but frown. What's the point of this?

"This toy is the size of an average human male. It's what your body is made to take. We want you to get used to this before we have sex. Otherwise, it'll hurt you too much to be enjoyable," Gray explains.

I glance between him and the toy. I've never put too much thought into their sizes before, but I didn't realize they were so much larger than humans. Silas has a good few inches on the toy, and I don't even want to try to measure the girth difference.

I assumed they would be about the same size, but I suppose that's a silly thing to think. Demons are taller and stronger than human males, so I guess it only makes sense their anatomy would be different, too.

"Untie me," Silas says, tugging at his restraints.

Gray stares at him in silent conversation before nodding and undoing the ties. Silas lowers his arms with a quiet sigh, shivering slightly as he rubs at his wrists.

"Did you like that?" Gray asks, a hint of vulnerability in his voice.

I lift myself off Silas's chest to give them some space.

"I did," Silas admits.

Gray beams before ducking and kissing Silas, and I swallow past the lump in my throat as I watch them. I like watching them.

They don't give me much of a show, though, and Gray pulls away moments before pushing me down on Silas. I grunt as my arms collapse under the sudden weight, and Silas doesn't hesitate to wrap me in his arms. He presses soft kisses to the top of my head as the toy is brought to me, and I wiggle against it as Gray begins to push it inside.

"Fuck, Charlie." Silas moans, squeezing me tighter. "Gray's going to get you good and ready to take us."

Gray uses the lube he bought earlier, but there's still a slight pinch as he pushes the toy in. It doesn't necessarily hurt, but it feels full and uncomfortable.

"It's cold," I admit, peering at Gray over my shoulder.

He frowns. I can tell he's unhappy with my level of satisfaction, but I had my heart set on taking one of them today. Gray meets my eye before he cocks his head to the side and a sly smile spreads across his lips.

I don't trust that smile one bit.

My hair's being yanked back before I can register what's happening, and I let out a loud gasp as I'm pulled off Silas's chest. I can't help but feel turned on by the sudden roughness, and Gray seems to know that as he works the toy further inside me.

It starts to hurt, but Gray continues until I've taken all of it.

"Sit," he orders, adjusting us so I'm sitting on Silas's stomach.

The toy's base presses against Silas's torso, and it shifts inside me when he flexes. Silas looks between me and the toy with evident enjoyment, and he presses his fingers against the toy's base to hold it steady. His other hand falls to my clit, and I let out a low whine when he begins to circle it with his thumb.

"You want us so bad?" Gray whispers in my ear. "Then prove

it. Show Silas how well you'd ride him."

"Can I… have your lust?" I ask, wanting something to take the pain away.

"No."

Gray grabs my hips and helps rock me back and forth. My muscles tighten as I try to relax around the toy, my body incredibly aware that there's something foreign inside me.

"That's it. You're doing so well, baby. So fucking good for us." Gray moans. His words are followed by a deep inhale as he feeds. "Sit up so Silas can fuck you with the toy."

I don't hesitate to do precisely that.

Silas is gentle as he cups the toy's base and begins to rock it in and out. It slides relatively easily, and I clench around it as I try to grow comfortable with the pressure. Silas continues to rub my clit, the only thing keeping me going.

"Do you feel stuffed, baby girl? Imagine how full you'll be when Silas and I fuck you. You looked so adorable trying to shove his dick in you—couldn't even get the tip in." Gray laughs in my ear.

My thighs tense and squeeze around Silas's waist.

"I want you to get nice and stretched so you can use me. My cock is yours. You know it's yours, yeah?" Silas chimes in. "Only for you."

I nod and drop my chest onto Silas. He adjusts his hand so he can continue to rub at my clit, and he slows the fucking of the toy into a slow rock. Despite his easy movements, I still feel an ache in my sex, and I shut my eyes to focus only on the pleasure coming from my clit.

Silas seems to sense it as he stops moving the toy altogether.

It helps, and in only seconds, I'm clenching around the toy as my orgasm rushes through me.

"Oh," I gasp.

Silas cups the back of my neck and guides my mouth to his, his actions distracting me while Gray lifts my hips and pulls the toy out. I wince as it's moved, shifting uncomfortably at the sudden emptiness.

"I don't, uh, I don't know if I liked that," I admit, burying my face in Silas's chest.

Silas kisses my forehead. Sex is always described as this fantastic, otherworldly thing in all the books I've read, but if that's what it feels like, I don't know if I'm a big fan. It wasn't necessarily bad, but it was uncomfortable and slightly painful.

Gray steps away and returns with a wet washcloth. He wordlessly runs the warm fabric between my thighs.

"Did I bleed?" I ask.

He shakes his head. "Of course not. We aren't brutes like human men. I'm just cleaning the lube off you."

Silas continues to trail his fingers up and down my spine as Gray wipes me, and I relax against his chest.

"Do you like it when we finger you?" Gray asks, pressing a kiss to my shoulder when I nod. "That's how it'll eventually feel with the larger items. Your body just needs to get adjusted to the size. We'll take it as slow as you need."

Gray tosses the cloth aside and plops down next to us. He removed his shirt somewhere along the way, but he still wears his pants. They do little to hide his erection.

I tentatively turn to Silas before grabbing his hand and placing it on Gray. Both men chuckle at my antics, but Gray's throat bobs as I crawl off Silas and pull down the incubus's pants and underwear. He likes it when I rub myself on him, and I sit on his bare length with a quiet moan.

Gray's hands fly to my hips, and they flex as he guides me back and forth.

"Kiss me," he says, turning to Silas.

Silas doesn't hesitate to lean over and kiss Gray, and I plant my hands on Gray's chest for more leverage as I continue rocking on him. My body is sensitive, and Gray's bare length rubs directly against my clit with each movement.

It feels good, and I lean closer when he tightens his grip and some of his lust begins to pour out. He struggles to hold it back when he gets close, and I greedily breathe it in as the ache between my thighs grows. It feels good, and my motions grow jerky as the pleasure builds.

Gray moans into Silas's mouth, and I let out a quiet whine as my orgasm slams into me.

My thighs clench around Gray's hips, and he curses before gently nudging me off him and taking hold of himself. I try not to let myself be annoyed that he still won't let me make him cum, and I trail my hands up his thighs as he thrusts into his fist and spills on himself.

Silas pulls away and flops onto his back, his lips swollen and red, and I can't help but giggle as I take in his heated expression. I think he quite likes being with Gray.

Both men watch me as I crawl over Gray and plop down on Silas.

Silas stares up at me with a weak smile, and I shove a stiff finger into the bridge of his nose.

"If you don't make right with the shifters tomorrow, you're not allowed to touch Gray or me ever again," I threaten.

Gray tries to argue, but he shuts up when I shoot him a playful glare. Silas chuckles and flips us so he's on top, his hips between my thighs and his hair dangling in my face. He kisses my forehead with a soft smile.

"Noted, my love."

Chapter Six

CHARLOTTE

AZIEL LOOKS LIKE he's holding in a fart as I say my goodbye to Silas.

I pretend I don't notice as I pull Silas into a tight hug.

He's been in good spirits since we woke up this morning, and I'm hoping it's because of what we did yesterday. Being with Silas still feels surreal, especially when I wake up to his body curling around mine, but I'm quickly growing used to it.

"We'll be back soon," Silas promises, pulling away.

Aziel makes a noise in the back of his throat, and I crane my neck to see him. He's lingering by the door, his face still upturned in an annoyed scowl. I have half a mind to say something snarky, but he's only meeting with the shifters to humor me and I don't want to piss him off and make him change his mind.

He's still annoying, but I admit that much of my fear of him has lessened.

It's comforting knowing both Gray and Silas have my back, and Aziel, despite his sour attitude, hasn't done or said anything threatening to me since my first days here. A small part of me also feels better after Gray snuck me into Aziel's dreams and I got to see firsthand Aziel protecting me against Shay, but I don't let my mind linger on that particular event.

What happened afterward still haunts me.

"Be safe," I say, turning back to Silas.

His smile grows. "I like that you're concerned for me."

That's good because being concerned is my specialty. I pull Silas into another tight hug before stepping back so he and Aziel can teleport to the shifter lands. They were given specific coordinates to go to, and they were threatened with harm if they don't go to the precise location. Silas says that's normal behavior for the shifters, though.

They're peculiar with whom they let on their land and where exactly they let them.

Silas disappears, leaving Aziel and me alone. I shift my weight from foot to foot, waiting for Aziel to go. He continues to linger, and I clear my throat before gesturing to the door he's standing in front of.

"Excuse me," I mutter, making it more than clear I intend to leave.

"Do you feel safe in this house?"

His words are rushed as they tumble from his mouth, like he's forcing himself to ask them.

I hesitate before answering, unsure why he's asking. "Yes?"

Aziel clenches his jaw. "I'm not going to hurt you."

I scratch the back of my neck. Aziel and I are rarely alone together, and when we are, it's usually by accident and only for a brief moment. He'll step into a room, realize I'm already in it, and leave.

I do the same.

It's awkward, but it works for us.

"I know you're not going to hurt me," I admit.

I didn't believe that for a long time, but I figured if he had plans to harm me, he would've done it by now. Seeing him interact with Silas and Gray only confirms my suspicions. Aziel pretends like he doesn't care about anybody or anything, but I see the way he watches over Silas and Gray.

He knows where they are every minute of every day, and he's almost always looking over Gray for signs of hunger. Aziel cares for my males, and I doubt he'd be willing to hurt me and risk ruining their friendship. I've gathered they're the only people he has in his life.

"Are you scared of me?" Aziel continues, his eyes darting to the clock above my head.

I'm sure Silas is wondering what's taking him so long, and it's only a matter of time before Gray realizes Aziel is alone with me and comes storming into the room to shoo the Wrath away.

"I'm uncomfortable around you," I say. "But I'm not scared of you."

It's true.

Aziel nods, seemingly pleased with my answer, before he vanishes.

I stare at where he just stood as I struggle to wrap my mind around his odd questions. I assumed he didn't care about my perception of him, and I hate how I feel strangely complimented that he does.

If I didn't know any better, I'd say he wants me to like him.

My lips curl into a slight smile as I step out of Silas's office and make my way to my own. I peek into Gray's office on the way, but he's busy on the phone, so I don't linger. I still can't believe he works for the forest service.

I never would've guessed.

Rock is already waiting for me in my office, and I shoot him a wide smile as I make my way to my desk. He's already laid down a math workbook for me, and I groan as I sit and open it up. Math is easily my least favorite subject.

"Oh, stop whining." Rock snorts. "It's either this or language."

Language is my second-least favorite subject. It was fun initially, but the demonic language Silas and Gray insist I learn is literally impossible. It's full of contradictions, and it's unlike anything I've ever heard.

A good ten percent of the noises don't exist in the human or universal language, and I feel stupid when I try. I'm relatively decent at reading and writing it, but speaking seems to be where my brain stops working.

I shoot Rock the most menacing glare I can muster as I flip open my workbook and reach into my desk drawer for snacks. Gray recently restocked it for me, and I grab two bars of the chocolate- and caramel-covered nougat.

Rock catches the one I throw in his direction, the man obsessed with them, and I tear open the other and munch on it while I flip to the page Rock bookmarked for me.

"Variables?" I ask.

"You ever heard of them before?"

I shake my head. "No."

I've never heard of math with letters, and I stare blankly at the page as Rock grabs his damned whiteboard and starts writing down a problem to go over with me. I rest my chin in my hand, not excited to learn what 'X' is and how I'm supposed to do math with a letter.

I flip onto my back and stare at Gray. He's sitting on the opposite end of the couch, his eyes locked in on the screen mounted on the wall. The TV is a new addition to the house, and I have a feeling it was added for me.

"Graaaaay," I sing, peering down at him.

I poke his bare thigh with my toes as I admire his profile. His sharp jawline and prominent cheekbones are every human's wet dream, and his full lips are to die for. He truly is one of the most beautiful men I've ever seen.

Gray sucks in his cheeks, no doubt sensing where my thoughts have strayed.

"I love you," I say.

That captures his attention, and I feel my cheeks warming as he turns and shoots me a toothy grin. His eyes fall to the spot on my neck where demons mark, and I scrunch my shoulders to hide it. Now's not the time for that.

"How much longer do you think they're going to be?" I ask.

Silas and Aziel left hours ago, and I'm beginning to get worried. I even convinced Gray to send them a few messages, but they haven't responded.

"I'm sure they'll be back soon," Gray says. "I'd be able to feel through my bond with Aziel if he were hurt, and he's perfectly fine."

I frown, happy to hear it but still worried.

I've never met a shifter before, but many rumors are floating around about them.

News clips always portray them as wild creatures, their bodies shifting between man and animal with ease. I've seen a few images, and they sure look the part.

The men are enormous, and they're always photographed wearing nothing more than short, leather skirts that hide very little. I suppose it makes sense they'd wear clothing that's easy to remove when they need to shift, but I couldn't imagine being comfortable being so exposed.

Gray grabs my feet and begins to gently massage them, his

thumbs pressing into my arches before moving up the soles. It feels incredible, and I let a quiet groan slip from my lips as I relax on the couch.

I'll give it one more hour before asking Gray to check on Silas and Aziel again.

We turn back to the TV and continue watching the human sitcom Gray put on. Movies and television shows aren't being created anymore, but he found a collection of old ones. I'm enjoying it more than I thought I would, and I even find myself laughing a handful of times.

"I have to go to the bathroom," I say, rolling rather ungracefully off the couch.

Gray moves to get up and follow me, but he freezes as I turn to glare at him. I can go to the bathroom by myself.

He doesn't look pleased as he sits back down, his lips pursed and arms crossed over his chest. I can't help but laugh as I bend and kiss him, and I feel him smiling against my lips as I pull away.

"I love you!" he shouts as I leave the room.

"Good!"

These men hear practically everything, and I go to the bathroom farthest from him for that exact reason.

Some things are meant to be private.

I whistle quietly as I head upstairs and into the bathroom I share with Gray. It feels nice to have some time to myself, and I take my time washing my hands and fixing my hair after emptying my bladder.

It feels like a new product has been added every time I come in here, and I apply some of the fancy hand moisturizer Gray bought me before reading the label on the back of some scrub I haven't had the chance to use yet.

It's written in the demonic language, so I only understand about three words, but it's three more words than I knew six months ago.

I twist open the top and smell the scrub. It's floral, and I lean in to give it another sniff when I notice some movement in the mirror. I drop the bottle with a gasp, my mind in a panic as it clatters to the floor.

My feet trip over themselves as I spin around, and I curl my fingers around the sink basin as Shay materializes in the room. Her cold eyes are locked in on me, and I instinctively clutch at the stone necklace Silas gave me.

Am I hallucinating? I won't hesitate to use my stone if she tries to hurt me.

Shay's lips curl into a smirk as she watches my reaction to her, but the expression falls when I open my mouth to scream.

"Wait, please!" she rushes to spit out.

She lifts her hands in peace, and I feel my blood rushing through my ears as I step back into the sink to place some additional distance between us.

"I'll cut to the chase," she says, her voice low. "Levia's in talks with the ogres. He's pissed about Aziel's findings and intends to start a war."

What? I struggle to wrap my mind around this information.

Shay makes no attempts to pretend she's not evaluating every inch of my body as I cower, her cold gaze calculating.

"He doesn't care about the protection of females, and he intends to use Aziel's findings to force female births and sell the women for profit," she continues.

My throat runs dry, and I tighten my grip on my necklace as she steps closer to me.

"Why would he do that?" I ask.

"He's the King of Envy. I don't know why he does anything he does."

"And why are you telling me this?" My voice shakes, and I

clear my throat in a sad attempt to hide it.

Shay rolls her eyes.

"Your males can attest to this, but I have a vagina. My loyalties lie with the females more so than Levia," she says, shrugging. "Barely."

Her remark about Gray and Silas makes my blood boil, but I push my anger deep down. She could kill me with the snap of her wrist, and I'd do well to remember that.

I don't even know if she's telling the truth.

As much as I want to believe somebody wouldn't lie about this, her prior actions make me skeptical. Shay's had it out for me since we met, and I know she has ulterior motives. She's made it clear that she intends to have Aziel, Gray, and Silas for herself.

"Levia agreed to Aziel's plan," I point out.

Shay pinches the bridge of her nose with a loud sigh.

"Yes, I was there for that," she says, speaking slowly as if talking to a child. "And I'm telling you he's lying. Do you know what that word means?"

I suck my cheeks into my mouth. *Bitch.*

She smiles and cocks her head to the side. I shift uncomfortably, hating every second I'm in her presence. She makes me uneasy, and I don't trust her one bit.

"Why are you telling me and not Aziel?" I ask.

"Aziel refuses to see me."

My face remains flat, but inside, I find joy in hearing that.

I clear my throat, trying to decide what to say, when Shay suddenly steps forward and reaches for the stone around my neck. Her abrupt movements have a scream tearing out of my mouth, the noise making her jolt and disappear just as Gray materializes in the space.

He looks feral as he grabs me and searches the room, his grip on my ribs bruising as he yanks me into his chest. I flinch at the pain his abrupt movements bring, but he doesn't seem to notice as he pulls me out of the bathroom and into his bedroom.

His eyes continue to dart around as he checks to ensure Shay's truly gone.

"Are you okay?"

"Yes."

Gray doesn't listen as he grabs my shirt and rips it off my body.

"Gray!" I shout. "She didn't touch me."

He unclips my bra before yanking my leggings and underwear down my legs. I frantically try to cover myself as he crouches to peer at the small red spots left on my waist from where he grabbed me too hard. His fingers ghost over them before he grabs my thigh and lifts it so he can check underneath.

I curse, grabbing his shoulder to remain steady while he maneuvers me like cattle.

"What's going on?"

I jump a good foot in the air and hide behind Gray as Aziel's voice floats through the room. He stands in the doorway next to Silas, and I can pinpoint the moment he smells Shay. His pupils dilate as he scans the room, checking for any sign of her.

"Where is she?" Aziel asks, shifting into the bathroom doorway and stepping into the spot where she stood only moments prior.

Silas follows him before changing his mind and approaching me. His eyes follow the same path Gray's did, and I feel my cheeks redden as he grabs my arms and pulls them away from my body.

"Guys," I hiss, embarrassed.

Aziel returns to the room and plants himself next to Silas. He bites at his bottom lip as he grabs my wrists and lifts them in the air. I fight to rip them out of his hand, but he refuses to let me go.

"I'm okay. She just wanted to talk," I promise.

Aziel's gaze on my naked body is clinical, a far cry from the heated one I'm used to seeing on him. He hardly glances at my exposed breasts as he searches for any signs of injury, but his jaw snaps shut when he finds the darkening bruises on my ribs from where Gray grabbed me.

He adjusts his hold on my wrists before bringing his free hand to the spots.

I hate how my skin pebbles up as he lightly runs his fingertips over them, and I look to Gray for help when my nipples harden for everybody to see. Gray doesn't seem to notice as he crouches to peer at the thigh he didn't get a chance to evaluate earlier, his need to protect me from Shay outweighing his desire to protect me from Aziel.

"What are these?" Aziel asks, still distracted by my tiny bruises.

Gray looks up. "Those are mine."

The temperature in the room seems to drop a good ten degrees as Aziel stills. Silas disappears behind me as Gray gulps.

"You hurt the human?" Aziel asks.

He releases my wrists and pushes against my belly until I stumble into Silas's chest. The fate wrestles a shirt over my head as Aziel turns to Gray.

I can't see the Wrath's expression, but I figure it's not friendly, given the look of fear that spreads across Gray's face.

"It was an accident," Gray says, gesturing wildly in my direction. "I heard her scream and panicked. Shay's scent was everywhere, and I grabbed Charlie too hard."

Aziel remains silent, and Silas wraps an arm around my waist to keep me still. I've seen Aziel and Gray fight before, and I will not sit here and watch them do it again.

I can tell Silas silently agrees with Aziel's actions by the way he's not trying to stop their impending fight, but I don't agree. Aziel backs Gray up against the wall, his fists clenching and unclenching at his sides.

Gray tries to sidestep him, and in fear, I stomp Silas's toe with my heel.

The momentary distraction is all I need, and I lunge forward the second I feel Silas's hold loosen.

Gray's eyes dart to me just seconds before my arms wrap around Aziel's midsection. The Wrath doesn't move an inch as I try to yank him back, his body still as a statue as I plant my heels into the ground and try pulling him away from Gray.

"No!" I huff, linking my hands together to trap his arms by his sides.

Gray looks shocked as he glances between Aziel and me. His eyebrow quirks as Aziel's taut muscles soften beneath my arms, and his lips curl into a full-blown smile as Aziel steps aside and makes room for Gray to slip away.

Aziel's hands move to my wrists, but I continue to latch on. I bury my face into his back as he tries to pry me off.

"Release me, Charlotte." He scoffs, his grip shifting rapidly between tight and loose as he tries to figure out how much pressure he can use without hurting me. I want to laugh, but I don't want him to know I find his actions funny.

I'm starting to think he doesn't hate me as much as he lets on.

Taking pity on him, I let him unwrap my arms from around his waist. He's disappearing and materializing in the corner a second later, his arms crossed over his chest as he glares at me.

The slight flush of his cheeks tells me there's another emotion he's feeling beyond anger.

"Aziel felt Gray's panic and brought us back," Silas says.

He pulls me into his arms, and I rest my face against his bare chest. The shirt he forced me into is his, and I breathe in his scent before pulling away to look at him.

"Shay said Levia's working with the ogres," I rush to tell them.

Silas's grip on me tightens, but it's the only reaction he gives.

"Go on," Aziel says from the corner.

I bury my fingers into the muscle of Silas's back as I recall our conversation.

Chapter Seven

AZIEL

I CAN'T GET the image of Charlie's bruised ribs out of my head as she shares what Shay told her. I only half-listen, knowing Shay is lying, but I nod as if Charlie has my full attention. Shay is known for her intricate schemes, and I've watched my males fall prey to them one too many times to be fooled.

My attention slides to Gray.

He glances at Charlie's side, his guilt as clear as day. It couldn't have been more than ten seconds from when he heard her scream to when we showed up, and if her skin's already red and swollen, I don't even want to think about how bad it will be tomorrow.

He could have broken her ribs.

I clench my jaw shut, angry I didn't show up earlier.

I could feel Gray's stress through the bond, and I took an extra few seconds to grab Silas rather than immediately teleporting here. I should've come here the moment I felt it. Gray wouldn't have panicked, and I could've prevented him from harming Charlie.

The shifters probably wonder what happened and why we left

in the middle of the conversation, but I'll send a message to them tomorrow explaining there was an emergency with our female. They're obsessed with theirs, and I'm sure they won't question it.

My eyes travel to Charlie's covered ribcage.

She and Silas are the only ones unaffected by her bruising. Silas rubs her shoulders and arms, comforting her in a way I find unusual. In all the time I've known him, I've never seen him so nurturing.

He's generally the most reserved of the three of us, but lately, he's been the exact opposite.

I know he's been whispering information about the fates to her, and he went against my wishes and told the shifters we're working on a cure for the females during our meeting. The fucker refused to meet my eye as he spoke, and he even dared to straighten his spine as if he were proud of himself for sharing our private information.

I'm sure he'll be all cheesy smiles when he tells Charlie about it, too. I did all the work to set it up, but it'll be Silas who gets his dick touched as a thank you.

Not that I want her to touch me, anyway.

"Are you okay?" Gray whispers as Charlie finishes retelling her interaction with Shay. "I'm so sorry."

Charlie nods, but Gray's guilt still pours off him in waves as he slips his fingers between hers. He should be sorry, fucking idiot.

"I'm okay," she comforts, squeezing his hand.

"You shouldn't trust what Shay says," Silas says.

Gray and I are quick to agree, but Charlie seems hesitant. She glances at Gray, her lips pursing, before turning to me.

"Will you speak to her?" she asks.

I perk up, happy she's asking me, not Gray or Silas. It's about time she realizes who's in charge.

She looks hopeful, and I take no pleasure in shaking my head *no*. It's not an idea worth entertaining.

I'm not sure what plan Shay's concocted in her head, but I don't believe she cares about the females for a second. I've watched that woman tear out the organs of weaker women simply because they looked at her wrong.

Not to mention how she took it upon herself to kill every female Gray slept with while they were together. She even tried to take me out in a fit of rage, sneaking into my room while I was asleep and attempting to rip out my heart.

It was a good attempt, one I found humorous, but Gray was mortified.

I wonder what he would do if Charlie tried to kill me. She'd fail, but I want to know if he'd grow as enraged as he did when Shay made her attempt.

I like to think he would.

Despite what he claims, I know he still feels our bond. He can pretend to be indifferent all he wants, but the guilty way he avoids eye contact whenever he's been recently intimate with Charlie or Silas tells me all I need to know. He hates the divide between us, and I'm sure he still secretly hopes I'll change my mind about Charlie.

Charlie presses her lips together.

"Please?" she tries.

I shake my head once more.

It's not worth the effort.

Charlie tilts her head to the side, the sight making my hands clench into fists by my sides. She looks like a fucking dog when she does that.

Despite my attempts not to, I glance at her covered ribcage once more. Silas's shirt covers her, and I want to know if her bruising has worsened.

"No," I repeat before she can ask again.

Charlie frowns, her expression matching my own as she tightens her grip on Gray's hand.

I don't understand why she's looking for his comfort when he hurt her just minutes prior. He was careless, and I hate how nobody else is angry with him.

He needs to be careful.

I'd lecture him myself if it didn't draw so much attention to my softness toward the human. I'm fully aware I'm having difficulty distancing myself from her, but I don't need anybody else to realize that.

The memory of Charlie's gangly limbs wrapping around my body and pinning my arms to my sides calms me, and I clear my throat before running a hand through my hair.

"Why not? There's no harm in hearing what she has to say," Charlie argues.

Her eyes are all big and bug-like as she stares up at me, and I resist the urge to step forward and push her lids shut. They're going to dry out.

"I don't want to," I say.

"Why not?"

I shrug. "Shay annoys me."

Charlie's face turns red in anger, the sight only provoking me to continue. I like when she gets mad at me, and I find the attitude that erupts from her to be exciting.

"You're being stubborn," she snaps.

She's not wrong, but I won't give her the satisfaction of letting her know I agree.

"And you're being gullible," I say instead. "I already know Shay's lying, and I don't want to waste my time listening to her try to spin some story to get us on her side. She's an Envy. It's what they do."

"Please, Aziel," Charlie begs, her voice lowering.

I press my tongue to the roof of my mouth and look away. Why does she have to use that fucking voice every time she wants something from me?

Her heart races as I clamp my lips together and shake my head, silently denying her request. I'm tired of letting her walk all over me. I'm in charge here, and I'll be damned if I let some puny, short human try to tell me what to do.

My eyes narrow as she steps out of Silas's arms and approaches. I back up against the wall, not liking her proximity under the watchful eyes of Silas and Gray. They get a kick out of seeing her make me uncomfortable, finding humor in my awkward reactions toward her.

Charlie steps into my personal space, and I stare at her with wide eyes and stiff muscles as she wraps her arms around my waist. I look to Gray and Silas for help as she rests her chin against my sternum, but they offer none.

Bastards.

I'm not sure where this sudden sense of confidence has come from, but I sure as shit am not enjoying it. I liked it better when she was scared of me, constantly scampering along the walls and staying out of sight.

She thinks she's got some pull over me.

"Please?" she asks again.

My body reacts to her begging despite me telling it not to, my tense muscles softening while other parts of my body do the opposite. Gray grins as he picks up on my arousal, and I know the way Charlie shoves herself against my bulge isn't accidental.

It feels good, and I hate every second of it.

I don't know what's been happening with Charlie's hormones recently, but she's been all over Gray and Silas. At this point, there's a noticeable thinned-out patch on my bed where I've been rutting against it, unable to stop myself when I listen to them.

It's almost always followed by self-loathing, and I can hear Gray rummaging around my room feeding on my residual lust every time I take a shower afterward.

Even now, I can smell slight arousal coming off her, the scent barely noticeable but still there. I can also smell that she will be getting her period any day now, and I wonder if it's a side effect of her menstrual cycle.

Demon women aren't afflicted with the same hormonal changes humans are, and from the research I've done, it seems humans have many of them.

"You're trying to manipulate me," I say.

Charlie giggles, and I want to stick my finger in my fucking eye.

"Yes," she admits.

Silas turns away to hide his laughter. Gray quickly follows suit, covering his mouth as he saddles up alongside the fate. I don't know why they find this so funny.

You would think they'd be angry watching their female all up on me like a bitch in heat. Do they have any sense of protectiveness over her, or do they intend to share her with every interested male? My pulse races at the thought of them offering her up to others, and I fight against the irrational wrath that stirs within my chest.

I'll kill any fucking male they try to share her with.

I reach down and try to pull Charlie's arms off me, but she refuses to be removed.

"Please, Aziel," she pleads. "Just one conversation. That's all I'm asking for."

Her fingers twist into the fabric of my shirt, pulling it taut against my chest. I tighten my grip on her biceps before loosening up in fear of hurting her. Gray may be more than happy leaving bruises all over her skin, but that's not something I'm interested in.

"You're being annoying," I tell her.

I know she can feel my erection digging into her stomach, her reddening cheeks giving her away.

She doesn't say anything, and after a silent stare-off, I groan and look up at the ceiling. Buying her was a mistake. If I were smart, I would've accepted Shay years ago when I had the opportunity. I hate her, but at least I wouldn't have to deal with this incessant human.

"Fuck!"

Charlie jolts but doesn't let go.

"Fine," I say. "You win. Just fucking let me go, and I'll talk to her."

Charlie beams up at me, and I fight the urge to shut her eyes for her as she finally fucking releases me and steps away.

I meet her gaze as I shove my hand into my pants to readjust my erection. She felt it, Gray smelled it, and I'm sure Silas noticed it the second she stepped back, so there's not much of a point in pretending it's not there.

My cock twitches as I pull it into my waistband to relieve some of the pressure, and I sink my teeth into my bottom lip as she backs into Silas's chest. Her eyes flash to where I'm holding myself, and her heart beating loudly in her chest.

I wonder what she'd do if I were to pull out my cock and begin stroking myself. Gray would love it, but Silas and Charlie are wildcards.

"Thank you," Charlie mutters, clearing her throat as I release myself and pull my hand from my pants.

She thinks she owns me, and I just gave her more reason to believe that. The realization pisses me off, and I turn and leave the room without responding.

I prop myself up on my elbows as Gray and Silas stroll into my bedroom. Gray is wearing one of Silas's T-shirts, which is odd. It's usually my clothes he's trying to steal.

I've done an excellent job avoiding them these past two days, but I should've known it was only a matter of time before they forced themselves into my private space.

I'm only wearing my sweatpants, and I glance at my shirt lying bunched up on the floor before turning back to my two intruders. I can't be bothered to get out of bed and dress.

"You promised Charlie you'd talk to Shay," Gray says.

I turn and look in the direction of Charlie's bedroom. If I listen hard enough, I can hear her breathing into her pillow. It's steady, signaling she's asleep, and I allow myself to listen for a moment longer before turning back to Gray and Silas.

They look pissed.

"It's not going to kill you to have one ten-minute conversation with her," Silas adds.

I beg to differ. I have no interest in speaking to Shay and even less interest in allowing Charlie to continue thinking she has some pull over me. I have enough to worry about, and I've been focusing too much on Charlie.

The room falls silent, and I listen as she lets out a quiet sigh. Her sheets rustle as she rolls over, and I hold my breath as I wait to see if she wakes up. She doesn't.

Cute.

"I'm too busy to waste time indulging Shay or Charlie," I say. "I spent all day trying—and failing—to catch up on everything I missed while in the pits."

It was foolish to leave for so long, and I'm paying for it dearly.

My days are busy enough without the added pressure of trying to figure out this whole female situation, and now I'm lucky to have even an hour to myself a day.

"We all know nothing good's going to come of it," I continue. "If I speak with Shay, she'll take that as an invitation and start showing up all the time. She's done it before, and she'll do it again."

The bed frame groans as I sit up further.

"You need to buy a new bed," Gray points out. "You can have mine once the wing is finished."

I sigh. He and Silas have been fixing up the unused wing of our home, and he's taking great pleasure in constantly bringing it up.

"If you're not going to talk to Shay," Silas says, "you need to tell Charlie. She's been asking when your meeting is."

I blink. "No."

Gray looks like he's about to burst an artery.

"And why not?" Silas asks.

I look down at my legs. "Charlie doesn't own me."

A loud laugh bubbles up out of Gray's throat before he turns to look at Silas. He's laughing at me, and I shift awkwardly as I wait for him to contain himself. This female is turning me into a whiny, pathetic male.

"Are you telling me that you, a thousand-year-old demon, are scared of how a twenty-five-year-old human perceives you?" Silas asks.

I choose not to respond to that.

Gray approaches my bed and hovers over me. He's trying to be menacing, and I let out a loud gasp and lift my hand in front of my face.

"Oh, no, Gray! Please, no!" I snort. "Have mercy!"

Gray's pupils dilate as he glares down at me, and I glare right back. We both know he's not going to hurt me, and I'm not in the mood to act scared just for his precious little ego. He's an incubus, and I'm the King of Wrath.

The list of things I fear is short, and he doesn't make the cut.

I turn to Silas. "Have you—" My sentence is cut short as a hand curls around my throat.

I've got about ten seconds before my wrath consumes me, and I rip Gray's hand off my throat before grabbing his shoulder and yanking him over me. He loses his footing almost immediately, and I spin so he's on his back and I'm kneeling over him.

My fingers dig into the sides of his neck, and I place just enough weight on his throat to remind him who I am.

Gray's face turns red as he claws at my arm, but even the scent of my blood doesn't stop me. First he hurts Charlie, and now he tries to choke me.

"That's enough," Silas says, pushing off the doorframe.

He grabs my shoulder and tries to ease me back. I loosen my grip on Gray's throat, but I otherwise don't move. Gray thankfully stops ripping at my arm, and I wince as my skin begins to heal.

"If you two need to fuck, I'm fine with it," Silas continues. "I'm sure Charlie will be, too."

Over my dead body. Gray slides his thigh between mine, and I clench my jaw as it presses against me. I didn't realize I was aroused until now, and I pull away from Gray with a quiet grunt. This can't happen.

"I'm uninterested in pretending to enjoy a thirty-second, poorly executed hump," Gray says as I climb off my bed.

I don't know why he keeps making digs at my virginity.

"Fuck you," I snap.

"You wish."

My eyes fall to his mouth before I catch myself and turn away. I may have once entertained the idea of what it would be like to be with Gray, but that's in the past. He's chosen the human, and I won't beg.

Gray holds eye contact as he slides his arms out to his sides and runs his hands along my bedsheets. He's not sly, and I purse my lips as his lust fills my lungs. He's pushing his scent into my bedsheets, and they'll reek of him when he leaves.

Silas clicks his tongue against the roof of his mouth and moves back to the doorway. I'm willing to bet he can hear Charlie better from there.

As calm as he's trying to be, I know he's worried about Shay. I hate to admit I feel the same way. I don't like how easily the female entered our home and spoke to Charlie, and a small part of me fears she will do it again.

I should have never brought Shay here to begin with.

Gray's movements are suspiciously lithe as he climbs off my bed and steps toward me. His lust pours out of him in waves, the scent affecting me more than usual. We've been holding in our natural scents for so long that I almost forgot how strong they are when released.

Especially Gray's.

Silas's doesn't affect me much, and I'm sure he'd say the same about me, but Gray's is different. Incubi's always are.

Gray places a hand on my hip, and I struggle to remain still as he weasels his fingers underneath my shirt. They press against my bare skin, and I hold back a shiver as our bond reacts.

I've gotten so good at ignoring our bond that it falls to the back of my mind most of the time, but it's impossible not to notice when he's touching me. Our souls are entwined, and I feel him pulling at mine as he steps farther into my space.

"Please meet with Shay," he begs.

For fuck's sake.

Gray wraps his arms around me just as Charlie did the other

day, and I resist the urge to disappear and materialize on the other side of the room. I don't know why I don't. Probably because it would hurt his feelings and there's a sad, pathetic part of me that doesn't want to do that.

He presses his cheek against my shoulder, and I suck in my cheeks when Silas steps forward and joins him in this infuriating hug.

"What the fuck is this?" I snap. "Don't you see how childish you two are acting?"

Silas wraps his arms around both me and Gray.

"You're big and scary, baby," Gray coos, mocking me.

I push my arms out to try to remove my intruders, but they only double down and squeeze me harder.

"I'll have Charlie say your name when she cums." Gray's offer captures my attention, and I stiffen as I wait for him to continue.

His lips brush my ear as he speaks, and I'm hopeless to stop my dick from twitching in my pants. Gray moans, the little fucker probably feeding on my arousal, and I curl my fingers around a wrist to keep myself steady.

Silas shifts, and I realize he's whom I've grabbed onto.

"Don't bother pretending you don't listen to us," Gray says. "I'll fuck her with my fingers and tell her to close her eyes and pretend it's you. She'll scream your name when she cums."

I gulp. "She'll never do that."

Gray runs his fingertips across the waistband of my sweatpants. His nail digs into my skin just hard enough to hurt, and I groan as my cock throbs. I fucking hate incubi.

"She'll do it," he promises.

His lips find my neck, and I grow entirely still as he grazes his teeth over the spot he's made abundantly clear he someday intends to mark. We've already got a bond, but he wants a physical reminder.

I tilt my head back to give him more room, and my grip on Silas's wrist grows impossibly tight as Gray turns and begins kissing Silas instead. Silas moans into his mouth, and I drag the fate's hand to my covered erection before I can talk myself out of it.

This is a bad idea. Silas takes hold of me, his grip tight.

"Fuck," I gasp.

Gray quickly grabs Silas's hand and pulls it away, and I curse as my hips jerk forward and meet nothing but air.

"Would you prefer I have her cry out 'Daddy' instead of 'Aziel'?" Gray asks.

I square my shoulders. I'm sick and tired of his games.

"'Aziel' will be fine," I say. "I want you to do it while you're fucking her with the toy."

Gray beams. "Only if you go to Shay now," he counters.

He unwraps his arms from my waist and steps back, and Silas quickly returns to the doorway. We all pause and wait until we hear Charlie's even breathing before returning to our conversation.

"It's the middle of the night," I point out.

"She's staying at her chateau in Lust," Gray says, ignoring me.

I sigh. "I'm only doing this to shut the three of you up."

Gray shrugs, clearly not caring, and leaves my room. He pulls Silas along with him, and I listen to their footfalls as they return to Charlie's bedroom.

The bedsheets rustle as they climb into bed, and I hear Charlie let out a particularly loud grunt before she whines and the sheets rustle some more.

"Did it work?" she asks.

Did what work?

Gray laughs. "Like a fucking charm."

I step closer to the door. *Did what work?*

Charlie giggles, and I frown as I listen to the three of them settle into bed. I'd kill to know what they're doing right now, and I'd materialize in there if I thought Gray and Silas wouldn't notice.

"I ended up agreeing to have you moan Aziel's name the next time I get you off," Gray admits.

Why is he telling her that? Did they set this entire thing up? I clench and unclench my hands as I imagine them getting together and concocting some plan for Gray to seduce me into doing their bidding.

Gray hisses, and I wonder if Charlie's pinched his nipple as she so enjoys doing. I hope so.

Silas moans, and I cock my head to the side as I hear more shifting.

"I accidentally got Silas all turned on, too," Gray admits.

There's another low moan, followed immediately by the unmistakable sound of a cock being stroked.

"You're so fucking needy. I want you to tell Charlie how embarrassingly desperate you've been tonight, rutting on and touching Aziel while I told him how I'm going to pleasure Charlie." Gray's voice is low, and I slide a hand down my own body as I listen.

"Silas!" Charlie scolds.

She sounds pleased, the fucking gremlin, and I force myself to teleport to Lust before I do something I regret.

Chapter Eight

SILAS

I TAP AIMLESSLY at my keyboard, unable to concentrate on a damn thing.

"I'm not changing my decision," Rock says, his voice slightly muffled as it travels through two doors and a hallway. "Just because you know a fate doesn't mean they aren't endangered."

Charlie huffs. "You don't know what you're talking about."

I shake my head, holding back laughter. She's gaining more confidence with each passing day, and I enjoy listening to her near-constant arguments with Rock.

"I can assure you, I do," Rock says.

Charlie doesn't respond, but the sound of paper being flicked makes its way to my ears.

"Would you care to ask Silas yourself?" Rock suggests.

I hope she does. She won't be happy with my answer, and I think she knows that as she quiets down and returns to her studying. She loves challenging Rock, and I'm glad we chose him as her tutor.

Most shadows in our home are desperate to appease her. They think it's a way to win our favor, but I like that Rock doesn't seem to care much for that. He pisses her off more often than not, and he doesn't back down despite how hard she occasionally pushes.

Their conversation is cut short as Aziel storms into her office, his footfalls loud as he stomps down the hallway and pushes open her door.

"I spoke with Shay last night," he says.

I lean back in my chair, eager to hear this conversation.

"And?" Charlie urges, my female clearly desperate to hear all the details.

Aziel clears his throat, an action he does whenever Charlie does something he thinks is attractive. He's been doing it a lot recently, and I can only imagine what she's done to provoke it this time.

"She had nothing to share other than what she's already said to you," Aziel says. "Shay's untrustworthy, and I hold Levia's word above hers."

There's a long beat of silence, and Aziel clears his throat once more before continuing.

"This was a waste of my time, and you've used up the one favor you'll ever get from me. I don't want to hear any more talk of Shay, and you're to stop trying to use my males to manipulate me into doing your bidding. You're a small human, insignificant, and you'd do well to remember that."

I raise a brow, fighting the urge to laugh. Aziel tries so hard to pretend Charlie isn't anything to him, but he's not fooling anybody.

Charlie hums, and I hear the faint sound of a pen being clicked a few times.

"We'll see about that," she says.

Absolute silence follows her words, and I can only imagine how infuriated Aziel is right about now. He's used to being in charge, and I can tell Charlie's lack of respect drives him mad. I think it's good for him.

He's been leading Wrath for a long time, and he's grown quite callous over the years. Charlie's been forcing him to think about his actions, and I'd go as far as to say she's softening him. He doesn't like to show it, but I can see it in the way he's always trying to evaluate and understand her emotions.

"We *will* see about that," Aziel eventually says.

He's storming back into his office a second later.

Even though his meeting with Shay was as unproductive as he thought it would be, he doesn't need to be so dramatic about it.

We're old, and one hour is hardly a loss.

Besides, it's a small thing to give Charlie peace of mind. She has trouble trusting us after learning about our initial reaction to the female information, and it's good for her to see that we're taking her concerns seriously.

Drawers slam shut as Aziel searches his office for something, his audible frustration growing as he leaves and makes his way down the hallway toward Gray's. He refuses to turn in my direction as he passes my open door, continuing forward until he busts into the incubus's office.

"Where's my keyboard?" Aziel snaps.

There's a snort followed by a loud clanging. I imagine Aziel shoved aside the chairs in front of Gray's desk in order to better hover over it and glare. Gray's probably got a sly grin on his lips, happy with the attention he's getting from Aziel.

It surprises me the lengths he'll go to get Aziel's attention, purposefully doing small, meaningless things to piss the Wrath off.

I should've known Gray wouldn't be able to help himself from tormenting Aziel, but he'll need to tone it down if he doesn't want to hurt Charlie's feelings. She's protective of her relationship with Gray, and quite insecure. It's easy to see she's scared Gray will end up choosing Aziel over her, and his subtle flirting will only backfire on him.

Charlie will get upset, and Aziel will get his feelings hurt when he eavesdrops on Gray comforting her.

"I didn't touch your keyboard," Gray says.

"No? Then care to explain to me what your greasy, stubby fucking fingertips are resting on right now?"

I shut my eyes and hold my breath to keep from making any sounds. As annoying as they are, I can't lie and say their bickering doesn't amuse me. It's better than the sharp digs and physical fights they've been resorting to these past few months.

I'll take an annoying, childish Gray over a bloody one any day.

Charlie starts up another argument with Rock before storming out of her office. She pauses outside Gray's, probably peering in on him and Aziel, before pattering my way. I lean back in my chair and wait for her to come, my pulse racing.

She pops her head in my doorway, probably making sure I'm not busy, before slinking inside. She holds her hands behind her back as she enters, taking her sweet time looking around before sitting in the chair opposite my desk.

Her eyes linger on the cleaning supplies that still clutter up the room. Gray was so proud of himself as he cleared out what was once our cleaning closet and turned it into Charlie's office, but now both his and my offices contain random items he couldn't find a home for.

I didn't mind him putting the cleaning products in here when I thought it was a temporary solution, but I'm starting to realize he has no intention of cleaning it up.

They ruin my aesthetic, and I don't want the chemical fumes damaging my books.

Not to mention how distracting it is to have shadows moving

in and out whenever they need things. Some of the more daring ones even seem to find humor in it, chuckling to themselves as they notice my glaring.

"How'd your test go?" I ask, not wanting Charlie to know I was eavesdropping on her tutoring session.

"I got one question wrong, which Rock refuses to change, but other than that, I did well," she says.

I lean forward and rest my chin on my palm. It takes everything in me not to tease her for her argument with Rock. Listening to her banter with him is amusing, especially when they speak about my kind.

"I want to take you on a lunch date," I say.

Charlie's expression brightens, a soft smile playing at the corners of her lips as her pulse quickens. She's only been on one date before, and Gray's bright idea was to take her to a pool bar.

Where's the romance in that?

"Where?" Charlie brings her hands together in an excited clap.

I pause before answering, unsure how well my idea will be received. Gray said it was a good idea, but I don't want to disappoint.

"It's a surprise," I say, standing.

Charlie jumps up from her chair as I walk around my desk and hold out my hand. The shadows I sent out earlier promised to have everything completed by now.

I pull my hand back to my side when Charlie hesitates to grab it. She hates teleporting, but it should be easier with me. Gray's not as experienced with it, so his teleportations are rougher on the body, but mine are smooth.

"Come here." I chuckle, pulling her into my arms.

Charlie buries her face in my chest, no doubt bracing for the sickness I'm sure she's convinced she's going to feel, and I press a kiss to the top of her head before taking her to our spot.

The sound of birds chirping is the first thing that makes its way to my ears as I materialize, and I hope it's loud enough for Charlie to hear as she grabs my biceps for balance. Her nails dig into the muscle, but it doesn't hurt.

"Are you okay?" I ask, running my hands down the back of her head.

Her body loosens one muscle at a time, and I take great pleasure in how she looks up at me with evident relief. Slowly, she turns, her heart pounding as she takes in her surroundings.

I brought her to a small, secluded island in Wrath. I found it a few hundred years ago, and as far as I'm aware, I'm one of the only ones who know about it. It's one of my favorite places to visit, and Charlie seems to enjoy it as she looks around with a slack jaw.

Her attention lingers on the lava pits surrounding the island before shifting to the sprawling trees behind us. I feel her skin to ensure the lava isn't too hot for her, but she seems to be handling it well.

The actual lava is far away, but Charlie doesn't do well with the heat. Many of her conversations begin with her complaining about how hot it is in Wrath.

"It's a picnic," I say, gesturing to the small table farther down the beach.

Charlie clears her throat. "This is amazing."

She steps back into my chest and grabs my hands. Her fingers intertwine with mine before she moves to the table, dragging me behind her. I happily oblige, glad she likes what I've done.

Charlie smacks her tongue against the roof of her mouth as she peers at the food.

"These are the traditional dishes of my kind," I explain, leaning over her shoulder.

The grip on my hand tightens as I point to each one and

explain what it's made from. I don't often ask the shadows to prepare the food from my childhood, knowing it's unfamiliar to them and can be tricky to make, but I wanted to show Charlie.

I can't tell her much about me and what being a fate entails, but I *can* share this.

"This is similar to human beef," I say, pointing to the dish closest to us. It's a stewed meat, and it's covered in a spicy vegetable sauce I was obsessed with as a child.

I grab a fork and scoop up a bite. Charlie watches, her eyes wide as I bring it to her lips.

Pleasure like I've never known spreads through me as she opens her mouth and tries the food. She hums as she chews, and I can't help but stare at the column of her throat as she swallows.

I am obsessed with her.

"It's good," she says.

Licking my lips, I pull a plate of baked sweet vegetables closer to us and scoop Charlie up another forkful. She looks pleased as she eats it, her lips curled upward and her eyes shining.

I love it, and I take a bite for myself with a content hum. It's been so long since I ate any traditional fate food, and I've missed it.

"You know, before the fates became endangered, we used to love holding grand feasts," I say, grinning at the sly joke regarding her earlier argument with Rock.

Charlie stiffens, catching on, before grumbling and taking a seat. I quite enjoy her pouting, and I sit next to her before continuing to show and feed her my food.

I haven't had the opportunity to spend much meaningful time alone with Charlie, and I can't keep my smile off my face as we eat. She eats more than I expected before getting up and dragging me around the island.

It's rich in fruits and animals, and her eyes grow comically wide as she stumbles upon a fruit tree. It's similar to the human banana tree, but the fruit's skin is hard and the taste is sour.

"Be careful," I warn as she tries to scale the tree to grab one.

Charlie scoffs, ignoring me before inching up higher. I position myself underneath so I can catch her if she falls, but she makes it to the top and shakes off the fruit without much trouble. She climbs back down with ease, and I sit at the tree's base.

She settles between my legs and leans back against my chest as I pull open the fruit and feed her a piece.

Her teeth sink into the skin of my fingers, and I press a kiss to the side of her head as I rip off another chunk. I'm content as I serve her, happy to have something to fill my time that isn't work.

I'm grateful to have Gray, too, an emotion I never imagined I'd feel. It's odd to transition from friend to lover, but Charlie's presence has made it easy. I've always had a slight interest in Gray, but my feelings were easy to cast aside with the knowledge that someday we'd have a female and she might not want her males together.

Charlie seems to love it when Gray and I are intimate. If anything, she's the one who provokes it, always grabbing our hands and placing them on one another.

"When do you want to bond with me?" Charlie asks.

My movements freeze as her question filters through my mind. In all honesty, it's not something I've placed much thought into. Charlie's still so young, and I don't want to pressure her into making a decision that will impact her for the rest of her life.

I refuse to let myself get excited about something she might end up deciding she doesn't want.

"I will happily bond with you the moment you're ready," I say, feeding her another bite.

Charlie spins in my arms. "I'm ready."

Her look of complete trust and adoration is enough to take my breath away, and I shut my eyes to collect my thoughts. There's no way I can tell her I think she should wait before making that decision without hurting her feelings. She'll accuse me of treating her like a child, which admittedly I am, but this isn't something I'm willing to back down on.

I know she loves me, but I'm not going to let her get blinded by her lust and make rash decisions. I mentally prepare for her wrath as I grab her hands and look into her eyes.

"I think we should wait," I admit.

She recoils, the reaction stronger than I was anticipating. *Fuck.*

"Why? Keeping your options open?"

Charlie crosses her arms over her chest, putting a physical barrier between us, before glancing timidly to the side. I raise a brow, unwilling to justify her question with a response.

I may like that tone in bed, but I'm not on a mattress and she should know better than to think so little of me. I've made my interest in her more than apparent, and I'm not one to say things I don't mean.

Her tense muscles relax when I don't acknowledge her harsh questioning, an apologetic look taking over her features as she lowers her eyes to my chest.

"I'm sorry," she mumbles, clearing her throat. "Why do you want to wait?"

I intertwine our fingers and kiss the back of her palm. Her breath hitches, and I give another kiss before lowering our hands to her lap.

"I've chosen you, and that's not going to change, but I could never live with myself if we bonded and you came to regret it," I admit. "I've waited over a thousand years for you, and I want you to be as sure about me as I am about you. Let's give it at least a year."

Her heart thunders as she stares at me, her glossy eyes hard to read.

It's times like this I wish I could read minds as Aziel can. If I had the ability, I would be in everybody's business twenty-four-seven, and I'll never understand how he manages to resist.

He can't enter the mind of a person who hasn't permitted him, but it would be easy for him to trick Charlie into giving him permission. He was able to fool me into giving it decades ago, and he found it a fun game in his younger years to force people to let him in.

Now, he uses it so infrequently that I wonder if he's forgotten he has the ability.

It wouldn't surprise me.

Charlie's lips purse as she plays with my fingers, her pulse continuing to race as she mulls over my words.

"Fine," she eventually relents. "But I'm not waiting one second longer than a year. I expect to feel your teeth in my neck the moment the clock strikes."

My chest vibrates with laughter.

Charlie scrambles off my lap so she can face me entirely, and she sticks out her hand in an odd gesture. I stare at it for a second, confused, before realizing she wants to perform the human tradition for agreement.

My eyes crinkle as I reach out and shake her hand, and Charlie makes a pointed effort to squeeze my knuckles.

"Deal," I say.

Charlie narrows her eyes before lunging at me, a loud giggle erupting from her chest as she pushes me onto my back and plops down on my stomach.

"I love you," I blurt out.

Charlie cups my cheeks and smooshes my lips together before bending and kissing me.

"I love you, too."

I sit up and wrap my arms around her waist, and we sit quietly until it's time to go home.

She gasps as I teleport us back to my office, the sounds of the birds and water vanishing as it's replaced with the silence of the manor. I pat her butt as she climbs off my lap.

I'd say this was a successful date.

Chapter Nine

AZIEL

I HOLD BACK an audible sigh as I check the time. It's gotten late, and I can already feel the effects of sleepiness taking hold of me. My handwriting grows sloppy as I rush to finish the last of my paperwork, my attention only half on my work as I listen to Charlie showering upstairs.

She's far enough away that I have to strain to hear her, but it's more than worth it. I can tell when she moves out of the water, the sound of the spray growing louder as it hits the shower floor, and I know when she steps back underneath.

Silas is in the room with her, his voice quiet as he tells her a story from his childhood. I was present for it, and I feel slightly offended by how he intentionally leaves me out.

Gray's approaching footfalls draw my attention, and I turn toward my office door just as he invites himself inside.

He wears only a pair of tight black briefs, and he leans against my doorway as he looks around my office. I was under the impression he was already in bed, and I must have been too busy listening to Silas and Charlie to hear him get out and walk down here.

Gray crosses his arms over his chest as he takes in my half-lidded eyes and stiff posture.

"It's time for you to go to bed," he says.

I snort. It's been a while since he cared enough to make such demands. His paternal instincts left shortly after Charlie arrived, his care for how many hours I slept or how much I ate disappearing.

"I'm busy."

I turn back to the paperwork on my desk. The issue with the females is taking up a significant portion of time, and I have to work late if I want to get everything done.

"Go to bed, Aziel," Gray says. "Silas and I will help you with your work tomorrow." His offer is appreciated but unrealistic.

"You don't know how to do my work, and teaching you will only be more of a hassle."

Gray lets out a frustrated hum. "Silas knows how to do it."

I lean back in my chair. Silas hates when Gray whores out his brain, even if it's for my benefit.

My lips purse as I recall when Gray went feral after a particularly bad haircut. He promised a witch that Silas would tell her her fate if she made him an elixir to grow his hair back, and Silas was so mad that he refused to speak to Gray for almost two months afterward.

Silas made up some story to tell the witch so she wouldn't come after Gray for not holding up his end of their bargain, but he was pissed.

"If you keep promising such things, you're going to find yourself upset when Silas gives you the silent treatment again," I say.

"I'll do it!"

I snap my jaw shut with a quiet click. Gray shoots me a cocky smirk as I glance toward the ceiling where Silas's shout traveled down from. I suppose I shouldn't be surprised he's listening to our conversation. He's always been nosy, interested and obsessed with everything that happens inside our home.

Charlie giggles as Silas explains he wasn't talking to her. I gulp, wanting to know what's happening as the sound of her bouncing on the bed makes its way to my ears.

She may be slowly opening up around me, but I've never seen the truly playful side of her that she so eagerly shows to Gray and Silas. The closest I get is listening to it through the walls, which doesn't feel great.

"I'm going to use the toy on her tonight," Gray says, changing the subject.

That captures my attention.

"If she's not into it, I'm not going to follow through," he continues.

I nod, having expected as much. I wouldn't want him to continue with something she doesn't enjoy. It took everything in me not to storm into their room when I heard her uncomfortable moans the first time they used it.

I clear my throat and set my pen on my desk. I don't remember picking it up, and I hate that Gray's presence has me fidgeting.

"Don't make her say my name," I decide. "I don't…." I trail off as I search for the right words. "She doesn't like me, and I don't want you to force it on her."

Gray's loud laugh only furthers my embarrassment, and I look away as my face and neck warm. He shakes his head and scratches his bare stomach before turning and leaving.

"Go to bed!" he shouts from the hallway.

I run a hand through my hair and recheck the time before standing. I'm not getting any meaningful work done, anyway. It won't kill me to rest and return with fresh eyes tomorrow morning.

I materialize in my bedroom as Gray makes his way upstairs,

and I rip off my clothes before sagging face-first on my mattress. My sheets still smell of Gray, the scent irritatingly comforting. Already, I can feel my eyes growing heavy, and I mindlessly listen to Charlie and Silas laugh and joke with one another.

They do this every night, and I tense when their happy noises are cut off by a sharp gasp. Charlie lets out a quiet moan and whispers Silas's name, and I turn my head to better hear.

Silas hums, the vibrations of his voice signaling that his mouth is busy. I try to imagine what part of her he has his lips on, and my body grows taut as her noises grow louder.

What's he doing?

My hips instinctively twitch into the mattress, my interest growing.

"You couldn't wait for me to come back?" Gray chuckles, stepping into her room.

"I—" Charlie lets out a shaky breath and clears her throat. "Silas started it."

She's such a tattletale. Silas hums again, but the noise is followed by the unmistakable sound of wetness. I sink my teeth into my bottom lip and grab my pillow. Is he licking her?

My throat grows dry as I recall her taste.

Fuck. It feels like years ago that I had the opportunity to put my hands on her, and I'm thankful I had the bright idea to put my fingers in my mouth afterward.

"I'm going to talk to you about Aziel tonight," Gray whispers, slight pauses between each of his words as he kisses her.

I freeze, my hips stilling.

I'm still fucking pissed they told her about our agreement.

"Stop bringing it up," I hiss, knowing damn well they can hear me.

Both ignore me, and the muffled laughter from Gray has me fuming. Is nothing sacred in this house?

They find it appropriate to share my private business with her, but I wonder what Charlie would think if she knew they were putting on shows for me well before they got her permission.

"Is he listening?" she whispers.

My arousal grows at her attempt to keep me from hearing, and I shove a hand between my body and my mattress so I can take hold of myself. I bury my face into my pillow to muffle any noises as I curl my fingers around my cock.

Fuck.

"He's got his hand wrapped around himself right now," Gray answers her, "and the creaking of his bed tells me he's fucking his fist listening to Silas lick you."

Charlie gasps, and I strain to hear her heartbeat. I frown when I can't find it. I want to know her body's reaction to Gray's words.

"That's good, baby girl," Gray moans.

Why's he saying that? What's she doing?

A low grunt slips from my lips as I shut my eyes and imagine Silas between her thighs. I bet her hands are in his hair, using it to guide his mouth.

She'd never get away with that if it were me.

"What does she taste like?" I ask.

I push my hips forward and fuck my fist. The tip of my cock rubs against the sheets as I thrust, the friction drawing another quiet moan from my lips.

Charlie pants, her breathy noises only further spurring me on.

"You taste so fucking good, Charlie." Silas moans, his words muffled. "You're addictive."

Gray quietly agrees. He's not much of an observer like Silas, and I'm sure he's assisting in some way. Gasps and moans accompany long kisses, and I hate not knowing exactly what they're doing.

I roll onto my back so I can better stroke myself.

"Sit up, baby. I'm going to use the toy on you," Gray says, gently breaking apart the Silas and Charlie love fest.

Charlie lets out an annoyed groan, the anger within it surprising. She doesn't want my involvement.

"Don't—" I start, pausing when Charlie begins to speak.

"I'm tired of the toy," she complains. "I want to have sex."

I clench my jaw and turn away, not wanting to hear that. It's one thing when it's a small silicone toy, but I don't think I can sit here and listen to them have sex. As much as I love to torture myself, that's too much.

Gray hums, thinking it over, before shuffling around on the bed.

"I'll give you my cock when you've been a good girl and deserve it," he says.

I bite back a moan as Charlie whimpers. She's so fucking tempting, and I massage the head of my cock before sinking to the base and squeezing tightly. Precum leaks out as I stroke myself, and I spread it with my thumb before easing my way down my shaft.

"Please," she whines.

Gray's low chuckle has goosebumps spreading along my skin, and I draw my hand away in a desperate attempt to hold my orgasm back. I don't want to cum too soon. He hasn't even started to fuck her with the toy yet.

"Soon, baby," Gray promises.

Charlie releases a sudden gasp, and I sink my teeth into my bottom lip as I hear the toy slide into her. I wait for the giggle she always lets out whenever it's in all the way, and I squeeze my length when I finally hear it.

I bet she looks so pretty when she's fucked.

She lets out a low moan, and I press my palm against my mouth to muffle my noises. There's no hiding the sound of my fist smacking against my pelvis each time I thrust into my hand, but I don't want Gray and Silas to have the satisfaction of hearing me moan.

They'd never let me hear the end of it.

Releasing a shaky breath, I plant my feet into the mattress and pretend it's Charlie I'm sliding into instead of my fist.

"Aziel's about to cum," Gray whispers, probably to Charlie. "He's trying so hard to be quiet, but I can hear how fast he's touching himself. You're going to make him finish so quickly. That's how pretty your noises are."

Gray speeds up the pace with which he's fucking the toy into her, and I groan when he matches my rhythm.

"This is how hard he's doing it, Charlie," Gray continues. "Silas is going to fuck you at the same tempo so you know exactly how good it'd feel to take Aziel."

The bed shifts as the two demons adjust. Clothing rustles, and Silas grunts a moment later.

Wanting to test them, I still my hips and slow to a painful pace. Almost immediately, Silas follows, and Charlie releases a loud whine. It takes every bit of willpower I have not to speed up and push myself over the edge.

This might be the only opportunity I ever have to be this close to Charlie, and I'll be damned if I don't savor it.

Charlie pants as she's fucked, and I stop trying to hide my moans as my abs tense and I fight off my orgasm. I've never tried not to cum before, and it turns out it's fucking hard.

I speed up as the tension inside me grows, a near-constant stream of curses slipping from my lips as Charlie begins releasing the noises she always does right before she cums.

"Gray," she cries, her voice cracking. "Please."

"It's not us, baby. This is Aziel fucking you." Gray chuckles. "If you want to cum, you're going to have to ask him."

Silas releases a deep moan just as Charlie lets out a loud whine.

"Please, Aziel. Please, I want to cum," she finally relents. "I'm sorry, I'm so sorry. Please."

I don't know what she's apologizing for, but I sure as fuck don't care.

Her cries push me to the edge, and I don't bother fighting it off as I curl both hands around myself and fuck into them.

"I'm so close. It feels so fucking good, Charlie," I moan. Gray repeats my words to her. "Cum, baby."

Charlie lets out a loud moan that ends in a whine. I assume that's her cumming, and I throw my head back with a shout as I do the same.

My hips twitch as I finish all over my fist and abdomen, and I lie rigid for a long moment before sagging back into my mattress.

I don't think I've ever cum so hard before.

Silas and Gray shower Charlie with compliments before continuing, and I block out the sounds so I don't get myself worked up again. There have been nights where I've ended up lying awake for what feels like hours masturbating, and even some desperate times where I was up long after they finished, unable to calm myself down.

"Shit." I sigh, glancing at the mess I made on myself. I should've grabbed some tissues.

Chapter Ten

CHARLOTTE

SHAY STANDS AGAINST the wall opposite my desk, her finger over her lips in the universal gesture to keep quiet. My palms grow clammy, and I gulp as she turns and shuts my office door.

I didn't expect to see her after her conversation with Aziel.

For once, I find comfort in knowing all the males in this house are always listening, their ears turned toward my office whenever I'm alone. They'll be here if I let out even the slightest sound of distress.

That's if Shay doesn't kill me first.

She turns away from my now-closed door, her hands still in the air. I lean back as she grabs a piece of paper and pen off my desk, her movements slow and cautious.

What is she doing?

My jaw clenches as I try to avoid showing too much fear. I don't like her knowing how afraid I am, especially when I know how much she enjoys it.

Shay glances at me before clicking the pen and writing down whatever she wants to say. I find a little pleasure in her choppy human grammar, and I crane my neck to read as she writes.

It's comforting to know she's not perfect at everything.

She spins the paper around and slides it in my direction.

Aziel believe me?

I purse my lips, unsure how much I should say.

Aziel is convinced everything she said was false. He thinks Shay is untrustworthy, and he holds Levia's word above hers.

I'm still unsure.

Shay may be a raging bitch who's been more than transparent in her goal to take Silas and Gray from me, but I have trouble understanding what she'd get out of this lie. It would be easier for her to kill me now and wait a couple of years for my males to mourn my loss. Then she could swoop in.

That would make more sense than this odd claim.

I gnaw at the skin on my bottom lip, unsure what to think, before shaking my head.

Shay pinches the bridge of her nose, seemingly genuinely upset, before yanking the note back in her direction so she can write something else.

Aziel need go to Queen of Greed. Mammon is allied to blessed breeds. Good people.

I shrug before grabbing the paper and writing a response.

Aziel says she's aligned with the ogres. Ogres hate Wraths.

Shay scoffs, the noise quiet but loud enough to make us both freeze. She straightens up and glances at the door, her body entirely still as she waits to see if anybody heard.

After a minute, she nods to herself and returns to the paper.

Broken alliance. Secret: Ogre rape Mammon's daughter. They do not

Shay disappears mid-sentence, her body vanishing just as Gray bursts inside the room. He wears a large grin, but it falls the second he smells Shay. I gulp, nervously touching the paper she was writing on.

"Silas!" he shouts, shoving the door against the wall as he storms inside and searches my office.

I cringe as Silas pulls open his office door. His body goes rigid as he rounds the corner to my room, his eyes moving immediately to me.

"Why was Shay in here? How long?" he hisses through clenched teeth. "Why the fuck didn't you call for us?"

Aziel's office door swings open the moment Shay's name leaves Silas's lips, and I cave in on myself as he comes storming into my office. The room feels suffocating with all three of them inside, and Aziel shoulders both Silas and Gray out of the way, his black eyes locked in on me.

"I—" I start, my voice cracking. "She just wanted to talk."

Aziel's nose crinkles as he snatches the paper off my desk and reads over our written conversation. His knuckles turn white as he grips the edges of the sheet, his fingernails digging into and ripping the thin paper.

He looks furious as he turns and hands the note to Silas.

I sink into my chair, avoiding eye contact. *Oh, god.* I hate it when Aziel gets mad.

His breathing is loud, and I avoid eye contact as Silas reads over and hands the note to Gray. Neither of them seems particularly concerned with Aziel's current emotional state.

"You've lost office privileges," Aziel says, his voice void of emotion.

Without waiting for a response, he steps forward and begins grabbing the items on my desk. I scramble to snatch my things back, alarmed by his actions.

"What?" I ask, disorientated.

"Until you learn that you can't sit around and have secret conversations with a female who wants to kill you, you won't have privacy," he decides, rudely ripping my stapler out of my hand.

I gasp, my anger flaring as Silas and Gray step forward and begin to help him collect my things.

"Hey!"

I struggle to grab as many of my things as possible, but all three men smoothly ignore me as they steal my items faster than I can save them. My eyes grow wet as they carry my things out of my room.

I know it was stupid not to call out when she appeared, but it's not as if she hurt me.

We should look into what she's saying.

I jump to my feet and follow them into the hallway, my cheeks growing red as they take my things into Gray's office. Aziel drops my belongings carelessly on the couch before going back for more.

"Stop! I'm sorry," I plead, reaching out and grabbing his wrist. "It won't happen again."

He shakes me off. Gray wraps a hand around my waist and tugs me aside.

Aziel seems to lose his last semblance of sanity and begins to full-on throw my things across the hallway into Gray's office. I wince as my precious treasures bounce off the floor, but I don't move to stop him. The last thing I need is to get caught in the crossfire of his pitching practice.

"Do you want to talk about what she said?" I whisper.

All movement stops, even from Aziel.

"No," Silas says, disappearing.

I stare at where he once was as Aziel returns to his launching. Thankfully, I don't have too many items, and it doesn't take long for Aziel to empty my office. Gray pulls me into the hallway and makes me watch as the Wrath slams the door shut and breaks the lock.

Aziel looks murderous as he storms into Gray's office and rips out the drawer I keep stocked with snacks.

"You'll get this back when you learn to stop risking your life for the lies of a jealous Envy," Aziel hisses, clutching the drawer to his chest.

I open my mouth to apologize, but I fall silent as he turns and storms out of the room. Gray's gone a second later, his comforting touch leaving as he begins to pick up the mess that's become his office.

Fuck.

They want to keep me safe, and this is the second time I've ignored their wishes.

Silas even went as far as to have his power put into a necklace so I could protect myself. I didn't think much of it at first, but Gray let it slip that making the necklace, even with the help of a mage, depleted Silas to the point that he was bedridden for almost two entire days.

I know they're worried about Shay.

Silas is almost always listening, and Gray checks in what feels like every ten minutes. Even Aziel frequently strolls past my office door, his nonchalance easy to see through, considering my office is the last one in the hallway and he has to spin around and walk back only a few seconds later.

"I'm sorry, Gray," I say, fiddling with the hem of my shirt. "I just wanted to know what she had to say. I want to make sure we're doing right by the females."

"I don't give a shit," Gray snaps, spinning to face me. "I love you and want to spend the rest of my life with you, and I can't do that when you're dead. You insist on holding on to this childish ignorance of yours, and it's fucking infuriating."

I recoil. That was harsh. Gray sits on the couch and drops his head between his knees.

"Will you go to Aziel's office?" he asks.

I sniffle. "Why?"

"Because I'm so fucking angry right now, and anything I say will hurt your feelings. Silas left to fuck-knows-where, probably burning off some steam in Wrath, and Aziel's the only other person here I trust you being around without me."

My bottom lip wobbles, and I shift my weight from foot to foot before leaving. Who knew rejection could sting so much? I don't allow myself to think about the fact that Silas got so angry he left. He's usually the voice of reason amongst the three males.

Aziel glares at me as I enter his office, and he wordlessly points to the couch.

I can't think of a time, except when I was first purchased, when Aziel was so angry with me. My skin burns where he stares at it, and I clear my throat before awkwardly lowering myself onto the couch.

"Are you—" I start.

"I don't care to hear anything you have to say right now."

My jaw snaps shut with an audible click, and I nod before turning away. I don't want him to see me cry.

I do my best to keep my breaths even, and I stare at the wall with my back turned to the angry Wrath. I'm sure he's still looking at me, probably enjoying the sight and smell of my tears.

The silence in the room is deafening, and after a few minutes, something soft smacks against the back of my head. My fingers curl into the couch's cushion as I spin around to glare at Aziel.

I understand he's mad, but throwing things at me is petty.

He's not looking in my direction, feigning ignorance, and I purse my lips before glancing at the floor to see what he threw. A package of chocolate donuts is lying on the ground, and I wipe my cheeks before picking them up.

I don't hesitate to rip open the package and shove one in my mouth.

I shouldn't overthink this. He's probably tired of listening to me cry and hopes to shut me up with the snacks he stole from me earlier.

Aziel clears his throat, and I turn to look at him out of the corner of my eye. He raises a brow and glances between me and the chocolate donuts. My face warms as I struggle to swallow what's in my mouth.

"Thank you," I whisper, knowing he'll be able to hear it easily.

"I don't like when you cry," he admits.

I blink, unsure how to respond to that.

Aziel turns back to his computer. I open my mouth a few times to say something, but I end up just shrugging off his comment and returning to my donut.

He's confusing.

I drop into a low crouch as I come up on Aziel's office door.

Things were awkward after our intimate moment by proxy of Gray, and the incident with Shay has only made it worse.

My pulse races as I peek into the open doorway. This is a quick errand, and I'll be in and out.

Sinking my teeth into my bottom lip, I straighten up and step into Aziel's office. He stands with his back to me, and I hold my breath as he grabs a giant book off his shelves.

I wish Gray would have brought Aziel the files himself.

He could teleport in and out in the time it takes me to hurry down the short hallway. My lips purse. Gray probably sent me here to get me out of his office. He tries to hide it, but I know he finds me being in his space all day distracting.

Especially when Rock's tutoring me.

I shift my weight from foot to foot. The sooner I get this over with, the sooner I can leave.

Clearing my throat, I raise my fist and knock on the inside of the doorframe.

Aziel hardly seems surprised by my presence as he turns and gestures for me to enter. My fingers dig into the edges of the papers as I step inside, and Aziel makes his way to his seat.

"Gray told me to bring you these," I say, holding out the files Gray shoved into my arms only moments prior.

Without meaning to, my eyes fall to Aziel's hands.

They're large, and I can't get the mental image of him touching himself out of my head. I wish Gray hadn't told me what Aziel was doing that night, and I regret how much I enjoyed it. Aziel's been nothing but rude to me, and I feel weak over how badly I still want him.

It's probably some unresolved childhood trauma rearing its ugly head. A sane person wouldn't find themselves attracted to the man who treats them like shit. They'd hate him.

Aziel grunts, his hands clenching into fists before he relaxes and takes the files from me.

I turn, eager to leave.

"Stop," Aziel says.

I freeze.

"Come here," he continues.

I wipe my palms on my pants before turning back to Aziel. He pays me no attention as he reaches into one of the drawers of his desk. I scratch the back of my palm as I wait to see what he's doing.

He keeps my candy in his desk now, and if he offers me a piece as payment for being Gray's errand girl, I'm going to throw myself over this desk and strangle him myself.

"Take this to Gray." Aziel pulls out an unopened box.

What's this? I cannot hide my curiosity as I take the item from him. There's a picture of a keyboard on the front, but it's lighter than I'd expect one to be. Without thinking, I give the package a little shake.

"Charlie!" Aziel stares at me like I've grown three heads.

I want to crawl into a hole and die. I avoid eye contact with Aziel as I turn and practically run to the door. Why do I always have to be so fucking embarrassing?

The box falls from my hands as I'm abruptly pulled into a hard chest. I gasp, my brain struggling to comprehend what's happening as Aziel wraps his arms around my torso and yanks me against him.

I grab at his arm, both alarmed and thrown off-balance.

"What?" My thoughts vanish as I spot a woman standing in the doorway.

Her long, silky black hair and equally black eyes tell me she's a demon, and her confident, graceful movements and coy smile tell me she's a succubus.

She crosses her arms over her chest as she watches Aziel's dramatic response to her arrival, and I curl my fingers into his forearm as I try to figure out where I recognize her from.

Aziel greets her. "Valentine."

She cocks her head to the side, her eyebrow raising as she slides her attention to where I'm holding Aziel. I loosen my grip but don't let go completely.

"What do you want?" Aziel asks.

Gray comes storming inside before she can answer. His shoulder bumps against hers as he places himself in the middle of the room. I expect him to take me from Aziel, but he makes no moves to do so as he crosses his arms over his chest and glares at his sister.

Valentine chuckles and glances down the hallway to where the other offices are. "Where's the third one?"

Gray scoffs. "Busy."

Valentine gives an exaggerated pout and turns to me. "That's unfortunate. Silas has always been my favorite."

I tighten my grip on Aziel and try not to think about how he's moving his thumb back and forth against my collarbone. Or the feeling of his warm breath hitting the top of my head.

He's just trying to calm me down, probably worried I'll say something snarky and make her mad.

I won't.

I've grown comfortable with Aziel, but I'm not dumb enough to talk to other demons the same way I do him. I'm fully aware of how easy it would be for them to kill me if I did.

"What do you want?" Aziel asks, skipping the pleasantries.

Valentine's smile grows. "Shay sent me. She said you'd kill her if she showed her face around here again."

She's met with complete silence, but she hardly seems bothered by the thick tension between us. If anything, she seems to enjoy it, her posture relaxed as she looks curiously around the room.

I'd kill to have that level of confidence, and I wonder if it's because she's a succubus. I'm sure it's hard to be insecure when you know you can have anybody you want at the snap of your fingers.

Her blank, almost bored expression vanishes as she turns to

Gray. She scowls at him, her black eyes glaring holes into his body. I don't like it, and Aziel seems to feel the same way as he shuffles us forward and grabs the back of Gray's shirt.

He yanks Gray against me, the two of them sandwiching me in.

It also cuts off my view of Valentine, and I frown as I try to peer over Gray's shoulder. I don't like not knowing what's going on.

"Oh!" Valentine teases. "Is somebody feeling protective?"

I slip my fingers underneath Gray's shirt and rest them against his lower back. I don't like being around demon women. They all treat me like a second-class citizen, their poor views on humans not exactly hidden.

They also seem to love making comments about being intimate with my males.

"You hate Shay," Gray says.

I wiggle to the side and peer around Gray's arm. Valentine looks amused as she watches my head pop out from behind Gray, her lips curling into a cruel smirk.

"No, I hate my competition. Right now, she and I share the same one," she admits. "Rumor has it that little Charlie's got two of you in the bag. Such a shame the only one who matters doesn't want her."

She looks me in the eye as she speaks, and I know she's telling the truth. Despite how much I like to think I have some hold over Aziel, he's made it clear he's not interested in ever being with me—even if he gets aroused by me.

Gray's quick to defend me. "You don't know anything about our relationship."

"You're right," she admits. "I only know what Aziel told me during his little visit to Lust earlier this week. We had a lot of fun, didn't we, baby?"

I release Gray so I can try to pry Aziel off me. Gray seems to feel the same way as he buries an elbow into Aziel's side.

I'm glad I'm not the only one who wasn't told about his visit with Valentine.

Aziel grunts as Gray's elbow finds him, his warm breath hitting the back of my head, but he doesn't release either of us. I'm sure Gray learning he's fucking around with his oldest sister wasn't in today's plan.

Valentine looks pleased.

"Your message?" Aziel asks.

She frowns, clearly unhappy with being shut down, before sighing and lifting her hand in a gesture of defeat. "Yeah, I'm not sure what Shay's on about, but she's acting unusually unhinged lately. She's paying me a pretty penny to tell you, and I quote, that she's 'telling the truth and you need to believe her.' I'm not sure what truth she's talking about, but she said you'd know."

"Is that everything?" Aziel asks.

She nods.

"Then you can leave."

Valentine cocks her head to the side, a look of confusion spreading over her face at his dismissal. I ignore it as I continue to fight with his hand, using both of mine to grab onto his fingers and pry them away.

He seems to think it's some game as he allows me to remove one, holding it away from my body, only to snap it back as I begin to work on the next. He only lets me remove one finger at any given moment, and I resist the urge to stomp on his toes.

"So you only want to be sweet with me when we're alone," Valentine says, licking her lips. "Noted."

She's gone before Aziel can respond, her body disappearing as quickly as it appeared. Gray snaps into action and yanks me out of Aziel's arms in the blink of an eye, and I trip over my feet as

I'm spun around and pulled into the incubus's chest.

"What the fuck was she talking about?" Gray asks.

Aziel shakes his head. "Nothing."

"Didn't sound like nothing."

Aziel looks stressed as he runs a hand down his face and leans against the corner of his desk. I don't like the thought of him with Valentine, and I force myself to ignore the painful tug in my chest as he fumbles for a response.

"Drop it, Gray," he finally says.

"No."

Aziel's eyes shift to me before returning to Gray.

"I went to a bar after speaking to Shay and ran into Valentine. I had too much to drink, and we chatted. That's all," he says.

"Chatted about what?"

"Why does it matter?"

"Because it does."

Aziel sighs. "Gray."

Gray sighs, mocking Aziel. "Aziel."

"Did you touch her?" I whisper, cutting them off.

It's none of my business, but I know I won't be able to stop thinking about it until I have an answer.

Aziel looks to the side before directing his attention to the floor. My lip wobbles, and before I can think better of it, I step forward and bring my hand to his cheek.

The pain in my palm doesn't register immediately, but the way Aziel's face hardens sure does. His pupils expand as my slap registers, and I flatten against Gray's chest in panic.

Gray doesn't move, his body serving only as a wall for me to pin myself against as Aziel stalks forward.

"Don't test me, Charlotte," Aziel says through clenched teeth.

I raise my chin.

"You're a piece of shit!" I retort, jabbing my finger against his chest. "Gray's sister is a new low, even for you." I pull back and jab him again. "It's fucking cruel."

My eyes water as Gray cups my hips. Who the fuck does Aziel think he is to go prancing around with Gray's sister like that? Gray's obviously in love with him, and while I never considered Aziel to be a particularly good man, this is just wrong.

Aziel's hand curls around my neck, but I find myself unafraid as I bury my finger as deep against his chest as it will go.

"You're a trashy, vindictive asshole," I continue, spitting whatever insult comes to mind.

Aziel leans down and presses his forehead against mine, and I angrily meet his stare as he pants onto my face.

Gray's hands slide away from my hips, and I watch out of my peripheral vision as he loops them around Aziel's shoulders. Aziel doesn't push him away like I expect him to.

"So what if I touched her? Would you be upset to hear that I put my mouth on her soft, wet—" The end of Aziel's words are cut short as Gray yanks his arms inward and smashes Aziel's mouth against mine.

Both of us stiffen when our skin touches, and I stare wide-eyed at Aziel as he slips his fingers into my hair and spreads his lips. He tugs my hair until I gasp, and he doesn't hesitate to take advantage as he forces his tongue into my mouth.

Aziel's kiss is frenzied and demanding, and he moans and presses the front of his body against mine. I grunt as he grabs my thighs and lifts me into the air. Gray helps to hold me up as I wrap my legs around Aziel's waist.

I hate how much I love this, and I grab Aziel's shoulders as he takes charge of the kiss. Low noises seep from his throat as he squeezes my thighs, the sound making me feel things I have no business feeling.

"You're fucking infuriating, Charlie," he says, pulling back and attacking my neck. "I didn't touch her. I'd never do that to Gray."

I drop my head against Gray's shoulder as Aziel bites and sucks at my sensitive skin. He's leaving marks I'm sure I'll hate later, but I can't bring myself to care as I wind my hands through his hair and hold him against me.

"I'd never do that to *you*," Aziel whispers, moaning as I scratch his scalp.

Gray's grip on my thighs tightens as I wiggle, but he gives no hints that he's struggling to support my weight. He easily holds me in the air, allowing Aziel to run his hands along the front of my body.

The Wrath's mouth on my neck makes me ache, and I arch into him for more.

There's movement to the side, and I turn just as Silas walks into the room. His lips twitch as he watches us, and with a subtle shake of his head, he drops a stack of files on Aziel's desk.

The loud noise isn't enough to stop Aziel, nor are my hands as I try to push him away.

"So while I'm running around doing the work you're too busy to get to, you're out here tonguing my female," Silas says, not looking nearly as upset as his words insinuate.

Aziel cups my chin and pushes my head back. His hands are everywhere, and I try to hide how good it feels when they slip underneath my shirt and press against my bare belly.

"You may be interested to hear that I ran into Shay while I was out," Silas continues.

Aziel pulls away with a low grunt. I move to unwrap my legs from around his waist, but he grabs and holds them. Gray readjusts, lifting me higher so my sex rests against Aziel's belly, not his pelvis.

I'm grateful not to have the hard erection sitting between my thighs anymore, the temptation too much.

"What'd she say?" Aziel asks, pressing his thumb against my bottom lip.

I'm unsure what he expects me to do with it, and I open my mouth just enough for him to wiggle the digit between my teeth and press down on my tongue.

"Suck," he orders.

I bite, hoping to hurt him enough to make him pull away, but it seems to have the opposite effect as his eyes roll back and eyelids flutter shut. Gray inhales, probably feeding, and drops his chin on my head with a whispered curse.

"She repeated everything she's already said," Silas says, entirely unbothered by the scene before him. "She claims that Levia will betray us and we need to talk to Mammon."

Aziel pulls his thumb from my mouth, and Gray sets me on my feet.

My knees feel wobbly, and I embarrassingly use Gray for stability as he leads me to the couch. Silas quickly follows, sitting to my right while Aziel pulls up a chair.

I lean against Gray's shoulder as he wraps an arm around my lower back and holds my hip closest to Silas. Silas slips his hand between my thighs and cups the one pressed against his.

It's an appreciated comfort, but it doesn't stop the anxiety I feel as I try to wrap my head around what the fuck just happened.

Aziel plants himself directly across from me instead of sitting behind his desk as usual. His knees touch mine, the man unnecessarily close.

"I believe her," I say. Shay's persistence has me inclined to believe she's telling the truth. "What other reason could she have to be pushing this hard? She's risking her life each time she does it. I don't imagine Levia would be happy to hear she's going behind his back."

Silas rubs his thumb against the inside of my thigh. He's still angry with me for not screaming when Shay came into my office, but he's slowly warming back up.

Aziel clears his throat and places a hand on my knee.

My neck cracks with how quickly I turn to look at it, my eyes bulging.

"What's this?" I point to his hand.

Aziel frowns and tightens his grip, doubling down on his decision as his timid eyes turn hard.

"I'm comforting you. Don't be whiny," he snaps.

I push him away, beyond pissed. I don't need the affection of somebody who's going to insult me. Aziel's frown deepens as I shove at his hand, and he retracts it with a loud scoff. I have half a mind to continue pushing him about his sudden weird inclination to touch me, but I change my mind and direct the conversation back to the females.

"It won't kill you to have a conversation with Mammon to feel things out," I say.

Aziel crosses his arms and leans back in his chair, and I deflate as I realize nobody is on my side. What more is it going to take?

"Charlie," Gray says, his voice soft. "Shay's a notorious liar."

"Has she ever gone this far for a lie before?" I ask.

The silence I receive is answer enough, and I turn to Aziel, knowing he's the final decision maker.

"Please," I beg.

He looks at the ceiling with a sigh, and I bounce my knees as I wait for a response. He's got to see how hard she's trying. I understand Shay doesn't have the best track record regarding these things, but there's no harm in having a conversation with Mammon.

I once told Silas I'd do whatever it takes to help the females, and I meant it.

Aziel finally answers. "I haven't spoken to Mammon in over a hundred years. If I suddenly start a conversation, she's going to dig into our lives for the reason why and I'm sure it won't take long for her to find it."

I shake my head, refusing to believe it.

Aziel's eyes soften as the tears in my waterline grow, and I turn away so he can't see.

"There has to be something we can do," I say, wincing as my voice cracks.

The hand Aziel removed from my knee earlier is returned, and his fingers curl and squeeze into the material of my leggings. Why does he keep touching me?

We've shared the occasional hate-filled kiss before, and he, without fail, always treats me like shit afterward. I will not fall into whatever emotional trap he's laid out for me.

"I trust Levia," he says.

"I don't," I grumble, fumbling for an idea.

My temples throb when I think of one.

"Rock told me you're a bit of a hot commodity," I say to Aziel. "What if you told Mammon you want to bond with her? I don't think it'd be too surprising. She's strong and everything, which is what you want." My voice is shrill, unintentionally giving away how much the idea upsets me.

Gray's spine straightens, and Silas leans back against the couch cushions.

Aziel blinks.

Nobody speaks for a long moment, and I cross my arms over my chest as I wait. It's a good idea, and we all know it.

"I don't want her, Charlie," Aziel finally says. He pushes the hair out of his face and glances at Gray and Silas. "It's come to my attention that you two aren't changing your minds about Charlie, and I, well, I don't want to split up. I've decided—"

I interrupt. "I'm not just some baggage you have to put up with so you can have Gray and Silas."

Aziel's eyes narrow, and Silas flicks Aziel's hand off my knee.

"Don't speak about her like that," Gray snaps.

My heart soars at how quickly my males jump to my defense.

"Well, you didn't let me fucking finish!" Aziel says, returning his hand to my knee. He clears his throat and levels his gaze with mine, the look serious despite the flush that spreads across his cheeks and down his neck.

I hold his stare, eager to get this over with so we can return to the topic of the females.

"I have come to care for you during your time here," he says, "and Gray's made good points in that both he and Silas are strong, fulfilling that need for my people. I've thought a lot about this, and while there may be complications from us having weaker, half-breed children, it's a risk I'm willing to take."

I cock my head to the side. Is he trying to be romantic?

He's still calling me baggage, just in a slightly nicer way. An 'oh, you're not ideal, but I don't hate you and as long as I have Gray and Silas, I think it'll be fine.'

No, thank you.

I'd be lying to myself if I didn't acknowledge that I have feelings for Aziel, but I want more than a man who provides only the bare minimum. Gray and Silas go out of their way to love me, but Aziel doesn't do much of that. I can't tell whether or not he actually cares about me or is just horny.

"Thank you for your…." I start, clearing my throat as I search for the right words. "Your honesty, but I'm not ready for that."

Silas rubs his thumb across my thigh, but he's not my concern as I turn to the incubus, whom I know wants this more than anything. Gray gulps and offers me a smile, but I see right through it. He can pretend all he wants, but I know it breaks his heart to see me reject Aziel.

"I'm so sorry," I whisper.

Gray plasters a shaky smile on his face.

"Don't ever apologize for the way you feel." He leans in and bonks his forehead against mine.

Aziel pushes off my knee and stands. No noise escapes him as he grabs the chair he pulled up earlier and returns it to its usual spot in front of his desk. His movements are eerily calm, and I hold my breath and watch him circle his desk and sit behind it.

He clears his throat and grabs the paperwork Silas set down earlier, his face devoid of emotion as he thumbs through it.

"I'm done with this conversation. Leave," he orders, jerking his head toward the door.

I gulp. "What about the females?"

Black eyes meet mine. "Get the fuck out of my office, Charlotte."

Chapter Eleven

CHARLOTTE

SILAS LOOKS AT me over his shoulder as I pull back the shower curtain and step inside. He moves aside so I can get under, his eyes half shut.

"Silas, please," I beg.

He's annoyed by my asking, but I'm not going to stop until they give me a good reason not to believe Shay.

Silas wraps an arm around my waist and guides me into the water before pressing himself against my back. I let my head rest against his chest as he pours some shampoo into his palm and begins to wash my hair. He seems to like doing these little things for me, and I can't say I don't enjoy it.

He works my hair into a good lather, and I let a quiet moan slip from my lips as he gives me a little scalp massage. Gray's too rough when he does this, but Silas takes his time.

"I know it's hard for you to believe, but Shay isn't a good person," Silas says. "Did you know she killed all the women Gray was having sex with when they first got together? Then she tried to murder Aziel."

I shake my head. I had no idea. But I also never thought she was good. That isn't the issue. "What if she's not lying?"

Silas disconnects the showerhead from the wall and begins rinsing my hair. It feels relaxing after the tense conversation with Aziel.

Rejecting him was the right decision, even if it hurt Gray's feelings. I know damn well Aziel will come to change his mind about me in the future, and I'd rather not allow my feelings to grow any further before he does.

"It would mean a lot to me," I continue, hoping to get Silas on my side, even if it's through pity.

Silas rinses the rest of the shampoo from my hair and reconnects the showerhead to the wall.

"I love you," he whispers, spinning me around. He kisses my cheeks and forehead. "But we can't ask around without drawing attention to ourselves. Wrath has been too secluded for too long, and to suddenly show interest will turn heads."

"I believe her," I repeat.

"I know, and I'm asking you to believe me more."

A cold breeze hits my side as the shower curtain is pulled back and Gray steps inside. His hand grazes my lower back as he squeezes past us to get under the water.

"We would've been out in a few minutes," Silas grumbles.

"I've been waiting for twenty, and I was feeling left out," Gray says, hogging the water.

I can't wait until our new bedroom is done and we have a bathroom with a shower large enough for the three of us. It'll even have two heads, one for Gray and one for Silas and me.

"There's a reason we don't like to shower with you." I laugh, pushing him aside so that at least a sprinkle of water hits me.

Gray huffs. "Silas likes to shower with me. Don't you, sweets?"

Silas gives a less-than-excited response as I wiggle

underneath Gray's arm. There's not enough space for the three of us to comfortably fit, and the realization only enforces my decision to reject Aziel.

Adding another male to our relationship wouldn't make sense if he can't even fit in the shower with us. I suppose I don't *have* to shower with all my men at once, but I'd prefer to.

Gray and Silas fight about the water before Silas gives in and leaves. I'm not far behind.

I shiver as the curtain is pulled back and the cold bathroom air hits my bare skin, and Silas tosses me a towel to dry myself off. He also throws me one of his shirts to wear, and I look away to hide my smile as I slip it on over my underwear.

We make our way to bed in relative silence, and Silas is already half-asleep by the time Gray finishes in the shower and joins us. It's been a few days since he fed, and I look over his black eyes with a low hum.

"Are you hungry?" I ask.

Gray climbs into bed and pulls me into his arms. I relax against his chest, happy to be held.

"A bit, but we can wait until tomorrow," he says.

Silas's breathing continues to slow, and I slide my toes along whatever legs I can reach to warm them up. Gray huffs as I make contact with his shin, but he doesn't say anything about my ice toes as he buries my face into his chest.

"Are you upset with me for telling Aziel *no*?" I ask.

Gray's throat bobs. "I'll never be upset with you for being honest."

"It wasn't a definite no," I continue, assuming Aziel can hear me through the walls. The demons seem to be able to hear everything. "I just want him to put in some effort." I pause and lick my lips, nervous to say this out loud. "He spent months treating me like a burden, and I don't believe he truly cares about me."

The sheets behind me shift as Silas rolls over and wraps his arm around my waist.

"We understand," Gray whispers, pressing a soft kiss on my head. "And we'd feel the same if we were in your position."

I clear my throat, even more nervous to ask my next question.

"Do you think he'll find another female like last time?"

Gray chuckles, his fingers lacing with mine.

"No. He's learned his lesson with Shay." Gray's quick to soothe my worries. "Besides, he's going to be much too busy begging for your forgiveness to pay attention to any other females."

I clench my jaw in a sad attempt to hold back my smile.

"Bringing me breakfast in bed would be a good start," I tease, hoping Aziel's taking notes. "And I'd like it to be handmade."

Gray snorts. "Good luck with that."

He lets out another laugh, seemingly quite humored by that thought, before giving me one more tight squeeze and rolling away. I stare at his back, tracing the strong muscles lining his shoulders. I want to lick them, but I'll wait until tomorrow to indulge.

Rolling onto my back, I stare at the ceiling as my thoughts fall to the females.

At this point, as much as I hate to admit it, there's nothing further I can do about Shay. I've begged and begged, and it's been made clear that my males aren't going to deviate from their original plan.

It's three against one, and my opinion carries the least weight.

Rock isn't going to be any help, either. The shadow is more than willing to take part in my silly pranks or provide the information my males try to keep from me, but arguing with them is a line he won't cross. It's one I won't ask him to, either.

I resist the urge to scream, and carefully, I slide out from under the covers.

A hand on my ankle stops me, and I turn to look at a bleary-eyed Gray.

"Where are you going?" he asks.

"To get some water."

He hums and releases me.

I do my best to remain quiet as I tiptoe toward the bathroom, but I pause in the doorway to peer back at them. Silas rolls into the spot I once occupied and throws an arm around Gray.

Gray tends not to love cuddling, preferring his own space as I do, but he sinks into Silas's hold with a content sigh. Before I can think better of it, I snatch Gray's phone off the dresser and open the camera.

They'll hate that I did this, but I don't care as I hold it up and take a minimum of twenty photos.

The distraction lifts my mood, and I clutch the device to my chest as I step into the bathroom and shut the door. I chuckle as I fill my cup and plop down on the toilet.

Gray's told me his password before, and I rack my brain for it before taking my best guess and tapping the numbers on the screen. It doesn't work, and I purse my lips before trying again.

When it goes through, I bounce on the toilet seat and hurry to find the icon that'll take me to Gray's photos. I don't use phones often, and it feels foreign as I click on one of the pictures I just took and set it as his background.

The photo is a bit dark, but there's just enough light to be able to tell they're all cuddled together. I'd have used the flash if I weren't afraid of waking them up.

My cheeks hurt from how hard I'm grinning when I see the option to send the photo, and I eagerly type in Silas's name so he'll have a copy. Nothing comes up, and I frown before finding my way to Gray's messages.

He probably saved Silas's name as something stupid, but I'm sure they've messaged recently and I can send the photo through the thread.

Rock's name is at the top of the screen, and I resist being nosy and clicking on it. I'm sure the conversation is about my schooling, and I'm uninterested in reading a subtle roasting between my tutor and my male.

Aziel's next. It takes everything in me not to peek, and I grudgingly continue down the list.

The name Shay stops me in my tracks, and the screen says that he was messaging her today. I click into the thread. They don't get to prohibit I speak to her while secretly keeping in contact through their personal devices.

That's bullshit.

I feel slightly better as I note that all the messages are from her. Do Silas and Aziel know about this? Gray's ignored every one of her messages, but I still take my time to read through them.

I've never been more thankful for Rock's lessons on the demon language.

Shay begs Gray to believe her. She promises she wants to help and this isn't about me, and she's even sent a few photos of documents that are too intricate for me to read. The blurriness tells me they were taken in a hurry, though.

I can even see Levia's prominent profile in one. His eyes are cast downward at his computer, not paying attention to the female who sneaks a photo over his shoulder.

She's doing everything she can, and I can't believe Gray's ignoring her.

Angry tears fill my eyes, and I have half a mind to storm into the bedroom and demand answers. He's just going to lie. That's all they've been doing.

Do they actually intend to help the females, or are they just stringing me along to make their lives easier?

I wipe my cheeks before making sure the phone is on mute and typing a message.

This is Charlie. They don't believe you.

I wait, my leg bouncing and body shaking. I can't believe them. This is probably really stupid—I'm fully aware of that—but I'm more than willing to take the risk. I'd rather die having tried my best to do what's right than sit back and find out later I didn't do enough.

Males are fucking enslaving us. We're sold like cattle and passed around like toys, and I refuse to sit around doing nothing. We deserve better than this.

I bring the phone closer to my face as I wait for her response.

Talk in person. Do not scream.

Shay's in front of me just as I finish reading the message, her hand held out. She wants to teleport me.

I gulp, hesitating, before setting Gray's phone on the sink and curling my fingers around hers.

We materialize a second later in a large sitting room, and I release her hand the moment I'm steady. My heart is pounding in my chest, and I bring my fingers to my necklace in case she tries to make another grab for it.

I look up and gasp.

I've never seen anything like this. The entire ceiling is glass, leading to a stunning view of the night sky with millions of bright stars.

"Mammon sure does love her décor," Shay says, looking through the glass panes. "It's a magnifying glass. That's why the stars look so big."

I clear my throat and force myself to look away, not wanting to get distracted.

"I have a rock I can kill you with," I say, hoping my words sound threatening.

Shay looks unconcerned as she eyes the jewelry I clutch in my fist. "I'm aware, but you won't be needing it. I have no intention of keeping you here longer than a few minutes. Your males are on edge, and I'm sure it won't take them long to discover you're gone."

I dig my thumb into the stone, hoping she can't hear my racing heart as she turns and takes a lap around the room. Why does everything she does have to be so ominous? We're in a sitting room, but this one is better decorated than the one back home. The warm-toned rugs and large cushioned furniture make it feel cozy.

Along the walls are hundreds of photos, each in a different medium but portraying the same family—or at least parts of it. The woman and man in the images never change, but the children are almost always different.

A cold sweat breaks out along my back as Shay lowers herself into a chair and gestures for me to sit opposite her. I don't immediately move. She lets out an impatient huff, which isn't too surprising. I've never pegged Shay as an exceptionally patient woman.

I bite the skin inside my cheek as I step forward and sit in the chair opposite hers. As suspected, I sink right into the cushion.

"I've tried speaking to Mammon myself," Shay says, "but she's as stubborn as your males and refuses to believe me. I want you to talk to her. You don't wear any marks, but everybody knows you belong to the Wrath Trio."

The "Wrath Trio"? Is that what people call them? It's fitting.

"You want *me* to talk to Mammon?" I ask.

I wouldn't describe myself as an expert communicator, and I won't have answers to the questions she's sure to ask. I could barely even read the report Aziel had done up, the language too complicated to follow.

My leg bounces as I turn and eye the door.

"Don't look so frightened," Shay says, snapping her fingers.

I jump back as a shadow appears. He hands some papers to Shay, and I recognize them as the female information Aziel shared with Levia. Did she steal this from him?

"Are you going to kill me?" I can't help but ask.

Shay pauses, thinking over her answer. "I wish," she admits after a moment of silence. "I don't like you, and I'm not going to pretend I do, but I cherish my life. Your males would have my head if I ever touched a pretty little hair on yours."

"Comforting," I deadpan.

Shay's lips twitch, and I take a moment to enjoy the sight of her trying to hold back a smile. She doesn't like me, but I don't think she hates me as much as she lets on.

"I need you to tell Mammon I'm telling the truth. Then I'll take you home. She and I can handle the rest from there," Shay explains. "Then you and your males can waste the next year making plans that'll never see the light of day."

I suck my cheeks into my mouth. They're going to be so mad at me.

"How do *I* know you're telling the truth?" I ask.

Shay shrugs. "Your males had fifty years to do the right thing. They didn't. You're not the only person who's been affected. Demon women have had it hard, too."

I roll my eyes, refusing to believe it. Even if they aren't experiencing new births, demons live forever, and the declines don't hurt them nearly as much as most other species.

Shay's back goes rigid at my response, her friendly

disposition changing into the cold one I last saw at the Lust party I was taken to forever ago.

"You don't believe me?" she hisses. "Would you like to see the video of me that was passed around after a visit with the ogres? They don't live such long lives, and they miss the attention of females. I'm strong, but when you have twenty of those fuckers holding you down, it's a bit hard to fight them off and teleport."

The chair armrest cracks as her hand tightens around it. I didn't know about this incident, and I wince as the wood splits beneath her palm.

Shay opens her mouth to continue, but she stills as the door behind me opens. My heart feels like it's lodged in my throat as I turn and watch a woman step inside. She's clearly a demon, with black eyes and short dark hair, and she wears a long, blue silk robe.

She barely looks in my direction, and I nervously pick at the skin of my fingers as I glance at the infant connected to her chest.

"This better be important," the woman snaps.

She makes eye contact with Shay as she lowers herself into the seat beside mine. The sudden movement lodges her nipple out of the baby's mouth, and I try not to stare as she groans and realigns the infant.

"The little thing won't latch," she complains to nobody in particular.

I gulp as her eyes flash to me.

"Who's this?"

"Charlotte. She's Aziel's female." Shay gestures between the two of us. "Charlie, this is the Queen of Greed, Mammon."

I'm unsure what to say or do, and I hope my shaky smile doesn't come off as impolite.

Mammon looks tired as she tries to coax her baby to take her nipple. Watching her is an excellent form of birth control, and I hold back a wince as the baby finally latches on and starts chewing her like she's a piece of gum.

"Please tell me they know she's here." Mammon sighs.

Shay cowers, her neck and head shrinking into her shoulders. Mammon shuts her eyes and sucks in a slow breath before turning to me.

"Let me put Cain down, and I'll take you home," she says, her soft eyes hardening as she turns to Shay. "You'll stay here."

Shay turns to me in a panic, and I give the same look right back.

"Wait," I call out as Mammon stands. "I'm here by my own choice. Shay and I need your help with the females." My voice cracks, but I continue. "Aziel knows how to fix the declines, and we have the information here."

Shay hands her the report, and I clench and unclench my fists as Mammon takes it and sits back down. She fingers through the pages, taking her sweet time to read every section.

I wipe my sweaty palms on my shirt, my nerves worsening as Shay begins to fidget. This was supposed to be a quick meeting before my males discovered I was gone, and with each passing minute, my worry grows.

"So, Charlotte," Mammon starts, setting the report on her lap. "You're willing to betray Aziel for this? Why?"

I clear my throat. "It's the right thing to do."

Mammon hums, her eyes darting between me and the papers she holds. "You're aware this is treason, yes? The Wrath Trio will execute you for coming here."

I stiffen. No, I did not realize that.

I feel like I'm about to vomit as it sinks in just how badly I'm fucking up. This isn't just me going against my males' wishes. I am going against the King of Wrath, one of the last remaining fates, and a Prince of Lust.

My back is sweaty, and I lean forward to disconnect myself from the chair I'm sitting in.

Shay chimes in. "They won't kill her. They claimed her."

Mammon adjusts her son before standing and approaching. I wring my hands together as she grabs the neckline of my shirt and tugs it down so she can see my skin. Her actions make me painfully aware that I'm only wearing one of Silas's shirts.

"She bears no marks," Mammon says.

She looks at Shay as she speaks, but I answer.

"They want to wait to make sure it's truly what I want," I explain.

Her finger slides across my neck before dipping down the front. I try not to look too creeped out as she presses her palm over my heart.

"I've never liked Aziel. I could tolerate Gray and Silas, but the Wrath has always caused problems. If I were anything like him, I'd kill you and send you back in pieces," she says, pulling her hand from my shirt. "Did you know that's what he did with my firstborn?"

I breathe through my nose to try to stop the overwhelming panic her proximity brings. Her power doesn't affect me as much now that I've gotten so used to being around Aziel and Silas, but she doesn't need that to terrify me.

"If I'm being objective, I suppose my son deserved it," Mammon continues. "He was stupid to be toying with the incubus's feelings, but I still didn't appreciate getting pieces of his cock delivered to me by a lowly shadow."

I gulp, unsure what response she's looking for.

Her fingernail scrapes the underside of my chin, and I shyly lift my head until I'm facing her.

"Look me in the eye. Are you lying about this information, Charlotte?"

Her nail digs into the soft skin of my neck.

"I'm telling the truth." I gasp.

Mammon seems pleased as she smiles and steps away, finally giving me space. The baby on her chest whines, and Mammon calmly switches him to her other breast before gesturing for me to follow.

"Then I need you to stick around for a few days," she says. "We'll meet with the shifters tomorrow, and I have some contacts with the high elves I'll reach out to."

My throat runs dry, and I look between her and Shay in a panic.

"I need to go home," I rush to say.

Mammon's eyebrows furrow. "Did you not come here to assist?"

"I did! That's why I've told you this information!"

"Yes, and in order for you to help me, I'm going to need your words. Leaving will only prolong the process," she explains, her words laced with disappointment as she heads to the door. "Shay will take you home if that's what you wish."

Shay stands and holds out her hand. I worry my bottom lip between my teeth as I look between her and Mammon's retreating figure.

Choosing to stay with Mammon will undoubtedly destroy my relationship with my males. My actions here have probably already done that, but not going home will cement it. I feel my heart pounding in my chest as I stand.

I love my males so fucking much, but I can't put myself before the females. I feel I can trust Mammon, and as much as I hate to admit it, Aziel sat on the information for decades.

My eyes water as I think about the young children I encountered at the facility, some too young to walk. They were ripped away from their families and will spend their entire youth stuck inside some white-walled, sterile building until they're sold to the highest bidder.

And they're the lucky ones.

Some species don't even treat their females that kindly.

Shay clears her throat and taps her foot along the ground, her impatience only furthering my stress.

"Come on," she urges, wiggling her fingers in my face. "I need to get you home before your males notice you're gone."

I turn to Mammon. She's paused in the doorway, her eyebrow quirked as she awaits my decision.

Chapter Twelve

CHARLOTTE

MY EYES ARE itchy.

I rub at them as I stare at the ceiling. The shadows are noisy as they walk up and down the hallway, their voices loud as they speculate about who I am and what I'm doing here.

It's a question I wish I had the answer to.

A part of me expected my males to come busting in here in the middle of the night to bring me home, but it's well into the morning and there's been no sign of them.

Mammon said she'd inform them I'm alive and well, but I still worry they won't get the message. Or that they won't believe it. The last thing I want is for them to think I'm injured or here against my will.

I run a hand through my hair.

I hope Mammon didn't send Shay as the messenger.

She disappeared when I decided to stay with Mammon, her eyes panicked. It feels odd to be worried about her, but I am. She seems like one of those people who always manages to weasel her way out of trouble, but I'm scared of how far my males will go to punish her for taking me.

They were furious when she so much as spoke to me, and taking me to Mammon will be seen as much worse in their eyes.

My jaw aches from how hard I'm clenching it, but I figure the pain is a fitting punishment. I hope my males don't think I chose to leave because I don't love them. I'd pick them in any other situation, but this is too big to put myself first.

I force myself to push thoughts of Gray, Silas—and even Aziel—to the back of my mind as I crawl out of bed. Mammon's shadow didn't say much as he led me here. I was told where to find the nearest bathroom and hygiene necessities before being left alone.

"Fuck," I whisper, looking down at myself.

I'm still in Silas's shirt. I lift the fabric to my nose, comforted by his scent as I make my way to the wardrobe in the corner of the room. The shadow said there would be some spare clothing in here, and as much as I love wearing Silas's shirt, I'd rather not meet the entire royal family in this state.

I have a feeling they wouldn't find it as endearing as my males do.

The wardrobe doors stick, and I drop my shirt and give them a hard yank. They open to reveal a small handful of dresses.

They're all incredibly long, probably made for the tall height of demon women, but I manage to find and slip on one that doesn't drag along the floor. I'm an average height for a human female, but even the shorter demon women I've met are a good few inches taller.

Both Mammon and Shay are the same height as my father.

I run my fingers through my hair and pry any lingering crusts out of the corner of my eyes before straightening my shoulders and heading to the bedroom door. My pulse races, but I shove my fear aside as I enter the hallway.

The few shadows around stop to stare, and I do my best not to look too nervous as I turn to the nearest one.

"Can you take me to Mammon?" I ask, rocking back on my heels.

The shadow nods and gestures for me to follow him. He doesn't try making conversation, and I remain silent as he leads me down a handful of identical hallways. This place is practically a castle, with echoing hallways and cold stone walls that give off an almost eerie feeling.

Even the long rugs and decorated walls can't hide it.

It makes me grateful for the smaller manor my males choose to live in. It's still more space than anybody reasonably needs, but it's cozier and harder to get lost in.

I hear Mammon before I see her, the woman loud as she speaks over screaming children.

The shadow comes to a halt and gestures to an open doorway down the hall.

"Thanks," I mumble.

He leaves, and I take a moment to collect myself before stepping into the room. The chaos inside has me pausing, my foot freezing midair as I take in the sight before me.

The room is large, which is unsurprising, and it looks like a dining area mixed with a family room. Half of the room is empty, save for an eight-person wooden dining table and several shadows standing along the far wall, and the other half sports an oversized sectional surrounded by children's playsets.

A toddler drags a pre-teen to a shelf full of toys, and I watch both boys whisper to one another, their eyes sliding to me before turning away in disinterest. A teenager is sitting on the couch watching the TV, his arm thrown over the back of it as he flips idly through the channels.

They're all spitting images of Mammon, and they don't seem to notice or care about my presence. My lips purse as I watch them, intrigued by the Queen's personal life. How many children does she have?

Guessing by the photos I saw hung up in the sitting room, I'd say at least fifty.

I suppose there's not much else to do when you live thousands of years.

"Good morning, Charlotte," Mammon says.

I jolt and spin in her direction, embarrassed to have been caught watching her children. She's sitting at the head of the dining table, the baby from last night sitting in her lap.

Unlike last night, though, he's awake and drooling all over himself. He's also gnawing at his arm, and he screeches before wiggling and shoving his fist down the front of Mammon's shirt.

It seems demon infants are similar to human ones. I've never met a human infant before, but I've read much about them in my books.

Mammon smoothly removes the drool-covered arm from her shirt and waves me over.

"Excuse the mess," she says. "I don't typically work out of here, but my husband's not home and I don't want to leave the heathens alone."

The heathens in question grumble as they hear their mom's casual insults.

"Come sit with me," Mammon urges as she sees me hesitating over what to do.

I glance at the kids one last time before sitting in the chair to her left. She pulls her chair closer and slides her work in my direction. All I can focus on is how her arm brushes mine and the feeling of her body heat seeping through the thin fabric of my dress.

The small action reminds me of my mother.

I haven't been around many women since being purchased,

and I didn't realize how much I miss it until now.

"I've been reading over the female report all morning, familiarizing myself with it, and I have a few questions," Mammon says, flipping through the pages.

My eyes grow comically wide as I see how marked up the report is. Mammon's made notes in the margins of almost every page, and I can't help but smile as I read over a few.

In the eight hours since she was given this report, she's shown more interest than my males have in the many years they have had it. Even when we met with Levia, they never bothered to mark anything up or discuss specifics.

It reinforces my belief that I'm making the right decision.

"I don't have much information beyond what's already in here," I admit.

Mammon laughs. "I don't expect you to. We're meeting with Aziel later this week to discuss."

I'm going to vomit.

I swallow past the lump in my throat, horror rendering me silent. I didn't anticipate her wanting to discuss it with him. I was under the impression they didn't get along, and I assumed that meant they wouldn't want to meet.

I thought she'd take this information and create a plan separate from Aziel's.

"Don't look so frightened, Charlotte," Mammon says, squeezing my wrist. "I'm not going to let him kill you."

Oh, my god.

"*Kill* me?"

Mammon nods. "Yes, but don't worry about that. He knows you're under my protection. You've given me the upper hand, and once I've secured our alliances with the shifters and elves, Aziel will be forced to submit and face punishment."

I'm sure I'm failing to keep hidden just how panicked I am,

and I shove my hands underneath my thighs to hide their shaking. I never wanted to hurt Aziel with this.

"We'll meet with the shifters over dinner, and I've arranged to meet the high elves tomorrow morning. They'll be excited to meet you," Mammon continues, politely ignoring my growing anxiety.

"I'd like to move quickly, and I assume the blessed breeds will also. We've worked together on several issues, so a decent level of trust has already been established. The Seekers are the largest agency for female collection, and I believe we'll want to start there." Mammon pauses to wave over one of the shadows standing along the wall.

The man stumbles over himself to get to her, and he skids to a halt to her right.

"Bring Charlotte something to eat," she says, turning to me. "Your stomach is loud."

I instinctively cover my belly. My body's gotten used to Gray shoving food in it first thing in the morning, and it isn't happy with the sudden change.

The shadow returns to the room with a plate of demon breakfast. It's some grain and meat dish I don't necessarily love, but it's better than nothing.

"Thank you," I say, accepting the plate.

Mammon returns her attention to the document while I eat. It feels awkward, and I hurry to empty my plate as quickly as possible. There's no water or anything to wash the food down, but I refuse to ask.

I'd sooner drink out of the bathroom sink than ask Mammon's shadows to get me a glass of water.

"Taking control of the Seekers should be relatively easy," Mammon says, resuming our earlier conversation. "The organization is disorganized, and I doubt they're interested in fighting. They'll disband quickly."

I nod and push my empty plate aside.

"The real issue will be with imposing regulations on stronger species, specifically the ogres." Mammon pauses when one of her children screams.

I turn, panicked, only to relax as the younger boy jumps on the couch and punches his older brother. The older boy hardly looks fazed as he palms the younger one's face and pushes him onto the floor, the action eliciting another scream.

Mammon excuses herself to take care of them.

The little boy giggles as Mammon scolds the older one, his eyes wide as he grins up at his mother. It's endearing, and for a brief moment, I wonder what it would be like to have little demon babies.

Gray and Silas would make excellent fathers. Gray would be an absolute pushover, bending over backward to make them happy, and Silas would be the one they come to when they're in trouble and need advice. I'm not sure if Aziel would be good with children, but I'm sure he'd tolerate them.

I lick my lips and turn to the female report.

I gave up that option when I chose Mammon.

"What will happen to me once this is all over?" I ask when she returns.

She squeezes my shoulder and sits in her chair. "You're free to stay here. In full transparency, I don't see a world where the Wrath Trio welcomes you home." Hearing that hurts. "As a thank you, I'd be willing to bond you with one of my sons so you can live here in Greed with an extended lifespan. Most of my sons are very handsome, and I'm sure you'll find one to your liking."

I blink once, twice, three times before shaking my head.

"I appreciate the offer, but I won't ask for that. If my males don't take me back, I'd love to spend my remaining years with my mother," I admit, hoping she doesn't take offense to my rejection of her kind offer.

I understand losing Gray and Silas is the consequence of my actions.

"I'm sure I can arrange for that," Mammon says, gesturing for me to stand. Her eyes travel down my frame. "We need to find you something better fitting for our meeting later."

Chapter Thirteen

GRAY

SILAS GROANS AS I unwrap my arm from his waist. He snatches my wrist and drags it back over the top of him, and I smile into his shoulder as I press myself against his back.

I didn't take him for a cuddler, but I shouldn't be too surprised.

The man hasn't had much physical contact these past few years, and as much as he likes to pretend he didn't miss it, I know he did.

I kiss the back of his neck before slowly pulling away. Charlie hasn't returned to bed, and I'm getting worried. I faintly remember her leaving for a drink, but I was half awake and fell asleep before she returned.

I assume she's in my bed.

This wouldn't be the first time she couldn't sleep and escaped to my room for a few hours, but with Shay acting up, I don't want to leave her alone. My feet drag against the floor as I walk through our connected bathroom.

My phone sits on the sink, and I tap the screen to see the time.

Instead of the image of Charlie I set as my background a few weeks ago, my screen brightens to reveal a sleeping photo of Silas and me. Charlie must have changed it. I'm surprised she even knew how to do it, and I smile as I admire the photo.

After figuring out where my human ventured, I'll have to send it to Silas.

I move through the bathroom and into my bedroom, but I pause in the doorway.

My bed is empty.

I gulp, a little worried as I leave my room and make my way to Aziel's.

Charlie was guilty about rejecting him, and I'm willing to bet she found her way to his bed sometime in the middle of the night. It's the only other place I think she'd go, and I refuse to entertain any other possibilities.

Charlie would've called for us if she were in trouble. She saw how upset we were after the last incident, and I don't see her doing that to us again.

I repeat that to myself as I head to Aziel's room. I bet he welcomed her right into his bed, probably sporting a childish, eager grin as he pulled back his bedcovers and urged her to crawl into his arms.

My steps quicken as I think about it. Aziel's had women throwing themselves at his feet his entire life, and I immensely enjoy watching him fumble to get my female's attention. Charlie's not making it easy for him, and I love that about her.

She knows what she's worth.

I push open his bedroom door and step inside. I do my best to remain quiet as I listen for her heartbeat, but when I only hear one, I lunge forward and rip the sheets off the bed.

Aziel sits up with a gasp, his eyes wide as he meets my frantic ones.

"Charlie's not with you?" I ask, already knowing the answer.

He turns to search the room before vanishing, and I hurry back into her bedroom to ensure I didn't miss her. Silas wakes up as I come busting inside, and he takes one look at my panicked expression before vanishing just like Aziel.

I run downstairs, unable to hear or smell Charlie anywhere in this fucking house.

My hands shake as I run them through my hair, my desperation growing as I rush into Aziel's office and then Silas's. Aziel promised that Shay wouldn't be messing with us anymore.

He should have fucking killed her the last time she showed up.

The sound of screaming draws my attention, and I hurry into the foyer to see what's happening. My eyes harden as I spot Shay sprawled out on the floor, her hands clutching her head as Aziel throws her to the ground.

She smells like Charlie.

"Where is she?" Aziel spits.

Silas appears a second later with her son, Don. The demon is gangly and weak, and he looks pitiful as he tries to fight out of Silas's hold. He screams, and Silas wraps an arm around his throat before sinking a knife into his abdomen.

Shay cries as she watches her only child bleed, but I don't have it in me to feel bad. She's done an excellent job hiding Don's existence from the world, but she should've known Aziel and Silas would have inspected every aspect of her life when she became close to me.

We long ago agreed to leave her son out of our issues, especially considering he's still relatively young, but desperate times call for desperate measures. Besides, in human years, he'd be considered elderly.

"Where's Charlie?" Silas asks.

His voice is unnaturally cold, and the power that radiates from him makes me shiver. I've never been on the receiving end of a fate's anger, and for once, I realize why so many hate his kind. He's fucking scary.

Silas cocks his head to the side and twists his knife in Don's abdomen.

The man cries out as his knees buckle. He may be a full demon, but sending him to be raised by the fairies made him weak. That species is much too soft for the world he rightfully belongs in.

Shay's done him a disservice.

"Charlie's safe! She's safe! You can hate me all you fucking want, but I did what needed to be done." Shay gasps, crawling away from Aziel.

He smiles as he stalks toward her, and I jump in the way and grab his shoulders to stop him. His pupils are fully dilated, and we don't need him losing control right now. Aziel curls his fingers around my wrist, his grip bruising, but he doesn't fight me as I pull him away from Shay.

Silas removes the knife from Don's stomach.

"Tell us exactly what you mean by that," he says.

I pull Aziel back another few steps. Watching a man being stabbed will only make it harder for him to calm down, but I already know trying to get him to step outside isn't going to happen.

"She came to me," Shay says, her voice shaky as her eyes dart toward her son. "I swear I didn't come for her. She asked me for help!"

Charlie would never do that to us, and one glance at Silas's crazed expression tells me he's thinking the same thing. Whatever Shay did to our female, she's lying through her teeth trying to cover it up.

Aziel grunts and tries to shove me aside, but I bury my face in his chest to distract him. My arms slide to his waist and squeeze, forcing him into a tight hug. He stiffens, and I let out a fake sniffle before nudging my face into the skin where his shoulder meets his neck.

He needs to be calm, and I'm not above pretending to cry to get him to do it.

I feel him hesitate, his muscles taut as he runs a hand down the center of my spine. It's about time he lets me settle him. We're bonded, for fuck's sake. This is my job.

Shay continues to spit her lies. "She messaged me off Gray's phone a few hours ago. She asked what she could do to help. I took her to Mammon, and she chose to stay there."

"Charlie wouldn't fucking do that," I snap. "What'd you do with her?"

Aziel be damned, I spin to face the female and her weak excuse of a son. Shay doesn't even look at us, her teary eyes focused only on the blood that pours out of her spawn's stomach.

"Go to Greed and see for yourself," she says, scrambling to her feet.

Aziel grabs the back of my shirt and buries his face in my hair, and while I'd typically be over the moon that he's using me, I can't bring myself to care. I need to know where Charlie is.

Shay's too smart to have killed her, but if she's done anything to harm my female, I'll let Aziel rip out her throat.

I can tell Shay wants to teleport, but she won't leave Don. She knows he'd be dead the second she disappeared, and it'd only be a matter of time before Aziel found and brought her back.

"I offered to take her home, but she chose to stay. I'm not lying," Shay continues, backing up against the wall.

I shake my head, refusing to believe it.

Silas slips his knife back into Don's abdomen, but this time, he punctures a lung. Don lets out a choked cry and hunches forward, the scent of his fear thick in the room. It's practically suffocating, and Aziel buries his face further in my hair to try to escape it.

Silas glances between me and the barely contained Aziel.

"Go," he tells me.

With a curt nod, I teleport to Greed.

My knees buckle as I materialize in Mammon's sitting room. The place smells of Charlie, and my nostrils flare as I walk to the chair that holds most of her scent.

Mammon worked with a coven of witches long ago to create a spell that prevents anybody from teleporting anywhere in her home other than into this sitting room. They offered Silas the same thing after he found and returned one of their lost great spellbooks, but he turned it down in lieu of getting a ring that allowed me to use less energy when I teleport. It was a waste of a favor, considering I took it as a sign of weakness and never wear it.

Charlie would be safe if we'd accepted the witches' initial offer.

Impatient for Mammon to arrive, I grab the chair Charlie sat in and whip it toward the ceiling. The glass pierces my skin as it rains down, but I heal before the pieces even settle on the ground. There's no movement beyond the guarded door that leads to the room, and I grab the coffee table and smash it against the armoire with a muffled grunt.

The force crushes both items, and I step over the debris before moving to the remaining couch and chair.

"For fuck's sake. You're acting about as irrational as Aziel," Mammon says, storming into the room.

"Where is she?"

Mammon glances around the room in disbelief. "She's in bed, just like you should be," she snaps, stepping over the shattered glass as she approaches. "She doesn't wish to return to you, and I will not let you take her."

I still refuse to believe it.

"You can't hold her hostage. We'll consider it an act of war," I threaten, ignoring the guards who pool into the room and stand along the far wall.

Mammon shrugs, seemingly unconcerned. "Are you really in a position to start a fight? Charlotte shared the report, and it's only a matter of days before every species you may think yourself aligned with turns against you," she coldly states. "I gave Charlotte the option to return to you, and she chose to stay."

I grind my teeth. Mammon's lying.

"I want to see her," I say.

Mammon sighs.

"I'm not leaving until I see her for myself, and I'm sure Aziel will find his way here if I'm not home soon," I continue. We both know it to be true.

Aziel is already on edge, and I doubt he'll be waiting long for my return.

Mammon gestures for the guards to follow as she turns and leads me inside. I'm not intimidated by them, and I practically step on Mammon's heels as I follow her.

Charlie's scent grows stronger as Mammon leads me down a maze of hallways, and I flare my nostrils as I search for any fear or blood. To my complete relief, there is none.

Mammon stops in front of a door and spins to face me.

"I was informed it took her hours to fall asleep, and if you wake her, you won't be welcome to visit again," she threatens, her voice low as she steps to the side.

My hand shakes as I grab the knob and inch open the door. I immediately recognize the tuft of hair sticking out of the sheets, and I step closer to get a better look. The scent of Charlie's salty tears is thick, and I frown and step fully into the room.

Mammon stops me from shutting myself in with Charlie, her stern expression unwavering as she holds her hand against the door to keep it open. My jaw clenches shut, matching hers, but I don't fight.

Charlie's breathing is deep and even as I walk to the side of the bed. It's too dark for her to make out my figure even if she were to wake up, and I take comfort in that as I crouch and stare at the dried wetness on her cheeks.

She cried herself to sleep, but she otherwise looks uninjured. She wouldn't have dozed off if she were being held against her will.

That's a hard pill to swallow.

Have we been so awful that she felt she had no option but to run to Mammon?

She's quick to anger and act on emotion, but this is beyond that. This is calculated treason. This is her putting us in the middle of a war we were working hard to prevent.

It's only a matter of time before Mammon and the blessed breeds come to us for retribution. We're strong, but we can't fight a war against all of them.

Charlie's breath hits my cheek as she exhales, and I resist the urge to wake her up and demand answers. I want to take her home, but I won't force her to live in a place she doesn't want to be.

She went through this much work to run away, and I'll honor that decision, even if it hurts. I'm not in the business of imprisoning females and forcing them to love me.

My fingers ache with how hard I'm clenching them, and I stare at Charlie for a moment longer before leaving the room.

Mammon wears a cocky smirk as she follows me back to the sitting room.

"I assume I'll be receiving visits from the other males tonight?" Mammon asks, her shoes clicking quietly against the ground.

I'm unable to speak.

Silas and Aziel will deny what I say, and they'll probably call me foolish for believing Mammon before coming here to see Charlie themselves.

"I'd like to meet with Aziel in three days to discuss the report. I have many questions," Mammon says. "You'll have the opportunity to speak with Charlotte then."

My lungs burn as I hold my breath, hoping the action will keep me from lashing out.

"We'll be there," I confirm.

"Have them bring Shay when they come tonight," Mammon continues. "She was supposed to be here by now, and I'm assuming you brutes have something to do with her absence."

I nod.

I'm not in the mood to fight over Shay.

We enter the sitting room, and I don't hesitate to teleport back home. The back-to-back travels are draining, but it's not like I've got many other options.

Silas and Aziel are still in the foyer with Shay and Don. All four pairs of eyes land on me, and I run a hand through my hair as I search for the right words.

"You lied to us," Silas says, pulling his knife out of Don's chest.

I gasp. "Wait!"

It's too late, and Silas's knife is slipping into the man's throat before the words leave my mouth. It's a fatal wound, and I wince as Shay screams and lunges for her son.

Aziel's in front of her in a heartbeat, his body shaking as he buries his hand in her chest. He shows no emotion, but his lips twitch upward as he grabs her insides and yanks his hand back out.

She falls to the ground with a thud, and Silas tosses her son on top of her body as I drop my head into my hands. Could they not have waited three fucking seconds for me to explain the situation?

Mammon's going to be pissed to learn we killed Shay. So is Levia.

He's not the most affectionate man, but he's kept an eye on Shay since his brother died long ago.

"Shay was telling the truth," I say, stepping over the bodies and throwing myself on the stiff couch.

"No," Silas snaps." She was lying, and now we have no way of finding Charlie." He turns to Aziel. "Way to go."

I shake my head.

"I saw her myself. She shared the report, and she's sleeping like a baby at Mammon's." The words are bitter on my tongue. "Mammon wants to meet with us in three days. We'll have the opportunity to speak with Charlie then."

"I don't believe it," Silas argues, reaching for Aziel.

They touch their arms and disappear. I'm sure they're in Mammon's sitting room right now, and I shift my attention to the bodies on the ground with a quiet sigh.

Aziel was stupid to kill Shay. Nobody liked her, but her death will only make it harder for us to convince Charlie to return. I'm sure she's come to think of Shay as some martyr, and this will most definitely piss her off.

Rock steps into the room.

We make eye contact, and he wrings his hands together as he glances between me and the bodies. He smells of fear.

"Will you have Charlie executed?" he asks, avoiding eye contact.

I clench my jaw, angry he's even asking me this.

"No," I snap. "Let the shadows know we want the boy's body returned to the fairies who raised him."

They'll be devastated to find their son's mangled body on their front porch tomorrow, but I don't have it in me to feel bad tonight. Life's cruel, and everybody comes to learn that at some point.

Rock nods and opens his mouth to say more, but with a shake of his head, he turns and leaves. I'm sure he's pissed with us, the shadow having grown fond of Charlie. I won't be surprised to wake tomorrow and discover he's run off to find her.

Shadows are loyal, and I have an inkling Rock's devotion has shifted from us to her.

I'm glad she'll have a friend to keep her company.

Fuck.

Charlie warned me she'd put the females before herself, but I never imagined it would come to this. Would she have decided to stay if we were more open with her?

Our discussions with the shifters were more fruitful than we let on, but we kept that information quiet so Charlie wouldn't get too excited before things were finalized.

I'm sure Mammon's already reached out to them by now, destroying that option for us. She doesn't even need to spin a story to turn them against us. We fucked up, and nobody will be inclined to believe us when we say we were trying to fix it.

They'll think we're saying whatever we can to save our asses, and having Charlie speak out against us will only cement that.

That's probably the only reason Mammon's keeping her around. The blessed breeds treasure their mates, and they'll eat up everything Charlie says like it's fucking soup.

Aziel and Silas are in the midst of an argument when they return, but I don't bother listening to the sharp words they spit. I listen to see if I find a third heartbeat with them, but when I only hear two, I stand and head upstairs.

I'm going to bed.

Chapter Fourteen

CHARLOTTE

I DIDN'T THINK it was possible for somebody to walk as quickly as Gray, but Mammon's sure proven my assumption wrong. I struggle to keep up as I adjust the bag on my shoulder. Several copies of the female report are in it, weighing me down.

"Are you sure I need to come?" I ask, hurrying behind her.

"Yes." She doesn't bother looking in my direction. "The shifters will want to hear what you have to say."

I doubt I have any insight that'll be fruitful to them, but I don't challenge her. If she thinks it'll help, I'll be there.

Mammon pauses once we reach her sitting room. I cock my head to the side as I peer around, a bit confused by what I'm seeing. The room looks the same, but something's different.

"New furniture," Mammon says, answering my unspoken question.

She holds out her arm. I hesitate, nervous, before grabbing her wrist.

The unmistakable weightlessness of teleporting spreads through me, and I clench my eyes shut until it's over. Nothing's as bad as Gray's travels, and it only takes a few seconds for me to regain my balance.

I release Mammon and look around, slightly surprised to see that we're in the middle of the woods. Mammon warned me that shifters tend to enjoy nature more than most, but I didn't realize that meant they live in the wilderness.

I just thought they'd have big backyards or something.

"Stay close to me," Mammon says, her fingers curling around my elbow and guiding me forward.

I follow her lead, struggling with the uneven terrain.

I've never walked through the woods, and I'm quickly learning that the ground is hard to move on. The heels Mammon gave me to wear sink into the soft dirt, and I find myself having to pry them out with each step.

I don't know how Mammon manages to walk so effortlessly, and I try to copy her smooth, easy motions with little success. She looks like an experienced gazelle, and I look like a newborn deer just learning how to use my legs.

We walk down a steep slope before rounding a large hill. Sweat pebbles along my temples when what I thought would be a quick journey turns into a good fifteen-minute venture. Why didn't she take us right to where we needed to meet?

I'm going to be a puddle of sweat by the time we get there.

Mammon leads us in the direction of an ominous, dingy cave entrance. It's carved into the side of a large mountain, and I stare at it in panic. Does she intend for us to go inside?

It's pitch black in there.

"I can smell your fear, Charlotte. There will be lights once we get farther in. Would you like me to carry you?" Mammon asks.

I clear my throat, hoping she can't see the redness spreading across my cheeks.

"I'm okay."

She holds my hand as she guides me inside, her voice quiet

and soothing as she tells me when to step over things or move to the side. As the air around us cools, an unwanted shiver makes its way down my spine. I don't like this.

I eventually spot some torches, and I sigh with relief when I finally begin to make out my surroundings again. Mammon turns and leads us through a wide crack in the stone wall.

Water drips and echoes around us, the noise blending in with the clicking of our shoes, but it vanishes as voices make their way to my ears.

What is this place?

We enter a room filled with giant shirtless men, and I break out in a cold sweat. These are the shifters. The men watch as we enter, their attention darting rapidly between Mammon and me.

I count twenty as I'm ushered to a large, round table in the center of the room.

The shifters wait for us to get seated before lowering themselves into their chairs. I flinch when a brown animal fur is draped over my shoulders, and I squeak out a quiet *thank you* as I clutch the warm carcass to my body.

It's freezing here, and I can't imagine how these men are comfortable in such little clothing.

The man directly across the table from us is the first to speak up. "It's been a long time, Mammon."

He's slightly larger than the demon males I've come across, and his overgrown blond beard and long hair make him look wild. His muscles bulge as he leans forward and places his forearms on the table, but the action doesn't seem overly threatening.

"Yes," she says, gesturing to me. "This is Charlotte, whom I'm sure you've heard of. She's the chosen female of the Wrath Trio, and she's come to me with information I think you'll be most interested in."

I reach into my shoulder bag and pull out the copies of the

report Mammon made earlier. My back sweats as I hand them to the men around the table. They stand and practically press their chests to the cold stone so I don't have to reach too far.

"I'll give you all a moment to read it over," Mammon says, turning to me.

Her voice lowers as she begins to address me individually. "These are the shifter alphas. They each have a red design on their thigh that will tell you what their animal form is."

I nod and slyly glance at the shifter on my right. He's one of the largest of them, his muscles bulging, and he shoots me a friendly smile before turning to read the report. His green eyes dart quickly over each word, and he worries his full bottom lip between his teeth as he flips the page. He doesn't have a beard like the other shifter, and his dark-brown hair is shorter, too.

Mammon leans over me to touch him, but he pulls away before her hand meets his skin.

"Stop being so dramatic, Kato. Show her your design," she says.

Kato doesn't look away from the page he's reading as he pulls up his leather skirt to reveal a red bear.

"Show her your mated mark, too," Mammon hisses before leaning closer to me. "Shifters don't let females who aren't their immediate family touch them."

Kato grunts and pulls his skirt up further. Above his bear is a thick, black line, the marking seeming to wrap around his upper thigh.

I think that's all there is to see, and I choke when he pulls the skirt up higher and exposes his soft penis. Instead of looping around his leg, the black marking angles up when it reaches his inner thigh and curves over the top of his pubic bone before traveling along the top of his penis.

"That's what a mated male looks like, so don't ever let one of them trick you into their bed if they have these markings," Mammon warns.

Kato drops his skirt with a huff and turns in my direction. His eyes narrow as he glares at Mammon, the look alone telling me there's more than a little bad blood between them.

"A shifter would never trick a female into their bed, let alone a mated one," he snaps.

Mammon shrugs, turning to the man next to her. "Show Charlotte yours," she orders.

The man side-eyes her before pulling up his skirt. His red marking is of a deer, but the mate line on his skin is white. I'm grateful he doesn't expose his penis like Kato did.

"That's what an unmated man looks like," she explains, gesturing for him to lower his skirt. "It will turn black when he finds his female."

A man across the table clears his throat, the message less than subtle, and Mammon whispers that she'll tell me more later before going silent. I tighten my grip on the fur around my shoulders as I wait for the shifters to finish reading.

My impatience grows with each passing minute.

They're reading so slowly.

"I want his head," Kato says, slamming his fist on the table.

The stone underneath his fist crumbles, and he brushes it away before grimacing at the man across from us. That man eyes the newly created dent before straightening his shoulders and peering around to see who needs more time.

A quick scan tells me they're all ready.

"Where and when did you acquire this?" the man asks.

I turn to Mammon. She gestures for me to answer.

"I found the report in Gray's office a few weeks ago," I admit. My voice shakes, but I force myself to continue. "All three of them had copies."

Mammon clears her throat. "They sat on this information for fifty years."

"And when did you discover this, Mammon?" Kato chimes in.

Unlike me, she appears strong as she levels her stare with the giant bear man.

"I was informed yesterday night. I'm sure you're aware this issue is important to me, and I can only imagine it's something that also hits close to you." Her voice is full of confidence as she turns to make brief eye contact with each man sitting around the table. "I want to enforce regulations on female capture and treatment, and I'm asking for your support."

Almost immediately, the men begin to chat amongst themselves, their voices loud as they speak over one another. It's hard to follow anything they're saying, and after only a few seconds, they transition from the universal language into a guttural one I'm unfamiliar with.

Their eyes occasionally flash to me as they speak, their actions making it clear I'm a topic of conversation. One man grabs the report and throws it to the center of the table, his wide arms accidentally smacking into the men on either side of him.

"Why did you come here?" Kato asks, his accent thick as he transitions back to the universal language.

"I want to help the females," I answer truthfully.

Kato hums. "Why?"

"Because the first twenty-five years of my life were spent in hiding, and the last one was spent in a facility and the home of an incubus," I say. "I won't sit here and tell you I don't care for the Wrath Trio, but my loyalty lies with the females. I'm willing to do whatever it takes to help them."

Kato grunts but doesn't question me further.

"And this information is accurate?" a man sitting farther down the table asks.

"Yes," I say. "Do you not have female births? I assume you would, given the rumors about how well you treat women."

The room falls silent. Every pair of eyes is on me, and I nervously twist my fingers into the fur on my shoulders. I shouldn't have asked that.

"Shifters don't speak about their females," Mammon says.

Kato shifts in his seat. "We'll overlook that," he decides, making eye contact with each shifter male. None look happy, but they don't argue.

Fuck. I pissed them off.

"And if it comes to the females and your males?" a man across the table asks. "Whom will you choose?"

I gulp, my throat dry and face hot. "I believe I've already answered that by coming here." The words burn my throat, but they're true. "I'm committing treason by sharing this information with you."

Kato fingers through the report, his eyes scanning over each page.

"How can we help?" he asks Mammon.

She perks up, and I pull out a rough proposal she created earlier.

It's not much, but it outlines a basic plan for securing ownership of the Seekers organization and a few potential regulations that could be enforced immediately. The more significant changes will take time, but with the shifters and elves on our side, we'll be in a place to move quickly.

The shifters are careful not to touch my skin as they launch themselves onto the stone table and politely take the papers from my hand.

Mammon handles the conversation with ease, brainstorming quick ideas and eagerly accepting their adjustments. My heart soars as they grab writing utensils and begin marking up their sheets.

They're taking this seriously.

Despite a good portion of the conversation going over my head, I can't stop myself from grinning as they make their way through each section of the proposal.

"We won't commit to anything until we see your luck with the elves," Kato says, speaking for the group. "We can provide men to fight, but we don't have the financials to support a war."

A war?

Mammon nods, her eyes darting to me. "We can stronghold Aziel into paying. He's not looking for a war, and now's the perfect time to strike. With you and the elves backing me, he'll have no other options."

I feel like vomiting.

"Aziel was looking to work with you on making a plan to help the females," I tell the shifters. "I'm sure he'll offer financial support without the threat of war."

I doubt it helps, but I want it to be known that the Wrath Trio was trying to fix the problem. They were going about it all wrong, but there were attempts. Mammon's making it sound like they'll have to fight Aziel and force his support, but I don't think that'll be the case.

At least, I hope not.

Mammon clears her throat and shoots me a sharp look. "They sat on this information for over fifty years."

"I can confirm I've had recent meetings with Aziel and Silas," Kato says. "They didn't outright share this information, but they did say they were conducting studies on the female decline and had some promising early results."

Kato eyes me, his gaze heavy, before turning back to the room.

Mammon helps to steady me as we materialize in her sitting room.

"That went well," she says.

I agree. The shifters seemed receptive, and our meeting lasted hours.

"When are we meeting with the elves?" I ask.

"Their leaders will be arriving tomorrow afternoon. Kato will be coming to speak on behalf of the shifters, and if all goes well, we should have a verbal treaty in place by the end of the day."

Mammon's lips flatten into a straight line as she looks me over, but whatever emotion starts to spread over her features disappears as she squares her shoulders and turns away. I follow her out of the sitting room, acutely aware of the guards who watch my every move.

I don't know why they bother. Even if I wanted to, it's not like I could hurt anybody here. Demons are stronger than even the largest humans.

I doubt I'd get as much as one hit in, and I have no weapons.

Well, except for one.

Thankfully, Mammon doesn't seem to recognize my necklace. I'm not sure who's stronger, her or Silas, but I'm willing to bet she'd demand I remove it if she knew what it was.

"I think I can get Asmod's support, as well, but he can be tricky," Mammon admits.

My lips purse at the mention of Gray's dad. It's safe to say I'm not a fan of the King of Lust.

Mammon comes to an abrupt halt, and I freeze as a shadow comes hurrying around the corner with her infant. The baby reaches for Mammon with a loud whine, and he wraps his tiny limbs around her neck as she takes him from the shadow.

"Did you miss me?" she coos, bouncing him on her hip.

The baby looks in my direction, and I make a goofy face. He squeals and gives me a gummy grin, and I hope that means he likes me. I've never interacted with a baby before.

"Will Shay be joining us tomorrow?" I ask.

I'm a bit shocked she didn't come with us today, but I wouldn't be too surprised to learn she's done something to piss off the shifters and was told to stay away today.

Mammon purses her lips and glances at her baby. The boy, whose name I can't remember for the life of me, grabs at the front of her shirt. I politely look away as she readies the baby for feeding, her voice soft as she apologizes to him for being gone for so long.

I don't think I'll ever get used to seeing a woman so openly loving her children. My mother loved me, but there was always a hint of fear and pain behind it. Mammon loves hers like she knows they'll never be taken away.

"It seems the Wrath Trio got to Shay before me," she says. "They brought her body here last night."

I stiffen. Her body?

"They killed her? They were here?"

Fear is thick in my voice, but I can't bring myself to care. Shay didn't do anything wrong, and I can't believe they would be so cruel as to kill her. It was I who shared the information and betrayed Aziel. Shay was only my form of transportation.

"Yes, to both. They wanted proof you weren't being held captive." Mammon says. "My promise to protect you still stands, though, so there's no need to worry," she continues, seemingly misunderstanding my horror.

"Proof?"

"Yes. I brought them to your room, but they left without a fight after ensuring you weren't harmed," she admits with a slight roll of her eyes.

She brought them to my room? My mind reels, and I place my hand on the wall for balance. I suppose I should be grateful Mammon didn't let them take me, but why didn't she tell me sooner that they'd come to my room while I'd been sleeping?

That's a big thing not to mention.

"We were with the shifters for longer than anticipated." Mammon's quick to change the subject. "Go to bed, Charlotte, and we'll discuss more in the morning."

I don't like her dismissal, but I don't want to seem rude by continuing to force conversation. Sending me off to bed is probably more for her benefit than mine, anyway. She's not like my males, and she has an entire family to look after.

Mammon leaves, but a shadow lingers behind and leads me to the room I've been staying in. I dread spending time alone, my thoughts of Gray and Silas all-consuming.

Especially knowing they killed Shay and visited me while I was sleeping.

I wonder if Aziel came, too, or if he was too busy torturing Shay to bother.

My lip wobbles at the thought of them, but I clear my throat and force my tears away. I can't avoid thinking about them forever, but I'd like to put it off for a little longer.

I'll have to face what I've done at some point, and I'm pretty sure that will happen when Aziel meets with Mammon in only a few days.

I've made my bed, and now I need to lie in it.

A familiar face enters my line of sight, and my footsteps slow as I stare at the man I'm confident is Rock. The shadow looks straight ahead and walks past me without a glance.

"Are you okay?"

I turn toward the shadow currently leading me to my room.

He cocks his head to the side, his eyes flashing to Rock.

I glance back, but Rock rounds a corner and is out of sight before I get another good look. I'm not dumb enough to blurt out that one of Aziel's shadows is lingering around Mammon's home, but I can't contain my shock.

Did they send him to spy on me?

"I'm fine," I say, turning back around. "It's just been a long day."

The shadow hums, sounding suspicious, but he doesn't push. I resume following him, but I make sure to get distracted a few more times so my run-in with Rock isn't an isolated event.

I'm not sure why he's here, but I don't want to get him in trouble. I've grown quite fond of my tutor friend.

"Here," the shadow says, pointing to my door.

I dip my chin and step into the room. Tears threaten to pool over, but I hold them back as I wait for the shadow to leave. They move quickly, but I still give it a few minutes before grabbing Silas's shirt and peeking into the hallway.

A guard watches my every movement, and I hurry across the hall into the bathroom. The door has a lock, thank the heavens, and I lock it before stripping down and stepping into the shower. They've always helped to clear my mind, but after five minutes of standing underneath the hot spray, I realize it won't cut it for me today.

There's too much happening to relax.

Today went well, but I could tell Mammon was annoyed when I told the shifters how Aziel was making plans to fix his mistakes.

I want to help the females, but actively planning with Mammon how to fuck over Aziel feels wrong. She wants to back him into a corner and force him to submit. From the sounds of it, she also wants him to report to her rather than rule Wrath independently.

I've also learned that Aziel's filthy rich. I figured the man wasn't hurting for cash, but being with the Prince of Lust and one of the last remaining fates gives him a hoard of wealth too large to count.

My muscles ache with how tense I've been lately, and I turn the temperature of the water up until it burns. What will my life look like once the initial work with the females is completed? This is a years-long endeavor, and I doubt Mammon will want to keep me around that long.

I also doubt I can live a normal life afterward.

Shay's death proves that Aziel is out for blood.

I finally drag myself out of the shower when my skin is sore and aching. The room's all fogged up from the steam, but I enjoy not being forced to look at my reflection as I slip on Silas's shirt.

My lips purse, and I glance at the oversized fabric with a quiet sigh. Do I think Gray would kill me? Probably not. If anything, it would be Aziel. Or Silas. I know the fate loves me, but he's too logical. He can put his feelings aside and act on facts alone.

Ignoring my heart's racing, I hurry back to my room and climb into bed. It feels empty without Gray and Silas invading my space and sweating me out, and I grab and tuck the pillows against the sides of my body for a poor approximation of the feeling of being embraced.

Chapter Fifteen

CHARLOTTE

I WIPE MY palms on my shirt, anxious to meet the elven leaders. They arrived at Mammon's castle a few minutes earlier, but she said it was best to wait until they've been seated before making an appearance. She says it's a status symbol.

She doesn't wait on them—*they* wait on *her*.

"Ready?" Mammon asks, drawing my attention.

I nod, and she pushes open the doors and steps inside. I follow closely behind.

Kato stands as we enter, his broad frame a sharp contradiction to the thin, dark-toned men sitting on either side of him. He rises to his full height while the elves only stand halfway, their conversation dwindling as they notice our arrival.

I've heard many rumors about the elves, and I can't tell if I should be fearful. They're known to be one of the more intelligent species, but they're incredibly cunning and notorious for holding long grudges.

There's a spot open next to Kato, and I rush to it while Mammon sits at the head of the table. I'm comfortable around him.

"Charlotte." He grunts, pulling out the empty chair for me.

I offer him a relieved smile as I take a seat. He grabs the bottom of my chair and pulls it toward him, careful not to touch my skin as he brings us close together.

The elves don't outwardly look, but I know they're paying close attention to everything happening. Mammon told me to be careful with what I say around them, instructing me to remain silent and let her do most of the talking.

That's a request I have no issues fulfilling.

"Good afternoon, Mammon," the elf to her left says.

His voice is soft, and he speaks in a pitch I'm unfamiliar with hearing outside musical notes. It's almost like he's singing.

Mammon nods in his direction but doesn't verbally respond as she looks around the room, inspecting each man.

I've seen her softer side that comes out around her children, and yesterday I witnessed the loud, ferocious personality she put in front of the shifters. This one, though—this one screams power.

"This is Charlotte," Kato says when it becomes clear Mammon's not going to introduce me.

I jolt, shocked he's gone out of his way to make my presence known. The elves scoff at his lack of social etiquette before looking at me. My face warms as their eyes scan my figure, and I instinctively turn toward Mammon for guidance.

She's too focused on Kato to notice me. Her lips twitch downward as she glares at him, clearly angry with his interruption.

"We've heard of you," the elf sitting across from me says.

He has dark spiraled hair, and deep-purple markings cover the entirety of his neck.

His eyes dart along my face before shifting to Mammon. "We were told you had information."

Mammon nods, and with a wave of her hand, shadows begin placing tablets in front of each elf. I'm surprised they're not getting stacks of papers like the shifters did, but I realize why as Kato shoves the tablet away.

He looks at me, hesitating, before also pushing my tablet aside. I'm shocked but silently grateful when the shadows supply two paper versions for us.

I'm unfamiliar with technology, and it's easier to sift through physical sheets.

I read once that humans used to make paper with trees, chopping them down to such an extent that our air quality was thinning. I think a lot of the deforestation had to do with infrastructure, but I'm not positive about that. It was so long ago.

Kato's body provides a comfortable warmth as I watch the elves' facial expressions shift as they flip through the pages. They do relatively good jobs at keeping emotions hidden, but I still catch sight of the occasional rage and shock.

"This information is inaccurate," the man next to Mammon says.

Mammon clears her throat and straightens her back. "I have my researchers testing this theory now, but after a thorough read, they've found the science and math to be accurate. It checks out."

Another elf shakes his head. "My mate loves me, but she has given me no females. We have several children."

Mammon looks mildly uncomfortable.

"Love isn't enough. Elves believe sex is only for procreation, yes?" Kato chimes in, his voice loud. The elf across from me nods, his narrowing eyes warning that Kato's entering sensitive territory. "You do not make your females squeal, and that is what makes the girls."

The meaning behind his words is clear, and my face turns red. The balls this man must have to tell ten elven leaders they aren't pleasuring their females. I could never.

The elves don't look nearly as offended as I thought they

would, and they glance amongst themselves before directing their attention to a male sitting next to Kato. I lean forward to see around the shifter's enormous body, but once I do, I spot an elf hunching in his seat with a look of shame.

Kato laughs and smacks him on the back, his rough touch accidentally shoving the man's chest into the thick, wooden table.

"Filthy," another elf spits.

It takes me a moment to understand what's happening, but once it clicks, I can't stop the loud bubble of laughter that erupts from my lips. This poor elf must have a baby female, and he's being inadvertently outed for his untraditional sexual habits with his mate.

"Filthy is not bad," Kato says. "Our mates love us to be filthy, and we've produced many baby girls to prove it."

I raise a brow, surprised he's mentioning shifter females. After the awkward silence that erupted when I asked about them yesterday, I was under the impression they would never be brought up.

Kato seems more open than the other shifters, though.

My throat runs dry at the mental image of him lifting his skirt and showing me his penis yesterday. Even the unmated man refused to show me his, probably out of respect for the female he hopes to have someday.

Maybe that's why the shifters chose Kato to be their liaison.

He's open enough to bridge the gap between the shifters' secrecy and the elves' reserved ways.

The men around the table look uncomfortable as Kato jokes about being filthy for his mate.

"That aside, how did you come across this?" the shamed elf asks.

Mammon opens her mouth to respond, but Kato answers before she has the opportunity.

"The Wrath Trio claimed Charlotte," he explains. "She found the report in the incubus's office and came to Mammon with the findings when her males were too slow to help."

Mammon looks beyond livid, her cheeks flushed as she works her jaw side to side. "They weren't *too slow*. They did nothing to help, and they sat back and watched while our numbers dwindled and theirs grew. They planned to attack when we grew too weak to fight."

My skin bristles.

My males might not have done the right thing, but they were trying to fix their mistakes. They were going about it all wrong, but they were trying nonetheless.

"They were working on securing an alliance with Levia, and they were starting conversations with the shifters," I clarify.

Kato grunts. "Can confirm."

The elves still look pissed, but I'm happy to note it's considerably less than it was moments ago.

"Aziel will still need to be punished," the shamed elf says. "Despite his actions of late, he allowed this to be sat on for decades. I assume you've thought this through, Mammon."

Mammon nods and gestures to the tablets. "Document two."

The elves flip through their tablets in search of it. The shadows didn't provide a copy for Kato and me, and after a tense moment, I grab the tablet Kato pushed away earlier. He watches as I fiddle with it, his hot breath hitting my shoulder.

I can't figure out how to turn it on.

"Stupid fucking..." Kato mumbles, snatching it from my hand and turning to the shamed elf.

The man scoffs as Kato steals his working tablet and replaces it with ours. An elf across the table laughs, but I avoid looking in his direction as Kato sets the new one on the table in front of us.

Hoping the slight tremor in my hand doesn't show, I swipe to the first page of the document and begin reading.

Mammon has outlined a six-month plan.

She wants to use Aziel's money to build protected facilities in every realm, and then she wants to create an entirely new organization that oversees the new facilities. It sounds similar to the child protective services humans used to have, where one person monitors the well-being of a set of females.

If there are signs of abuse or the women are unhappy, they'll be rehomed to the nearest facility. The long-term plan is for all females to be given access to land and money, but that will have to wait until the risk of being snatched has decreased.

Mammon suggested chipping every female so they could be tracked, but the shifters shut that idea down yesterday.

"And if Aziel doesn't agree to pay?" the shamed elf asks.

I don't like how Mammon's eyes dart to me, nor does Kato if his shifting shoulders are anything to go by. Mammon looks me over before turning back to the men in the room.

"Aziel isn't prepared for war, especially not one at such a large scale," she says.

It takes everything in me not to flinch when Kato's fingers touch the outside of my exposed thigh. Mammon had me wear a shorter dress today, and he casually pulls up the hem of it as she answers questions.

I tighten my grip on the tablet as my skirt fabric reaches my waist, and I stare intently at it as a piece of folded-up paper is wedged between my hip and underwear. Kato leans forward and uses his free hand to swipe to the next page as he pulls my dress back down my leg.

I saw how the man recoiled when Mammon reached for him yesterday, and even though Kato is a bit more forward-thinking than the other shifters, touching a female who's not part of his immediate family is a big no-no.

The paper stabs into me, but I resist the urge to move it.

He was much smoother than I could ever dream of being, and I'll draw unwanted attention if I move. I'll wait until I'm alone to even think about the note.

"And what happens when Charlie runs back to Aziel and shares our plans?" the shamed elf asks.

The room falls silent.

"I doubt they'd bother listening to a word Charlie has to say before executing her," Mammon says. "They killed her counterpart already. They made her watch as they slit her son's throat, then they ripped out her heart."

Did Shay have a son? I didn't know that, and I especially didn't know that they went as far as to kill him, too. Will they hurt my mom?

"You underestimate him," the elf across from me says. "It's not just Aziel we're challenging, but the Prince of Lust and a fate."

The group begins arguing about how much power Aziel holds, and I gulp as I realize I know something they don't. They think Gray holds standing with Asmod and has the Kingdom of Lust supporting him.

My pulse races as the elves shut down good ideas because they think Asmod will counteract them, and I debate whether or not I should speak up. This plan is for money, and it's not as if they've truly gone out of their way to look for other options.

Not once have they discussed paying for this endeavor themselves.

"Who will pay if Aziel doesn't?" I ask, clearing my throat when my voice comes out squeaky.

Kato throws his hands in the air. "Shifters have no money. We live off our own means."

Nobody seems too surprised. It's been said before that the shifters are most helpful for their physical strength. Both

Mammon and the elves remain silent, however.

"Yes, Mammon. You talk about the costs, but from what I understand, you have quite the hoard of wealth yourself," somebody points out.

If it were possible for looks to kill, all of us in this room would be dead ten times over. Mammon's face turns a light shade of red, and her lips purse before she sucks in a deep breath and squares her shoulders.

"We will be receiving the money from Aziel. I am not concerned about it," she eventually says.

Kato snorts, but the noise goes ignored.

"Let's move on," Mammon continues, changing the topic.

Mammon storms from the room the second the last elf leaves. This meeting didn't go the way she wanted, but the fact that the elves agreed to give their public support was a win.

They didn't seem too keen to provide men or money, but they did offer technology.

Technology so advanced it makes me wonder how they didn't discover the fix for the female decline before. Most species were thrown into a panic when the declines began. They invested their money and resources into facilities over science, but the elves didn't have that issue.

Gray would say it's fate, and Silas would awkwardly look away and avoid the topic. He does that every time fate is mentioned.

The table groans as Kato leans against it, his weight too much for the wooden frame to support.

"Mammon will calm down shortly. She always does," he says.

He adjusts his leather skirt and brushes the nonexistent dust particles off it. The man's a freaking barbarian, and I can't help but wonder what he's like around his loved ones.

Given his protectiveness and pride whenever he mentions his children, I can tell he's a family man. I chuckle at the mental image of the large man playing with small children.

"You and Mammon are close?" I ask.

Kato frowns before shrugging.

"She's my brother's mate," he explains, sounding displeased. "She turned him into a damned fool, then sent him away." His voice deepens as he speaks. "Vont is a good man, and she's treating him as nothing more than a breeder. He's been moping around my house for six months, waiting for her to call him for another baby."

I gape, shocked by how openly he's airing their dirty laundry.

"Stupid woman and stupid babies. They are all ugly like her," he continues, gesturing for the guards to come over.

"Take me home," he orders.

I bite my lip to stop from smiling as four guards prepare to teleport him. It makes sense he'd need more than one. The man's a bear, after all. They leave, and I turn and follow the shadow who's been leading me around these past few days.

I need to know what's in the note Kato slipped into my underwear. The paper digs into my hip as I walk, but I ignore the slight pain.

"Thanks!" I blurt out, rushing past the shadow when I see my door.

I hurry inside and slam the door shut. There's no lock, so I lean against it as I lift my dress and grab the note. My hands are so shaky, it takes me a few tries to unfold it, and I can't help but frown when I finally do.

It's coordinates.

What the fuck am I supposed to do with that? I turn the note over to ensure I'm not missing anything before folding and returning it to my underwear. It's uncomfortable, but I don't want to risk it being found by one of Mammon's shadows.

I'm sure they search the room whenever I leave.

With a quiet groan, I rest my head against the door and stare at the ceiling. Now what?

I should apologize to Mammon and make sure all is well between us. She's the only thing protecting me from Aziel, and I'd like to stay on her good side.

I turn and pull open the door, pleasantly surprised to see my shadow is gone.

He probably didn't expect me to leave my room, and I kick off my shoes to remain quiet.

Wanting to remain inconspicuous, I stick to the wall and keep my head low as I move through the halls. The only human in the castle is probably hard not to notice, but I'm surprised to see it works as the few shadows I encounter don't even look in my direction.

I must be smoother than I thought.

I keep my eyes peeled for Rock, still convinced it was him I saw yesterday evening.

I'm not sure where Mammon stormed off to after the meeting, but I make a guess and head toward her office.

It doesn't take long for me to get lost.

My fingertips graze the stone wall as I continue forward, hopeful I'll encounter a hallway or room I recognize. I'm surprised I haven't run into any guards yet. I must not be in a high-traffic area of the castle.

"He's not reacting how I expected him to."

I pause as Mammon's voice floats down the hallway, and I flatten against the nearest wall to eavesdrop. Silas is rubbing off on me.

"You're underestimating him."

The harmonic pitch of the voice tells me she's speaking to an elf.

"I agree," another elf adds.

What's going on? Why's she meeting in private with the elves? I doubt Kato knows about this secret meeting.

"I thought he'd be more opposed to the idea of war. The Trio has gone out of their way to avoid it in the past," Mammon says. "It's not ideal, but Charlotte is our only leverage."

What?

An elf laughs. "How so? They want her dead."

"Not exactly. They're demanding regular updates on her health, and the incubus has gone as far as to send me a list of food she likes." Mammon huffs. "I've been speaking with the ogres, and they've agreed not to kill her until we have what we need from Aziel."

She's met with silence.

What's that supposed to mean? I thought Mammon hated the ogres. They're one of the cruelest species, and they burned their bridges with Mammon when one of them forced themselves on her daughter.

I shove my hair from my face and do my best to steady my labored breathing. The last thing I need is to grow all panicked and be overheard.

"I disagree with this. We want to help the females, and sending one off to be raped and tortured directly contradicts that." The elf's voice grows cold.

"We sacrifice one female to save thousands. It's an easy decision," Mammon argues. "I don't like it, either."

"Aziel will kill us."

"Aziel will be too distracted trying to save Charlotte. He doesn't have the capacity to fight the ogres *and* us, and he will choose her."

I take a step back. I've heard all I need to hear, and I need to get out of here before I get caught. My arms flail as my back comes in contact with a rigid body, and a hand covers my mouth before I get any noises out.

My eyes practically bulge out of my head as I'm dragged down the hallway, the person moving so quickly that the walls blur. I curse my decision to wear only socks as my heels make no noise against the floor, the entire kidnapping silent.

I try to bite the fleshy palm covering my mouth as I'm pulled into a dark room and spun around. My body instinctively relaxes at the familiar face of the shadow, but my brain remains on edge.

Rock puts his finger in front of his mouth, signaling to be quiet before releasing me. I suppose that answers my question about whether or not he's solid beneath his hazy form.

The small closet he's pulled us into reeks of stale bread and cleaning supplies, the unpleasant smell making me scrunch my nose. Rock hardly seems to notice as he bends so his mouth is directly next to my ear.

"It's time for you to come home," he whispers. "It's not safe for you here."

I shake my head. "It's not safe for me in Wrath."

"Yes, it is. I promise you."

I clench my jaw, not believing it. I heard what they did to Shay.

Rock looks panicked as he cups my cheeks. It's the first time he's ever truly touched me, excluding the occasional hair tousling and back pat when I'm walking too slow, and it's weird. He seems to feel the same way as he grimaces and moves his hands to my covered shoulders.

"I stole this from Gray," he says, holding up a gold ring. "It will give me enough juice to teleport you."

I run my hands through my hair, panicked. I can't stay here, but I can't go home.

Kato.

I rip up the bottom of my dress and grab the note he shoved in my underwear. Rock looks disgusted as he takes it from me and unfolds it.

"Where is this?" he asks.

I shrug. "Not sure. A shifter gave it to me. Take me here." I point to the coordinates.

Rock looks hesitant, his grip creasing the paper. He hands it back, and I return it to my underwear.

"I'm only going to be able to teleport you once," he warns. "Even with the ring, it will take everything I have."

I'm grateful he's not immediately shooting down my idea. I have no idea where these coordinates are, but I trust Kato. The man's a tactless brute who showed me his penis within minutes of meeting him, but fuck if I don't trust him.

I double down. "This is where we need to go."

I just know it.

Rock groans and throws his head back, visibly annoyed.

"You're infuriating. I can only teleport from the sitting room. Follow me," he says, giving in.

He opens the door and peeks out. My heart's practically beating out of my chest as he grabs my hand and tugs me down the maze of hallways. I'm grateful he seems to know where he's going.

A few shadows give us sideways glances as we pass, but it's not until a guard catches sight of us and turns to follow us that Rock speeds up. He pulls so hard, I'm sure my arm's about to be yanked from its socket, and eventually, he moves so quickly he's full-on dragging me.

Fucking demons.

Rock shoves open the sitting room door just seconds before a guard reaches us. The room around me vanishes, and immediately, I can tell this is about to be the worst travel I've ever experienced.

Chapter Sixteen

CHARLOTTE

I'M PRETTY SURE my eardrums have burst. If they haven't, I'm pretty sure they're about to.

I squeeze my eyes shut and cover my ears in the hopes of stopping the agonizing ringing, faintly aware of the ache in my knees as I drop onto some unknown hard surface. Light flashes behind my closed eyelids, and I hear the faint sounds of talking behind my covered ears, but I can't make out anything specific.

My body instinctively curls into a ball, my forehead pressing into the ground as I dry heave.

Somebody's touching me, and I shoulder them away as another loud cry rips from my throat.

What the fuck did Rock do to me?

I feel embarrassed for how I sob into the ground, the dirt sticking to my cheeks and finding its way into my mouth, but the pain is so consuming. I can't stop.

It feels like every vein in my body has burst and every nerve ending's been fried.

Air struggles to make its way into my lungs, and I rock back and forth as I wait for the pain to diminish. Objectively, I know it won't last forever, the uncomfortableness from teleporting typically only lasting a few minutes, but when it's happening, it feels never-ending.

"Charlie, Charlie!" Rock chants, running his hand up and down my back.

I release my right ear so I can shove him away.

"Where did you send us to?" he continues, pushing at the hand I shove against him.

My heart pounds, and I force myself to get up on my knees and look around. It takes a second for my eyes to adjust, my eyelids fluttering as they try to shut and cut off the bright light.

I'm not surprised to see we're in the middle of the forest, but I am slightly taken aback by the army of giant men surrounding us. Their leather skirts tell me they're shifters, but their bulging arms crossed over their chests and prominent frowns tell me we're not welcome.

"Who are you?" The one closest to us steps forward as he speaks.

He's tall and muscular—all the shifters are—and I spot the red marking of a bear on his thigh. I can barely make out a white line above it, but only a sliver of it peeks out below his skirt.

He clenches his jaw and shoves his brown hair out of his face before holding out a hand. I wave it away, knowing he doesn't want to touch me but feels obligated. He doesn't offer Rock the same help, but I'm not surprised.

Rock grimaces as he stands and helps me up, his arm wrapping around my hip to support most of my weight. I appreciate the gesture and lean into his side.

It's the least he can do after trying to kill me.

"I'm Charlie," I say, clearing my throat when my voice comes out croaky. "Kato gave me this address."

When the shifter doesn't respond, I yank up my dress and pull out the note I've got stashed there. The men gasp and turn away as my underwear is exposed, but I can't bring myself to care about modesty as I step forward and give the paper to the one who spoke.

It's not signed or anything, but it's all I've got.

There's a collective sigh when my dress is returned to its usual position, and the shifters turn to the one holding the note. He grunts and runs a hand down the front of his face, his bright green eyes darting over the numbers.

"You can call me *Chev*. Come." The man turns before waiting for our response.

The other shifters look wary as they let us through, their narrowed eyes darting between Rock and me. They all have the same bear mark, and I wonder if this is Kato's pack.

Rock explained during one of my tutoring sessions that the shifters tend to live in large groups with those who share the same animal.

"Shifters don't take kindly to unwelcome guests," Rock whispers, angling his face toward mine so he isn't overheard. "I hope you know what you're doing."

I gulp. Fingers crossed I don't get us killed.

My steps are jerky as I try to navigate the ground, but Rock helps to keep me steady. I don't know what to make of the fact that Kato gave me coordinates to his home, and I hope he intended for me to use it in case I was ever in trouble.

I can't imagine why else he'd give it to me.

It takes a few minutes of walking before I begin to see some variation in the wilderness. The trees are thinner, and I spot some houses and large communal buildings out of the corner of my eye. I make a pointed effort not to look anywhere near the shorter, feminine bodies that move around, not wanting to offend the shifters.

"Dad!" Chev shouts.

I spot Kato just as he spins and sets down the three children who cling to him. They don't look like him, their hair stark white, and they latch onto his legs as he approaches.

Kato is Chev's dad?

"Chev." Kato hugs Chev tightly before turning to me. "Charlotte," he says, eyes wide as he looks me over.

His lips purse as he takes in my lack of shoes and ripped dress, the fabric having torn while Rock dragged me down Mammon's hallways. His eyes briefly flash to Rock, his expression unreadable.

"Charlotte?" Chev asks, turning his back to us as he faces his father. "Like the Wrath's Charlotte? Are you kidding me?"

Kato frowns, his attention sliding from me to his son.

"She was with Mammon." Kato shrugs like that answers everything. He nudges his son aside and turns back to me. "You're welcome here, although I didn't anticipate you arriving so quickly and with a demon male." He waves away the men surrounding us.

The shifters hardly look happy as they return to whatever they were doing before they found Rock and me. Chev is the only one who sticks around, and he stumbles when the children I've been doing an excellent job of keeping my eyes away from transition from Kato's legs to his.

They don't seem to care that a human female and shadow are infiltrating their land, too busy trying to climb up and knock down the large men.

"This is Chev," Kato says, gesturing to his son. "He is my oldest baby," he continues, frowning as he eyes the other man. "Although now you are big. Almost as big as me."

Kato cups Chev's head like he's about to pop it. I stare at the two, shocked. Of all the things I was expecting to encounter here, watching a father have an existential crisis over the adulthood of his son wasn't one of them.

"Mammon wants to give me to the ogres in order to back Aziel into a corner," I blurt out, wanting to be upfront.

I like these people, and the last thing I want is for them to be caught off guard if Mammon comes to collect me. Kato releases his son, his lips curling into a snarl. I hope it's not directed at me, and I press myself further into Rock's side.

"I knew she was up to something," he snaps. "Come with me. We've got a cabin prepared for you. The shadow can stay, but I don't want to see him messing around my lands." He shoots another glance in Rock's direction before turning and leading us farther into the pack.

Kato had a cabin prepared for me?

Rock tightens his grip on my waist and pulls me along. Thin twigs and rocks burrow into the bottom of my socks and dig painfully into the soles of my feet, but I ignore them.

I'm glad Kato could sense something was up with Mammon and doesn't seem intimidated by the fact that she has use for me. Mammon is hellbent on Aziel paying for this project, and I honestly have no idea how far she's willing to go to get what she wants.

Chev follows us, his footsteps eerily quiet despite his proximity.

I can only imagine what Rock's thinking right now. He's probably wondering how I got into this mess and what part of my brain is malfunctioning. I hope asking him to bring me here wasn't a mistake.

The old Charlie would have thought I'm cool—running away from my males and venturing on my own. I feel far from cool right now, though. I'm in way over my head.

"You can call me *Charlie*," I say as Kato turns and leads us toward a small cabin.

It's far from the others, which isn't a surprise. I'm sure they want to keep some distance from Rock and me.

"Charlie, huh? I like it." Kato steps to the side and gestures to the wooden front door of the cabin. "Everything you need should be in there, and I'll have a cot brought in for the shadow."

I offer him a grateful smile.

He offers a polite nod of his head. "Chev will stand guard to ensure no Greeds show up to try to snatch you. I must leave for a meeting, but my daughter will probably make her way over when she hears you arrived. She has many questions about your incubus. Don't answer them." Kato speaks as if he's reading off a mental checklist. "There's food in there, but my mate will probably insist on bringing you dinner."

This is a lot.

"I have things to do today," Chev complains, gesturing angrily to the woods beyond the cabin.

Kato shrugs. "Yes. Watching Charlie." His tone leaves no room for discussion.

Kato and Chev glare at one another, neither seemingly wanting to give in. My gaze darts between the two as I wait to see who'll be the first to submit. I'm not entirely surprised when it's Chev, his shoulders slumping forward as he plops down on the small patio built around the front of the cabin.

Kato's eyes soften as he watches his son, his chest expanding as he sucks in a deep breath and pats the man on the head.

"You're safe here," Kato promises.

My body is sore and exhausted, and I let Rock bring me inside and set me on the couch. The place is surprisingly cozy, the front door opening up to a tiny living area and kitchenette. Directly across from the front door is a short hallway, no more than three steps deep, with one door on the left and another on the right.

Rock moves to the kitchenette and pulls open the fridge while I force myself back to my feet and move to see what's behind the doors. The one on the left opens to a bedroom, the room just large enough to fit a twin bed and dresser, and the door on the right opens to a small bathroom.

I'm surprised by the sheer amount of toiletries. Kato wasn't lying when he said the place was stocked.

"Charlie, come here!" Rock shouts, his voice gargled.

My nose scrunches as I exit the bathroom and round the corner leading into the main living area. Rock stands behind the kitchen island, shoving food in his mouth. He holds an odd-looking brown meat chunk out to me, and with a chuckle, I step forward and take it.

"It's Ucka, a very rare animal that only grows in the shifter lands," he says, shoving another large chunk in his mouth.

I set the Ucka on the table. I'll try it in a bit, but we need to talk first.

"Tell me everything," I say, pulling out one of the two stools tucked underneath the island and sitting on it. "Starting with what happened after I left. Did Gray and Silas send you to watch me?"

Rock clears his throat and sets down his meat.

I take a moment to glance at the open shelving behind him. I recognize some of the food on it, the staples like rice and beans, but most of what's here is unrecognizable.

"Your males went ballistic when they found out you were gone, but I honestly didn't stick around for long," he says.

There's a creak from outside the front door, and I turn to look through the thin crack in the wood. I make eye contact with Chev as he peers through it, the nosy shifter probably wanting to hear the story.

My cheeks heat as I look away, unsure what to make of him. He doesn't seem unfriendly, but he's clearly wary of us being here. Rock and I are strangers looking for refuge from two demon royals. It's not exactly an everyday occurrence, or a welcome one.

"They didn't send me," Rock says, "but I was worried about you and came myself. I was following you around the castle and overheard what Mammon was saying. I'm not letting you be pawned off to the ogres." His voice lowers as he speaks about Mammon.

Rock purses his lips, contemplating, before continuing. "I need to tell your males you left Greed. They won't come for you if you don't want it, but it's better if they know not to believe the lies Mammon will undoubtedly feed them."

My head throbs, and with a huff, I grab the meat off the table and carry it to the couch. I ignore the eye peeking through the gap in the door as I throw myself onto the soft cushion.

I need a minute to think. Also cry, but mostly think.

Chapter Seventeen

GRAY

I ROLL TO the side and look at Silas. He stands at the foot of the bed with his arms crossed over his chest, clearly pissed.

"Get up, Gray," Aziel snaps.

Silas is a fucking snitch. I glare at him, annoyed he ran to Aziel.

"We're meeting with Mammon in less than an hour, and you need to feed," Aziel continues, yanking the covers off my body. "We can't have you going hungry. It'll look bad."

I shrug. What's the point?

Rock teleported here last night to tell us that he and Charlie were no longer in Greed. The fucker refused to give any specifics other than to say they are safe, and it seems Charlie has no interest in seeing or hearing from us.

It breaks my heart, but I can't force her to come home. As frustrating as it is, I understood why she left for Greed. She was doing what she thought was best for the females, but that excuse doesn't apply here.

She just doesn't want to come home.

"I'm not going," I say.

There's no point in meeting with Mammon if Charlie won't be there.

"Yes, you are. Mammon doesn't know we know about Charlie's disappearance, which puts us at an advantage," Aziel argues, kneeling on the bed when I try to roll away. "We need all the advantage we can get right now."

I hum, pretending to listen as I bury my face in Silas's pillow. It smells like him, and I breathe it in as my eyes slip shut.

I'm not hungry.

"I've tried touching him, I've asked him to touch me, and I've tried touching myself, but he won't feed," Silas says, infuriatingly updating Aziel on my current sexual status.

I frown. It's not any of Aziel's business when I've last fed.

I'm not dying, and I have no intention of feeding until Charlie's back. Besides, I doubt Mammon will notice if I'm the tiniest bit hungry.

"You're acting like a petulant child." Aziel's voice is thick with annoyance, but I don't care.

He grabs my shoulder and rolls me onto my back, and I let out an undignified gasp as I smack at his hands. He pins me to the bed, and I lift my leg and try to knee him as he climbs over me.

"Get the fuck off me," I huff, not in the mood for this.

Aziel grabs my hands and shoves them underneath his knees as he sits on my stomach.

I turn to Silas for help. He holds eye contact as he climbs onto the bed next to us, and I can't help but lean into his hands as he cups my face and brings his mouth to mine.

"You need to feed," he whispers against my lips.

"No."

I can tell I've hurt Silas's feelings by the way he curls in on himself and moves back. My heart lurches, my emotions conflicted. I've never felt this way about feeding before.

I'm an incubus, for fuck's sake. Sex is nothing more than a necessity.

Objectively, I know my guilt stems from the way Charlie perceives it. Will she see it as cheating? Will she refuse to return home if she thinks I've moved on with Silas and forgotten about her?

Silas clears his throat and glances to the side. I don't think I've ever seen him looking so awkward before, and guilt hits me in the chest like a sledgehammer. He's just trying to help me.

"Do you love me?" I blurt out.

Silas looks startled, and he glances between Aziel and me before nodding. "Of course I do."

Aziel releases one of my shoulders and grabs the back of Silas's head. He weaves his fingers through Silas's hair before pushing his face into my neck. Silas doesn't fight it, and I hold back a moan as he buries his face in my skin and smells me.

My body responds despite my best attempts to remain calm, and I feel my lust pour out in response to the touch. It pisses me off. I want to be pouty, and I want to starve myself in rebellion.

"Look at me," Aziel commands, his rough voice sending an unwanted shiver down my spine.

My hips twitch, and I do my best to look unaffected as Silas begins to strip. He rips his shirt over his head in one smooth motion, and his abs flex as he leans back and removes his bottoms.

Aziel grabs my chin and forces my eyes away from Silas as he begins to push down his underwear. I want to see him.

"You're our incubus, Gray," Aziel says. "Let us feed you."

I throw my head back, and Aziel seems to take advantage of that as he leans in and licks my neck. *Fuck.* He licks the spot where demons mark, and I squeeze my eyes shut as my lust thickens.

Silas gasps, and I turn to see why. He's naked, and I watch through narrowed eyes as he breathes in my lust and swells in his hand. He curls his fingers around the base of his shaft and gives himself a slow tug.

I like it, and Aziel lets me continue watching as he pulls out of my neck and slides down my body. I don't push him away as he works to undo my pants.

Silas moves forward and presses the tip of himself against my lips.

"Make me feel good. Please, baby," he moans.

One of his hands lands on the headboard while the other curls around Aziel's shoulder.

I should tell him *no*. Silas is patient while I hesitate, but Aziel doesn't seem to share the same feelings as he shoves his thumb between my teeth and yanks my bottom jaw down.

My tongue presses against his finger, subtly licking the skin as he pries open my mouth.

"Good boy," Aziel praises, his pupils blown out.

I know the dirty fucker's enjoying the control as he turns my open mouth toward Silas. Silas seems hesitant, his cock softening.

"Feed him, Silas," Aziel orders.

Silas sucks in a shaky breath before pushing his hips forward and slipping himself between my lips. He's thick, and I have to open my mouth wide so he can fit.

My eyelids flutter shut as his taste hits my tongue, and my lips instinctively move to close around him before being halted by Aziel's thumb. Silas tastes so good, and I moan as he fills my mouth.

"It feels good," Silas coos, pushing my hair out of my face.

Of course it does. I'm an incubus. I know how to suck a dick.

Silas gently rocks himself in and out, and I suck him the best I can when Aziel's thumb is in the way.

Aziel chuckles as he watches my struggle, and he presses harder against my tongue before removing his finger. I close my lips entirely around Silas the moment I can. He hits the back of my throat as he fucks my mouth, the action causing my eyes to water.

I want him to make me choke.

"Would you look at that? We knew our incubus couldn't resist a warm cock in his mouth." Aziel says.

He continues removing my pants before doing the same to himself. I try to turn my head so I can look, upset his dick is out and I can't see it. He never exposes himself to me. Not unless I trick him into it.

"Fuck." Aziel moans, grabbing my hand and placing it on his length.

Silas turns to watch, his hips jerking.

"Come on, Gray," Aziel says. "You're always begging for my cock, and this is your opportunity to have it."

He knows exactly what buttons to push to lure me in.

I curl my fingers around him, loving how he twitches in my hand. I've wanted to feel Aziel for so long, and I take my sweet time running my fist from his base to tip.

"I want you to be full, Gray." Silas gasps, his thumb stroking my cheekbone. "You're going to look so healthy and strong. Charlie's going to love it."

I nod as much as I can when my mouth's being fucked, gargling on my spit as he cups the column of my neck so he can feel it expand with each of his thrusts. My eyes roll back as I feed on their lust.

It's fucking good.

Silas slows to a stop before pulling out of my mouth, and I cry as I crane my neck and try to chase him. What's he doing? He and Aziel exchange glances, and I don't like it.

They've discussed this behind my back.

I release Aziel and move to sit up, but he places a hand on my chest and pushes me back down.

I ball my hands into fists, ready to lash out, when Aziel reaches for me. My entire body stills, and I do a poor job hiding my surprise as he takes hold of my cock. Aziel's never touched me before.

"Let your arousal out," he says, giving me a painful tug.

How does he even know about that?

My lips flatten into a straight line as I shoot Silas a pointed glare and shake my head. I don't like letting it out, finding the thick liquid that seeps from my cock humiliating. Most incubi only produce a small amount, just enough to help our dicks glide, but mine makes too much.

"I wasn't asking," Aziel continues as I hold it back.

He strokes me harder to try to force it out, tugging on me like I'm a fucking cow. My eyes screw shut when it works, and I feel it leaking out onto his fist and my lower abdomen. Silas bends and kisses me while Aziel covers both himself and me with it.

"Please," I cry.

Silas trails his fingers up my shaft before covering himself, too.

I sink my teeth into my bottom lip to stop more from coming out as I feed.

"Show me how good you can make me feel, Gray," Aziel says, straddling my thigh and pressing his cock against mine.

Silas is quick to do the same, and I know I must be hallucinating as he grabs my hands and brings them to where all three of our bodies connect. It's about time they give in and let me pleasure us all. I've been wishing for this to happen for decades, and finally seeing all three of our cocks pressed together is better than I ever imagined.

My lips curl into a sly grin as I stroke us with both hands. The positioning's a bit awkward, but I make it work.

"I told you I don't want to feed," I moan, needing to say it out loud so I feel better about how much I love this.

"I don't care what you want, Gray," Aziel says, ripping open my shirt and planting his hands on my bare chest. "You're mine. That means your cock is mine, your arousal is mine, and your entire fucking body is mine. If I want you to make me cum, then you're going to make me cum."

Silas pants and rocks his hips forward, too lost in his pleasure to pay attention to what's happening between Aziel and me.

"Let me into your head," Aziel whispers.

I gasp as both men begin to thrust into my hands.

"Let."

Aziel kisses my ear.

"Me."

He moves to my neck, trailing his lips over my sensitive skin.

"In."

It takes everything in me to deny him, not wanting him to have access to my thoughts and memories the way he does with Silas. He's only doing this because Charlie's gone and he's feeling needy. He wants an additional layer of control so we can't run from him, too.

"Let me in, baby, and I'll let you sink your teeth into my neck," Aziel promises. "Everybody will know I'm yours. They'll all know I belong to you."

My mouth opens in a silent moan. Everybody knows we've bonded, but letting me put physical proof on his body will show that he's accepted me.

"I'll let you touch me whenever you want. I'll let you into my dreams and…" He pauses, clearing his throat. "I'll let you fuck me once. I know you've always wanted to."

It's not the promise of sex that does it for me, but the string of desperation and fear I feel through our bond that crushes my resolve. Charlie's leaving hurts him more than he cares to admit, and if letting him eavesdrop while I think about wet pussy and warm mouths all day is what's going to help, then so be it.

Silas stills with a choked moan as he reaches his peak, and I eagerly stroke him through it as he covers both Aziel and me with cum. I love him so much.

"Okay, okay. You can come in." I gasp, throwing my head back as I breathe in everything Silas releases.

Aziel barges into my head. I can't even begin to imagine what he's seeing or searching for in the mess that's my mind, but I can't bring myself to care as my movements grow frantic.

It feels so fucking good having a slick cock rub against my own.

I'm not sure if Aziel knows what will happen, but I hardly care as I stiffen and find my release. Aziel almost immediately drops onto me, his arms going limp as my orgasm hits him. Finishing an incubus is pleasurable, and Aziel's learning firsthand just how true that is.

He shivers as he cums, his face buried in my neck.

Who's the good boy now?

"You're not biting the Wrath," Silas says, surprising me.

I didn't realize he was even listening. I shoot him a soft smile. "I know, baby. I didn't even consider it."

Aziel leaves my mind and rolls away.

He avoids eye contact as he heads to the bathroom to clean himself. If I'm honest, I'm disappointed by how quickly he grew cold. Silas seems to sense my thoughts as he peppers my face and neck with kisses, distracting me until Aziel returns fully clothed.

"We're going to be late," he says, gesturing for Silas and me to get up.

I still don't want to attend this meeting, but I don't make a fuss as I climb out of bed and reach for my pants.

Chapter Eighteen

CHARLOTTE

MY TOE CATCHES against the doorframe as I finally drag myself out of the bedroom, and I hiss and jump as pain shoots up my leg. Rock's sitting on the couch scarfing down the food that was dropped off in front of our door last night, and he laughs as he watches me hop around.

"You okay?" he asks.

I nod, grimacing as I gingerly return my foot to the ground.

Rock shakes his head and stabs his fork into a chunk of meat. I'm grateful whoever brought it, probably Kato's mate, didn't stop to chat or investigate. Chev must have left, too, his shadow no longer lingering behind the door.

"How long did I sleep for?" I ask, pushing back my hair as I walk into the small kitchen.

"About eleven hours." Rock's words are muffled as he speaks around a mouthful of food. "You were snoring so loud, I'm surprised you didn't wake yourself up."

I roll my eyes, not in the mood to deal with his jokes. It's way too early for that.

"Have you just been hanging out in here? Do you know if

we're allowed to go outside?" I ask, serving myself some of the leftovers.

There's a pan left out from when Rock heated his up earlier, but I don't have the patience and eat it cold. It tastes just as good, and I hum quietly as I take a few bites.

Mammon strictly ate demon food, and while I don't necessarily have a problem with it, it lacks flavor. The shifters seem to enjoy spices, which is a blessing.

"The shifters will have my head if I leave the cabin," Rock says. "Kato came by while you were asleep and said Chev would be by shortly to show you around." He kicks his feet up on the coffee table.

It's odd seeing him so relaxed.

"Did he say when?" I ask, glancing at the clock.

Instead of answering, Rock stands and stomps toward me with a deep-set frown. My hand freezes halfway to my mouth as I take in his angry expression, unable to understand where it's coming from. He comes to a halt and scans my face and torso with a scowl.

"Where's your necklace?" he asks, taking it upon himself to yank down the front of my shirt.

I gasp and shove his hands away as the action exposes my bare breasts, but Rock hardly seems to notice as he searches for the tiny stone.

"In the bathroom. I took it off to shower," I explain.

Rock drops my shirt, and I clutch my stretched-out neckline to my chest as he spins and storms into the bathroom.

His sudden outburst is shocking, and I remain frozen until he returns with the necklace clutched delicately in his hands. He moves slowly, careful not to do anything to set it off as he approaches and holds it out for me to take.

"I'm not risking my life in the shifter lands only for you to be careless with the best form of protection you've got," he scolds.

"Don't take it off again."

"I'm sorry," I say, clasping it around my neck. "I try to keep it from getting wet so the chain doesn't get ruined."

Rock scoffs and gestures to the thin metal. "Do you think Silas didn't think of that? It's enchanted, and it will take more than a little water to ruin it."

My cheeks warm as I nod. I hate when Rock scolds me, but he has a point. I'm usually careful to put the necklace back on after my showers, and I never took it off when I was staying with Mammon, but I feel comfortable around Rock and let my guard down.

It was thoughtless.

"Did you tell my males I'm no longer in Greed?" I ask, changing the subject.

Rock returns to the couch. "I told them last night. They weren't happy about it, specifically Gray, but they won't be bothering you."

I'm not sure how much I believe Rock's claim that they won't bother me, but I don't argue as I force myself to eat before Chev gets here. I can't lie and say I'm not nervous about leaving Rock, but I don't want to insult the shifters by telling them *no*.

My heart is pounding when a quiet knock echoes throughout the room, and I suck in a shaky breath before approaching the front door and pulling it open.

Chev stands on the other side.

"Good morning," he says.

He's wearing the usual leather skirt, and I can't help but immediately notice the material's ridden up to show most, if not all, of his thighs.

"You're exposing yourself," Rock shouts, finding no issues letting the shifter know.

Chev grunts, looking embarrassed as his chest turns red and

he tugs down his skirt. "I ripped my bottoms hunting, and I'm borrowing a pair from a smaller male," he explains, wrestling with the fabric.

I wonder if they've ever heard of pants, or even a skort, but I can't bring myself to ask. I don't know these people well enough to joke around with them.

"Would you like me to show you around? My sister wants to meet you." Chev steps back and gestures in the direction where the heart of the pack resides.

I glance at Rock, wanting his thoughts on whether or not he trusts these people. He gives a thumbs-up, and I clear my throat before nodding and stepping outside.

"Thank you," I say. "I wasn't sure if I was allowed to leave the cabin."

Chev seems confused, but his expression quickly shifts to fear as he watches me trip over the first root I come across. He hesitates, his arm twitching by his side, before he holds it out for me to take.

I offer him a small smile and shake my head, not wanting to disrespect him just because I'm incapable of walking through the woods. How embarrassing.

"You're welcome here, but we'd ask that you don't walk alone," he explains. "Shifters have good hearing. You can yell for me when you want to leave, and I'll come running."

My lips quirk upward at his word choice. Chev's a bit more serious than Kato, but he's just as friendly.

Chev continues to make polite chitchat as he leads me to the center of the pack lands. It's warm, but there's a decent breeze that keeps the air from feeling too hot. I enjoy it.

Shifters stop and stare as we pass, and I take solace in the fact that nobody seems outwardly hostile—a few even wave. I gradually grow steadier on my feet, too, and after a few minutes,

I'm not making a complete fool of myself.

"This is my home. I made it and moved in when I turned twenty," Chev says, his chest puffing up as he gestures to the small wooden home we're passing.

I'm surprised it's the same size as the cabin Rock and I are staying in. I assumed he'd have a bigger home, but I suppose it doesn't make sense for him to put all the work in if it's only going to be him.

"You made it yourself?" I ask, impressed.

Chev nods, a smile toying at the corners of his lips. "Shifters always make their homes. I'll add to it when I find my mate, and I'll build a new room for each baby we make." His visible excitement warms my heart.

The shifters sure do love their families.

Chev's quick to change the subject as he turns and resumes walking. He continues to tug at his skirt as he shows me the pack training room and hospital, and he orders another man to bring him a larger one before taking me to the playground and education center.

"Chev!" a feminine voice rings out, halting his words.

I turn to see a woman sprinting toward us. She looks exactly like Chev and Kato, minus the bulging muscles, but she has the same dark-brown hair and bright green eyes. She wears an identical leather skirt as the men, but she also has a thick wrapping around her chest that holds her breasts firmly against her body.

"You must be Charlie!" she says, saddling alongside Chev. "You said you'd tell me when she wakes up."

Chev shrugs, completely unapologetic. "I was going to bring her to you after the tour. I just have the tavern left." He turns to me. "This is Echo. My sister."

Echo grins and wraps her arm around my shoulders. I grunt as I'm pulled around, and I look to Chev for help as she squeezes me against her chest.

"Be gentle with Charlie," he snaps, concern thick in his voice as he watches my body mold around hers.

"Of course, of course." Echo huffs, releasing me and giving me some much-needed space.

This is far from what I anticipated when Rock and I escaped from Greed, but I'm not complaining. The shifters are kind.

"I'll take her to the tavern," she says. "Dad needs your help with the toddlers, anyway. They're having trouble with their axes."

My eyes bulge out of their sockets at the mention of toddlers with axes, but I quickly taper down the shock. The shifters love their families, and I doubt they'd put children in danger.

Their toddlers are probably better equipped to use axes and survive in the wilderness than I am, anyway.

Chev grimaces and turns to me with an apologetic huff. I stare blankly at him before realizing he's looking for my permission. My cheeks warm as I give a timid nod, the gesture all he needs to turn and rush into the woods.

Echo watches him leave before turning to me with a sneaky grin.

"Dad doesn't need help, but I wanted to get to know you without him lingering around," she whispers, crouching slightly so she can link our fingers together and lead me to the tavern. "I never get to meet any non-shifters, and I'm sure you could use a drink or two after all your travels."

I open my mouth to let out a polite chuckle, but I wince when all that erupts is a semi-loud squawk. Echo gives me a concerned glance out of the corner of her eye, but thankfully, she doesn't comment on my odd noise.

Maybe she thinks it's a human thing.

"They keep you pretty tucked away, don't they?" I ask,

blurting out the first thing that comes to mind.

Echo shrugs. "In a way. We have free rein here, but our males are concerned with us meeting non-shifters. There are many women here, and we don't want to draw attention to our lands. Especially with the species who can teleport."

We turn right, and I spot what must be the tavern up ahead. There's a sign above it I can't read, but the doors are open and I can see people inside drinking. Echo doesn't acknowledge my suddenly sweaty palms as she pulls me inside.

There's a lot of chatter, and I pray it doesn't go silent when I enter as it does in the movies.

A few people glance over, but most don't even notice my presence. *Thank the lord.*

I stick out like a sore thumb in my dusty blue dress.

Everybody else is wearing dark leather, and even the females are easily twice my size.

Echo releases my hand and leads me to a table in the center of the room. A small handful of shifters turn to say *hello*, and Echo greets them happily before grabbing my arm and introducing me.

"This is Charlie! She's Dad's guest," she says, gently squeezing my shoulder.

The man and woman she's speaking to shoot me wide grins, their friendliness surprising. They give a polite *hello*, but Echo tugs me away before I get a chance to respond.

She's a bit demanding.

"I'll get us something to drink," she says, making an odd gesture to the bartender.

The woman behind the counter nods and holds up her thumb. Apparently, the thumbs-up gesture is universal. Interesting.

She finishes serving her customers before pouring and bringing us two large cups filled with a beige, foamy drink. I accept mine with a grateful smile and set it on the table between us. Their cups are enormous, and I have to use two hands to avoid spilling.

"How'd you end up here with a shadow?" Echo wastes no time getting to the meat of her questions.

I shrug and take a sip of my drink. It's bitter, but I don't hate it.

"That's kind of a long story," I admit.

Echo's smile grows. "Even better!"

I take another sip of my drink and let out a long sigh before launching into my explanation. What I intend to be a ten-minute story turns into a thirty-minute one, my lips loosening due to Echo's friendliness and the alcohol.

She has me cackling more than once, her wild facial expressions and dramatic gasps making the more somber parts of my story feel lighter.

"So you're telling me you lived with an incubus, who's totally obsessed with you, for months, and never once had sex with him?" Echo gasps and slams her empty cup on the table.

I snort, shaking my head as she gestures for a refill. "Is that all you got out of my story?"

She has the decency to look mildly guilty as she shrugs and hides a smile behind her hand. The squinting of her eyes gives her away, though. "It's arguably the most important part. Besides, I've been dying to hear the inside scoop on Gray's life since he participated in the show."

I pause. "*The show?*"

Echo's face goes red, and a flush spreads across her cheeks and down her neck.

"I don't think I'm supposed to tell you about that," she admits, hiding behind her drink. "We don't talk about it."

I shake my head and pull her drink away from her.

"If I can sit here and tell you all about my failed excuse of a love life, you can tell me about the show," I argue.

Echo throws her head back with a loud groan.

"Well," she starts, lowering her voice and glancing around. "We're abstinent until we find our mate, which is great and all, but that leads to many questions about sex that are too embarrassing to ask our family about. Every ten years or so, our leaders bring in an incubus and succubus to provide a demonstration and answer our questions."

I lean in. "A demonstration?"

Echo huffs, her blush deepening. "*Charlie*," she whines, clearing her throat. "We group up and go into a private building with the opposite sex demon so they can show us their bodies and explain how, logistically, it works. Then they answer our questions."

I place my fingers over my mouth, trying and failing to keep my face flat. Echo looks away, her lips twitching as her eyes dart in my direction every few seconds to see my expression.

"Stop laughing." She frowns as my lips twitch.

Her anger breaks me, and I drop my head into my hands to hide my giggling.

"Echo! That's some of the weirdest shit I've ever heard." I cackle. "And Gray did that?"

I'm not surprised. He probably volunteered himself, much to Silas's and Aziel's annoyance.

"Shut up!" Echo shouts, her lips spreading into a wide smile as she tries and fails to stop her own round of laughter. "We take it very seriously!"

I hold my belly, struggling to breathe. "I'm sure you do."

Echo rolls her eyes, giving up, and gestures for me to finish my drink. My mind feels lighter, and much of the stress in my muscles is gone after telling her my story and getting a good laugh. It still hurts to think about my males, but seeing and hearing her angry reactions to my recap of their actions makes me feel better.

For once, it feels like I'm connecting with somebody who doesn't have some wild ulterior motive. Echo just wants somebody to gossip with.

It's refreshing.

"Do you want to help me hunt our meat for tonight's dinner?" Echo asks as we leave the tavern. "Or I can take you back to your cabin."

I squint, the sudden bright light momentarily blinding me. It takes a moment for her words to sink in, but I let out an excited gasp once they do. "You'd let me go with you?"

Echo grins. "I'll let you do more than that. I'll let you hunt the meat yourself!"

Chapter Nineteen

AZIEL

MAMMON WEARS THE smirk of a woman who thinks she has something over us. I clench my hands into tight fists below the table, struggling to contain my wrath.

I'm convinced Mammon's made it her life's mission to piss me off. She's succeeding.

Silas sits to my left, his features calm, but I know he's as livid as I am.

Gray doesn't have the same ability to hide his emotions, and he sits at my right outwardly glaring at Mammon. He's going to be a problem today, and I hope he can keep it together for this meeting.

The last thing I need is to navigate another screaming match between Gray and Mammon, especially when I'm already on the verge of losing control.

Charlie's in the shifter realm, my female sneaky in her multiple escapes, but I need to keep peace with Mammon to keep her safe. I got Rock to tell me where she is, and while the shifters may be notoriously kind to females, I don't need Mammon finding out my human is with them.

I need her thinking she's got the upper hand, the woman careless when she's cocky, while I slip in and turn the shifters on my side. I'm sure they're pissed by Mammon's plans to sell Charlie, and I think I can get them to flip sides.

The shifters are soft and quick to forgive, and I'm going to use that to my benefit.

"Where's Charlie?" I ask, glancing at the door.

"Charlie chose not to come," Mammon lies. "She doesn't want to see you."

If only she knew how true that statement is. The shifters haven't told her that Charlie's with them, and I assume all she knows is that one of our shadows broke in and took Charlie away.

She probably fears Charlie's back in our possession.

It would make everything so much easier if she were. Instead, she had to run off to the fucking shifters to do god knows what. That species isn't good for much beyond fighting, so I doubt she will enjoy her time there.

Charlie's many things, but a warrior isn't one of them. The poor female probably couldn't even hurt a fly. It's a miracle she lasted as long as she did in our home, my males and I rarely backing away from a fight.

I suppose that was part of the problem, though.

She didn't enjoy our constant fighting and went as far as to cut her neck when the fights grew too frequent. It was dramatic—but effective in making us stop.

I wonder if Mammon will reveal that Charlie's escaped or if she'll try to play us. Probably the latter.

I clear my throat and place my hand on Gray's thigh when he grows fidgety. It would've been wiser to have him sit next to Silas, the fate better at keeping him calm, but I let jealousy get the best of me and forced myself between them.

"And Charlie is well?" I ask, cocking my head to the side.

Mammon's eyes narrow as she tries to read us. I'd love to be in her mind, and I suck my cheeks into my mouth as she clenches her jaw and nods.

Lying sack of shit.

I wonder what Charlie would think if I killed Mammon. She'd probably be pissed. She always is.

"She's doing as well as a person can when the Wrath Trio is hunting them," Mammon says, poorly hidden anger lacing her words.

I grin and lean back in my seat.

It's always entertaining when Mammon gets angry, the woman prone to sharp, snarky remarks and poorly executed insults. We haven't spoken since I was forced to deal with her son, and if her clenched fists and tight jaw are anything to go by, I'd say she's still pissed about it.

I suppose I don't blame her, though.

I'd kill anybody who dared to harm so much as a hair on my child's head, and I'm sure she feels the same way. It must be frustrating to sit across from the man who murdered your firstborn child and not be able to do anything about it.

Mammon's no match against me, and I'm sure that knowledge kills her. She'll never be able to avenge her oldest, and I won't be surprised if I find a cluster of her children on my doorstep someday trying to do just that.

I'll be merciful, though, and I'll have my shadows return them alive.

"Hunting Charlie? We all know that's not true." I chuckle, enjoying how her guards shift along the far wall. "I hope you haven't been telling our female those lies."

It's a good play on her end, even if it is annoying. Mammon's genuine in her efforts to help the females, but I know her hatred of me overshadows that.

That's the only reason she wanted to give Charlie to the ogres.

"I've only been telling her the truth," Mammon says after a moment's hesitation.

Silas and Gray bristle, the men identical in their movements as they shift and straighten their backs. My fingers dig into Gray's thigh to stop whatever manic thoughts are brewing in his head. I want to seep into his mind and see what he's thinking, but now's not the time for that.

His mind is new to me, and I can't maneuver around it as easily as I can with Silas.

Gray will feel my attempt and get riled up, and the last thing we need is him losing control inside Greed. If he gets violent, I for sure will.

Even Silas won't be able to stop me. Our friendship is strong, but it's not enough to outweigh the emotions Gray feeds me through our bond.

I really should've had them sit next to one another. As much as I hate it, Silas has taken my place as Gray's person. The incubus cares for him more than he does me, and Silas is better equipped to help keep him calm.

The thought makes me angry, and I shut my eyes and breathe in the desperate hope of calming my pounding heart. Gray didn't even consider marking me when I offered it, his loyalty to Charlie and Silas keeping him at an arm's distance.

His rejection was humiliating, and I'll never ask again.

Mammon looks elated by my visible struggle, and I clear my throat before wiping all emotion from my face. She doesn't even know what I'm upset about.

"What's it going to take to get Charlie back?" I ask.

Mammon laughs. "She's going to cost a pretty penny."

I stiffen.

Charlie would be devastated if she knew she was being talked about like this, especially after her history of being very literally auctioned off. My human isn't for sale.

"We have no interest in buying her from you," Silas adds, taking over.

Mammon gulps, her eyes darting from me to Silas. It's never a good sign when I'm unable to continue interacting, and it's making her nervous. Good.

Gray runs his thumb along the back of my hand before prying my fingers off his thigh and flipping it over so he can trace the lines on my palm. It distracts me enough that I can smell his lust, the man probably pushing it out for my benefit.

It's a good thing we fed him before coming. He would've been too hungry to do this earlier.

"You need to pay for what you've done." Mammon pivots, getting to the real reason she called us here. "The blessed breeds know of your lies and are far from happy. We know you're looking to avoid a war, and we're willing to forgive your deceit if you support our efforts."

Silas grabs my leg when my anger doesn't settle, his fingers curling into my thigh as mine did to Gray's thigh earlier.

While my relationship with Gray has always been complicated, I've never crossed any bridges with Silas. I can count on one hand the number of times we've willingly touched skin. It's never been something we do, but if we want to bond with Charlie, we'll need to get comfortable with it.

I let my fingers fall between his.

I don't necessarily want to do all the things Silas and Gray do with one another, my attraction toward men limited, but I'm willing to try. Especially since Charlie seems to enjoy it so much.

My little female will demand I get fucked at least once.

My desire for Gray grew after our bonding, and I'm sure the same thing will happen with Silas. Even now, I don't dislike

Silas's touch. It's foreign and feels odd after being nothing more than friends for so long, but that doesn't mean it's unwelcome.

If he moved his hand higher up my thigh, my body would react.

"Support your efforts?" Silas asks, ignoring the way Mammon glances at our connection. We're giving away more than we should. "We're going to need more information than that."

"We want your money. Our plan includes extensive infrastructure and operational expenses." Mammon lists off items with a snap of her fingers.

I tighten my holds on Silas and Gray, needing something to keep me from launching myself at her.

Gray stands and weasels himself between me and the table. I huff as he plants himself on my lap. Instinctively, I wrap my arms around his waist and rest my hands on his thighs, the only comfortable place to put them when we're in this position.

What did I do before he was in my life?

Killed a lot more, that's for sure.

Silas turns to us with a raised brow, his hand flexing before he yanks it back to himself. It probably hurt having it smashed between Gray's and my bodies.

"Oh? And how much are *you* providing?" he asks, propping his elbow on the table and resting his chin in his hand.

Mammon doesn't immediately respond, her lack of answer telling me all I need to know. She has no intention to pay, and she fully intends for me to bear the financial brunt of this endeavor.

I have no issues helping, wanting to show my support to the cause, but I'll be damned if she makes me out to be a fool.

I've been embarrassed enough by Charlie running to Mammon and sharing our secrets. Levia's furious with me, threatening war and publicly mocking my inability to keep my female under control. The last thing I need is to come across as weak by submitting to Mammon.

She plans to drain me and attack while I'm down. It wouldn't be the first time she tried.

My lip curls at the memory of her feigning interest in helping teach me to lead after my father was removed from power. It only lasted a few years before her true intentions came to light. The woman's always wanted my kingdom, and I know she's willing to do whatever it takes to get it.

"We're supporting in other ways," she says, avoiding Silas's question.

I hum, craning my neck to see around Gray's hair. He moves the exact moment I do, and with a quiet sigh, I reach up and nudge his head out of the way. *Fucking incubus.*

"I'm willing to support in other ways, too," I retort.

The guards along the far wall continue to shift, their eyes darting between Mammon and me. They're scared I will attack, and if it weren't for Gray, I probably would. She only stationed a few guards inside the room, but I'm willing to bet dozens more are lingering just beyond the doors.

"We don't need, or want, that." She clears her throat, her earlier confidence wavering.

"But you want my money." I shake my head with a humorless chuckle. "And, let me guess, your plan spares no expense? Only the best for Mammon and her humanitarian causes. You can take your plan and shove—"

Silas interrupts. "We're willing to help, but we won't support the entirety of this project. Send over a list of what you need, and I'll set aside some budget for you."

Mammon's fists slam onto the table, cracking the surface. Oh, fun. I like it when she's angry.

"You'll be paying the amount I tell you."

I raise a brow, mildly entertained. Ballsy to assume I'll be paying her anything with that attitude. I'm only considering this because I know Charlie will want me to, and at this rate, I'm willing to do anything to get on the human's good side.

Beyond my selfish reasons for wanting her back, my males are struggling. Gray's hunger strike is unheard of, and while Silas is putting on a calm façade, the growing bags under his eyes tell me he's not getting much sleep.

They feel betrayed.

Rock said Charlie's been made aware we aren't a danger to her, but she still chooses to send us on a fucking scavenger hunt. The shadow's purposely elusive, too, refusing to give us meaningful information on what she's doing with the shifters.

I'd wring his throat if I didn't appreciate him keeping her safe and providing her comfort.

Besides, I'll enjoy hearing her tell me herself when she returns. I'll wait patiently for her to share before punishing her for leaving. I'm done moping around, waiting for her to choose me.

She's mine, and she's going to know it.

Silas and Mammon continue going back and forth until Mammon gives in and has a shadow bring over a stack of paperwork outlining the specific items they need money for. It's pages thick and will be a headache to sift through.

Charlie better fucking appreciate this.

"We're prepared to fight if you don't agree to these terms," Mammon says, her threats going in one ear and out the other.

Let her try.

Chapter Twenty

CHARLOTTE

ECHO GIGGLES AND smacks me on the arm with her stick.

"You bitch." I gasp, clutching my side in pain.

"Come on, human," she taunts, poking me in the belly with the tip. "Show me what you've got."

Kato and Chev sit on the ground a few yards away, their laughing distracting as I roll my shoulders back and lunge for Echo. She screams and dodges me, but I still manage to draw a tiny sliver of blood with my sword.

My head aches from all her loud noises, the shifters finding it best to fight while yelling like a bunch of banshees, but it does make things more entertaining. Plus, they gave me a real sword to fight with. It's thin and lightweight, and it's proving to be a lot of fun.

I was offended at first when they gave Echo a stick and me a sword, but the dozens of tiny nicks I've made on her skin with it have me feeling a bit better.

She heals in seconds, but the blood still stains her leather.

"Our little prodigy!" Kato shouts, clapping as Echo hisses and turns to stare at her cut arm.

Rock chimes in with his own shouts from the porch. He's still not allowed to leave the immediate vicinity of the cabin, but Chev was kind enough to bring him a small chair to sit in while watching.

I can't help but smile, appreciating their compliments, even if I know they're a bit over the top. Echo could probably kill me with her flimsy stick if she wanted to, but that doesn't make the sparring any less fun.

It only took three seconds of Echo watching me try to take down an animal to declare that I needed some training, which I thought was a joke until she arrived at my cabin at the butt crack of dawn with a thin sword and her damned stick.

"Go for her left leg. It's weak!" Chev yells, grunting as Kato frowns and hammer-fists him in the thigh.

"No cheating," he scolds.

They were walking through the woods with axes when they saw Echo and me fighting, and they promptly sat themselves down to observe. I guess watching me embarrass myself is a fun source of entertainment.

"When I raise my arms like this, your best bet is to lift your leg and kick me in the groin, bladder, or liver," Echo explains, raising her stick with both arms to demonstrate. "You're too small to meet my strike with your sword."

I nod, wiping the sweat off my brow before lifting my arms and getting into position. Echo moves slowly as we practice a few times, her patience unwavering as she gives slight adjustments.

"Okay, now we do it for real," she says, her relaxed posture tightening.

I gulp, my eyes narrowing as we circle one another. My arms will ache tomorrow morning, the muscles not used to this level of effort, but it'll be well worth it. Learning these simple defense maneuvers makes me feel strong, and I need that.

I don't stand much of a chance against the stronger species, but having this knowledge is better than nothing. It makes me feel powerful and fills me with the hope that I won't always need somebody to protect me.

Echo lunges with a low cry, her eyes flickering all around my frame as she tries to read my body language and guess my next move. When she raises her arms, I plant my weight onto my left foot and lift the right into the air.

My knee bends toward my chest before I propel it into Echo's belly. She grunts and twists her torso at the last minute to try to deflect it. It throws her off-balance and allows me enough time to jump to the side and avoid the downswing of her stick. She didn't teach me what to do after this, but I operate off instinct as I step forward and try for her neck.

Her eyes widen as she grabs the end of the blade, effectively halting my motions before I can nick her throat. Blood pours down her palm, and she releases my sword with a sharp hiss. I drop my sword to the ground, struggling to catch my breath.

"That was so good!" Echo praises, turning to her dad and brother. "Did you see that?"

I plant my hands on my thighs and spin in their direction. Kato sits with his head between his knees while Chev rubs his back and murmurs quiet words I can't make out from this distance.

"You just about gave Dad a heart attack seeing that blade so close to your throat," Chev scolds, his eyes darting to me. "The human trains with a stick now, too."

I bounce on my heels and turn to Rock, grinning as he stands and gives me two enthusiastic thumbs-up. It looks like I'm too dangerous to train with a real sword.

"Charlie," I grunt, shoving my thumb into my chest. "Shifter Slayer."

Kato howls and rolls onto his side at my self-given title, his laughter making me frown. He won't be laughing like that when I'm coming at him with my sharp reflexes and even sharper weapons.

"I can't watch this any longer." He wipes his eyes as he stands and approaches Echo. "Family dinner tonight. Don't forget again. I love you, my baby."

He turns to me and nods. "I have a meeting with Mammon tomorrow afternoon. We'll regroup after to discuss." He gestures toward Rock. "Your shadow can join."

Rock *whoops*, his ears picking up everything despite how quiet the shifters try to be. I can tell it annoys them, but they haven't said anything about it. Secretly, I think they're just jealous the demons have better hearing.

Echo kicks my sword to the side. "We're going to learn how to fight with our fists now," she decides.

The blood that spews from my lip at her first punch is enough to have Chev standing and rushing off, his laughter loud as I accuse him of being a baby.

By the time we finish, I can barely stand, and I lean onto Echo for support as she leads me to her parents' cabin.

"My mom made some food for you and your shadow," she says, wincing when I stumble over a tree stump.

I let her throw me over her shoulder like a sack of rice, and I hang limply as she walks to the cabin and kicks open the front door.

"Hi, Mom!" Echo yells, carrying me into the kitchen.

"Oh, fuck," a feminine voice rings out as I'm dropped into a chair.

A dark-haired woman is in front of me a moment later. She's arguably one of the most attractive women I've ever met, with jet-black hair, black eyes, and full lips I can't stop myself from glancing at.

"This is Emily, my mom," Echo says.

Emily frowns as Echo explains that she's teaching me how to fight, and she rolls her eyes when Echo goes on to say that learning how to take a punch is just as important as being able to give one.

My eyes fall to Emily's lips before I catch myself and look away.

"It's okay, Charlie. I'm half-succubus. It's a natural reaction for your body," Emily explains, patting my hand before ordering Echo to get a first-aid kit.

I'm only slightly relieved to know I'm not going crazy, and I try to push my embarrassment aside as she begins to apply antibiotic ointment to the cuts on my face.

I'm going to go out tonight and break Echo's stick into twenty little pieces.

Emily places one last bandage on my forehead before handing the kit back to Echo. Echo carries it out of the room before returning a second later with a small handful of leather.

"You'll wear our clothing now," Echo says, setting them on my lap.

My cheeks ache as my lips curl into a smile, and I finger the fabric before unfolding and holding it up in front of me.

"They're going to be big. Let's get them fitted," Emily suggests, glancing between my chest and the top I hold.

I accept her outstretched hand and stand with a slight groan, my legs shaky as she helps me remove my clothing.

A small part of me feels silly having my muscles so sore that I can't do it myself, but my joy over being accepted by the shifters outshines that. Besides, it's not like I have any parts they haven't seen before.

My pride is all-consuming as I put the leathers on and stand before the pair. Emily and Echo grin as they start marking where the skirt and top need to be taken in.

"You're going to look so good," Emily praises. "I'll sew these for you tonight and have Chev bring them over tomorrow morning."

She steps back as I carefully slide the leather top off and hand it over. She and Echo politely look away while I reach for my shirt.

"My mate!" Kato shouts, shoving open the front door.

I gasp and cover my chest at the exact moment he screams and spins around. The cabin shakes with how hard he slams his shoulder into the doorway trying to escape, and he blindly reaches back and shuts the door behind him.

Emily laughs, patting my shoulder. "He's going to stress about that. I'll see to him," she says, excusing herself with a subtle shake of her head.

I nod, my face warm as I rush to finish getting dressed. Echo folds the leathers and places them on the counter before grabbing the food Emily made and tucking it under her arm.

She loops her other arm around my waist to help me walk.

I didn't realize just how badly my body got worked out today, but with each minute of rest, the ache in my muscles grows. I'm not getting out of bed tomorrow, and Rock will have to bring and feed me my meals like a child.

There's no other way.

Still, I'm proud of myself for stepping out of my comfort zone and giving this a genuine attempt. I look forward to Echo teaching me more.

Kato lies on his belly on the ground directly outside the cabin, his face buried into the dirt while Emily sits at his side and runs a soft hand down his back.

"I hope you enjoy the food, Charlie. Have a good night," Emily says, her friendly smile unchanged as she rubs her mate's back.

Kato groans and curls his arms around his head, and I avoid

looking at his exposed butt from where his skirt flopped up. He must've thrown himself on the ground immediately after leaving the cabin.

Poor guy.

His walking in was awkward, but I don't feel nearly as awful about it as he does. Accidents happen, and it's not like he ogled. I doubt the man even saw anything during his sheer desperation to leave.

I hesitate, debating whether or not I should say anything to him, when he lets out another loud groan and wraps himself around Emily's knees. She shakes her head and fixes his skirt before kissing his temple.

Kato's dramatics remind me a lot of Gray, and Emily's calm demeanor makes me think of Silas. I miss my males, and I feel a lump forming in my throat at the thought of them. Even Aziel, whom I thought I'd be glad to be rid of, has wormed his way into my heart and made me miss him. He's annoying and rude, but I know he cared in his own way.

I refuse to wonder what would've happened between us if I hadn't left. Gray seemed to think he would fight for me, but I'm not sure about that. Aziel's not the type of person to plead.

Rock comes hurrying out of the cabin as Echo and I approach, the shadow unable to hide his concern as he runs to the perimeter Chev gave him and waits impatiently for Echo to bring me over.

He curls his arms around my body the second we reach him. I wince, but he's gentle enough that I'm able to keep from crying out. Echo grunts and jumps away as his arm accidentally bumps hers, but she doesn't say anything about it.

I'm sure Chev and Kato would be here in a heartbeat if they knew Rock had touched her, but thankfully, she doesn't seem to take too much offense. The shifters, while firm in their beliefs not to touch the opposite sex, don't seem to dwell too much on the occasional brush or helping hand.

"You look like shit," Rock says. He takes the food from Echo with a quiet "Thank you." She nods and leaves.

I feel bad about how much the people here dislike him, but he doesn't mind. Rock doesn't share much about his personal life, but I've gathered that he has more than a few lovers that keep him busy.

Rock's a little ho.

"I spoke to Aziel," Rock says, pushing open the door to our cabin.

He deposits me on the couch, and I gesture for him to continue. "He wants you to talk to the shifters and get them to reconsider their alliance with Mammon. Aziel wants to flip the script, with Wrath leading the effort and Greed paying."

Chev grabs my arm as I pivot forward, his grip tight as he keeps me from toppling over. I grimace and clutch my animal carcass to my chest, paranoid about dropping it and making a mess.

"Careful," he warns, holding back a laugh.

I shoot him a glare, unappreciative of the teasing. I don't have the years of experience they do walking on rough ground, and while I've gotten better these past few days, I still haven't mastered their smoothness.

Chev's grip remains until I've righted myself, and I gently wave him off with a friendly smile.

He's been kind to escort me each morning to the traps I laid out earlier this week, and not once has he complained when we make the long walk only to find them empty.

Today, though—today, I caught a fox.

Chev needed to steady my shaking hands to prevent me from

accidentally prolonging the kill, and my cheeks were stained with tears by the time I worked up the courage to sink in the knife, but I'm still proud of myself.

"And you'll tell Echo I've fallen sick with a human illness and want to be left alone this morning?" I ask, eager to ensure he's got the plan down.

Chev snorts and clicks his tongue against his teeth, a gesture I've learned is the equivalent of a human eye roll.

"Yes, Charlie, I will tell her, but I cannot promise she won't come over," he warns. "Echo likes you, and she'll want to see that you're okay."

I hope she doesn't. She'll ask questions if she learns I've been sneaking out every morning with Chev, and I'm not a good liar.

Blood smears over my arms as I struggle to carry the fox, and I stop walking so I can readjust.

My catch is on the chunky side, and the animal easily weighs twenty-five pounds. Chev watches, but he doesn't offer to help. He learned his lesson the first time I snapped at him.

I want to do this myself.

My pace quickens as Emily and Kato's house enters my line of sight, and Chev follows me quietly to the front door.

"Have fun," he says, reaching around me to open the door.

"Thanks!" I chirp, hurrying up the steps.

Kato's sitting on the floor of his living room as I bust inside, and he watches with shock as I kick off my shoes and shuffle through his house with my bloody carcass. The door slams shut behind me, and out of the corner of my eye, I watch him stand and follow me into the kitchen.

My panting is embarrassingly loud as I drop the fox on the kitchen island. Blood pools below it, and I grab a towel and wipe it off while Kato examines my treasure.

"This one's good." He lifts the limbs to get a better look. "You won't get a full set, but this should be enough for a top."

I beam as he flips the animal over and continues his evaluation.

"You think Echo will like it?" I ask.

Kato nods, his shoulder bumping mine as he holds back a smile.

"She enjoys fox leather, and she'll love that you've gifted her something so special," he says. "You've done well, Charlie."

His praise makes my heart race, and I clear my throat before turning back to the animal. Emily enters through the back door a second later, her cheery expression growing as she notices the animal I've haphazardly thrown on her counter.

She's quick to copy Kato and evaluate it, loud compliments slipping from her lips as she picks it up and orders Kato to lock the doors so Echo doesn't come over and ruin the surprise.

"We usually do this outside, but we'll do it here since this is a present," she explains, grabbing a tarp from the closet and sending Kato to collect several knives.

I grab the fox and set it on the tarp, and Kato returns quickly before kneeling to my right and explaining how to skin it. Emily politely ignores my wet eyes, but she grabs a tissue to wipe at my cheeks when the animal in front of me begins to blur.

"It's okay," she whispers, grabbing my hair and pulling it out of my face. "Chev cried so hard that he vomited the first time he did this, and it took Echo a good year before she could do it without Kato's help."

Kato's voice is comforting as he guides me through each step, his even tone soothing my guilt-ridden heart. Thankfully, my tears stop by the time we've finished removing the skin.

Emily grabs the meat and moves it out of my view.

"Kato, why don't you ready the chemicals while Charlie and I remove the fur?" Emily suggests, grabbing a bucket from underneath the sink.

She fills it up and returns to the tarp. "Come here." She gestures for me to drop the skin in the bucket. "We'll soak it for a bit, then remove the fur with a knife. Help me massage the cleaner in."

Her hands cover mine as she shows me how to clean and wring out the skin, washing all the excess blood and guts off. It feels gross between my fingers, but her touch distracts me so much that I don't mind.

We continue to work the fur until the water's red, and I spread the skin on the tarp while Emily dumps the bucket. She's back seconds later, her body wrapping around mine as she shows me how to remove the fur.

I hold in a gasp as her fingers lace between mine, her teaching intimate. I've learned that shifter women tend to be big on hugs and physical affection, but I usually avoid Emily. I was around Gray long enough that her natural scent doesn't throw me into a frenzy, but it still calls to me.

"You did amazing today. Everybody's been talking about how impressed they are with you," she whispers. "We enjoy having you here."

My jaw clenches, and I let my eyes slip shut as my body reacts to hers. Her breasts push against my back, and when coupled with her sweet scent, it has me holding back a shiver.

She hums quietly in my ear and pulls away as we finish. Emily has been kind to me, and it's wrong to lust after her like this. She turns to me with a soft smile, her eyes ever-knowing as her nostrils flare.

I feel the blood rush to my cheeks, and I turn away to hide my shame.

"It's okay, Charlie. Honestly," she says, helping me to my feet. "Please don't feel guilty."

I shake my head, overwhelmed with guilt as I follow her to the sink to clean my hands.

"I'm sorry," I whisper as she tries again to assure me I've done nothing wrong. "I don't mean to, and I know you're mated to Kato."

Emily laughs. "Kato doesn't mind."

I doubt that very much.

I drop to my knees and begin cleaning the tarp. My guilt refuses to let me acknowledge that she's a succubus and probably gets this all the time.

It's not nearly as embarrassing for her as it is for me.

Kato returns shortly with the chemicals. He grabs the skin from Emily and coats it with the smelly liquid. I move to help him, but he waves me away with an exaggerated huff.

"The chemicals are strong," he explains as Emily steps out of the room to put some things away.

"How long until it's finished?" I ask.

Kato shrugs. "About a week."

That's not too bad. I fold up the tarp, and Kato hangs the skin on a rack while I try to put the tarp back on the top shelf of the closet they took it from. Kato washes his hands with a laugh as I struggle to reach.

"Humans are so short," he teases, approaching.

I shoot him a glare, but my body quickly stiffens as he grabs my hips and lifts me a few inches into the air so I can reach. My fingers shake as I shove the tarp onto the top shelf, and Kato sets me back on the ground in one smooth motion.

The action presses his chest against my back, and I let out an embarrassingly loud, shaky exhale at the feeling of his bare skin touching mine. Kato's an attractive man, a fact I've been working hard to ignore and pretend I don't notice, but it's near impossible not to when he's covered in Emily's scent and pressed against me.

I should move away and put distance between us.

Kato doesn't seem to notice my arousal as he drops his hands from my hips and steps back. I take a moment longer to move.

I'm a horrible person. Kato and Emily are happily mated, and I still don't know what's happening between me, Gray, and Silas. I'm still slightly convinced they're out to kill me, even if Rock promises they aren't, but I shouldn't do anything until I have clarity.

Kato turns to look at me, his eyebrows pulled tightly together.

"Are you okay?" he asks.

Unlike his wife, Kato seems blissfully unaware of my reaction to him, and his growing comfort toward me only worsens it. I almost miss the days when he avoided me like the plague, but now he sees me as a friend and has no issues with the occasional touch.

Kato looks good, but it's his mate's scent that does me in. It turns me on, especially when he's so close, and it urges me to act on my attraction.

Would it be so bad if I did?

As much as I love Gray and Silas, I'd be foolish not to acknowledge the power imbalance in our relationship. Most of my life has been spent in hiding, and when they purchased me, the only experience I had outside of my home was from the month I spent in the secure Seeker facility.

I want to know who I am outside of Gray and Silas, and shouldn't discovering who I am sexually be a part of that? How can I say my males are genuinely who I want when I don't even know who I am and what I want?

"Charlie?" Kato asks when I don't answer his question. "Are you okay?" he repeats.

I clear my throat and nod, but it doesn't seem as convincing as I'd like it to be as he steps forward and ducks to my level. He looks me over, and a quiet hum emerges from his throat as he straightens up and pulls me into a tight hug.

I wish I'd chosen to wear my usual clothing instead of the leathers Emily and Echo gave me. The bandeau top leaves most of my chest exposed, and the feeling of Kato's bare skin against mine is doing more to me than I'd care to admit.

"Life has been hard for you," Kato whispers, running a hand down the center of my spine.

I shiver.

He's trying so hard to comfort me, but my body isn't getting the 'this is innocent touch' memo. My face warms as my cheek presses against his chest, and I listen to his heart beating as I clench and unclench my fists.

Kato's large, and it's next to impossible not to realize it when I'm wrapped in his muscular arms. I breathe in, my body softening as Emily's residual scent fills my lungs. Every inch of his body is coated in her, and while it's diluted, it's still distracting.

It smells so good.

My thighs clench as I rack my brain for a response, my mind coming up blank despite how hard I search for one. I flinch when Emily walks back in, and I meet her gaze with wide eyes.

She raises a brow at our positioning, the woman able to easily see how intimate it is, even if the shifter hugging me is clueless.

"Tell me what's wrong," Kato urges, his voice rising in pitch.

He struggles with strong emotions, and he gets especially nervous when he can't determine what's causing them.

Emily rolls her eyes as Kato panics.

"Charlie's fine. She's just turned on."

Kato gasps, his body stiffening as he pulls back to look down at me.

"Are you aroused?" he asks.

Emily leans against the counter to watch, a smile toying at the corners of her lips. She thinks this is funny.

She kicks off the counter, and her hips sway as she approaches and slides her body between Kato and me. He quickly steps out of the way.

"Can I kiss you," she asks me.

I pause, hesitating. Would it be so bad if I said yes? I'm aware she's mated to Kato and this doesn't mean anything, at least not what it meant when I kissed Gray and Silas.

It's just for fun.

I should be allowed to have fun. I deserve to have fun.

My eyes flicker between Emily and Kato before I give a jerky nod.

Emily's lips curve into a sensual grin. "Use your words, Charlie," she urges.

She places her fingers below my chin, her touch gentle as she tilts my chin upward. I pant into the air between us, more than a little nervous.

"Kiss me," I say.

Emily's lips are on mine a second later. They're surprisingly soft, and a low moan slips from her throat as her tongue meets mine. My hands twitch by my sides before I work up the courage to bring them to her waist.

What am I doing?

"Emily," Kato says, stepping closer. "We can take a trip to Lust if you're needing."

She ignores him, and her fingers slide up my hips before she turns and walks me backward into Kato's chest. He doesn't move, but I can feel his heart pounding against my back as she grabs his hand and drags it to the front of my body.

I moan, enjoying the touch, and Emily pulls away with a smile before shifting her attention to Kato. He's as still as a statue behind me, and Emily slides his hand up my thighs as she kisses him over my shoulder.

I turn to watch, my body shaking with need.

After a few seconds, Emily reaches around me to touch Kato. His leathers shift against my back, and he grunts as she slides her hand underneath them.

I should put some space between us, but I don't move.

Emily strokes Kato, her arm rhythmically moving back and forth as she pleasures him.

"Please," he begs.

Emily giggles, and I moan as she returns her lips to mine. I have no thoughts as she kisses me, and I'm only faintly aware of Kato's length pressing between my thighs as I feel the bare skin of Emily's waist.

She's soft, and she smells so fucking good.

Kato rolls his hips with a quiet hiss, his body rocking against mine as he squeezes my inner thigh. His mouth is on my neck a second later, and I whine into Emily's mouth as he sucks a dark hickey into the spot where demons mark.

I'm sure the location doesn't mean much to a shifter, but Gray and Silas loved to kiss me there.

It was a silent promise.

I continue to inhale Emily's lust as Kato thrusts into her fist. It's growing stronger as she feeds, and I find myself quickly falling victim to it.

"My dirty mate," Kato breathes.

He slides his fingers further up my thigh, and I rest my head against his chest as he cups my sex. One of his thick fingers slips into me a second later, and I clench around it as Kato moans.

His thrusts grow faster, the tip of his cock pressing between my thighs with each movement.

"*Shit.*" He lets out a choked cry, and something warm coats the back of my thighs and slit.

Kato curls his finger inside me, rocking it in and out. It feels too good, and my back arches as an orgasm rips through me. It's intense, and I tighten around his finger as he works me through it.

Emily pulls away, seemingly shocked by our quick releases.

She cups Kato's chin to hold him still as she peers into his eyes, and after a moment, she roughly turns to me and does the same. Kato continues to ease his finger in and out of me, and my eyes roll back as another wave of her scent fills my lungs.

"Fuck," Emily hisses.

She's on the opposite side of the room a second later, her back plastered against the wall as her eyes dart frantically between Kato and me.

I drop my chin to my chest, the distance between Emily and me helping to clear my mind. Kato removes his finger, and I wince as his movement brings to attention the slight sting inside me.

It's identical to how I felt when my males used the toy on me for the first time, and my body goes painfully rigid as I draw that connection.

My eyes dart to Kato's finger, and I clench my jaw as I see the wetness still coating it. What have I just done?

Chapter Twenty-One

CHARLOTTE

EMILY PLACES A hand over her chest as I scramble away from Kato.

This was a mistake.

I stumble over my feet, and Kato reaches forward to catch me before I righten myself and wave him away.

"I'm so sorry, Charlie," Emily rushes to say. "I shouldn't have let things go so far."

I was okay with some light flirting, maybe a kiss or two, but I shouldn't have let it go beyond that. My sex is sore from Kato's finger, the slight ache a painful reminder of what I've just done.

Kato's gone pale. "I'm sorry, Charlie." His voice is hoarse. "Have I dishonored you? Oh, fuck, I'm so sorry."

My bottom lip trembles as I wipe my wet cheeks, unable to make eye contact with either of them. Kato's cum drips down my inner thighs, the feeling of it only worsening my anxiety.

He begins to pace the room, the man very clearly out of his element. Emily steps forward and grabs his shoulder, halting his nervous movements.

"I need to go home," I say, hurrying to the door.

"Let me walk back with you," Emily says, still holding Kato. I'm sure he will panic the second I'm out this door, and Emily should be here for that instead of with me.

"I'll be fine! It's a quick walk," I assure her, gesturing wildly in the direction of my cabin.

I don't wait for a response before turning and escaping out the front door. My bare feet slam against the rough ground, and I curse myself for forgetting I took off my shoes shortly after arriving with my fox.

I'll get them another time.

Sticks bury into the soles of my feet as I rush to the cabin I share with Rock. The last thing I want is to run into any shifters who can smell what I've done. I can't face the disgust I'm sure they'll show as they realize who the male dripping down my thighs is.

There's no way to hide it from Rock, but that's a bridge I'll cross when I get to it.

I gasp and scurry off the path when I spot a shifter ahead. I'm sure he already knew I was there, but hopefully, he won't think anything about me steering away at the last minute.

I clench my thighs together as he keeps walking, his attention focused solely on the large log of wood he carries.

That was a close call, and I push my hair out of my face as I venture further off the trail to avoid running into anybody else. I'll cut back in once I reach the cabin, but I should stay out of the main walking areas.

Tears continue to pour down my cheeks, my hatred for myself only growing.

"You smell nice."

I freeze, my body going rigid as I turn toward the voice. A man with black eyes stares at me, and I instinctively step away as I take in his unnaturally enticing features and realize he's an incubus. He shouldn't be here.

He cocks his head to the side as his nostrils flare, and I take another step back as his gaze slides to my thighs.

"Naughty female." He chuckles, shoving his hands into the front pockets of his jeans.

I glance behind him, desperate for a shifter to come barreling through the woods as the man rocks back on his heels and bursts out in full-blown laughter. Despite my fear, I square my shoulders in the way Echo taught me and widen my stance.

"I came here searching for a pretty girl to feed on, but it looks like I found something much more valuable. My dad will be thrilled to see you," he says, still smiling.

His dad?

His grin falls as I open my mouth and release the loudest scream I can manage. I pray it's enough for Rock to hear as the man hurries toward me, and I slam my eyes shut as his body hits mine and the world around me crumbles as we teleport.

My fist makes contact with a hard jaw as the ground beneath me materializes, and I drop my shoulder and shove it into the man's belly before he grunts and pushes me away. Pain radiates up my tailbone as I fall to the floor, but I ignore it and kick the incubus's knee as hard as I can.

When it turns inward, I scramble to my feet and run away, my legs carrying me down the unfamiliar hallway. The man behind me screams, but I don't dare look back as I brace myself and slam into the large double doors at the end of the hall.

They fly open, and I skid to a halt as I see the room I've just thrown myself into.

Asmod stares at me from the large seat in the center of the room, his excitement visible as I spin and try to leave. I hear his laughter as the doors shut in my face, and two incubi move in front of them.

My palms grow sweaty, and I resist the urge to clutch my necklace as I spin toward the Lust King.

Asmod's already approaching, a sinful smile spreading over his lips as he watches me like I'm some small prey he's about to devour.

"Charlie! What a surprise," he says, waving to the demons blocking the double doors.

They take hold of my arms, and I grunt as I struggle to free myself. My thighs clench together when Asmod glances at them, his eyebrows raising before his nostrils flare and he releases a loud laugh.

"Gray always falls for the unfaithful ones."

I flinch, the truth of his words cutting deep.

The doors behind me open, the wood smacking loudly against the wall as the man who brought me here storms in.

"The fucking bitch broke my kneecap," he says, walking around me to stand next to Asmod. "I want her."

Asmod shakes his head, denying the request, as he steps forward and runs a finger down my cheek. I yank against the hands holding my arms as I try to move away, but they force me to remain still. The other incubus looks pissed, but he doesn't argue. He must also be one of Asmod's sons.

How many children does this guy have? More than I'd care to meet.

I breathe through my nose as Asmod's intoxicating scent fills my lungs, and I hate myself for how it makes my body react. Asmod seems pleased by it, and I resist the urge to knee him in the face as he ducks and licks the inside of my thigh.

His tongue smacks against the roof of his mouth as he tastes Kato, and his smile grows as he straightens back up.

"I've met this shifter before. He's a strong man, but I'll cover his scent easily," he says, stepping away and gesturing for the guards to follow.

A scream tears from my throat as they drag me, unaffected by my fighting. I try to dig my heels into the ground to slow them, and I even reach for my necklace, but every attempt fails.

The guards tolerate me for a short while before glancing at one another and lifting until my feet dangle and I have no leverage to try to fight with. I still try, my arms practically twisting out of their sockets as I wiggle back and forth.

The one on my left laughs at my attempts, his enjoyment causing Asmod to look over his shoulder and see what he's missing. He rolls his eyes as he watches my embarrassing positioning.

I try to bite the incubus to my right as we halt in front of a set of gold doors, but he shoves me through them before my teeth make contact. My knees burn as they scrape against the floor, earning a pained hiss from me, and I spin and crawl away from Asmod as he traps us alone in the room.

A quick glance tells me I'm in a bedroom, and I use the leg of the bed frame to help me stand. My feet wobble, the muscles protesting after the sheer amount of tumbles I've taken in the past ten minutes.

"Aziel will kill you if you touch me," I threaten, skirting around the bed and backing up against the far wall.

Asmod's eyes return to my thighs, and I tug down my skirt to hide them from view.

"You're dripping shifter, Charlie. Don't lie to me."

I hold out my hands to push him away, but I sway when the full extent of his lust hits me. My pulse races at the exact moment my sex clenches, and I instinctively lean toward him for more.

Asmod's all too happy to comply, stepping into my space and allowing me to bury my face in his neck. His hands soothe my growing burn, and I grab his shirt and pull it toward me with a loud moan. I want to be inside this man's skin.

There's a lingering pain in the back of my head as he shoves his knee between my thighs and pulls me up onto his leg, but it's impossible to focus on it through the fog that's become my brain.

"I'm going to ruin you," Asmod says, cupping my waist.

I nod, happy to hear it. I *want* him to ruin me.

"I'll enjoy telling Gray how much you begged for me. Maybe if you're lucky, I'll let you give him a show," he teases, trailing his fingers up my arm.

The burn grows the longer he prolongs his touch, and I bury my face into his chest in the desperate hope of stopping it. It feels like my every nerve ending is on fire, and he's the only thing that can cool me.

Asmod laughs when I grab his arm and try to shove his hand up my skirt. My hips rock against his thigh, but my mind trails to Silas and Gray.

Asmod grabs my chin and forces me to look him in the eye, his face similar to Gray's but not quite as pretty. My eyebrows furrow as I look away, wanting my incubus to soothe my burn more than this man.

"Where's Gray?" I slur, my eyes slipping shut as Asmod encourages me to slide my hand underneath his shirt.

I try to move away, not wanting this. Asmod tuts, the sound of disappointment bringing tears to my eyes. I want Gray. My anger flares when Asmod doesn't let me move, and I glare at him before craning my neck and smashing my lips to his.

He doesn't hesitate to return the kiss, and he lets out a throaty moan as I curl my fingers around my necklace and tear it from my neck. Asmod's too distracted to see what I'm doing, and I slam the stone against the front of his throat as he grabs a fistful of my hair.

His body stiffens before dropping, and I follow as his hand

knots in my tangles and yanks me down. A loud cry slips from my lips at both the pain on my scalp and the abrupt pullback of his scent, the burn intensifying until it takes everything in me not to scream.

I grab a piece of cloth off the floor and shove it in my mouth as I scramble to Asmod's bedside table and rip it open. There's a lot of random shit inside, but just like in Gray's bedside table, a small knife lives at the bottom.

My skin drips sweat as I drop to my knees next to the unconscious man's body, but I hardly feel the same guilt I did with the fox as I bring the knife to his throat and slip it into the big vein on the side of his neck.

Blood pools and coats me and the floor, and I scream into the cloth between my teeth as I pull the knife out and sink it back into his throat to ensure he doesn't wake up. Then I do it again for good measure.

Asmod's blood soothes my burn, and I cry out as I desperately spread the red liquid on my skin to alleviate it.

Chapter Twenty-Two

AZIEL

I TRY NOT to let my annoyance show as Gray sprawls on the floor in the center of my office. His mind's a fun mixture of boredom and arousal as he turns toward Silas and me, but it quickly shifts into anger as he feels me prodding around in his head.

He tries to kick me out, but I ignore his wishes and continue searching, enjoying seeing the years of thoughts he's had about me. It turns out my incubus has been more obsessed with me than I ever realized, frequently watching me sleep and keeping tabs on how often I'm eating.

His eyes narrow as I bring his memory of Silas once catching him in my bed to the forefront of his mind. Silas laughed and teased him until I returned a few days later, but Gray still snuck into my room each night despite it.

Cute.

Gray tries harder to force me away, his regret over giving me entrance prominent as I finally pull back and let him have his privacy—for now.

Silas watches the exchange with a raised brow. I'm sure he

remembers me doing this to him when he first permitted me to enter his mind. I don't do it much anymore, but maybe I should start up again.

"You two are being stubborn. Just give her the money," Gray says, rolling onto his belly and propping his upper body up on his elbows.

I ignore him, focusing on the spreadsheet Silas is showing me. I'm grateful he put in the extra hours to finish this, even if I disapprove of the dark bags under his eyes.

He can't avoid sleeping forever, and sooner or later, it will catch up with him.

I let out a quiet sigh and turn to Gray. The incubus isn't looking much better, and he's growing gaunt now that he's returned to his hunger strike.

"And what do you propose we do when Mammon attacks and we have no money with which to support ourselves?" I ask, pushing Silas away when he reaches for my shoulder. "Do you want to be the one to tell the Wraths we can't protect them because we brought ourselves to ruin for the affection of one individual human?"

Gray frowns and scrambles to his feet, his movements clunky in his hungered state.

"Don't give me that shit. I know damn well you've got the funds to cover this. It'll be a squeeze, but it's entirely doable." He approaches my desk and spins the computer in his direction.

I sit back and wait for him to read it over. He's not wrong in his claims, but that doesn't mean I'm going to roll over and hand Mammon the money before exploring other options. It'll put us in too defenseless of a position, and it's not worth the risk.

It'd be too easy for Mammon to turn around and attack me after she gets my money.

Our best bet is to turn the shifters on our side. We've managed to implement similar programs already, and it makes sense that we'd be best suited to lead at a larger scale.

Mammon's in over her head, and I need the other species to see it.

"If Charlie can talk to the shifters, we won't have to pay much of anything," I point out, turning to Silas for confirmation.

He nods, but he's hardly paying me any attention. Gray sways and sets the computer back on my desk before sinking onto the couch along the far wall.

He needs to feed.

Silas meets my eye before subtly shaking his head. He doesn't want to force Gray, but at some point, that's what it will come to.

"We told Rock to give Charlie the message days ago, and she still hasn't responded," Gray says.

Silas's fingers burrow into my shoulder as he leans over my back and messes with the computer. He's been touching me more recently with small gestures like this, and I find myself distracted by them every time.

Gray watches as Silas's hand slides to the neckline of my shirt. I lean back in my chair, my skin growing warm as I let myself enjoy the touch. Gray sits up with a huff, his eyes narrowing as he tries and fails to hide his attention.

This is the most interest Gray's shown in days, and I'll be damned if I let the opportunity slip. His resolve is weaker when he's hungry, and I'm not above taking advantage of that.

"On your knees, Silas," I demand, spreading my legs so Silas can kneel between them.

My desk cuts off Gray's view as Silas drops to the ground, and I turn to make eye contact with him as Silas gets to work undoing my pants. Gray cranes his neck to see us, his frown deepening when I shift to block his view.

I bite back a smile and run my fingers through Silas's hair

before gesturing for Gray to come over. He hesitates, his teeth sinking into his bottom lip as his lust begins to fill the space.

He's going to give in.

"Come join, Gray. I know you're hungry," I say, stiffening as the air around us begins to move.

I turn toward the source, my body on high alert as Silas fixes my pants and bounces to his feet in the time it takes me to blink. Gray's a bit slower to react and doesn't realize what's happening until Rock materializes inside my office.

The shadow pants as he sorts himself out, his eyes darting around before settling on Silas and me. He blinks a few times to clear his vision, his panicked expression enough to have me rounding my desk.

"Charlie's gone," he says, holding out his arm.

My throat runs dry as the words process, and I grab Silas before taking Rock's arm. Letting somebody teleport you to an undisclosed location is generally a bad idea, but I don't bother asking for details as I bear the brunt of the shift and let Rock lead the way.

It takes more effort than I anticipated, but I find the answer to my unspoken question when the world materializes around us and I realize a certain incubus decided to hitch a ride.

Good. I'm glad he didn't teleport himself. He should save the little energy he has.

Rock steps away as I look around the forest he's brought us to, and Silas pushes Gray protectively behind me as we notice the two large shifters standing nearby. My nostrils flare at the exact moment Gray lunges, and I wrap my arms around his midsection to hold him back as I scan the man who smells of Charlie.

Her scent coats him, and it doesn't take an expert to know the only way it would've covered him so thoroughly.

Our human has taken advantage of our temporary split.

Gray twists in my hold, and I wince as his hatred courses through our bond. A quick check on Silas tells me he's feeling something similar, his rage concealed by a calm demeanor but just as violent.

"What's going on?" I ask, struggling to hold back Gray as he claws at my forearm.

The man next to Charlie's toy speaks.

"Charlie's gone missing," he says, protectively stepping before his counterpart. "We heard her scream, but she was gone by the time we arrived."

If this is Mammon's doing, I'm going to kill every fucking person in her bloodline. My skin warms as my panic grows, and I follow Charlie's scent to see where she was taken from.

She smells strongest a few steps away, and I lower my gaze, only to be distracted by a thick, white splotch on the grass. Charlie's toy shifts uncomfortably. He finished on or inside her, and she dripped him while she was taken.

I suck in my cheeks, familiar with the anger accompanying infidelity after spending years with Gray. I may not have recognized the bond, but my body did, and the pain whenever he fed felt the same as this. Over time, I've grown used to it, and I'm proud of myself for not immediately lashing out.

There are more pressing matters to focus on.

I release Gray and examine the spot where Charlie was taken. The sound of Gray colliding with Charlie's toy is loud, but I'm sure it'll be over shortly. Gray can fight when he needs to, but he's not a match for two full-grown shifters when he's this weak.

"When was this?" I ask, struggling to keep calm as I crouch and breathe in the unnatural scents.

Every fiber of me wants to stand and fight, and I shut my eyes and do one of the stupid fucking breathing exercises Silas has been urging me to practice when I get worked up. I suck in air until my lungs hurt, and I imagine ripping off the balls of the shifter who smells of Charlie as I exhale.

It works, but barely.

Charlie's toy allows Gray to land a few hits before shoving him away. I've seen this man before, and I drop my gaze to his marking as he kicks at my incubus like a stray dog.

Kato. He's the leader of the bears, and he's rumored to have a succubus as a mate. I suppose that explains why a man with a blackened mate mark has fucked my human.

Gray grunts as he's thrown to his back, and he bounces to his feet, only to be dropped again. Silas comes up alongside me, his fingers ghosting over the grass as he tries to find any footprints or scents that give away who came here.

He lifts his hand when he encounters the few drops of cum, his fingers flexing before he avoids the area and brings his hand to a different blade of grass. His mind opens, welcoming me, and I slip inside to listen.

"It smells like an incubus," he thinks.

I nod, the movement slight so we don't draw attention. My ability to enter minds is kept quiet, and Gray's in a state that if he sees us, he'll loudly call it out and demand we share the whispers with him.

There's a pinpointed ache in my skull as I linger around Silas's mind, but when nothing else comes, I slip back out. His memories are easier to find than his present thoughts, and it takes a lot to create a live feed.

"It hasn't been long—fewer than five minutes," Rock says, crouching beside Silas.

He's clever to place Silas between us, and I turn away and suck in another deep breath. Hurting Rock isn't going to get me anywhere.

"Why'd you take so long to get us?" I ask through clenched

teeth.

A lot can happen in five minutes, and the wilderness covers scents quicker than I'd like. We'd have been able to tell precisely who took her had he gotten us here sooner.

My anger flares as Rock jerks his head toward the shifters, but Silas wraps his arm around my waist before I make any rash decisions. They might be able to keep Gray on his back, but I'll have their heads before they realize what's happening.

"Come smell this, Gray," Silas orders, his voice low.

"This is my land, with my mate and my children," Charlie's toy says, releasing Gray. "You're the King of Wrath, and if it were anybody but Charlie, I would've said *no*."

I move to the side as Gray approaches, and I bury my face into his mop of curly hair before responding.

"It must be tough to watch your plaything be taken—" Silas says, the rest of his sentence cut short as my fist cracks open his cheek.

He stumbles away, his eyes speaking betrayal as he grabs at his face. I ignore the shocked gasp from the shifters as I connect my other fist with his temple.

"Don't speak about Charlie like that," I spit, gearing up to hit him again. "She's our female."

Silas moves behind Gray, his eyelids lowering as his surprise shifts to anger. I can feel his outrage, the emotion swirling like a tornado, but I can't tell whether it's directed at Charlie or me.

Probably both.

"She fucked the shifter. I'll help save her, but she's no female of mine," he says, straightening his back and meeting my glare head-on.

I glance toward Gray, waiting to see what side he takes, and I clench my fists when he stares at the ground. Very well, then.

"Leave."

I don't need their help. If they want to abandon her over this, then they'll live with the regret of doing so completely. They won't get the satisfaction of having helped save her.

The muscle in Silas's jaw twitches as he hesitates, his stance wavering, before he wraps a hand around Gray's bicep and vanishes. I don't waste time dwelling on their betrayal as I stomp toward Charlie's toy and the shifter accompanying him.

"We're going to Lust," I say, holding out my arm.

Rock latches on before I can tell him he can't come, but his support is all the shifters need as they take hold of me.

It turns out that teleporting two giant bears and a shadow is hard, and I grind my teeth as I pull them into Asmod's home. It's well known that Asmod is interested in her, and any incubus who found her would know to bring her here.

"Chev, my baby," Charlie's toy cries as the world materializes around us. He pulls the other man into his chest before scanning him over.

I roll my eyes. The younger man scoffs and rips his father's arms off him, his lip curling as his eyes travel to the other man's skirt.

It seems my males aren't the only ones disgusted by the shifter's relationship with Charlie.

A tense silence settles over the two men as they take in the sounds of debauchery from within Asmod's estate, the skin slapping and screaming moans intense for a first-time guest. I hope Charlie's toy feels pain knowing this is where his mate is from.

She was once one of the moaning females he is listening to now, her body used by men and women daily.

I hope that knowledge destroys him.

"Follow me," I order, gesturing toward the corridor that'll lead us to Asmod's throne room. I can smell her.

Rock breaks from the group and wanders away as I lead the shifters down the vast halls of Asmod's castle. Being a shadow has its benefits, and I'm sure he'll return with good intel.

Lust demons aren't known for their fighting, and I hardly find myself worried as I approach the large double doors and shove them open. The interior's about as overdone as Asmod is, and I wince at the sheer amount of gold detailing and red fabric.

"Gaudy" would be a kind word to describe it.

The space is bristling with excitement, incubi and succubi engaging in all corners of the room, but they silence and scamper when they notice my presence. I scan the room for Asmod before turning to one of his older sons.

Felix, I think. It's hard to keep track of them all.

He lounges against Asmod's throne with a cocky smile, and I enjoy watching it fall as Charlie's toy and his son shift into their bear forms. They stand taller than I do, and I glance at the younger one with an impressed hum.

They're bigger than I expected them to be.

It's good to have them on my side, and I like how they don't hesitate to prepare for a fight. It's what shifters are known for, and it's a welcome change from the peaceful negotiating Silas and Gray are always trying to shove down my throat.

I turn to Felix. "Where is she?"

The guards along the wall stiffen, waiting for the command to fight, but I know they won't receive it. Asmod didn't prepare his men, and most of them are missing vital parts of their armor due to the entanglements they were in before we arrived.

It would be a massacre, and the Lust demons are too soft to willingly throw themselves into one.

Felix hums, his eyes instinctively darting toward the doors that lead to Asmod's private chambers. My blood runs cold, but I refuse to let it show as I jerk my head and signal the shifters to search in that direction.

Charlie's toy leaves—a good choice—his large body barely fitting through the doorway. Chev remains by my side, his fur brushing against my arm as he drops to all fours and circles my legs.

I'm not sure what the fuck it means, but I hope he's not thinking of attacking me. I'm not in the mood to fight a full-grown bear shifter right now.

Felix watches with a laugh, but his eyes anxiously follow our every move.

"You're aware that's the male your human was filled with. He's quite" —he gestures to the hallway Charlie's toy disappeared down— "virile. I could smell him dripping from her a mile away."

I don't respond. I'm furious, but that's an emotion I'll save for when Charlie's safe.

"Is she even worth it?" Felix asks. "I was under the impression the Wrath Trio were looking for a respectable female."

He's incredibly cocky for a man about to have his throat torn out, and he regards me with little concern as I approach. A subtle wave of his hand has the guards stepping forward, but they recoil when the bear behind me snarls.

Felix grows visibly panicked. Did he think his people would back him up? It's a cute thought, but he shouldn't have overestimated his men.

There's a reason Asmod does his best to stay out of conflict, and it's a shame he made such an idiotic mistake today.

I look toward his chambers as Kato's howl echoes down it, and my legs follow without thought. The beginnings of a scream tear from Felix's throat as Chev takes the opportunity to attack, but even the gargling of his blood filling his lungs doesn't satisfy me as I dart around the corner and spot Charlie's toy clawing at a door.

A few guards along the long corridor hesitate, debating what to do, before standing back when the blood-coated bear runs past me.

One incubus does try to attack, grabbing a knife out of his belt before lunging for me, but I grab his wrist and spin his arm until the metal's lodged into his eye. He screams, clutching at his face, before I drive it in further and he drops like a sack of beans.

That was just sad.

Chev doesn't slow as he comes up on Asmod's door, his body only picking up speed as he lowers his head to his chest. The bears are fucking huge, and he barrels into the gold-encrusted wood and knocks it clean off the hinges.

My lips purse as his body goes limp, the man probably concussed, before he twitches and shakes it off.

He'll be fine.

I materialize in the doorway. It takes me only seconds to find Charlie, the woman half-naked as she sobs over Asmod's body.

I lick my lips, shocked as my eyes flicker over the gory scene. What the fuck is happening?

Charlie doesn't seem to notice us as she smears herself with Asmod's blood, her hands shaking so deeply she misses her shoulder the first time she reaches for it.

Chev whines, but he's smart enough to stay back as I rush through the door.

Kato moves in front of me, heading for her, but I grab his neck and yank him back before he can step inside the room. The bear turns and snaps his teeth, but I ignore it and shove him to the side.

He can snap all he wants. I'll break his fucking jaw.

I drop to my knees beside Charlie, unable to hold back any of my power. It pours out of me, the sight of the female I've chosen covered in death making me too anxious to hold it in.

Charlie screams as I pull her away from the corpse, but she

gasps and lunges the moment her blown-out pupils land on me. I don't have time to absorb that she killed Asmod as she screeches and tries to climb me, her nails digging into the skin of my arms and drawing blood.

"Fuck, Charlie." I groan, grabbing her hands and prying them away.

Her skin drips with sweat as she rocks against me. "Make it stop," she begs. "Please."

I slide my hands down her back and hold her to my chest, desperate to soothe her as the shifters return to their skin forms and guard the door.

Demons peek in the doorway and hurry away with pained gasps, no doubt rushing to spread the news that Asmod's dead. That will be a headache, but it's a problem for future me.

I gesture for the shifters to come over, wanting to get out of here before any more of Asmod's guards find it within themselves to play the role of martyr. The two men look petrified as they stare at Charlie, but they snap their gazes away as she tries to rip off my shirt.

She yanks on the neckline, borderline choking me with it as I grunt and wave my arm impatiently.

"Come on," I snap. "We need to go."

I grab Asmod's ankle just as the shifters latch onto my arm. We'll need his body.

I heave, the effort it takes to bring everybody back to the shifter lands making me sick. Charlie's clawing hands move to my pants, distracting me, and I snatch them up as the world around us disappears.

The shifters stumble away as their forest materializes around them, and the older man forces his son to the floor so he can inspect his head wound.

I focus on Charlie, and I hurry to tug off my shirt so she can have skin-to-skin contact. Her body is hot to the touch, and I don't know whether my heat is making it better or worse as she cries into my chest.

"Charlie," I whisper, pushing her hair out of her face to capture her attention.

Asmod's blood smears from her skin to mine, the substance slick and cold. I can't even fathom why she covered herself in it, and I try to wipe her neck and shoulders clean as she rubs herself against me.

"What's wrong with her?"

I'm not sure who asks, but I don't bother looking as I curl my arms around her waist and hide her body from the shifters. She moans and grabs for me, her words incoherent as her skin burns under Asmod's lust.

"Fuck off," I snap, sucking in a deep breath as I realize I've exhausted myself teleporting them here.

Silas or Gray will be by shortly to help. I'm sure Gray can feel how drained I am, and he'll probably demand Silas come get us. My muscles ache as I stand and lift Charlie, holding her wiggling body tightly as I turn toward the shifters.

"Where's the nearest body of water?" I ask.

There's only one other thing that will make her feel better, and she's not going to want it from me. My forehead knocks against hers as I kiss her cheek, claiming her in front of the shifters before walking in the direction her toy pointed.

They're smart enough not to follow, lingering behind and beginning an argument over who's in charge of carrying Asmod's body back to their home.

I run my hands down Charlie's bare back, hoping my touch soothes her ache. She continues to rock against me, and I grab her hip as a large lake comes into view.

Thank fuck.

I don't bother removing my pants or shoes as I stomp down the bank and walk into the water, continuing until we're submerged to our necks and her body's shivering against mine.

Charlie instinctively tries to climb up me to escape it, but I pull back and plug her nose before shoving her head under the surface. I hold her for a second while she fights, and her glare when she pops up has me breathing out a sigh of relief.

A mad Charlie isn't ideal, but it's better than one high off Asmod's lust.

"What the fuck?" she snaps, her feet kicking my thighs as she tries to lift herself onto my shoulders to get out of the cold.

I shake my head, refusing to let the water dip below her collarbones. We will stay here until she's back to normal, or at least mostly so.

"Aziel," she whines, changing course and slapping her body against mine.

Her lips are tinted blue as she holds back shivers, and I run my hands up and down her back. Comfort isn't my area of expertise, and I turn toward the shore and wait for my males to show up as Charlie subtly grinds herself against me.

I pretend I don't notice, not wanting to embarrass her for something I know she can't control, and I spin us in circles so she thinks I'm too distracted to realize.

Her breath hits my neck in warm puffs, and I place a hand underneath her butt and urge her to wrap her legs around my hips as her squirming grows more violent. I can tell she's embarrassed by how she cries softly into my skin, but her self-control is little to none right now.

"It's okay. Use my hip," I whisper, pressing her harder against me.

Charlie nods with a soft cry, her arms looping around my neck so I can't move away. I'm grateful for the chill of the water as she uses me, the frigid temperature preventing me from breaking my composure.

"I'm sorry," she moans, her voice breathy as her eyes roll back.

Her body relaxes as she comes down, and I gently pry her away before scooping up a handful of water and pouring it over her shoulders. I need to get this blood off her. The sight of it is enticing, and I only have so much restraint.

She refuses to make eye contact as I clean her, and I listen to her racing heartbeat to distract myself.

"You have to go under so I can clean your hair," I say, wincing as my finger gets stuck in one of her tangles. She has chunks of Asmod's flesh caught in it.

"There are tangles," I whisper, not wanting her to know there are body pieces in her hair.

Thankfully, she doesn't seem to realize as she brushes her foot against my leg and sighs.

"There's a shower in my cabin," she admits.

I freeze. She has her own cabin? I wish I knew that before I cleaned her with dirty pond water.

Charlie holds back a laugh at my annoyed expression. The sight of her twitching lips brings about a smile of my own, even if it's at my expense. I can't tell if she realizes I know about her and the shifter, but I don't bring it up as I carry her out of the water and set her on her feet.

She never made any promises to me, so I don't have a right to be mad over her actions. Even if I do want to rip the dick off that fucking shifter.

I also want to rip the dicks off Silas and Gray. Their willingness to sit back and let Charlie be taken to Lust has my blood boiling. They can be mad all they want, but they lost my respect when they left.

Charlie crosses her arms over her chest in a sad attempt to cover herself, and I grimace before trying to teleport to where I took my shirt off earlier. I realize it's not going to work immediately, and I settle with pulling off my wet sock and holding it out for her to use.

She cringes and jerks her head to the left.

"It's this way."

I lift a brow as she spins and begins leading the way, and I bite my tongue to refrain from launching into a tirade of questions. Her skin is covered in bruises and wounds, all in various stages of healing, and I'm dying to know why.

I doubt the shifters are abusing her.

The muscles in her back flex as she walks, and I can't resist reaching out and tracing one of the long scratches on her shoulder. Her steps slow at the contact, but she doesn't tell me to stop so I move to the next one and repeat the action.

"Where are Gray and Silas?" she whispers.

I don't respond, not knowing what to say, but that seems to be answer enough. The scent of her tears reaches my nose a moment later, but she's trying to keep them hidden. She did her males wrong, and I won't lie and tell her it's okay.

"Do you know where Chev and Kato went?" she asks.

"No," I admit. They won't stay hidden for long, and I'm sure we're currently being watched.

I'd be more alert if Charlie weren't so distracting, but it's not like I can do anything even if I spot them. I can't teleport myself right now, let alone with Charlie, and there are too many shifters here for me to fight off myself.

I'm at their mercy, and I'm sure they know it.

Chapter Twenty-Three

CHARLOTTE

AZIEL WALKS AROUND my cabin, inspecting everything. He makes the room feel small, and I stand against the far wall as he does a lap of the place I call my home. I wish Rock were here to ease the tension, but Aziel said he chose to remain in Lust.

Aziel's lips twitch as he spots the braided leather I've been working on, Echo having asked me to help her tie the strands together during my free time.

"Why are you here?" I ask as Aziel pulls open my fridge.

He shuts it after seemingly deciding there's nothing of interest inside, and his body tenses as he turns to me. I try not to wilt under his gaze as he leans against the counter and crosses his arms over his chest.

I didn't mean my question to sound so unappreciative, but Aziel hardly seems offended as he shrugs and peers down the short hallway leading to my bedroom and bathroom.

"Would you rather I had left you in Lust?" he asks.

I shake my head.

"I mean, why are you *still* here?" I clarify.

Aziel runs a hand through his hair and shoots me a crooked

smile. I don't know how to react to it, so I don't.

"I used all my energy bringing the shifters to and from Lust. I can't leave," he admits.

A small part of me hoped he was here by choice.

I'm not sure how long it takes him to regenerate his energy, but I doubt he's planning to stick around any longer than necessary. The thought makes my heart ache, but I ignore it.

After what I've done, I don't have the right to ask him to stay. I missed him, all of them, but I fucked up too much to ask them to take me back.

"And you don't want to execute me?" I ask.

I'm sure he'd have done it by now if that was his plan, but I need to hear him say the words.

Aziel rolls his eyes. "No, Charlie. I'm not going to execute you."

My palms grow sweaty as I wait, knowing he has more to say. His silence when I asked about Gray and Silas speaks volumes, and I know they're aware of what I've done. Even now, I'm sure he can smell Kato and Emily on me.

My anger flares when he doesn't say anything. We're both thinking about it, and I'm ready to hear his judgment. I don't have an excuse for what I did, and I know I fucked up, but his silence is killing me.

"Say it," I beg after another long moment of nothing.

Aziel sucks in a deep breath, his eyes fluttering shut as he tilts his head back, before he slowly exhales and levels his stare with mine.

"We aren't in a relationship," he finally says. "What is there for me to say?"

I clench my jaw. That's not true, and he knows it.

Things were tense, but we had an unspoken agreement. It started well before he admitted his feelings for me, and I'd be hurt if he'd been with anybody new in my absence.

"We weren't *not* in a relationship," I point out.

Aziel nods, acknowledging my words, before stepping forward. I step back. I want him to yell at me and be angry. This Aziel is one I don't recognize, and his calm reactions are putting me on edge.

I can practically see his wrath pushing to come out, and for the first time in my life, I relish the sight.

"What do you want me to say, Charlie?" Aziel asks, running a hand through his hair. "That I'm disappointed in you? That I think it was selfish to break my male's hearts for a quick fuck?"

There's a dried smear of blood on the back of his arm, and I stare at it until he lowers his hand back to his side.

Yes. I want him to say all those things.

"You already know that to be true, and I'm not in the mood to make you feel worse than you already do," Aziel continues, his eyes darting toward the cabin door.

I turn and spot Chev's eye peeking through the crack. It slides to me before returning to Aziel and narrowing. He has no shame in his spying.

"He does that. Just ignore him," I say.

Aziel doesn't acknowledge Chev as he turns back to me.

"Go shower. I'm tired of smelling the shifter on you," he orders, jerking his head toward the bathroom.

I don't hesitate to leave, grateful for the excuse to be alone. This day's been a lot, and I need a minute to decompress before completely breaking down.

The low vibrations of Aziel's voice make their way to my ears as I close the bathroom door, but I don't bother listening to what he's saying to Chev as I lean against the counter and stare at my reflection in the mirror.

I look crazed, my skin stained red and my eyes wild and

unfocused. My hair's wet and limp, and it still has chunks of flesh and dirt tangled within it. There's a dark mark on my neck I refuse to look at, the hickey a glaring reminder of today's mistakes.

I don't know whether it came from Kato or Asmod, but neither seems better than the other.

Maybe it's for the best that Silas and Gray refuse to see me. They're already hurt by what I've done, and I'm sure seeing me like this would only make it worse. My bottom lip wobbles, and I clench my jaw to stop it before forcing myself to look away from the mirror and turn on the shower.

The pain of them abandoning me is one I will shove deep inside and ignore for now.

The front door slams shortly after the shower starts, and I wonder if Aziel will still be here when I get out.

I don't have the guts to ask how long he'll be stuck here or what his plan is for leaving. His loyalty lies with Silas and Gray, and I'm sure he will leave the moment he's able. He won't force them to see me if they don't want to.

It's just going to be Rock and me. Maybe Echo and Chev, too, if they can see past my interactions with their parents.

Fuck.

A scream threatens to tear out my throat as I bring my fist to the shower wall. I hit it as hard as I can, but the tile takes no damage even as the skin of my knuckles rips open. The pain feels good, and I find myself punching it again and again until the bathroom door slams against the wall and I'm being pulled against a hard chest.

Aziel holds me against him as I sob, his voice unnervingly calm. "It's okay. You're okay," he whispers, running his hands down my back.

I don't believe him, not one bit, but I don't fight him as he tugs off his clothing and drops them on the shower floor.

I cry as he grabs my shoulders and spins me around. "I'm so sorry."

"You're okay," he repeats, grabbing my soap.

I stare at the shower drain as he washes today's mistakes off me. He starts with my hair before moving down my body. Even when the physical remnants are gone, the feeling of filth remains.

"Spread your legs," he orders.

Aziel brings two sudsy fingers to my sex. I hope it doesn't give me an infection, the soap probably messing with my body's natural balance, but I'll let him clean me if it makes him feel better.

He takes his sweet time, and I bite my lip when the fingers inside me turn from clinical to pleasurable. Asmod's remaining lust has me sensitive, and I grab Aziel's wrist to stop him from doing something he regrets.

I'm sure the last thing he wants is to make me feel good.

"Don't fight me, Charlie," he says, pressing his front against my back as he rocks his fingers into me. "I'm going to be the last man inside you."

My pulse races, and I hold back tears as he kisses my shoulder and places his mouth over the mark already existing on it.

He sucks on my skin with a quiet moan, his erection rubbing against my lower spine. I let my head rest against his chest as he fingers me at the same leisurely pace as his rolling hips.

"Did you cum with him inside you?" Aziel asks, curling his fingers.

I whine, not wanting to answer. Kato's finger was very much inside me when I came, but I'm ashamed to admit it.

Aziel nips my shoulder, not accepting my silence as an answer, and he holds my skin painfully between his teeth until I nod.

"Then you will cum with me inside you," he says, shoving his fingers deeper into me.

He wraps his other arm around my waist and finds my clit. My foot slips as he rubs the swollen nub, but Aziel easily supports my weight. It takes him a moment to find a rhythm that works best, his fingertips switching between a hard rub and gentle skim before he settles on one that draws the loudest gasps from my lips.

"You're going to finish on my fingers, and then you'll bend over and spread your pussy for me," he says, sucking another hickey into my shoulder.

He moves all around my neck and shoulders, covering me with his marks while he moans into my skin and rocks himself against my back. I shudder as my pleasure grows, and I squirm against his fingers until my eyes roll back and I find my release.

It's hard to feel dirty when Aziel's gasping so loudly behind me, his movements quick as he places his hand between my shoulder blades and pushes me down. I brace against the wall before reaching behind and spreading myself as he ordered.

"Fuck," Aziel mutters.

Water pours down my back and onto my face as he begins to stroke himself, his fingertips digging painfully into my flesh as I listen to the wet sounds of his fist smacking his skin.

He's careful not to touch his dick to me as he steps between my legs and lines himself up, his breaths loud and choppy as he grunts my name and cums.

I'm not sure how much ends up inside me versus on me, but Aziel seems to be on top of that as he yanks me out of the water and shoves his cum-soaked fingers inside my sex.

"You will smell of me," he says, shutting off the water. "And you will not wash it off."

I nod, a sick part of me enjoying his claim. I'm tired of fighting with him, with all of them, and I want to go home. I'm ashamed it took me being with another man and then being kidnapped to realize that.

Aziel looks pleased with himself as I spin and reach for him. I squeeze his still-hard length before capturing his remaining cum. His eyes darken as I spread it on my chest, desperate to show how sorry I am. I don't want anybody else.

I want my males, and I hate that I ever doubted it.

"Put it in your mouth," Aziel instructs.

I don't hesitate to slip what's left between my lips. His cum is salty, and I curl my tongue around my fingers before dropping my hand back to my side.

Aziel and I stare at one another for a long minute, but before I can let my self-hatred sink back in, he bends and kisses me. His kiss is softer than I imagined it would be, and I curl my fingers around his wrist as he cups my cheeks.

"That's my girl," he whispers, pulling away.

Aziel steps out of the shower to grab towels. He smiles as he pats me dry, and his praise makes me feel better than I have in weeks.

He follows me into my bedroom and grunts when I reach for my leggings.

"That's not what you want to be wearing," he says.

I nod, not bothering to deny it.

I'm proud of my leathers. They're the only thing I've ever truly earned, and I have many scars from Echo's thin sticks and pointy fists to prove it.

I hold back tears as Aziel grabs my backup pair off the rack. He holds them out with a slight nod, ignoring my sobs as I slip them on my body.

"Say you're mine."

He wants me to say that? My heart lurches at the hope that blooms in my chest. If he still wants me to be his female, then there's hope to fix things with Gray and Silas.

"I'm yours," I promise.

"You'll wear my cum every day while we're in the shifter lands, and if I ever see you looking intimately at somebody who's not me or my males, you'll be punished." Aziel pushes my hair out of my face. "I'll make you look them in the eye as you shove my cum in your holes, and then you'll watch me tear out their throat."

I can't tell if he's serious, but I don't intend to find out.

Aziel's smile is infectious, and I didn't realize how much I missed it until now. A grin of my own spreads across my lips, matching his. There's still a lot of apologizing to do and mistakes I need to make up for, but this feels like a good start.

Chapter Twenty-Four

SILAS

GRAY'S UPSET.

He steps into the bedroom and leans against the doorframe, his attention sliding to the bed I'm lying on. He doesn't want me in here, but I don't care.

There's no reason for me not to be.

This wing was renovated for all of us to share, but I don't see the point in waiting. If I can't have Charlie, I've got no interest in finding another female, and this bed's too comfortable to pass up.

Besides, it's not like I've got anywhere else to go. Gray's bed is dirty, and the last place I want to be is in Charlie's. I suppose I could go to my room, but that wouldn't be nearly as spiteful.

I want to ruin everything I held special for Charlie, and this bedroom, built for all of us to share, was the most meaningful one.

"We shouldn't be in here," Gray says as I pull back the covers and slip underneath.

I shrug. "Why not?"

Gray's eyes narrow, but I don't care. I want to sleep in this bed, and there's not one good reason why I shouldn't.

"We should give her the opportunity to explain," Gray repeats for the tenth time tonight.

How he's not absolutely enraged right now is beyond me. He's holding out hope for Charlie, and I know he's desperate to find an explanation.

There isn't one. She cheated on us with that shifter, and I have no interest in learning any additional information. It's all I need to know. I doubt hearing in detail what she allowed that male to do to her will make me feel better.

Unless he forced her, which I doubt, she cheated.

I don't care if she did it once or a thousand times, or if it was with him or the entire fucking shifter pack.

Cheating is cheating, and I have no interest in it.

Gray looks around the room, his attention lingering on the dresser before he approaches and pulls open the drawers we filled with clothing for Charlie. I've already removed everything and filled it with my things.

A few drawers remain empty, but I'll have Aziel fill them in when he returns. He's got more clothing than Gray and me combined, so I'm sure he needs the additional room.

"What're you doing?" Gray asks, pushing the drawer shut and turning to me.

I roll onto my back and prop myself up on my elbows. Acting like a spoiled child is what I'm doing, but I refuse to admit that.

"Going to sleep," I say, dropping back down.

Gray frowns, and I can tell he's debating whether or not he wants to continue arguing. He's unhappy with this entire situation, and I'm sure he feels terrible about leaving Aziel, but I won't let myself feel guilty for that right now.

I was dumb to sit here believing Charlie's silence and insistence on running away was only temporary.

I thought she was discovering herself with the shifters, finding passions and making friends. A small part of me, despite how worried, was happy for her. She was living, and she was doing it all on her own.

It never crossed my mind that she'd be fucking them.

My lips purse as I grab one of the decorative throw pillows we bought. Gray and I picked out green ones, Charlie's favorite color, and I pause to glare at the design before throwing it off the bed. They're fucking hideous, but Gray said it's what humans like, so it's what we bought.

Humiliation is a light word to describe how I'm feeling.

Charlie didn't even have enough respect to say anything to us. She let us sit here waiting, rocking on our heels in anticipation of her return, while she ran around with that man. Rock told her we were eager to have her home, so it's not like she didn't know.

She just didn't care.

I'm stupid for having fallen for her. I knew she was young and didn't know what she wanted, and I shouldn't have let her convince me otherwise.

She just seemed so earnest when she promised it was us. We've dated hundreds, if not thousands, of women, but none have ever seemed so genuine in their love. Stupid fucking humans.

My shame for leaving in her time of need will fade, but her infidelity will never. She's stained our relationship, and I have no interest in tying myself to a woman who can't go without us for even a month before running into somebody else's arms. Absolutely not.

I'm okay with worrying about her health and safety, but sitting around stressing about whose cock she's touching is where I draw the line. I'm too busy for those games, and I'm too old to find them exciting.

"We should go to Aziel," Gray says, interrupting my self-loathing. "I can feel his power is all used up, and if we don't get him, it'll take a few hours for it to regenerate."

I take a moment to think as I grab, scan, and throw the tiny square pillows on the floor. Fate was cruel to keep her future hidden from me.

I thought it meant she would become a vital part of my life, but I was wrong. They got my hopes up for nothing.

Gray shifts, his concern for Aziel ever-growing. I'm not too worried.

Aziel's adaptable, and after being around him for so long, I don't worry about his safety. The man's more equipped to protect himself than anybody I've ever met, and he could probably take down the entire shifter pack if he needed to.

It'd be challenging, and he'd sure as shit be bruised and injured, but he'd be alive.

The Wrath demons have always been hard to kill, and he's by far the most powerful of them. He'll be fine.

"You can go get him," I say, knowing damn well he can't.

Gray's so weak he can barely stand, let alone teleport to Aziel and bring him back. I'm not going to fish them out of the inter-dimension space when he inevitably gets them lost, either.

At least not right away. I'll let them linger there for a day or two.

"Silas."

"Gray."

Gray crawls onto the bed. "You always get like this when you're hurt. You can't just shut off your emotions and pretend you're not upset," he says. "And you can't just run away until you're feeling better, either. I chose you today, but I will not defend your actions."

He sits on my belly and leans over my face, leaving me no choice but to look at him. His sunken cheekbones and chapped lips are alarming, and if he doesn't feed soon, he'll go into a frenzy.

"Tell me how you're feeling," he demands.

I purse my lips, hating the level of vulnerability admitting my emotions makes me feel. I did it for Charlie once, tucked my fear away and told her how much I loved her, and she spit it back in my face.

I've always felt emotions were overrated, and now I *know* they are.

Gray grabs my chin and forces me to stare into his wet eyes. "You don't get to pull away from me, Silas. I haven't done anything wrong."

I know he hasn't. Gray stands by his promises, even if it hurts him. His current hunger is proof enough of that. He was willing to hold out as long as he could, starving himself until his inner incubus takes over and forces him to feed.

He doesn't deserve my ice.

"I feel stupid," I blurt out.

Gray nods, unsurprised. I'm sure he feels something similar.

I wonder if he ever told Charlie about Nicolette—about how his first love left him for his father. She was ruthless in her goals and willing to step on Gray's throat to reach them. As much as I'm hurting, I doubt it's anything compared to the pain rushing through *his* veins.

Gray takes his promises seriously, more so than most, and he had one of fidelity with Charlie. He's a fucking incubus who agreed to feed off only her, an act that would inevitably always keep him weak.

Charlie doesn't have enough to sustain him long-term, but he was willing to agree to a life of unfulfillment for her.

And she thanked him by fucking a shifter.

"You feel so stupid that you abandoned Charlie in her time of need?" Gray challenges.

I look away, not wanting to think about that.

"You left with me," I point out.

"Would you have come back home if I hadn't chosen you?" Gray doesn't wait for an answer. He doesn't need one. "Besides, Aziel and two shifters are more than capable of getting Charlie from my dad. I would've just held them back."

I look at the ceiling, avoiding eye contact. I want to wallow in self-pity, not own up to what I did. It was wrong to leave, but I couldn't bring myself to stand there and panic over her with the man she left us for.

She made her decision, and it isn't us.

Gray sighs before lying on top of me, his support welcome. I let him bury his face in my neck and breathe me in, his touch helping to soothe my guilt. It grows with each passing minute, and I wrap my arms around Gray when it starts to make my chest burn.

The shifter reeked of her, his entire body covered in her scent, and the cum smelled of them both. Did she even think of us before giving herself to him? How long did it take for her to welcome others into her bed?

The questions rip through my mind like fire, fueling my anger.

It makes sense why she didn't want to come home.

She probably doesn't even think of this place as home, which makes me feel even worse about how desperately we were working to create a space for her. Even Aziel helped to paint this stupid room.

Fuck.

I still shouldn't have left like that.

Charlie may have been hurtful in her way of leaving us, but that doesn't mean she deserves to be abandoned in Lust. The incubi wouldn't hesitate to do awful things to her.

"Are they okay?" I ask, unable to hold back my curiosity.

Gray can reach Aziel through the bond, and while I'm sure he would've spoken up if he felt something was wrong, I want to hear confirmation.

Gray pops his head out from my neck and meets my gaze. I can tell he's debating whether or not to answer, his body tensing, before he subtly nods.

"There was some panic shortly after we left, but Aziel's been calm for hours," he admits.

Was Charlie surprised when Aziel came to her rescue without us? A small part of me hopes she asked where we were.

I cup Gray's head and bring his mouth to mine to stop my thoughts. I don't want to think about Charlie anymore tonight. She makes my body ache, and I'm tired of sitting around like her little lap dog.

Gray's tears land on my cheeks as he drags his mouth to my neck, his teeth nipping at the skin before latching on. I can tell he wants to mark me, but I shake my head and move his lips away from that particular area.

Not tonight.

Gray huffs, annoyed, but he doesn't push it as he sinks down my body.

I run my fingers through his hair as he slides off the bed and begins to strip. His bones are visible through his skin, and I can't help but frown as I eye them. He must be starving.

Gray reaches for me, and I lift my hips to help him pull down my pants. His eyes darken as he looks at my body, his lust filling my lungs and expanding my cock despite my sour mood.

"If she wants you back, what will you do?" I want to know if I need to prepare for our split.

If he forgives her, he'll end up bonding with her.

It's a serious thing, a life tie, and I won't do it to somebody I'm unsure about. I can't do that to myself, even if it means leaving my males and life behind.

Gray pauses, his hesitance making me worry. Fingers trace up my thighs before curling around my cock, and I hiss at his rough grip. Fuck, that feels good.

"I'll stand by your side, whatever you decide," Gray eventually says.

I look down and meet his eyes, wanting to see his truth. He's already staring at me, having expected this, and he holds eye contact as he shifts back and lowers his mouth to my skin.

It looks like he's done with his hunger strike. Good.

Chapter Twenty-Five

CHARLOTTE

THE SHIFTERS DON'T bother hiding their annoyance as Aziel struts through their land, their sharp gazes sliding from him to me. I shrink guiltily as he follows me around.

I only needed a few hours of napping to feel better, and I need to catch something if we want meat for dinner. Echo hasn't come by with food, which isn't surprising.

I'm sure she's pissed.

"Where are you taking me?" Aziel asks.

Chev told him to stay inside the cabin, but he's chosen to ignore that order. Aziel doesn't do well with people telling him what to do.

"We're going to check my traps."

Aziel pauses, his footsteps coming to a halt. "Your *what*?"

"My traps," I repeat. "Unless you want vegetables for dinner, we need to catch our meat."

I'm not the same woman I was when he last saw me, and he's about to see that firsthand. I hope he's impressed with my independence, but I don't want to embarrass myself by asking.

Aziel doesn't question me further, and I take that as a good sign and lead him deeper into the woods. This is the first time I've gone there without Chev, and I hope I'm not going in the wrong direction.

"Charlie!"

Fuck. Wincing, I squeeze my eyes shut and turn toward Kato.

This isn't going to be fun. I mentally prepare myself for the clusterfuck that's sure to happen, but I freeze when I open my eyes and am met with Aziel's back. He stands large in front of me, and in one smooth motion, he reaches behind and grabs my hips so I can't move. I try to shove him aside in a panic, scared he'll hurt Kato.

This isn't Kato's fault.

Aziel doesn't move, but he does lift his arm so I can shove my head underneath his armpit to see.

Kato comes to a halt a few feet away, his nostrils flaring as he throws a sideways glance at Aziel. I guess that answers my question about how well the shifters can smell his cum.

"Yes?" I ask, hoping my interaction doesn't anger the already on-edge Aziel.

It feels wrong to hate and ignore Kato after what happened, but it also feels like I'm betraying my males if I don't. Aziel presses down on my head, squeezing it between his arm and side, which I take as a warning.

Kato's eyebrows furrow as he watches Aziel's actions toward me, his disapproval clear. Shifters don't treat their females like this, and they'd probably cut off their limbs before squeezing their mate's head.

I don't mind it, though. It doesn't hurt, and the dominance makes me tingly.

"What do you want? Was fucking my female not enough for you?" Aziel's chest vibrates as he speaks, his voice booming through the trees.

"Look..." Kato sighs, running his hands nervously down his leathers. "I don't know the human traditions, but the shifters don't classify what happened between us as fucking. I didn't have sex with Charlie."

Aziel stiffens, the action so subtle. I wouldn't have noticed if it weren't for my head being squished against him, but he doesn't otherwise react.

"My mate encouraged our interaction, but the shifters are still angry," Kato continues, meeting Aziel's eye. "I'd appreciate it if you didn't spread further mistruths."

This is the first time I've seen somebody challenge Aziel so brazenly, and I'm shocked at how well the Wrath's handling it. His chest expands as he sucks in a deep breath, continuing until I'm sure his lungs will explode, before he slowly exhales.

I watch in shock.

"Anyway..." Kato changes the subject, turning to me. "I've spoken to my children at length about what happened, and I've come to warn you that Echo's quite angry. It would do you well to find a large stick for your training tomorrow morning."

My throat runs dry, and I wiggle against Aziel until he lets me move in front of him. His hands latch onto my hips and pull me flush against his front, not allowing any space.

"She still wants to train with me?" I ask.

Kato cocks his head to the side, confused, before bursting out in laughter. "Of course, Charlie. They're aware of Emily's unique sexual desires, and I made it clear she and I instigated."

Kato glances between Aziel and me before cracking a smile. "I'm happy to see you've not taken after your father," he says, clearing his throat. "But your presence makes my people uncomfortable. If you insist on leaving Charlie's cabin, stay off the main paths and away from any buildings."

Aziel grunts, and Kato takes that as his cue to leave.

"Have you been letting me believe this entire time that you fucked the shifter?" Aziel asks once Kato disappears. He's as still as a mountain as he leans over my shoulder and peers down at me.

"Tell me in detail what happened between you two," he orders.

My palms grow clammy, and I gulp as I try to think of the best way to avoid his anger. I didn't want to sound like I was making excuses or trying to justify my actions.

"Charlie," Aziel urges when I don't respond.

I clear my throat, wishing for the world to swallow me whole.

"Emily and I kissed, and she touched Kato while he fingered me," I croak, pressing my hands to my cheeks to stop a blush from forming.

Aziel says nothing, and I shift before continuing my humiliating explanation.

"It was only one time, and I felt horrible afterward. I panicked and left once we finished, and that's when I ran into the incub—"

My sentence is cut short as Aziel spins me around.

His lips are on mine, and my mind goes blank as he frantically kisses me. I'm not sure what to make of it, but I prefer this over his silence.

"You infuriating woman." He groans and picks me up.

He's hard, and I gasp as he steps forward and presses me against a tree.

"I'm going to be the first to fuck you, and I will give mine to you as well." Aziel speaks his words as a promise, and I hope he means them.

We're far enough from the main pack lands that nobody's around to see us grinding against one another, but I doubt Aziel would care if we were. He's not been secretive about his feelings since arriving.

He's made it quite clear where he stands, and I appreciate it.

My knees wobble when I'm finally returned to my feet, a fact Aziel takes great humor in, but I quickly find my stride and rush into the woods. Aziel has no issues keeping up with my attempt at a hurried pace, his quiet laughter warming my bones.

I don't know what's gotten into him, but I like it.

The distance was good for us, giving me time to grow and him to learn how to control himself.

I jump and squeal when I spot an animal inside my trap, and I drop to the floor beside it with a wide grin. This is exciting. I ignore the tears that fill my eyes as I grab a knife out of the waistband of my skirt and reach in through the back grates to hold the animal's neck.

Aziel lowers himself next to me, his face entering my peripheral vision as he looks at my wet cheeks.

"Charlie?" he whispers, moving to take the knife from my hand.

I jerk away. "I'm fine."

He retreats as I readjust my grip and bring the blade to the animal's throat. It looks like some giant hairless bunny, and I assume it's an animal native to the shifter lands.

It snarls and tries to move away, but I remain firm in my hold despite how awful I feel. My hand shakes as I hesitate, and after a moment, I admit defeat and turn to Aziel.

"Will you hold my hand steady so I don't miss? I don't want to hurt it more than necessary," I say, hating how my voice cracks. It was one thing to kill Asmod, a man who was actively attacking me, but this animal is innocent.

I wanted to do this by myself to show how strong I've become, but it isn't worth it if I accidentally torture this poor animal. Chev couldn't stress enough the importance of respecting wildlife, and I agree with everything he taught me.

We need to co-exist, which means merciful kills and hunting

only for need.

Aziel's lips graze my forehead as he wraps his arm around my shoulders and takes my hand. He holds it steady before guiding my knife into the animal's neck.

I choke back a sob as it screams, and I lean against Aziel for support as it dies in my hands. He hums and hugs me from behind, bringing to attention his erection. I stiffen.

"I like seeing you kill. Ignore it," he admits, pulling away so it's no longer touching me.

Aziel holds me until I've settled, but he still seems hesitant to let go as I open the cage and pull the animal out. It's heavy and full of good meat, and I grunt as I pick it up.

This thing's going to be a bitch to carry back.

My cheeks warm as I glance at Aziel and see the approval in his eyes, and I clear my throat before straightening my shoulders and jerking my head to the left.

"Let's check the others."

Aziel throws his head back with a moan, the noise low and filthy, and I trip over my feet in my attempt to hurry away. He laughs as I stumble to catch myself and the animal, and he seems disappointed when we discover the other traps are empty.

"Let me carry it for you," Aziel says.

He tries to take the animal from me, but I yank it away with an angry shout.

"No!"

Aziel's eyes darken, the man clearly annoyed, before the animal is ripped from my hands and I'm face-down in the dirt. I jump to my feet and bring my knee up in the way Echo taught me, and I take great pleasure in the way Aziel's face goes red as I slam it between his legs.

I know I've managed to hurt him as his jaw goes slack and he sucks in a sharp breath. *Good.*

I take advantage of his momentary distraction and rip my animal out of his arms. I like this game we're playing, and I let out a loud laugh before sprinting toward my cabin.

It doesn't take long for me to hear footfalls behind me, but Aziel's too slow as I hurry up the steps and slam the door shut in his face. I'm sure he let me win, but I still count it as a victory as I lean against the kitchen counter and catch my breath.

Aziel pushes open the door, and I pretend like nothing's happened as I grab my knives and set them on the counter with my animal.

"It's about time you caught up," I tease, my voice shaky as I struggle to catch my breath. "Be a dear and ready this guy for me, will you?"

I don't want him to know I'm asking him to do it because I don't know how, but Aziel seems to get the hint as he walks around me and takes my hands. The guilt that courses through me is intense, and I clear my throat before working up the courage to speak.

"I feel like I'm supposed to tell you that Kato helped me skin an animal like this," I admit.

Aziel pauses, his grip on my hand tightening. "Thanks for telling me, but I don't need to know everything you two did together." He presses a soft kiss on my cheek.

I still feel guilty as he teaches me how to butcher the animal. I'm continually distracted by his low voice as he walks me through the steps, his age shown through the sheer amount of information he knows.

I guess being old as dirt has its benefits.

Aziel doesn't give me even an inch of space as we cook and eat, and he even follows me into my bedroom when I decide it's time to sleep.

"What're you doing?" I ask as he crawls onto my bed.

Aziel looks confused, his lips pursed as he glances between me and the mattress.

"Going to bed?"

I hold back a smirk and point to the cot Rock sleeps on. Aziel snorts and makes himself comfortable on my bed.

"You're more than welcome to sleep on that, but I sure as fuck will not be," he says when I continue to stare.

His lips twitch as I huff and crawl in next to him, my body stiff until he curls around me. For the first time since he rescued me, he's not hard, and I realize just how tired he must be after all the work it took him to shift back and forth to Lust.

I wait until I'm sure he's asleep, his breaths deep and steady, before turning and kissing his cheek. I have no idea why he's being so kind, but I like it.

Echo stands above me with a devious smile, and she smacks the back of my thighs with her stick as I scramble to get up. Kato wasn't lying when he said she wouldn't go easy on me.

"Son of a bitch," I cry, landing in an ungraceful heap on the ground.

"I'm the daughter of a bitch, thank you very much," she retorts, still not entirely up to speed on human expressions.

"Hey!" Chev shouts, eager to jump to the defense of his mother.

He hasn't spoken much to me, not that I blame him, and I shoot him a friendly smile before Aziel steps in front to block my view. He crosses his arms over his chest, and I assume he's angry by Chev's presence and my willingness to be smacked with a long stick.

Still, I'm shocked he hasn't put a stop to it. Aziel's been

making genuine efforts not to limit me, which I appreciate, but it's starting to freak me out. Maybe he got a head wound while he was in Lust and it scrambled his brain.

I should check for one later.

"Get up," Echo says, her stick swiping my shoulder blade.

I groan and bury my hands into the ground as I struggle to stand, my movements slow and uncoordinated after the sheer number of hits I've taken today. I even sent Aziel out while the sky was still dark to find me a new, bigger stick, but it's not helping.

Echo circles me like prey, her eyes darting around as she decides where to strike next. I jump to the side and swing for her neck when she lunges, and I barely graze her skin before I'm knocked to the ground by a pointy elbow. My skirt flies up at the force of my fall, but Echo bends and fixes it in a heartbeat.

I appreciate the gesture and roll onto my back with my arms sprawled.

"Get up, human," she taunts, crouching over my limp, pained body.

I close my eyes, ready for death.

Aziel interjects. "That's enough."

Echo seems to quietly agree as she grabs my arms and helps me stand. My knees buckle almost immediately, but I get myself steadied with minimal help.

"I feel much better after this," she admits, patting my shoulder and dropping her stick. "Thank you for letting me beat you."

I snort. I wouldn't necessarily say *letting* is the correct word. I would've stopped it if I could.

Echo pulls me into a warm hug and squeezes me until I groan.

"I'm happy you and the Wrath are getting along so well, but I feel I should tell you we can smell his ejaculate on your skin," she quietly whispers.

I clear my throat and back away, absolutely humiliated. I know they can smell it, but I hoped nobody would comment. It's wishful thinking, though, and I should've known Echo would bring it up.

She has no shame, and she's mentioned multiple times that she finds it fun to make my skin red.

"My turn!" Chev shouts.

He grabs our sticks off the ground before turning to Aziel.

"My bloodline makes me stronger than the other shifters," he explains, throwing my stick at Aziel's feet. "I want a challenge."

Aziel looks hesitant, but I bounce on my toes in excitement. I've seen Chev spar a few times, but it's never by his request and he always comes out on top. He looks bored most of the time, grudgingly accepting the challenges the shifters throw his way.

Echo gasps and drags me away from the small clearing as Aziel picks up the stick, her movements too fast for me to keep up with. She hardly notices as she pulls me aside and plops on the ground. It takes me a bit longer to sit, my sore limbs making the action awkward.

"I'm not fighting you with a stick," Aziel says, tossing the wood aside.

I turn to Chev, looking for answers, only to choke and turn away when I catch sight of his penis. My eyes land on Aziel as Chev transforms into his bear form, his expression speaking volumes.

Aziel's going to punish me for that. That thought used to frighten me, but now it evokes a different emotion.

"We can smell your arousal, too," Echo whispers.

"Then stop sniffing," I snap, ignoring Aziel's cackle.

Aziel turns to look at us just as Chev lunges. My hands find Echo's and squeeze as Aziel's tossed across the clearing, and I feel my stomach in my throat as he lands in a heap and springs up to his feet.

The two men are brutal in their fighting, with fast and calculated movements that usually end with blood. Chev's enormous in his bear form, and as he and Aziel circle one another, I realize I've never truly seen either of them fight.

Aziel's cocky smile gradually falls as the minutes pass, his confidence wavering as he struggles to get Chev to submit. I think he's got the shifter a few times, but Chev always manages to rip out a chunk of Aziel's flesh and wiggle out of the hold.

I'm sure Aziel would've just gone for the throat if this were a real fight, but he sticks to punches and kicks. Who knew Aziel could fight without losing control?

I sure didn't.

Echo takes it upon herself to cheer on Chev, and after a slight hesitation, I decide to do the same with Aziel. His lips curl into a smile the first time I shout his name, encouraging me to continue.

Chev tackles Aziel to the ground with a snarl, and I sit up straight as Aziel wraps his arm around the bear's midsection and flips them around. He repeatedly punches Chev in the jaw, his movements too quick for me to follow, until Chev stops moving.

Aziel rolls to the side the second Chev goes limp, and he sprawls on his back the way I did earlier.

I stand and hobble over. Echo does the same, but she makes her way to Chev while I approach Aziel.

"You okay?" I ask, prodding Aziel's ribs with my toe.

He swats me away, and after a few seconds, he stands.

I look him over, my breath hitching. He's almost already healed, but his shirt is soaked in blood.

"I suppose that explains why you're all torn up," he says, reaching for one of the cuts on my shoulder.

His touch is featherlight, but my torn skin is so sensitive that it still stings. Aziel traces the line of my wound as Chev groans and stumbles to his feet. He approaches from the side and knocks his fist against Aziel's temple.

"That was fun," he says, letting his sister lead him away.

I watch a bite on Aziel's shoulder heal as they leave, the muscles knitting together grotesquely.

"I'm surprised you did that without losing control," I admit.

Aziel shrugs. "Silas has been teaching me breathing exercises."

I place a hand over my mouth to hide my smile. Breathing exercises? Aziel smirks, fully aware I'm laughing at him, before wrapping an arm around my waist and helping me back to my cabin.

Aziel fits in surprisingly well here, and I hope he isn't in a rush to leave. He's made it clear he thinks of me as his, but we haven't discussed anything beyond that. We should, but I'm hesitant to bring it up.

We still haven't heard from Gray or Silas, and I'm scared to face them.

I'm scared to face what I've done.

Aziel is letting me off easy, but I know it won't be the same with the other two. We were in a committed relationship, and even though my leaving blurred our status, I shouldn't have been intimate with anybody else.

I should have fought harder to distance myself from Emily. I knew how her scent affected me, but I still chose to be around her.

"What're you doing?" I gasp when I realize Aziel is leading me away from my cabin.

The shifters made it clear they wanted him to stay out of the central pack lands, and he's heading straight for them. I dig my heels into the ground, but Aziel doesn't slow.

"Aziel. Stop!" I snap, reaching up his torso in search of a nipple.

He hisses and yanks my hand away when I find and twist the nub, but thankfully, he stops walking. I make a mental note that the nipple trick works for all three of my males as I step in front of him and block the path.

"I need to talk to Kato," he says.

My head whips from side to side so quickly, I'm surprised I don't scramble my brains. There's no reason for Aziel to speak with Kato right now, and I worry that fighting with Chev got him more riled up than I realized.

"I don't want you two to fight," I beg. "Please leave him alone."

These people have become my family, and I can't let Aziel hurt them. Despite my regrets and desperation to keep my males happy, I won't back down on this.

"You ignored my request to talk to Kato about helping us with the females, and I don't intend to wait any longer," Aziel explains. "I wish to ask if he'd be willing to work with us instead of Mammon. I've implemented similar programs within Wrath, and I'm going to invite him and the other shifter leaders to come view them." Aziel pauses, tilting his head toward the sky as he thinks. "I also need to figure out where he put Asmod's body."

I blink. Then I blink again.

Is Aziel telling me what he's thinking? That's new.

I take a moment to absorb the information, my mouth gaping like a fish before I snap my jaw shut and cup his chin. My eyes narrow in a gesture I hope looks threatening.

"Can you be in a room with Kato for an extended period of time and not lose control?" I ask.

Aziel glances away, the muscles in his jaw twitching, before he lets out a long sigh.

"I'm not sure," he admits.

I gulp, hesitating, before kissing him. It's the first time I've ever taken the initiative to touch him like this, and I hope it works as he closes the space between our bodies. His hands find my waist, and he trails them up my exposed sides as I pull him toward my cabin.

The glint in his eye tells me he knows exactly what I'm doing, but he doesn't put up a fight as I lead him away from Kato's. Whatever he wants to talk about can wait until he's not all excited from fighting Chev and he's a little more confident he won't hurt anybody.

I groan as Aziel sits beside me, his heavy body causing the mattress to sink.

"It's time to get up, Charlie," he says, pushing my hair out of my face.

I whine. "I'm tired."

Aziel laughs, the sound loud and deep, before he cups my cheek and kisses my forehead. His outward affection is taking some getting used to, and I feel my lips curling as I roll onto my back and sit up.

I slept most of yesterday away after my early morning training with Echo. Aziel practically forced it on me, and I'm pretty sure he almost popped a blood vessel in his eye when I insisted I go out and check my traps.

They were empty, but I'm hopeful there'll be something in them today.

"I found some Ucka in the fridge and warmed it up for you," Aziel says, luring me out of bed with the promise of food.

It reminds me of Gray.

My throat runs dry at the thought of the incubus, and I get out of bed before Aziel can see my sour expression. He follows me into the kitchen, and I sit on a barstool and mindlessly begin to eat.

Aziel's pissed our men haven't tried to check-in. He admitted he told Silas to leave, but he never actually expected Silas and Gray to abandon me. He especially didn't anticipate them remaining gone for so long.

I could be getting passed around Lust right now, and they'd have no idea.

Aziel steps into the room and trails his fingers down my back, starting at the nape of my neck before sliding to the base of my spine. I shiver, his touch causing goosebumps to pebble up along my skin.

"You're beautiful," he says.

I laugh. I look like a hot mess right now. My hair is still messy from sleep, and I'm sure there are imprints on my cheek from the seams of my pillow.

Aziel's body heat warms my back as he traces my healed cuts, barely grazing over one before moving to the next. I can tell they make him uneasy, but he hasn't voiced any complaints.

"Why haven't Silas and Gray come yet?" I whisper.

The question's been heavy on my mind. I know they're mad, but I thought they'd at least have shown up by now to see Aziel. We're going on three days here.

I spin in my chair.

Aziel's face is pinched, and he flicks my hair behind my shoulder so he has a better view of my chest. My eyes narrow, but I don't say anything as he trails a finger along the top of my leathers.

This is all new to him, and I don't blame him for being curious. I remember fondling Gray on multiple occasions, eager to learn his body.

"Gray has been checking on me through the bond," he says.

"They're giving us space."

I scoff, knowing that's far from the truth. "They're giving *themselves* space. From me."

"You cheated, Charlie." Aziel doesn't bother sugarcoating his words, not that I'd expect him to. "They probably think you had a full-blown relationship with Kato, and I'm sure they'll feel better after hearing the truth."

I look down, embarrassed. I fucked up big time, and I'm starting to doubt they'll ever forgive me. My chest expands as I debate whether or not I should ask.

Aziel won't lie to me, at least not about this.

"Do you think they'll ever forgive me?"

Aziel reaches around me and grabs a piece of Ucka meat. He brings it to my lips, and I sigh as I open my mouth and eat. It tastes good, and he does this until the plate is empty.

"I think it will take them a long time to forgive you," he finally answers.

I refuse to cry.

"What are we doing?" I ask. "What's this between us?"

Aziel shrugs, his eyebrows furrowing like he doesn't understand my question.

"You're my female?"

"If Gray and Silas aren't willing to forgive me, where does that leave us?" I clarify.

I stare at my knees, hoping to calm my racing heart. As much as I love playing house with Aziel, it won't last forever. It's only a matter of time before he's ready to go home, and I want to know what that means for me.

"You're my female, and they're my males," Aziel says. "That's not changing. They'll come around with time."

I hum, sucking my lips into my mouth. Those words aren't the most comforting.

"Let's not talk about this until we have a better idea of what Gray and Silas are thinking," Aziel continues, his cocky smile returning as he dips his finger into the top of my leathers and pulls it down.

My nipples harden as they're exposed to the cool air, and Aziel sinks his teeth into his bottom lip and circles them with his thumbs.

"Fuck," he whispers, spreading my thighs and stepping between them.

"How can you be aroused at a time like this?" I ask, gesturing to his hips.

Aziel shrugs. "I'm a thousand-year-old virgin, Charlie. What do you expect?"

It's the first time I've ever heard him say this, and I can't stop a laugh from bubbling up out of my throat. Gray always calls Aziel a virgin to insult him, and there's something about hearing him say it so casually that does me in.

Aziel beams as I giggle, and he pulls me into his arms before storming into the bedroom. He tosses me on the bed, and I grip my stomach to try to stop my laughter as he pulls me to the edge of the mattress.

My humor vanishes as he strips and kneels on the floor between my thighs. I grab at his forehead in a panic, trying and failing to sit up as he puts his palm on the flat of my belly to keep me still.

"What're you doing?" I gasp, squeezing his head between my thighs as he leans uncomfortably close to my sex.

Aziel's black eyes meet mine as he grabs my thighs and pulls them apart.

"I'm going to put my mouth on you, and then I'm going to cum on your belly," he explains, kissing my inner thigh.

It's hard to stay focused when he's staring at me like I'm the most tempting thing he's ever seen.

"We can't," I say, wiggling away. As much as I'd love to feel Aziel's mouth on me, I'm not going to risk further angering my males. "I don't want to further upset Gray or Silas."

Aziel groans and drops his forehead on my belly. I raise a brow at his dramatic reaction and comb my fingers through his hair.

"Fine, but I'm still going to cum on you."

He climbs up my body, looking mildly annoyed as he strokes himself. I clench my thighs together in a sad attempt to keep the scent of my arousal hidden, but I still find myself panting as I watch him. There's something so erotic about seeing him pleasure himself.

I hesitate for a brief moment before spreading my thighs.

"Fuck," Aziel moans, releasing his length.

He moves too quickly for my eyes to follow, but the warmth on my sex provides an answer before my brain can register what he's doing.

My body spasms as Aziel curls his arms around my thighs and licks the length of my slit.

"I've waited a thousand years to taste a cunt, and I'm not going to wait any longer because my males want to pout," he says, pulling back just enough to make eye contact with me. "If they get mad, which I doubt they will, I'll let them know it was all me."

He's back before I have time to process words, his wet tongue flickering over my clit at a speed only the demons can manage. I throw my head back, overwhelmed by the sensation, before curling my fingers through his hair.

I give it a yank as I do with Silas and Gray, but it has the opposite effect on Aziel as he snatches my hands, grabs my wrists, and places them on my belly.

"Not with me, baby girl." He laughs and returns his mouth to my sex.

His tongue is everywhere, and I cry out as he brings his hand between my thighs and works two fingers inside. He scissors them, stretching me, before carefully rocking them in and out in a motion I'm confident he learned from Gray.

My head slams against the mattress as he slows, testing out different motions and pressures to see what makes me squirm. At one point, I snap my thighs around his head to hold him in place, but he yanks them apart before sinking his teeth into my inner thigh.

It hurts, and I yelp as he soothes the skin with his tongue and returns to my clit. Lesson learned.

"Gray's prodding at my head, begging me to let him in," Aziel suddenly admits, pulling back with a grin. "Should I let him?"

His lips and chin are soaking wet, and he licks his lips as he crawls over me and slots his hips between my thighs. I gasp as I feel his cock sliding through my folds.

"I'm going to be fucking Charlie in about five seconds. You can be here for that or not, but it's going to happen either way."

Aziel reaches between us and lines up with my entrance. My body is burning for him, and I resist the urge to roll my hips and ease his blunt tip inside.

Aziel speaks to my face, but I'm not the intended target. He's talking to Gray through the bond. His eyelids flutter as he brings his focus back to me, and I shrink underneath his heated gaze.

"I'm going to fuck you, Charlie, and you'll be mine forever. If you don't want my bond, now's the time to speak up," he warns, pressing in.

My response is immediate, no thought necessary.

I know what I want, and it's my males.

Chapter Twenty-Six

AZIEL

CHARLIE'S BREATH HITCHES, and I duck my head to hide my smile. She's so responsive, always making little noises whenever I say dirty words or touch her skin.

I like it, and I tighten my grip on my cock as I press it against her slit with more pressure.

Her hands slide up my waist as we wait to see if Gray and Silas show up, but I don't have the heart to tell her they'd be here by now if they were going to. I don't dwell on their absence as I plant my palms into the mattress and bring my face to hers.

"Are you sure this is what you want?" I ask, pressing wet kisses up the column of her neck.

Charlie nods, another gasp slipping from her lips as I lick her jaw. Murder taints her skin, and I hold back a moan at the taste of it. It was stronger after she killed the animal yesterday, and I almost regret not fucking her then.

Gray prods at the bond, but I shove him away. If he wants to know what's happening so badly, he can come here and see for himself. I can feel that Silas fed him, so nothing's holding him back.

"Say it with your words," I order.

Nodding isn't going to be enough for me. This is big, and I need her verbal confirmation before proceeding. My excitement grows as Charlie opens her mouth and rocks her hips, attempting to lower herself onto my cock.

She's desperate. I fucking love it.

"I want this. I want you," she promises.

Soft fingers touch my hips, digging into the firm muscle as I grin. I like hearing her say that, and I line myself up with her entrance before gently pushing forward. Her eyes screw shut as the tip of myself sinks inside, and I pause to let her adjust before rocking in a bit more.

I'm glad she's not asking about Gray or Silas, not wanting them to ruin this for us. I'm honestly happy they didn't show. This moment is for Charlie and me alone, and they don't deserve it after abandoning her.

Her walls strangle my cock as I push another inch inside. My fear of hurting her grows as she sucks in a shaky breath, the action provoking a feeling of insecurity inside of me that I'm unfamiliar with.

I want this to feel good for her.

Gray always made the females in my dreams love everything I do, and I sink my teeth into my bottom lip as I wiggle and try to figure out how exactly I'm supposed to do this. I understand the basic logistics of sex, but the motion feels unfamiliar.

Fuck.

"You're doing so well, baby. So fucking good for me," I say, squeezing the base of my cock as I fight the urge to snap forward and sink all of myself inside her.

Charlie sucks in a slow breath and shifts underneath me, her thighs brushing my sides as she lifts her butt and welcomes more of me inside. I clench my jaw and squeeze my eyes shut, struggling to keep my composure.

I've imagined what it would feel like to fuck Charlie a thousand, if not a million, times, and it's better than I could've ever imagined. She's warm and wet and *fuck*, so fucking soft.

Gray was an asshole to make her feel rough in my dreams.

It's his fault I'm embarrassing myself.

Charlie's heart races as I pull out most of the way and glance at where our bodies connect. Half my shaft is wet from where it was inside her, and I smirk at the sight before sinking back in. I don't stop where I did before, and I continue forward until our hips are flush.

She stretches around me, her skin pulled tight as it swallows my thickness.

Fuck.

I should take a picture and frame it in my room.

"Are you okay? Do you want me to stop?" I ask, looking up.

Charlie's face is red, and I freeze. I'm significantly larger than the toy my males were using on her, and she complained about it hurting the first time they penetrated her with it.

"I'm okay." Charlie gasps, grabbing my shoulders. "I can feel the stretch, but I like it." She pauses and clears her throat before continuing. "You make me feel full."

I moan, dropping to my elbows as she clenches around me.

Charlie giggles, and I slam my lips on hers to swallow the noise. Her tongue brushes against mine as I thrust, finally starting to fuck her. I move slowly so it doesn't hurt, easing myself out until only the tip remains before rolling my hips forward until she's taken all of me.

I smile as her giggles come to an abrupt halt, and I'm satisfied when they shift to breathy gasps and loud grunts.

I'm unsure what her body can take or what feels best, and I test out different rhythms until she buries her nails into my back and arches.

"Say my name," I order, sitting up straight so I can watch myself sink into her.

"Az—" Charlie slams her head against the pillow. "Aziel!"

I drop my hand between our bodies and press my thumb to her clit, remembering Gray's instruction. For once, I'm grateful for his impromptu sex lessons over the years, and I rub the swollen nub with the pad of my finger.

Charlie takes me so well, her pussy greedy for what I have to give. I'm sure she'll be sore later, but I'll put her in the bath we put in our new wing before putting her to bed tonight.

This bed isn't big enough for us, and I want my males to listen to her taking me while they sulk in their bedrooms.

Charlie's mine, and they're going to know it.

Just like the shifters do.

Charlie squirms, and I take that as a good sign and continue what I'm doing. Already, I can feel my body screaming to cum, but I want Charlie to finish first. I want her to be spent and satisfied when I spill into her and bond us together.

She covers her mouth with a cry, and I snatch her wrists and place them on her legs.

"Hold your legs open for me," I order, shutting my eyes so I don't finish too quickly. "Be a good girl and give me a good view to fuck into."

Charlie's walls clench as she grabs hold of herself, her fingers digging into her thighs as she pulls them apart. I shouldn't look, but the sight's too tempting not to.

I'm obsessed.

Charlie's red cheeks have my need growing, the physical reaction to her embarrassment provoking me. I like that she's shy about doing these things. My female's a whore only for me.

"Do you want to cum, my little warrior?" I tease.

Her thighs squeeze my hips, the weak muscles trying so hard to hold me in place, before she wraps her legs around the back of my lower spine and hooks them together. The action shifts my thrusts into a slow rock, which feels just as good.

My cock twitches inside her, and I keep steady as her wiggling grows. She's close.

"That's it, baby girl," I grunt. "Cum for me."

Charlie's knee slams into my bicep as she spasms, her limbs jerky as she screams and clenches. I have to stop moving as her walls strangle me, the muscles fluttering in a way that feels dangerously good.

I throw my head back with a low moan, fighting my orgasm as her body goes soft.

My lips curl as she sags into the mattress with a loud sigh, and I happily make eye contact with my red-faced female.

She's so fucking beautiful.

Charlie's legs tighten around my hips before I feel her heels digging into my butt, silently urging me to keep moving.

"I'm going to cum in you," I warn.

She nods, and I drop to my elbows so our noses are touching.

"I'm going to fill you with me, with my cum and my babies," I continue, fucking into her.

Charlie moans, her eyes screwing shut as she wraps her arms around my waist in a tight hold. I like her possessiveness, and I quicken my thrusts as the heat in my abdomen grows.

She's mine, and I'm hers.

"Please." Charlie licks my throat before moving to and latching on to the spot where demons mark. "Please, Daddy."

I curse, my ears ringing at the title. It's good she knows her place. I have half a mind to pull away as I feel her teeth grazing my skin. Gray will be offended I let her mark me before him, but I can't bring myself to care about that right now.

"Can I —"

I cut her off. "Yes."

Placing a hand underneath her head, I hold her mouth to me and bury my own in my pillow so I don't instinctively return the favor. I can bond without a bite, and I want to leave her skin soft for my males.

They'll have a spot on either side of her neck.

The feeling of her flat teeth forcing their way through the layers of my skin does me in, and I still with a choked moan. My eyes roll back at the pleasure of it, and I can't stop the cry that slips from my lips as I find my release.

Charlie tilts her hips to welcome in more of me, my female greedy.

It's a want I'm more than happy to fulfill.

I can feel the bond between us forming as my back curls and she pries her teeth from my neck. Humans can't mark, but I still hope my body will recognize her bite as an attempt and leave behind a scar.

The bond I created between us should help.

The power I usually keep locked away pours out as I roll to the side and pull her onto my chest. Charlie curls against me, her heavy breaths warming my skin.

My cock slips out of her, and I frown before reaching down and shoving it back in. I want to stay inside for a bit longer.

"Do you feel the bond?" I ask, trailing my finger up her belly.

It's where I feel the bond forming inside myself, the connection deep in my gut as our souls merge.

It hurts, her body needing a lot from mine, but I don't mind. I'd rather she be greedy and strong than take nothing and remain weak. The more she takes, the better off she'll be, and I press a soft kiss to the top of her head as the smell there begins to change.

I'll miss her natural human scent, and I breathe in as much as

I can before it's gone.

"It feels good," she says, flexing her hands between our bodies. "Your scent isn't affecting me at all."

I smile, happy to hear it.

After another moment, she pushes at my chest and wiggles her way on top of me. I fall out again, but I've gone too soft to stay inside. Charlie's sex is wet and dripping with my cum, but we both ignore it as she plants herself on my belly and stares at me with wide, shocked eyes.

Those eyes fill with tears as they dart around the room.

"I can see better," she says.

My hands find their way to her hips, and I hold them as she looks at herself. Cuts still litter her skin, and I frown as I find a fresh one and push into it. She winces, and I pull back and wait to see if she heals.

She doesn't.

There are limitations to what my bond can provide, but maybe when she has both Gray's and Silas's, she'll see improvement in her healing.

"Bummer." She pouts.

I snort, shifting underneath her. "Are you sore?"

As much as I love watching her discover the benefits of my bond, I want to know how she's feeling.

Charlie wiggles, her nose scrunching, before she gives a timid nod. She will be exhausted once the bond solidifies, and I urge her to lie on my chest so she's in a comfortable position when it does.

I plan to take her home while she's napping, and I want her to wake up in the wing we had made for her. I think she'll like it, and I hope it'll lift her spirits to be back in Wrath.

She'll probably miss being here, but maybe I can install a portal in our home for her to use. I'll have to get it programmed to only travel to set locations, which I'm sure Charlie will be pissed about, but it's worth it if it prevents her from accidentally going to some foreign, dangerous realm.

I'll have to put a portal here, too, which will definitely be an issue with the shifters. They seem to have a soft spot for Charlie, though, so I think they'll let me do it.

Her toy will not be welcome to use it.

Only the shifter female she loves to fight and the brother who's always staring.

"Was it good for you?" Charlie whispers, her voice cracking.

I can feel her pain through the bond, the feeling slight, and I know she's thinking about Gray and Silas. She seems to always think about them whenever something good happens, the action a subtle way of punishing herself.

"Best sex I've ever had," I quip.

Charlie hums, too tired to pick up on my joke. I don't mind, and I continue running my fingers through her hair as her breathing slows.

"Can I have access to your mind, baby?" I ask.

I want in her thoughts and, even more than that, her memories. She's young, and it won't take me long to replay her entire life for myself.

"No."

The answer's immediate, and I frown but don't fight it. She'll let me in eventually. Silas did, Gray did, and it's only a matter of time before Charlie does, too.

Chapter Twenty-Seven

CHARLOTTE

EVERYTHING SMELLS LIKE Aziel, and I smile as I bury my face in the sheets and inhale. I always thought he had a pleasant scent, and this confirms it.

I'm sore, and I tense my muscles before shoving a hand between my body and the mattress to prod at my sex. I've been cleaned, Aziel's cum no longer sticking to me. The skin is sensitive and tender, but it's not unbearable.

Despite the slight ache, I feel really fucking good. My body buzzes with energy, and I feel like I could run a marathon without breaking a sweat. My eyesight and hearing have improved, too. When I focus, I can hear the gears in the fan above my head clicking as they push the blades in motion. It isn't very pleasant, and I'm willing to bet it will take a while to get used to.

I prod between my thighs a bit more before finally moving away.

Aziel was careful not to hurt me, his movements surprisingly soft and gentle despite his generally brutish behavior. I didn't know it was even possible for him to be anything other than rough.

I loved it, and I feel my cheeks warm at the memory. I want

to do it again.

"Aziel?" I call out.

I'm met with silence, and I groan and push up off the mattress.

I stiffen when black sheets meet my eye. These are Aziel's sheets. I blink at them before slowly turning and looking around. Aziel's bedroom looks the same as the last time I was here, with dark décor and moody lighting.

He brought me home.

Aziel's nowhere to be seen, and I hold back a frown as I push the sheets off and climb out of bed. I'm annoyed he didn't ask for permission before bringing me here. I would've said *yes*, but having the option would've been nice.

I didn't even get to say goodbye to Echo.

She's going to wonder where I've gone, and I'm sure she will be sad I'm no longer around to beat with her stick. Although maybe not so much, considering I was intimate with her parents.

Conversation with Kato has been tense since our encounter, and Emily's been practically nonexistent. She usually keeps to herself, but I have a feeling Aziel's presence only exacerbates her absence.

Kato's probably worried Aziel will hurt her.

Aziel's mentioned a few times that she manipulated me, but I don't see it that way. What happened between us was an unfortunate mistake, but I wasn't manipulated.

The floor is cold against my bare feet, and I scratch the back of my neck as I search for something to put on. Aziel left me naked, and I mindlessly poke at the marks he left on my chest and neck as I grab one of his shirts.

His bedroom is messy, clothing scattered about, and I hold back a smile as I lift the shirt to my nose. It smells like Aziel, and I straighten it out and slip it on. I think he'll like seeing me in his clothing.

He seems to have a thing for my smaller size, and I'm pretty sure he'll be turned on by how big his shirt is on me. Sometimes I spot him measuring parts of my body with his, and the action is almost always followed up by him trying to kiss me.

There's still no sign of him anywhere, and I turn and peer into the floor-length mirror before leaving his room. My hair's a mess, and I rush to fix it and calm my racing heart. I want to look good when I see Silas and Gray.

I've got my apology all planned out. Aziel says I should start by clarifying what happened between Kato, Emily, and me, but I don't think I will. Doing that will make me look like I'm making excuses and trying to downplay what I did.

Instead, I intend to apologize and own up to my cheating. I'll make it clear that I know I fucked up, and then I'll beg them to give me another chance.

My palms are sweaty as I fix Aziel's shirt and comb my fingers through my hair one last time. It's now or never.

I straighten my shoulders and keep my chin high as I open Aziel's bedroom door and sneak into the hallway. I've not spent much time here, and I quickly peer around.

Curiosity gets the best of me as I walk to the double doors directly across from his bedroom. I'm not often left alone in his part of the house, and I want to know what Aziel's private space looks like.

My eyes widen as I pull open the doors and am met with the most immense walk-in closet I've ever seen. It's full, and I gawk at the sheer amount of clothing before shutting the doors. I had no idea Aziel owned so many things.

Shaking my head, I move to the room farther down the hallway.

There's no door, just a large archway, and I let out a quiet gasp as I peer inside.

Aziel turned the room into a cozy sitting area. A giant couch is pushed against the far wall, and an expensive-looking television hangs from the ceiling. I didn't take Aziel as a lounging type of person, and I hold my cheeks as I step inside and investigate.

It's hard to imagine him sitting here in his pajamas after a long day of work.

I do a lap of the room, stalling, before working up the courage to seek out Gray and Silas. I can't avoid this forever.

My pulse races as I walk down the long hallway leading to the circular landing at the top of the stairs.

The sound of yelling reaches my ears as I exit Aziel's corridor, and I cock my head to the side as I try to figure out where it's coming from. I recognize the yelling voices as Gray's and Aziel's, but they're speaking in the demonic language, so I can only make out what feels like every tenth word.

They sound pissed, though, and my nerves spike as I tiptoe in their direction. I'm scared of what I will be greeted with as I make my way down the empty corridor nobody ever uses. We were going to build a new bedroom here at one point, but I left before anything was completed.

My heart is pounding out of my chest when I reach the door the yelling is coming from, and with a slow exhale, I push it open and step inside.

Oh.

Gray, Silas, and Aziel are standing at the foot of the most enormous bed I've ever seen. Gray is half-hidden behind a stoic Silas, and Aziel faces them with his typical angry expression. They fall silent as I step inside, and Aziel offers me a soft smile.

I don't know what to make of this, and I clear my throat as Aziel faces me entirely.

"I thought you'd be asleep for a while longer," he says, frowning.

His words go in one ear and out the other as I look around the room. It's been furnished, but it's a complete mess. Pillows and sheets are strewn about, and a large pile of what looks to be my clothing is sitting in a heap in the corner. What happened here?

And why are my clothes on the floor?

I open my mouth, but then I lock eyes with Gray and Silas and freeze. My entire speech disappears from my mind as I look them over, my nerves making it impossible to remember.

Silas isn't showing any emotion, that alone a colossal tell, and Gray looks pissed, his face red and lips pursed.

Aziel blocks my view of them as he approaches. I try to step around him, but he grabs my waist and lifts me in the air before I make it far.

"Hey!" I huff, grabbing his shoulders as he lifts me onto his chest.

He responds by slamming his mouth on mine and pressing me against the door. My body wants to enjoy his touch, this weird urge that I think is the bond pushing me to give in to him, but I fight it and shove at his shoulder.

"Put me down," I say, wanting to talk to Gray and Silas.

This is the first time I've seen them in so long, and Aziel pawing at me isn't exactly the reunion I had in mind.

Aziel growls, literally fucking *growls*, seconds before he squeezes me so tightly that my lungs deflate.

"Mine." Aziel pants, burying his head against my neck. "You're mine."

What is he going on about? It takes every bit of willpower I have to place my hand on Aziel's ear and push his head to the side, clearing up my line of sight.

Gray holds his hand in front of his lips, but I can tell he's fighting back a laugh by the slight shaking of his shoulders. He loves intimacy, and I'm sure he enjoys seeing this despite his anger.

Silas remains unchanged, his arms crossed over his chest as he stares at Aziel and me. He doesn't bother hiding his disgust as his lip curls, and I hold back tears at his disapproval.

"I missed you," I say, clearing my throat.

Silas shuts his eyes and shakes his head, and Gray runs a hand through his hair with a deep exhale. Neither of them looks pleased, and I tap my fingers against Aziel's shoulders as I try to find the right words to say.

"You missed us?" Gray scoffs and looks away. He stares at the wall beside me, avoiding direct eye contact. "I imagine you were too busy fucking the shifters to think about us."

I recoil, shocked by the amount of hatred that seeps into his voice.

Silas licks his lips as I turn to him, waiting to see what he has to say. He only stares, refusing to acknowledge Gray's words. I wasn't expecting them to be happy about my return, but I didn't anticipate this level of vitriol.

It's not like they're perfect, either.

They abandoned me to be raped by Asmod. I cheated, but that punishment doesn't fit the crime.

Aziel cups the back of my head and moans into my neck, utterly oblivious to what's happening between Silas, Gray, and me.

"Look, I know I messed up, but I wasn't *fucking the shifters*," I say.

Aziel licks up the column of my throat, acting absolutely feral. "That's right, my little warrior. Tell them."

"Which shifter *did* you fuck, then?" Silas asks.

I smash my teeth together. "You're staring at the back of the only person I've ever had sex with."

Silas slides his attention to Aziel, a look of shock briefly taking over his features before the expression disappears and he turns back to me.

"The shifter reeked of you, and you were dripping his cum," Gray points out.

I gulp, hesitating, before lifting my chin and meeting their gaze head-on. They deserve the truth, even if it's hard to admit.

"I was intimate with Kato and his mate, Emily. She's a succubus, and I let things go too far. She pleasured Kato, and he touched me with his fingers. When he came, it landed between my thighs," I say, wanting to be honest. "It only happened one time, and I left immediately after. An incubus found me while I was returning to my cabin."

Aziel rubs my back, comforting me as my voice grows thick. I refuse to cry, and I blink away tears as Gray and Silas shift uncomfortably.

"You have no idea how much I regret it. I hate what I did, and I promise nothing like that will ever happen again." My voice cracks, but I ignore it and continue. "I love you two so much, and I know what I did was wrong."

My hands shake as I grab Aziel's shoulders, and I appreciate that he doesn't comment on how clammy my palms have grown.

"Why didn't you let Rock bring you here when you overhead Mammon discussing selling you to the ogres?" Gray asks.

"I was scared," I admit. "I knew you killed Shay and her son, and I was scared of what I'd encounter when I came back here."

Gray shakes his head. "You thought we'd hurt you?"

"I don't know, and it's not like I had much time to think about it. Rock and I needed to leave immediately, and the shifters felt like the safest option."

I clear my throat as both men stare blankly at me, and my pulse begins to race when they don't respond. Gray turns and looks at Silas, and the two have some silent conversation while

Aziel whispers crazy ramblings into my chest.

"I can't do this right now," Gray says, disappearing.

I stare at the spot where he once stood before shifting my focus to Silas. He licks his lips and looks at Aziel, and I wish he weren't so impossible to read.

"I should stay with Gray," he decides. "He's been having a hard time."

He's gone a second later, and I swallow past the lump in my throat as Aziel turns and carries me out of the room. My bottom lip wobbles, and I clutch Aziel's shoulders as I try to wrap my mind around what just happened.

That wasn't how this was supposed to go.

"They'll come around," Aziel says, taking me to my bedroom. "They're surprised to hear you didn't have sex with the shifter, and they're running away to hide their shame over abandoning you."

I clear my throat and wiggle against him. "You don't know that."

Aziel laughs and kisses my temple before setting me on my feet. He steps into my closet and grabs a change of clothes, and I accept them with quiet thanks. I can't remember the last time I wore my own clothes, and I finger the fabric of my leggings before getting dressed.

"We have a busy few months ahead of us," Aziel says, leaning against my dresser. "I'd like you to handle the shifters while I work with Mammon and the elves. Do you think you can do that?"

I blink, struggling to follow what he's saying.

"What?" I give in, asking for clarification.

Aziel grabs my hand and leads me downstairs. It's weird being back, and I stare at the floor as he comes to a halt in front of my office and pushes it open.

The room's been put back together after the dramatic freak-out he had all those weeks ago, and I scan the space before turning back to Aziel.

"I need you to get the shifters to agree to work with us on the female issue, and I also need you to figure out where they've hidden Asmod's body," he says. "Gray doesn't have a strong claim to the throne without it, and the shifters are being weird with it. We need it back. You'll also need to convince them to let me build a portal in their realm. I don't mind taking you there and back, but it'll be easier if you don't have to work seeing them around my schedule."

Aziel grins, his lips pulling back to reveal a set of perfect teeth.

I have no words.

He pats my butt with a laugh before turning and leaving, and I stare at his retreating back with a slack jaw. *What?*

Chapter Twenty-Eight

GRAY

SILAS SETS THE books in his hand on the floor, and I lean back in my chair as he grabs a small pile next to his right foot and stands.

"I don't want to say I told you so, but I did," I say as he sticks the books on the shelf. "I did tell you so."

I sit in a little corner chair in the library and cross my arms over my chest when he doesn't respond. Silas can pretend not to notice me all he wants, but I know he's watching me just as much as I'm watching him.

I'm pissed, mostly at myself, but he's taking it to the next level.

We should've spoken to Charlie, or Aziel, sooner. I feel stupid for what I said to her, and I would've taken a different approach had I known the truth.

Fuck.

I should've been there for Aziel and Charlie's bonding.

I've been planning and thinking about Aziel's virginity for a good hundred years, and I was excited to watch him lose it with Charlie. I'm sure Aziel doesn't care if I was there for his first time, but I wanted to be. I would've been an excellent help.

I slam my foot against the leg of the chair, frustrated. The shifter smelled so much like her, and I jumped to conclusions.

Silas whistles quietly as he reorganizes his shelves, the act within itself indicating his wrecked emotional state. He's changed up his library twice the entire time I've known him, and he spent weeks prepping both times.

Today was a spur-of-the-moment decision, one I'm sure he'll regret when his emotions settle.

I grab a book off the floor and scan the title page before setting it on the table beside my chair. The skin on my hand looks fresh, and I inspect my fingers before glancing at my arm.

Silas has been good about feeding me, and I would like to know if that will change now that Aziel and Charlie are back—especially if we're kicked out of our room. Aziel is dead set on us leaving so he and Charlie can share it, but he's in for a rude awakening if he thinks I'm giving up the room without a fight.

Charlie's half our size, and the two of them can easily fit in his bed. Silas and I need the extra space.

My jaw clenches at the memory of Aziel's wide, hurt eyes when he realized the room was occupied. He's already pissed at me for leaving, and us taking up residence in the wing we built together only further aggravates the situation.

I kick the leg of the chair again.

Aziel even let her mark him, claiming him in the spot I've wanted for years.

He didn't even bother hiding it, practically flaunting the little human bite mark on his neck when he returned. I can't believe the damn thing even stuck, and I lift my hand to prod at the spot where Charlie once bit me for fun. It healed in minutes.

I'll cover the mark she left on Aziel with mine someday, and my teeth will sink in much further than her flat ones.

"Emily instigated," I say as Silas changes his mind on the shelf he's spent the past hour on. "You know how hard it can be to turn down intimacy with a succubus."

Silas rips the books off it at a tenth of the speed it took him to place them there, and I wince as a few land awkwardly on the floor. He'll be upset about that when he's done pretending he doesn't have feelings.

Silas treasures his books, and ruining them is seen as treason in his mind.

"Emily is strong, but she wouldn't send Charlie into a frenzy," he argues, turning his back to me. "Charlie would have gotten a little high, enough for her inhibitions to lower, but not enough for her to lose control. Succubus or not, Charlie still cheated."

I raise a brow.

Charlie seems genuinely apologetic, and I liked listening to her promise she's going to earn our forgiveness, both me and my inner incubus turning to putty at the words. Nobody's ever fought for us before.

I throw my head back and stare at the ceiling. Saying something and showing something are two different things, and Charlie's promises of affection don't mean anything when she follows it up by cheating on us.

Even if Aziel is confident she'll never do it again.

He's been wild since returning, constantly walking around with his dick reeking of her.

"She and Aziel are bonded, and we need to find a way to coexist." The words are bitter on my tongue, but I force them out anyway.

Silas turns to me with a frown, his eyes scanning over my form before he approaches and snatches the book I was fiddling with earlier. He's so fucking grumpy.

"That's fine. I have some work I need to get done with the

dragons, anyway, so I'll probably be gone for a while," he mutters. "I'm sure she'll be long swollen with his baby by the time I return, and they'll have a set routine by then that I can work around."

I straighten, my body tensing. Silas promised not to leave me, and I'll kill him if he tries to up and disappear. I'm willing to bet Aziel won't let it happen, either, the man adamant in his claims that Silas and I are now his males.

We're on a short leash, and he'll drag us back if we stray too far from Wrath.

"Aziel won't let you do that," I say.

As angry as Aziel is at me, he's twice as pissed at Silas.

Aziel's never expected much from me, and it's well-known that I tend to have strong reactions to situations that might not always call for one. Silas, though, has always been the voice of reason. He's calm, and he thinks things through before making decisions.

"Say you won't leave," I demand. "If you try, I'll follow, and you don't want me in the dragon realm. I'll make a mess of everything, and you'll spend the entire time trying to keep me from getting my head bit off."

Silas raises a brow. His lips twitch as he fights a smile, and after a second, he blows out a slow breath and nods. We both know I'm being serious.

"Very well."

I open my mouth to make him say more, but the sound of Charlie's hurried footsteps distracts me. She doesn't so much as look in the doorway as she rushes past, the female making a pointed effort not to acknowledge us.

Silas and I both watch her pass.

"She's been busy these past few days," Silas acknowledges.

I'm aware of that.

Just because we haven't been speaking doesn't mean I'm not

keeping tabs on every little thing she does. I try not to, but I can't help myself.

"Aziel's taking her to the shifter lands tonight," Silas continues.

That I did *not* know. I gesture for him to explain, but he only shrugs before returning his focus to his books.

Why would Aziel be taking her to the shifters?

I know he has her working on a list of tasks, but I don't see why she needs to go to the shifter lands to complete them. Aziel has a phone she can use, and he gave her a laptop so she could communicate through email.

The shifters have fucking email, don't they?

Most species picked up the human form of communication over a hundred years ago, and it's widely used across most realms. They should have fucking email.

Silas sighs as I stand and leave the library, and I hear him following me as I storm to Aziel's office. Silas steps into the room behind me and leans against the wall.

"Yes?" Aziel asks.

"Why are you going to the shifter lands?"

Aziel shoots Silas a hard look before turning back to me. "Charlie and I are going to be speaking to them about their alliance with Mammon," he explains.

I tap my foot against the ground. We've been handling the female issue as a group, and I don't like that he's segmenting the work.

"And why didn't you inform me?" I ask.

"Are you about ready to—" Charlie's voice trails off as she steps into the room and sees Silas and me.

Her cheeks turn impossibly red, and I gulp as I notice a giant piece of hair she forgot to put in her ponytail. My fingers twitch with the need to fix it, and it takes everything in me to hold back.

She cheated on me, on all of us, and I'm not going to forgive her just because she's cute and soft. No amount of apologies will remove the shifter's touch from her, and I don't trust her not to do it again when she feels lonely.

My heart aches as Aziel grins at her. He's so childlike in his love, and I hope she doesn't end up hurting him.

Cheaters don't change, and I suck my lips into my mouth as Charlie approaches his desk. She appears so fucking genuine as she looks at him, but I refuse to be fooled by it. Not again. She looked at Silas and me the same way once upon a time—she still does—yet she had no issues letting another man and woman touch her.

Silas's hand on my waist settles me slightly, and I lean against his chest for more. I'm sure it's not fun for him to watch me obsess after the female who betrayed us, but I can't help it.

"Come here, Silas," Aziel orders.

What the fuck does he want with Silas? Silas frowns as I pull away, his eyebrows furrowing as he steps forward and approaches Aziel. I watch them through narrowed eyes, not trusting Aziel as far as I can throw him.

He's in one of his moods, and while I usually enjoy his conniving side, it's not so fun when directed at me.

Aziel smirks and makes eye contact with me as he grabs Silas and pulls him in for a kiss. He stands as he does so, and he curls his fingers into Silas's thick hair before yanking it like Charlie always did.

I know what he's doing.

Silas lets it happen, his back stiff as he grabs the sides of his pants and clenches the material. He doesn't know what to make of Aziel, his logic and emotions in two different places. Aziel's made it clear we're his males, and I'm sure he's having a fun time forcing us to realize it.

Aziel pivots so I can see as he slips his tongue into Silas's mouth, claiming it as his own before he pulls away with a smirk. He's looking at me again, silently challenging me to say something about it.

"Are you all right?" he teases, glancing at my hips.

He thinks I'm the weak link, but I refuse to prove him right as I place my hands over my bulge. It's none of his business whether or not I'm hard.

Charlie clears her throat and stares intently at the paperwork on Aziel's desk. She's been holed up in her office the entire day, scouring over forms and old documents from the female transition facilities we put in place years ago.

Aziel smirks as he notices me staring at her.

"Charlie and I will be gone for a few hours," he says, smoothing Silas's eyebrow with his thumb.

Silas returns to me, and I cross my arms over my chest as Charlie grabs her things. She struggles to hold all the paperwork, and Aziel quickly swoops in to carry them.

I raise a brow, surprised by his chivalrous behavior, before recoiling when she yanks them out of his arms and holds them to her chest. Oh?

"I can carry my things," she insists. "Thank you, though."

Silas and I blink, dumbfounded, as Aziel snatches them back before cupping her chin and forcing her to look into his eyes. I expect her to cry at his rough behavior, but she holds his glare with an equally vicious one of her own.

Charlie's always been sassy, but this feels different.

"Will you catch us meat for tonight?" Aziel asks.

I have to step back, my mind unable to wrap around what the fuck is happening right now.

Charlie's the first to break, her lips twitching before spreading into a full-blown smile. Silas looks just as confused as I feel, which is good. These two are being weird.

"You want me to?" Charlie asks.

Aziel nods, grinning. "Yes. I'll also teach you how to hunt on these lands if you'd like. The animals are bigger, so I don't want you going alone, but I'm sure one of us will always be happy to accompany you." He grabs her hips and spins her around.

Charlie bounces on her heels, clearly excited as she turns to Silas and me.

"Do you two want to come with us?" she asks, looking hopeful. "I'd love to show you my cabin and traps."

Her *what?*

"I'm busy, but I'd like to speak to Charlie before you two leave," Silas says.

Charlie's lips twitch, her hope poorly hidden as she nods and turns to me. I clear my throat, debating, before shaking my head. Being around her isn't good for me, and I need space to think.

Although it would have been nice to be invited from the beginning.

Her visible hurt makes my pulse race, and I rush out of the room before I can change my mind. I don't know what Silas wants to speak with her about, but I'm sure he'll fill me in later.

Chapter Twenty-Nine

CHARLOTTE

SILAS FOLLOWS ME into my office, and I tug on the hem of my shirt as I push open the door and walk around my desk.

Aziel shouts Gray's name before his footsteps quicken into a slow jog, but I don't try to eavesdrop on their conversation as I turn to Silas.

He's wearing his usual formal attire, and I can't help but notice the slight wrinkles in his pants and shirt. Silas is always so uptight about his clothing, and the lack of care in his outfit is shocking. His hair looks a bit unkempt, too, the shorter strands I love to run my fingers through now long enough to cover his ears.

I gulp and sit in my chair as he scans my office. Should I sit or stand? I'm not sure what's appropriate.

Silas doesn't seem to care either way, his attention darting from the items on my desk to the wall of photos behind me. Most are random flowers and objects I've collected over the years. Gray helped me frame them a long time ago.

Silas takes his time looking each one over, though, an action he's done dozens of times. His lips purse as he pauses on one, and I can tell by the clenching of his jaw that it's the photo of him,

Gray, and Aziel. I found it while snooping around Gray's office, and after a good thirty minutes of giggling, I convinced the incubus to help me hang it up.

Aziel and Silas look less-than-excited as they stand on either side of a beaming Gray, both men clearly having been forced to take the photo. Gray has a hand around each of their waists, holding them tightly while they visibly squirm.

They look awkward, but it's still one of my favorites. I know Silas felt complimented when I hung it up long ago.

He pushes a piece of hair out of his face before sitting opposite my desk, his attention finally moving to me.

I haven't been alone with him or Gray since returning, and the unknown has me wary. I knew coming back would be challenging, but I never expected this. My hands clench into fists at the memory of Gray and Silas's painful judgment, and I move my arms below my desk to keep them hidden.

When another minute goes by and Silas doesn't speak, I glance at the clock and fidget. The shifters are expecting Aziel and me soon, and I don't want to keep them waiting.

My tongue darts out to wet my lips as Silas scans the files on my desk.

"I want to apologize," he finally says, clasping his hands over his lap.

I'm shocked, and I stiffen in my seat as the words filter through my brain.

"It was wrong for me to abandon you in Lust," he continues, clearing his throat. "I'm sorry."

He gives me a moment to collect myself, watching silently as I push my hair behind my ears. I didn't think I'd get an apology, and I appreciate it.

"Why did you?" I ask.

I'm not going to like his answer, but I need to hear it. His actions are ones I'd expect from Gray, the incubus prone to emotional decisions, but not Silas. He's always the voice of reason, thinking through and weighing the consequences of everything he does.

"Rock came to get us right after you were taken. The shifter was there, and I was angry when I smelled you on him and realized you'd been intimate. I thought you had sex with him, and I got into a fight with Aziel about it." Silas pauses to run a hand down his face. "I was embarrassed and felt dumb, so I left."

I nod, happy to have an answer, even if it isn't one I like. I never would've abandoned them in a dangerous situation like that. My actions are inexcusable, but so is leaving me to be abused and raped in Lust.

"Did you regret it before discovering what happened between Kato, Emily, and me?" I ask.

My knees knock together as I wait for a response. I worry he only feels bad because he was wrong, but I think he should regret it either way. Even if I had had sex with Kato, his punishment doesn't fit the crime.

I cheated, yes, but that doesn't mean I deserve a lifetime of being abused by Asmod. Especially when it would've been so easy to save me.

It's not like it was a lot of work. It took Aziel, Kato, and Chev less than an hour, and considering the demons live practically forever, that's a quick task.

"Yes, I regretted it before I knew the truth. I knew Aziel was capable of getting you back himself, and I used that to justify my actions," he admits. "It's not an excuse, though, and I should've stayed to help even if I wasn't needed."

Instinctively, I move to fiddle with my necklace, but I pause when I remember it's no longer there.

Silas follows the action, his eyebrows furrowing as he spots my bare neck. He seems to want to comment on it, but I interject before he has the opportunity.

"Would you have left if Aziel hadn't been there?" I ask.

I'm met with silence, Silas's attention still captured by my bare neck.

"Of course not. Where'd your necklace go?" he asks, changing the subject. "You should be wearing it always."

I touch the skin between my collarbones, missing the weight of the stone. I wonder if he'd make me another if I asked, but I have a feeling I already know the answer. He was bedridden as a result of the first time, and I doubt he'd be willing to endure that again.

Especially given he can barely even look me in the eye right now.

"I used it," I say, flushing.

I don't remember all the details, but I know I slammed it into Asmod's neck just like Silas taught me. I don't like to think about the aftermath, but I'm pretty proud of the first half of his death. I protected myself against a demon royal without any help.

Silas looks shocked, his eyes widening before he tapers the expression back down. "When?"

I straighten up, my chest puffing. "I used it on Asmod. It turns out I didn't need Aziel to save me, and I killed—" I start, squeaking when Silas lunges over my desk and slaps a hand over my mouth.

I blink, dumbfounded, as he looks around and moves closer. I'm sure my heart's about to beat out of my chest as he brings his lips to my ear, his warm breath tickling the skin.

"No, Charlie. I'm a fate, and the death of a demon royal is a fated action. It throws things off-balance," he hisses, his voice so low I can barely hear it despite his proximity. "Aziel killed him, and he's the one who will face repercussions. Never speak about what happened again. Not to me, not to Gray, not to anybody."

A bead of sweat drips down my inner arm as I nod. Silas doesn't move for a long moment, his cheek pressing against mine before he tightens his grip and curses. I didn't realize it was supposed to be a secret.

That would've been helpful for Aziel to mention at some point.

Sometimes I think he forgets how new I am to this world, and the things that may seem obvious to him aren't always so to me.

Silas looks in pain when he finally pulls away, his hand cautiously sliding from my mouth as he drops to his knees between my thighs. I wish I could read his thoughts like Aziel can. It'd be a huge help when he's being all weird.

"Tell me exactly what happened that day," he requests, grabbing my wrists.

I gulp, feeling like this is some test. He just told me not to speak about it.

"Asmod took me to his bedroom. I used my necklace, which knocked him out. Aziel came storming in shortly after and killed him. He stabbed him with a knife he found on the floor before taking me back to the shifter lands," I lie, hoping this is what he's looking for.

Silas nods, tapping his temple before his eyes glaze over and roll back. I forget he's got a whole world inside his brain, and I try to contain my fear as I stare at his blank, empty face. His hold on me remains, preventing me from moving until he blinks and refocuses on me.

The panicked look in his eye is gone as he lets out a deep exhale. His chin lowers to his chest before he tilts his head to the side and cracks his neck, the bones popping underneath his skin. It sounds gross, and I cringe at the unusual behavior.

Silas going to the fated world isn't uncommon, but the weird behavior he displays the few seconds after returning always has my heart racing. It's like he's a different person, and he has to take some time to return to the Silas I've grown to know.

He's a fate before he's Silas, and every time I forget, he does something to remind me.

"Thank you," he says, squeezing my wrists before releasing me.

He looks a bit guilty as he steps away and gives me space. I'm surprised Aziel didn't come busting in when he felt my fear, but I figure he trusts Silas enough to give us alone time.

"You're trying to get yourself killed, Charlie," Silas mutters, running another shaking hand through his hair before moving to my office door.

With his back to me, I feel like I can finally breathe, and I scramble to my feet before he can leave. This is the only real interaction we've had since I returned, and I don't want it to go to waste. I appreciate his apology, and I don't want to fight anymore.

I want to be his female. I want to be together like he and Gray always talked about—all four of us.

"I'm sorry, too," I say, rushing up behind him. "I made an awful mistake, one I know I can never take back, but you have no idea how much I regret it. I love you, Silas."

I place my hand on the small of his back when he doesn't turn around to face me, and I wait a minute for him to push me away before sliding my fingertips underneath the fabric of his shirt.

He's as soft as ever, and I place the flat of my palm against his spine before wrapping it around his waist. His abs are hard underneath my fingers, and I put my hand over them as I press my cheek against his back.

I hold him as tears fill my eyes, and I sniffle quietly before continuing.

"I told myself you and Gray didn't care for me and that our

relationship was already over because of my leaving," I whisper into his spine. "I thought I'd find myself if I experienced intimacy outside of you guys, but I was wrong. I was wrong, Silas, and I'm so fucking sorry."

He spins, his shirt twisting around his torso as it catches on my thumb. I readjust my hold, letting his shirt fall back into place, before sticking my chin into his sternum and looking up at him. He looks pained, the sight of his sadness intensifying my guilt.

I don't want him to hurt, especially because of me.

"Fuck, Charlie," Silas grunts, his hands barely grazing my hips. "I can't."

I can feel his heart hammering in his chest, the muscle getting a workout with how hard it's beating.

"And I know that's so fucking selfish, considering all the shitty things I've done to you, but every time I look at your face, I see his, and when you touch me, even like this, I think about how much more potent your scent was on him than it will be on me when you let go." His vulnerability is shocking.

I release him and step away. "Then put my scent on you," I offer, backing into my desk and spreading my legs.

I'm sore and don't like the idea of having anything inside me right now, but I'll do it for Silas.

He smiles, but it doesn't reach his eyes. "I'm not Aziel, Charlie. Claiming you won't make me feel better. I want to co-exist with you, and I want to help the females and earn my forgiveness for my wrongdoings, but I can't look you in the eye and tell you I'll ever be open to a relationship again."

Silas sucks his bottom lip into his mouth, his eyes lingering where my necklace once sat.

"I'll have a new one made for you," he promises, clasping his hands behind his back before nodding to himself and leaving.

I stare at his retreating form, trying and succeeding to keep any tears from leaking out of my eyes. I appreciate his apology, and I know Silas will forgive me with time.

He has to.

I'm serious about wanting him and Gray, and even if they don't believe it now, they will eventually. I've got lifetimes to prove it now that I'm bonded with Aziel, and I can be patient.

Aziel comes wandering in a minute later, his expression cautious as he evaluates me. I'm sure he heard every word between Silas and me, and I shake my head to signal that I don't want to speak about it.

I know this puts him in a weird position, and I don't want him to feel like he has to take sides. Gray's got to be ecstatic with Aziel finally accepting their bond, and I don't want to make Aziel feel guilty for connecting with his males.

"How'd it go with Gray?" I ask.

Aziel shrugs, trying to hold back a smile. His lips are puffy, which I'm taking as a good sign.

He's made it his mission to annoy Gray as much as possible these past few days, and it seems to be working. I don't quite understand it, but they've always had a weird relationship, so I'm not questioning them.

I told Aziel to sleep with them last night instead of me, but he's insisting on waiting until I'm also welcome to join. I feel guilty, but Aziel isn't one to be pressured into doing something he doesn't want.

"Are you ready to go?" he asks, stepping forward and wrapping his arms around my waist.

I grab my documents and bury my face in his chest until we're in the shifter lands.

Aziel taps my back to signal the transition is over, and I do my best to push thoughts of Silas out of my head as I drag Aziel toward Kato's cabin.

He squeezes my clammy palm with a slight smile, seemingly unconcerned about the sweat accumulating due to the warm air and his tight grip. I know he notices it, our skin contact uncomfortably slick.

We make it two steps before I trip over a root, but Aziel quickly catches me.

"Let me hold these." He laughs and takes the documents out of my arms.

I thought being bonded with Aziel would help me be smooth on my feet, but it hasn't helped. I want to be like a mountain goat, climbing the trickiest terrain with ease. Instead, I'm like a bull in a china shop, tripping over everything and embarrassing myself.

"Are you going to be on your best behavior?" I ask, worried about Aziel and Kato being in a room together.

Aziel pinches my butt.

"What are Silas and Gray thinking? About me?" I pry, changing the subject.

I want to know how effective my apologies are, and Aziel's got the inside scoop. Silas seemed receptive to my apologies and touch earlier, but Gray's impossible to read.

"You know I'm not going to tell you that," Aziel scolds, pulling me against his side when Kato's cabin comes into view.

I frown, growing desperate for help. "I won't tell anybody."

Aziel shoots me a sideways glance, his eyebrow quirked. He's getting a kick out of this, and I'm sure he's secretly enjoying not being involved. For once, there's trouble in the house that he isn't the cause of.

How lucky for him.

"My males are entitled to their private thoughts and feelings just as you are, my nosy warrior." He chuckles. "Although maybe I'll feel generous if you let me into your head."

Would it be that bad to let him in? It's not like I've got a lot to hide, and I do like the idea of hearing and speaking to him through my mind. Still, it feels like a recipe for disaster. Aziel's nosy, and I just know he'd constantly be in my head.

Aziel seems to sense my softening stance as he ducks and brings his lips to my ear.

"It would let me enter your dreams as Gray does," he says.

I suck in a shaky breath, my resolve slowly crumbling as I shake my head. Not today.

Aziel huffs but doesn't push the issue as we arrive at Kato's cabin. My pulse races as I stare at the door, and with a slow, nervous inhale, I knock.

I'm pulled against Aziel's chest in a heartbeat, his possessiveness getting the best of him as he wraps his arms around my belly and holds me in place. I'm sure he wants to push me behind him, but he's smart enough to choose the tight hold instead.

I'm not some toy he can move around whenever he pleases.

The door opens to reveal a brooding Kato. Aziel tightens his hold as the shifter smiles and steps outside, cutting off the view of a crying Emily. I recoil, worried about what's got her so upset.

Emily's usually full of smiles, the woman hard to bring down.

"She's upset she's not allowed to speak to you," Kato explains. "She feels awful about everything that happened, and she wants to apologize."

I frown. "Why can't she speak to me?"

Kato doesn't immediately respond, but the way his eyes slide to Aziel is answer enough. My jaw clenches as I turn to face the Wrath, annoyed with his involvement. I've told him repeatedly that what happened isn't Emily's fault. She made my desire grow, yes, but I was still in control.

I open my mouth to explain that again, but I fall silent when Kato steps forward and places a hand on Aziel's shoulder. Aziel goes rigid, his expression turning cold.

"Can I help you?" he spits.

Kato shrugs, doubling down on his hold. "Take me to the meeting cave."

I suck in my cheeks to stop from laughing. I've never seen anybody tell Aziel what to do before, let alone try to use him as a mode of transportation. My fingers hook into the Wrath's pants, subtly holding him still as his black eyes narrow.

"Why the fuck did you tell us to meet you here if the meeting's at the cave?" Aziel snaps, shoving Kato's hand off him.

Kato frowns, looking offended, before placing his hand back on Aziel. "There was a last-minute change of plans. I don't want the wolf shifters on my land, and they didn't tell me they were coming until today. Come on, Aziel. We don't want to be late." Annoyance takes over his features.

My gaspy breath is loud, drawing the attention of both males. Kato looks confused as he stares at me, the poor shifter not realizing how inappropriate this is. Demons aren't pack animals, and they don't help one another the same way the shifters do.

"I don't want to be late," I say, shrinking when Aziel's glare turns to me.

He's frustrated, but helping the females is more important than his dislike for Kato. It's bigger than all of us.

Aziel licks his lips before lifting his hand and pressing his thumb against my mouth. I know what he's doing, and my cheeks warm as he adds pressure until I open and let him in. He presses against my tongue, stroking the muscle with the pad of his thumb.

I can't believe he's doing this in front of Kato.

"I'm going to put my cock in your mouth when we get home," Aziel says. "Do you want that?"

My teeth graze against his skin as he pulls his thumb out and squeezes our bond. My knees buckle, but he easily supports my weight.

Kato stares at the sky.

"Do you want that, Charlie?" Aziel repeats.

I clench my jaw, hating the way his actions turn me on. "Yes."

Aziel grins and squeezes our bond one last time before the world disappears.

He grinds his teeth as the mountain solidifies around us, but he otherwise shows no reaction. The shifters are heavy, and I know they take a lot of energy to transport. Kato hardly seems thankful as he pats Aziel on the shoulder and heads inside the mouth of the cave.

I move to follow, but a hand wrapping around my arm stops me.

My pulse races as Aziel leans over me from behind, his breath tickling my ear.

"That's the last bit of leniency you're getting from me," he warns. "Next time, I'm bending you over and making him watch you beg for my cock."

Aziel holds a lot of anger toward Kato and Emily, and I don't blame him. I'd feel similar if I were in his position. I just wish I knew how to fix it. We have to work together to help the females, and it will be best if we find a way to coexist.

Aziel kisses my temple before he grabs my hand and leads me inside. The cave's just as intimidating as it was the first time I was here, and I force myself not to show any fear. My eyesight is better now, and I shiver at the sheer number of spiders lining the wall. Absolutely terrifying.

Aziel squeezes my hand as we reach the opening of the meeting room, and I spot Kato and Chev the second we step inside. They nod in my direction as the other shifter leaders stand and greet me. Some even wear smiles.

"Thank you all for coming," I say, clearing my throat when my voice comes out shaky.

I need to sound confident. Taking my papers from Aziel, I plaster a smile on my face as I bring them to the center of the table. The shifters move immediately, taking their seats and grabbing a sheet.

"I want to discuss your alliance with Mammon," I continue, moving to sit.

Aziel pulls me onto his lap before my butt makes contact with the wooden chair. He wraps his arms around my stomach and rests his hands on my lap, and I debate insisting on sitting in my own chair before accepting my fate with a low sigh.

I've seen the shifters do this with their female mates many times, and that knowledge is the only thing that keeps me from feeling completely humiliated. This is normal for them, and nobody even seems to notice I'm sitting on Aziel's lap.

Kato clears his throat and turns to a man I haven't met before. Behind his long, messy, black hair are startlingly bright green eyes, but they're full of poorly concealed anger. I'm surprised by the outward hostility, and I hold my ground and stare right back.

Aziel tightens his fists on my lap, but he doesn't intervene.

Progress.

"Leave," Kato orders the man.

The man's frown deepens as he turns to Kato.

"I have every right to be here," he argues.

Nobody speaks up to defend him, and after a few moments, Kato repeats the order. The man still doesn't move, but he hurries to his feet when Chev stands. I watch silently, not understanding what's going on.

Chev ushers the man out before posting up by the door, probably to ensure the man doesn't try to sneak back in. I'm not surprised Chev's acting as the muscle. His mixture of shifter and demon blood makes him an absolute unit.

"That was Vont. My brother and Mammon's mate," Kato

explains, gesturing for me to continue.

I glance nervously at the doorway. What stops him from running to Mammon and telling her we're here?

"He knows to keep his mouth shut. Please continue," Kato says, shooting me a not-so-subtle thumbs-up.

At least somebody's on my side.

"We know you've aligned yourselves with Mammon, but I believe we're in a better spot to help the females." I pause and look around, letting that information sink in. "She doesn't truly have the females' best interest in mind, and her trying to sell me to the ogres is proof of that."

The shifters readjust at the mention of Mammon's plan to sell me. They've all been informed, and they aren't pleased.

"The Wraths have implemented several successful rehabilitation f-facilities, and we'd l-love for you to look at them before moving any further with Mammon." I trip over a few words, stammering slightly with nerves, but my voice is smooth and even for the most part.

Aziel grabs a cup of water belonging to the shifter next to us and holds it out for me to take. I blush, glancing at the man who's had his beverage stolen, but he doesn't seem to care. He's one of the ones who like me.

My hand shakes as I accept the cup and sip, hydrating my throat.

"We've compiled a list of the facilities and the number of females we helped. There's also an itemized list of costs and a detailed outline of the process used," I say, pointing to the papers I handed out earlier. "Everything should be in the papers you've got in your hands."

Aziel runs his fingers up and down my thighs, the touch comforting. He sniffs the back of my neck, too, but I pretend I don't notice as I fold my hands together on the table.

"Why should we believe a word you say?" a shifter at the far end of the table asks. "That question is directed at Aziel," he's quick to clarify when the man behind me lets out a low, threatening hum.

I grab Aziel's wrists, squeezing my nails into them as he sucks in a slow, deep breath. He's doing one of his breathing exercises.

"I'm not asking you to trust Aziel. I'm asking you to trust me," I answer for him. "We've spent much time together these past few weeks, and you know I wouldn't be sitting here if I didn't believe in Aziel."

My words are met with silence, which I don't think is a good sign.

Aziel chimes in. "We're not asking you to commit to anything today. I can arrange for my men to come in a few days and bring you to Wrath to look at the facilities yourself."

The shifters murmur amongst themselves, flipping through the report before coming back with detailed questions only Aziel can answer. I'm grateful for how much knowledge Aziel has on this, and I have a feeling he did some refreshing before coming.

He's so busy, and I like that he took time out of his day to read over the reports and familiarize himself with them. It looks good for us when he has all the information ready.

After much debate, the shifters agree to visit the facility. Some are hesitant, but at least they're giving us a chance.

It's all we can ask for.

The bond between Aziel and me hums at my excitement, radiating through me and into him. He responds with pride, and I have to hold my chest at the intensity of it. I'm still not used to the feeling of the bond, its presence weird and foreign.

"You did well today," Chev says as the shifters filter out of the cave.

He steps away from his position by the entrance, slowly

approaching until he's close enough to knock his knuckles against my temple. The touch makes me grin, happy with the action I've learned to associate with him.

Chev hesitates as he stares at Aziel, his fist hovering in the air, before he does the same to the Wrath. Aziel grunts and moves away, but Chev doesn't seem to mind the less-than-friendly reaction.

"How would you two feel about us building a portal in my cabin?" I blurt out. "That way, we can meet without needing Aziel to transport me back and forth."

Kato and Chev lock eyes before Kato gestures for Chev to answer.

"Let me think about it," Chev says, sounding hesitant.

I nod, happy with that. It's not a no.

"Kato will not be welcome to use it," Aziel interjects.

Kato frowns, looking mildly offended.

Aziel doesn't seem to care as he picks me up and carries me out of the cave. I overhear Kato brag to Chev that Aziel's warming up to him as we leave, and I roll my eyes at the plotting of the two men as Aziel brings me to my traps.

They're empty, and we find fresh nuts to place inside.

"Silas is stressed about his books," Aziel says after a long moment of silence. "He doesn't like the disarray, and he's frantic about how long it's taking him to put them back. Gray's angry because he feels you're trying harder with Silas than you are with him, but more than that, he's upset you haven't been lusting over him. It's a product of our bond, and he knows that, but it still hurts his feelings. I'd recommend starting there with them."

I freeze, my fingers on the latch of my trap, before I spin and throw myself at Aziel.

Chapter Thirty

SILAS

CHARLIE'S MOP OF messy, brown hair is hard not to notice as she peers at me from behind the bookshelf, her actions not nearly as sneaky as she seems to think they are.

She's taken it upon herself to watch me lately, her bare feet quietly pattering around the house whenever she's not working with the shifters. I don't know what to make of it, and I hate how it makes my body warm.

I pretend I don't notice her, but I can't stop myself from spinning in her direction when she continues to stare.

Her eyes widen when she realizes she's been spotted.

She squeaks and darts back behind the shelf, and I hold back a smile as I walk down the aisle and peer around the corner. Her knees are bent so she's low to the ground, the stance taught to her by the shifters.

It does nothing to help her blend in.

"Are you okay?" I ask, stepping back to give her space.

She stands, her cheeks turning red under my gaze. The human truly believed I didn't know she was there? Cute.

"Do you need help?" she asks, ignoring my question.

My lips purse as I debate what to say, and I turn to look at the mess that's become my library. I don't know why I decided to redo it, and I'm seconds away from giving up on the entire thing and lighting a fire.

It's not productive, and I'm wasting too much time here when I should be working on my dragon issue. They stole some gems from my favorite mage, and he's refusing to make another stone for Charlie until I get it back. He's lucky I consider him a friend; otherwise, I'd send Aziel after him for denying me.

I cock my head to the side and watch Charlie squirm.

I'm not doing a very good job keeping my distance from her, and she's not trying to make it easier for me. My fingers twitch as I fight the urge to touch her, scared of the slippery slope that's sure to lead to.

"Can you help me put my books up on the shelves? I've already got them organized by genre." I gesture to the piles on the floor. "I like them to be ordered alphabetically by author."

Charlie nods as I explain exactly what I want her to do, her nose crinkling as she attempts to memorize my every word. I appreciate the care she takes to do it right, and I only monitor for a few minutes to ensure she's got it down before returning to my organizing.

I should've never messed with the library in the first place.

The silence between us is comfortable as we work, the quiet a welcome change from the conversation Gray's always trying to force on me. I love the incubus, but sometimes it feels like he doesn't have an off switch.

I frown as I grab a book and notice the bent cover, the precious object damaged during my aggressive unshelving. Lowering myself to the floor, I sit cross-legged and get to work fixing it without causing further damage.

When Charlie clears her throat and crawls over to me, I pause and give her my attention. Her cheeks are tinted pink as she holds a book for me to look at.

"This one doesn't fit in the pile," she says, pointing to the stack she's working on.

I glance between the pile and her book, scanning the cover, before agreeing.

"You're right. Thanks for catching that," I say, grabbing and setting the book on the floor next to me.

I'm unsure where the gnome pile is off the top of my head, and I'll have to search for it after I finish fixing my bent cover.

Charlie holds back a smile as she leans forward to look at the book in my hand, the action moving her hair around her shoulders. My nostrils flare as I inhale her scent, its sweetness tinted with Aziel.

I wonder if she knows she's pregnant, but I decide not to say anything in case she doesn't. He's been loud in his desire to fill her with his children, so at this point, I'd be surprised if she hasn't started to suspect.

They're not using protection, and he's been finishing in her regularly.

I inhale, searching for and finding the cum that lives inside her even now. Last night I heard her moan Gray's name while Aziel took her, the action surprising. I was even more shocked when Aziel continued, teasing her for thinking of Gray when he was balls-deep inside her.

Gray sure seemed to like it if his aggressive masturbating was anything to go by. The man practically lunged at me when she cried his name for the second time, his mouth on my cock to muffle his moans.

I didn't comment on the wet spot he forced me to sleep on afterward, Gray covering my side of the bed with his arousal before happily rolling to the dry area.

Fucking incubus.

My lips purse when Charlie traces the cracked book cover with her fingertip, the scent of the baby inside her hitting me again. It'll be months before she begins to show, and I can't wait. My pulse quickens at the thought of her swollen belly, instinct pushing me to lock her away in a room where she can't be hurt.

It's a miracle Aziel hasn't done so already. I can tell it angers him to watch her run back and forth between our estate and the shifter lands, but he's been good about keeping his possessive urges at bay.

I've been doing a lot of research on human pregnancies, and I stare in wonder at the sliver of belly exposed at the bottom of her shirt. I hope Charlie gets the stretch marks her kind is prone to. I'd like her to carry a physical reminder of the presents she gives us.

My chest aches. The presents she'll give Aziel.

My body responds to the thought of her being pregnant with my baby, and I shift to hide it from her. Little Wraths will be cute, but fates are known to be the most well-behaved children. It's in our genes, our temperament calm for the sake of keeping balance in the world.

I wonder if she'll be upset when her children come out with no human traits. Our demonic genes will overpower all of hers, leaving them with nothing that resembles her. Maybe the sclera of their eyes will be white instead of black, the color not meaning much in terms of genetic progression.

Probably not.

Still, I think she'd love fate babies the most. Wraths will eat her alive, just as incubi will.

Charlie will be a good mother, though, and I'm sure Aziel will ensure their children don't overrun her. I'm happy to help, too, and Gray will provide them with good entertainment.

My eyes slide away from her stomach as she returns to her

pile. I wonder if she'd be open to letting me put a baby inside her after she's had time to heal and adjust to Aziel's.

My anger flares at the thought, and I wince as the cover in my hands further cracks.

Fuck.

I don't deserve to put a baby in Charlie. She may accept my apology, but I don't. I ignored her safety for my own selfish reasons, and that action doesn't deserve forgiveness. At least not yet.

Even when I do atone for my mistakes, I still can't give her my trust. It gives her another weapon to stab me with, and I'm still bleeding from the first.

"Thanks for all your help," I say after an hour of silence.

Charlie hums and turns to me with a grin. Her eyes dart to the clock on the wall, and I know it's about time for her to leave. The shifters will be here soon, and she doesn't want to keep them waiting.

She's been working tirelessly to get everything ready for them, even going as far as to send Aziel out like an errand boy to kill and bring back Ucka. He dragged Gray with him, and it took everything in me not to laugh at Gray's horrified eyes when they came back with three in tow.

It probably would've been good for Aziel to warn him they scream like children when being killed.

Still, it's a delicacy I'm sure the shifters will be excited to eat. They usually hunt in large groups to bring one down, and they're rarely successful.

Charlie stands and wipes her hands on her pants, the action one of anxiety, and I find myself doing the same as she approaches.

"Thanks for letting me help you," she says.

I shrug. She's careful with my books, and I enjoy the

company.

My lip twitches as she steps forward and invades my space. The logical part of my brain screams at me to move away and stop her advance, but the emotional part of me I've been working hard to ignore keeps me still as she grabs my shoulders and lowers to her knees to kiss me.

I'm holding her hips before I can stop myself, and I tilt my head upward so she can better reach my lips.

Her grip on my shoulders tightens, her fingernails digging into the muscle as I open my mouth and connect my tongue with hers. It feels better than I thought it would, and despite every inch of my body screaming at me to stop, I pull her flush against my front.

I'm vaguely aware of the eyes on us as I let her climb on my lap, our lips connected the entire time. She pushes against my chest until I give in and lie flat on my back, letting her straddle me properly.

My book's long forgotten as Charlie explores my mouth with her tongue, a quiet moan leaving her throat before she cups my chin and squeezes the sides of my neck. It cuts off my oxygen, and I slam my head against the ground as my hips instinctively roll against hers.

This female's going to be the death of me.

"I love you," she whispers, pulling back.

I squeeze my eyes shut, not ready to hear it again.

"Look me in the eyes, Silas," Charlie demands, her voice low as she moves her hand to my chin.

I blink at her, my jaw hanging open as she stares down at me with her big eyes.

"I love you, and someday it won't hurt when I say that. You're going to smile and kiss my forehead like you always did before saying it back," she promises, bringing her lips to my ear. "I want you to say it for the first time while you're fucking me. I want you to cry with how much the emotion's bursting out of you."

My hands clench into fists as I resist the urge to squeeze her.

She giggles, tapping my chin with the tip of her pointer finger. "Do you understand?"

My eyes narrow at her condescending tone, and I tighten my grip on her waist to hold her in place. I'll regret this when she's gone and my arousal no longer clouds my mind, but I couldn't care less right now.

She's an evil tease, and Gray taught her well how to put me on edge.

"Do you understand, Silas?" she repeats.

The door creaks as somebody, probably Gray, pushes it open to peer inside. I'm prepared to ignore it, and I curse Charlie's enhanced hearing as she swivels to see.

Gray steps inside with a frown, but I can smell the lust pouring off him in thick waves.

"Don't tell Silas what to do," he orders.

Charlie hardly seems intimidated, and she straightens up as he stands next to my head. His pants are tented as he glares down at us, but I know his anger is fake. He's only mad because he thinks he should be.

He's been hopelessly in love with Charlie since day one. She could try to kill him, and he'd forgive her with a single bat of her eyes.

His anger's all for show. He just wants her to fight for him.

"Why not?" she teases, staring at him through her eyelashes.

I'm not falling for the innocent act, but I stay silent as Gray immediately falls victim to it. His face softens before he realizes this and plants his little frown back on his lips.

I suck in a shaky breath as he crouches and brings his face to hers, trying and failing to look like he's in charge. It's hard to give the impression of being angry when your dick is leaving a wet stain on the front of your pants.

Charlie notices it, her eyes honing in on the spot to watch as it grows. Gray's been having difficulty holding his arousal in lately, his glands producing more as his body grows used to using it.

"Did you pee yourself?" Charlie giggles, reaching out and trailing her finger along the spot.

She knows damn well what it is, and she takes great pleasure in Gray's embarrassed flush as she pulls back and pops the finger in her mouth. Gray squeezes his eyes shut, refusing to watch as she sucks the liquid off and stands.

Her knees are a bit shaky as its effects hit her, and Gray instinctively reaches out to stabilize her until she's gotten her balance and leaves with her chin held way too high.

"She's playing us," Gray mutters.

I nod, still breathless.

"I kind of like it," he continues.

Again, I nod, propping myself up on my elbows as I stare at the doorway she just left through. She's fucking with my head, and I struggle to wrap my mind around it as I urge my cock to soften. It doesn't, continuing to ache as Gray hums and reaches for my discarded book.

"Put that down," I snap.

He frowns, clearly offended, but returns it to the ground without complaint.

He's not nearly as careful with them as Charlie is.

Chapter Thirty-One

CHARLOTTE

AZIEL LOOKS UP as I shove my way into his office, and he raises his hand in a gesture for me to remain silent while he finishes his conversation. I pin my lips together and sit on his couch, bouncing excitedly.

His eyebrows furrow as he yells at whomever he's speaking to, his words transitioning into the demonic language as his anger grows. It sounds so angry, full of hard consonants and abrupt cut-offs.

I feel bad for the other person on the line, Aziel's tone a reminder of why I was so terrified of him when we first met.

Aziel can be scary when he wants to be.

He slams his phone down with a low grunt before straightening and turning to me. Grinning, he gestures for me to come over as if his angry conversation never happened, and I raise a brow before sliding to his desk.

I sit on the corner of it and swing my legs over his.

"You smell like Silas," he comments.

I dip my head, flushing. I know he heard everything that happened back in the library.

"The shifters will be here soon," I say, glancing at the clock with a nervous sigh.

The shifters are not excited about the number of demons Aziel had to send to their land in order to teleport them here, and they've been changing the meetup location what feels like every hour. Kato's been working hard to have the meeting spot on the wolf lands, his grudge toward them growing the more they push him to allow Echo out to find her mate.

The alpha there is convinced she's his, apparently having smelled her on Kato once.

Kato doesn't believe it, naturally, but I think he's just scared to see her leave. Echo doesn't seem particularly excited about finding her mate yet, either. She calls herself a *free bear* and insists any mate of hers would try to take away her sticks.

"And the Ucka's all prepared?" I ask, desperate for everything to be perfect.

We're going to show the shifters the facility before returning here for dinner. Aziel and Gray got fresh Ucka to eat, and I think the shifters will enjoy it. It's one of their favorites.

I jump when Aziel's office door swings open, and I spin just in time to watch Gray and Silas storm inside. Well, Gray does the storming. Silas walks in calmly behind him.

"All right, let's go," Gray says, clasping his hands together.

My legs accidentally knock against Aziel's shins as I jump off the desk and straighten my clothing. I didn't realize they were coming. Whenever I ask Silas or Gray to join us, they say no with some shitty excuse before running away to hide.

I thought this would be the same, so I didn't bother asking.

"You're coming?" I ask, not caring how evident my excitement is.

Silas acts as if everything in the library didn't just happen as he walks past me and checks the schedule I've drawn out for today. The paper is sitting on Aziel's desk, and he scans it before giving an approving hum and handing it to Gray.

"Yes, we think it'd be best to show a unified front. If not for the shifters, then for the Wraths," Silas explains. "This will be their first time meeting you, and we'd like to ensure they know we're one."

His referring to us as *one* has my heart doing backflips, and I turn to hide my smile. Does this mean he's coming around?

Silas glances at me, his eyes darting to my slightly curled lips before he clears his throat and looks away. I just about burst into tears as his mouth forms a breathtaking smile. It's with teeth and everything.

"Who's taking me?" Gray asks, looking between Silas and Aziel.

Aziel grabs my bicep. "I'll take Charlie." There's a possessive note in his voice that I'm unfamiliar hearing used with Gray or Silas.

Even Gray looks taken aback, and he reaches for Silas with a scoff.

"I didn't want you to take me, anyway," Gray says.

He sounds hurt, and Aziel seems to recognize the pain, too, as he releases me and steps toward Gray. Aziel cups Gray's cheeks and runs his thumbs over his cheekbones before leaning in and kissing him.

Gray immediately moans and sinks into the hold, and I can't help but stare as Aziel tilts his head to the side and takes charge of the kiss. Gray lets him, his eyelids fluttering shut as he succumbs to the desires of the stronger demon.

"I'm yours, Gray," Aziel promises, pulling away. "And I want you just as much as I want Charlie and Silas."

I lean against Aziel's desk as Gray ducks, his cheeks red. It's nice seeing Aziel comfort him like this after all the arguing they've done since I was purchased. I'm not sure what happened between the three of them while I was gone, but whatever it is, I'm happy about it.

Gray's flourishing under all the attention, and Aziel is less irritable.

Silas is acting more unhinged than usual, but I think much of his stress comes from the library mess. He spends all day trying to organize it, and I've heard whispers from Aziel that he's getting behind on his work.

Gray trails his fingers along the mark I left on Aziel's neck. I wasn't thinking when I bit Aziel, and I had no idea I was stealing the spot Gray had claimed. Nobody's outwardly said anything about it, but I can tell it upset Gray.

Aziel doesn't seem to care, but he's not sentimental.

"You want me more," Gray decides.

Silas turns to hide his laughter, and Aziel snorts before giving in with a curt nod.

"Yes, Gray, I want you the most," he agrees.

We all know Aziel doesn't mean it, but Gray enjoys hearing it nonetheless. Gray once privately pulled me aside before everything went to shit and made me tell him I love him more than Silas, and I'm confident he's done the same thing with Silas, too.

I think it's an incubus thing.

Aziel gives Gray one last kiss before returning to me.

He buries his fingers into my waist as he transports me to the facility, the transition smooth and quick. I hold on to his forearm as the room around me materializes. Aziel brought us to the reception area, the place resembling one of those corporate buildings in all the old human movies Gray and I have been watching.

There's a large reception desk built into the wall to the left, and to the right is a lobby with surprisingly comfortable-looking sitting chairs. Very fancy.

The shifters aren't set to arrive for another thirty minutes, but ten Wraths are already waiting in the lobby area. Three are top scientists who worked on the study that led to the female findings, five are employees who used to work in the facility before it was closed, and two are Aziel's war generals. The giant, stern-faced men are impossible to miss, and I shrink into Aziel's side before deciding better of it and stepping away.

Their scent doesn't affect me now that I'm bonded with Aziel, but their imposing figures sure do.

I told Aziel I thought it would be beneficial to have a rehabilitated female here who could discuss her experience, but it seems none were comfortable doing so. They don't care to relive their trauma, nor are they interested in being in a room full of shifter leaders.

Aziel admitted that most Wrath females don't leave the Wrath kingdom. They're fearful of what would happen if they venture too far away, and I remember what Shay told me the ogres did to her when she tried visiting their realm.

It makes me sad, and it explains how Aziel's actions could go undetected for so long. The only people who know about their treatment of females and see the sheer number of young, newborn girls are those who have access to enter Wrath.

That number is low.

I clear my throat and step forward.

I've been working hard to stand my ground, even when surrounded by a group of men I'm uncomfortable with. The Wraths are intimidating, especially the war generals, but my males won't let anybody hurt me.

The Wraths don't bother hiding their contempt as they look me over. I doubt I'm what they wanted in a queen. I clench my hands into tight fists by my sides. *Shit. I'm a queen.*

Silas and Gray show up a second later, and Gray quickly breaks apart from Silas with a scowl. He doesn't like people knowing that Silas and Aziel teleport him places.

"Sir." One of the facility employees steps forward and gives a slight bow in Aziel's direction. "It's an honor to have you here. Would you like a tour before the shifters arrive?"

He doesn't look directly into Aziel's eyes, instead staring at his chest.

"Yes. Has the place been cleaned?" Aziel asks, his voice taking on a tone I'm unfamiliar with.

It's firm and authoritative, and it has me gulping. I want him to talk to *me* like that. His grip on me tightens as he feels my interest through our bond. He knows I like it when he's bossy, and I have a feeling he's been playing nice because of everything going on with Gray and Silas.

The demon nods, turning red as he shuffles his feet and clears his throat.

"Yes, sir."

"Great," Aziel says. "Let's begin."

He nudges me forward, and I ignore all the eyes glaring daggers into me as I follow the demon down the nearest hallway to our left. My males trail behind, their presence bringing me comfort. I'm sure they're doing it on purpose, putting me in a position to lead and show the Wraths my confidence.

The man quickly shows us around, walking us through the spacious bedrooms before moving to the dining area and lounge rooms. This place is thousands of times nicer than the facility I lived in, the walls painted bright colors and the lounge rooms containing enough hobbies to keep even the most obscure person busy.

We return to the main entrance just as the shifters arrive, each teleported by two or three Wrath warriors.

These Wraths give me the same disgusted looks as the others, but I refuse to react. They disapprove of me, which is a bit hurtful. I wasn't expecting Aziel's people to accept me with open arms, but I wasn't anticipating they'd look at me with such hatred.

I know they wanted him to choose somebody with more strength, preferably another demon, and they're both confused and upset I was his choice. Aziel said they should feel happy he has a fate and an incubus. Wraths typically only bond with one person, but Aziel is choosing three.

Two of whom are reputable and strong in the eyes of the Wraths.

Well, Silas is, but his people have already grown used to and come to accept Gray.

A few of the shifters stumble to the room's corners and get sick as they materialize, their backs curving as the travel upsets their stomach. I'm not usually queasy, but the sight has me turning away with a deep heave. Hands wrap around my stomach and move me into a corner, pulling my hair out of my face as I gag.

"This brings back some fun memories." Gray chuckles, referring to the first time he teleported me.

I wince at the memory of getting sick all over his shoes. Gray refuses to let me go as I fix my shirt and clear my throat, feeling weak. I wanted to make a good impression today and vomiting all over the floor isn't exactly showcasing my strength.

The shifters are dramatic in their recovery, loudly shouting at Aziel's men for their painful transitions. Kato and Chev stand to the side, chatting with a worried-looking Aziel. Aziel's eyes dart to me before he places his hand on the nape of Silas's neck, silently keeping the fate from attacking Kato.

I've never seen Silas look at somebody with such hatred, and I find myself intimidated by its intensity. His eyes soften when they land on me, and they slide down my body to ensure I'm okay before returning to Kato.

"Sorry," I say, speaking quietly so only Gray can hear.

He laughs. "It's fine. I'm good with things like this, especially spit-up and poop. I have many little siblings, and I oversaw handling a lot of the day-to-day care when—" Gray's rant is cut short as he notices the glares Aziel and Silas are shooting in his direction.

If looks could kill, he'd be long dead.

Gray quiets and leads me back to Aziel. Aziel quickly wraps me in his arms while we wait for everybody to settle. Some of the more dramatic shifters take a while, but they quiet once they see we're waiting.

"It's unfortunate the travel wasn't ideal for you. I'll provide those of you with weaker stomachs an additional Wrath for your return journey," Aziel says, his words causing everybody to straighten up.

If there's anything the shifters hate, it's being called weak.

I step out of Aziel's arms, not wanting to look like I'm relying on him for support. This is my project, and I want everybody to see that.

"This is one of the largest facilities, and over ten thousand females were successfully assimilated back into Wrath from this building," I say, my voice surprisingly strong. "Women born before the decline stayed for about eight months, usually just until they found work and secured a place to live. The women born after stayed for about four years, learning trades and filling gaps in their education before leaving."

I suck in a deep breath before continuing.

"It took about seven years to reach a point where the facilities were no longer needed, and now there are three females born for every five Wrath couples," I continue, hoping I'm explaining everything properly.

The shifters nod, taking everything in. I pause to see if they have any questions, and I turn to our tour guide when none come up. Everything I just said was detailed in the documents I shared with the shifters the other day, so I hope the lack of questions means they read through it.

Aziel introduces our guide, a tall, muscular demon with a name I struggle to pronounce, before stepping to the side so the shifters can pass. They do so quickly, speaking quietly to themselves and even taking pictures.

I'm sure more than one of them has been told by their mates to bring back images, and I smile as Kato tries to figure out how to use his camera. He's hopeless. Chev ends up taking it from him so he can take the photos himself.

Aziel and the guide take turns answering all the shifters' questions, the men curious about everything from the food served to the amount of money the females were given upon release. They seem intrigued, which is good, and even the most hesitant shifters find something to get excited about during the tour.

We move significantly slower than we did on our trial run, and the guide provides much more detail and color to his explanations. There's a bounce to my step by the time we finish and head home for dinner, and the shifters are much less whiny about their transportation after Aziel's subtle dig.

Aziel pulls me onto his lap when we sit at the dining table, his body warm as he feeds me Ucka and vegetables off his plate. Silas and Gray sit on either side of Aziel and me, and Kato's smart enough to find a spot as far away from the two men as he can get.

Silas won't stop glaring, and I can tell it's making the shifter nervous.

"Well?" Aziel asks, shoving a large piece of Ucka between my teeth. "What do you think?"

"We'll discuss privately and come to you once we've settled

on a decision," Chev says, speaking for the group.

I press my hands to my cheeks and smile, happy it's not an immediate no. That's got to be a good sign. Aziel continues to be a perfect host, supplying everybody with alcohol and Ucka until some more daring men lean back and loosen the ties on their leathers.

I drink water to keep a clear mind, refusing to let myself think too hard about why Aziel's so aggressively keeping the alcohol from me. I want him to tell me himself.

When only Kato and Chev remain, I purse my lips and debate asking about Asmod's body, but a quick glance at Silas tells me I better wait. He's weird about Asmod's death, and I'd rather ask when he's not here.

I trust they're not doing anything bad with Asmod. They probably just stuck him somewhere and forgot about him.

"We've made a decision on the portal," Chev says as Kato stands and gestures for three Wrath guards to take him home.

Gray and Silas lean forward, both anxious to hear the response. They don't love the idea of me going back and forth without one of them present, but I trust the shifters. Aziel does, too, and that says a lot.

"You can build one in your cabin as long as it's not connected to the entire system and only travels here and back. If anybody comes through that's not you, we'll kill them and ask questions later." Chev shoots Gray a warning look.

Gray sinks into his seat with a frown. He was probably excited to use it and terrorize all the females. He knows they have crushes on him.

Kato and Chev leave shortly after, and I spin in Aziel's lap the moment we're alone.

"That was good?" I ask.

He nods and gently pushes me off his lap so he can rush to the bathroom and pee. I watch him leave, loving the way he practically sprints. He must have been holding it for a while.

"I'm hungry." Gray grunts.

He finishes his drink and turns to Silas, his eyes wide and pleading.

"Silas," he whines.

Silas waves him away with a frown, too busy reading something on his phone to entertain the idea.

"I'm busy."

Gray gasps. "Too busy for me?"

"Yes."

I watch the interaction with a soft smile, enjoying the normalcy of this moment. I missed this.

Chapter Thirty-Two

GRAY

CHARLIE'S CLEARLY PISSED as she storms out of Aziel's office. I turn to watch her short legs carry her down the hallway, the limbs pumping. It's nice to know she *can* move faster than a snail's pace.

"Why's Charlie mad at you?" I ask, stepping into Aziel's office.

Aziel frowns and runs a hand through his hair, clearly stressed about whatever Charlie's found herself so pissed about. It's late, and she's usually winding down for bed around this time.

Sleepy Charlie is one of my favorite versions of her—Aziel's too—and I smirk as I realize he's just now learning how quickly it turns into Angry Charlie.

"I don't want to talk about it," he says, shaking his head.

He turns to his computer and reads over something, the man seemingly not feeling the least bit guilty about making Charlie upset. I applaud him for it, remembering how quick I was to chase after her and apologize.

Silas was a little better than me, usually searching for a compromise, but Aziel is unwavering. He dotes on her, but he has no issue making her angry.

I listen to her storm upstairs, her bare feet loud against the wooden steps.

"Have you gotten a response from the shifters yet?" I ask, leaning against the doorframe.

"Yes."

I roll my eyes when Aziel offers no further explanation. Why does he always need to be so damn elusive?

"And what did they say?" I pry, annoyance seeping into my tone.

"They want the final say on regulations, and they want to decide on the punishments for those who disobey." Aziel rubs his temples with a low sigh. "They also want to take the lead in hiring and managing the social workers."

Aziel's not used to giving up power, and the shifters are asking for a lot. They've already reached out four times this week to demand changes to the decisions Aziel's made.

Charlie has no issues giving in to the shifter demands. I don't like her lack of faith in us, but I know it's justified. It's not like we've proven to be the most reliable regarding females.

"And you said *yes*?" I ask, taking a seat on Aziel's couch.

His jaw clenches. "Charlie said *yes* before discussing it with me." He glares at the door she disappeared through.

Ah. So that's why they're fighting.

I like Charlie's initiative on this, and I can't help but chuckle at how it's so clearly upsetting Aziel. I'm sure many things she does drive him insane, the woman headstrong.

I continue to watch Aziel work, the silence between us growing as he frowns and types away at his computer. He hasn't fed me since returning, and I'm debating trying with him when he lifts his head and locks eyes with me.

"Will you check on her?" he asks.

I frown, unsure if that's a good idea.

"You're good at calming her down," he continues. "Better than I am."

I flush, happy with the compliment. I *am* the best at calming Charlie, the female quick to anger but even quicker to be settled with a few soft touches and kind words.

"I suppose," I say.

Aziel doesn't react, but our bond tightens as I stand and leave. He wants us to forgive her more than he lets on, and I don't know how to feel about that. Every part of me wants to forgive Charlie, to squeeze her in my arms and claim her as mine, but something in me resists.

It'd be easier to push her away if she weren't bonded to Aziel. Knowing she'll be in my life indefinitely makes keeping my distance feel pointless, especially when she's dead set on having us back.

My thoughts continue to race as I make my way to Aziel's bedroom. I don't smell her, and I move from his bedroom to his lounge area before scratching the back of my head and heading down my wing.

Maybe she wants to be in her old bedroom? All of her knickknacks are still in there.

"Charlie?" I call out.

Her bond with Aziel allows him to keep tabs on her location and emotions, so I know she's still in our home. He'd be breaking down walls the second she left the manor.

I don't find her in her bedroom or mine, and I clench my jaw as I make my way to Silas's. Where the fuck did she disappear to?

Charlie is a sneaky woman. I push Silas's bedroom door open with a huff, my eyes scanning the space before I turn and walk to the bedroom we had built to share. I know she's upstairs, and this is the only place left. I shift my weight as I stare down the corridor, my heart clenching painfully.

She's been careful to avoid the room, and even though I've caught her peering down the hallway with a wobbly bottom lip a few times, she's never tried to come inside. Her scent intensifies as I make my way down the hallway, and it's overpowering as I push open the bedroom door.

I listen to her racing heart as I slide my hand along the wall and flick on the light.

Charlie blinks as her eyes adjust to the sudden brightness.

I cross my arms over my chest and lean against the doorframe.

"What're you doing?" I ask.

Charlie grunts and sits up. She's not wearing a shirt, and I follow the slope of her neck before eyeing her exposed breasts. Her arms twitch as she fights the urge to cover herself, the human still shy about being seen bare.

"I was sleeping," she lies.

I raise a brow, letting her know I don't believe it. Her heart was beating too fast, and she's much too alert for having just woken up. Charlie needs a good ten minutes before being able to form a sentence.

"Why are you in here?" I ask.

"Aziel told me he doesn't allow brats in his bed."

I resist the urge to laugh. I doubt he meant she couldn't sleep with him. Charlie's clenched jaw tells me she already knows that, though, and she's playing stupid to piss him off.

It'll work.

"I went to my old bedroom, but you stripped the sheets and Silas told me to stay when I came here to ask where they were," she continues, lying back down.

I stare at her, frozen, as she adjusts the blankets around her shoulders and pulls them up to her neck. What the fuck?

Silas *would* tell her to stay instead of helping her search for fresh sheets—any excuse to keep her close. I have half a mind to leave and find somewhere else to sleep, but I'll be damned if I get kicked out of my bed by some tiny little human.

I shoot her my frostiest glare as I strip bare, and Silas turns off the shower just as I crawl into bed next to Charlie. She's taken my spot, and I gently nudge her before grabbing her hips and rolling her when she refuses to budge.

My bed. My spot.

"Hey!" she snaps.

"Move!" I snap right back, but I fail to hold any actual anger.

If anything, I'm excited to watch Aziel realize she's not in his bed. He'll come to collect her, and I have a feeling she's not going to go without a fight.

Then I'll get to listen to him punish-fuck her into his mattress.

Silas wastes time in the bathroom, probably trying to give me time to calm down, before joining us. His footsteps pause as he sees Charlie and me glaring at one another, her arms crossed over her chest as I sprawl and claim my spot.

He flicks off the light and climbs into bed, smartly deciding not to ask.

I gulp as we lie side by side in the dark. This feels awkward.

"I can hear your hearts beating when it's quiet like this," Charlie whispers.

The sheets move as Silas turns toward her, his face scrunched as he struggles to respond. I offer no help, having no idea what to say. Interacting with her during the day is one thing, but it's different when we lie next to one another in the dark.

This feels intimate.

Thin fingers curl around my wrist, and I know Silas is receiving the same treatment as his heart begins to race. Charlie squeezes, her touch warm and a bit sweaty.

I want to pull her against me like I used to, but instead, I lie still, unmoving.

Silas does the same, his body just as stiff as mine. Charlie probably wants us to make the first move, the act of touching our wrists alone sending her pulse into a scary pace.

I turn and scan her profile, hoping she can't see me in the dark. Her eyesight has improved since bonding with Aziel, but I have no idea how much. The way her eyes dart over my face tells me she can't see well, so I continue staring.

"Gray," she says, pausing with a grimace as Aziel squeezes our bonds.

She doesn't breathe for a moment, the intensity of his anger more than she anticipated. I smirk and shake my wrist free. I'm excited to see what comes of this.

It takes only seconds for Aziel to come barreling inside the room, the man not even bothering to turn on the light as he crawls onto our bed. The sheets are pulled down, the sudden chill earning a groan from both Silas and me.

"Care to tell me why the fuck my bed is empty?" Aziel snaps, reaching for Charlie's leg.

She kicks, hitting him square in the chest.

I raise a brow. I didn't see that coming.

"You told me you don't allow brats in your bed," she says, her breathy voice giving away her excitement.

Aziel sucks in his cheeks and rubs at where she kicked him. His nostrils flare as he breathes in her arousal, and I subtly feed on it as I wait to see where this leads.

"You're excited for your punishment," Aziel observes.

Charlie falls silent, the female not having a retort for the first time in forever. He's right, though. She loves pissing him off, and even more than that, she loves the way he fucks her after. She's a brat through and through.

"Silas told me I could sleep in here," she squeaks, backing up against the headboard.

Aziel blinks at her and cocks his head to the side.

"You're willing to go to such extremes to get me to fuck you, baby, when all you have to do is ask," he says, his voice deceptively soft.

Charlie licks her bottom lip as her muscles soften. His voice soothes her, and I take great pleasure in watching her lower her head and give a jerky nod. She's a fool.

Aziel crawls the rest of the way up her body.

I watch, excited, as he brings his lips down on hers. Is he going to fuck her in here? I expected him to take her back to his room, but I'm not against him doing it here. I usually have to wait until she falls asleep before sneaking into Aziel's room and feeding on the residual lust, but it's better when it's fresh.

And it makes me look less desperate.

Aziel buries his head in her neck, inhaling, before pulling away and turning to me. I nod, assuming he's asking permission to take her in our bed.

"But you didn't ask, did you, Charlie?" Aziel asks, grabbing my leg and yanking me flat on my back.

I grunt. What the fuck? He turns and crawls over me, his movements predatory. It takes everything in me not to moan as his body cages in mine. He hasn't been intimate with me since returning, at least not to the level I'd like, and I'm desperate for the attention.

"No," Charlie breathes. "I didn't ask."

Aziel grins, happy with her answer, before bringing his lips to mine. His tongue slips into my mouth when I gasp, and he quickly takes charge of our kiss as he slots himself between my thighs. I'm already naked, my cock hard and heavy where it rests on my belly.

Aziel kicks off his clothes as Silas sits up to see better.

"You can't cum by anything other than a thigh tonight, Charlie, and ours are busy," Aziel says, his smile growing when she grows stiff and glances at Silas.

I want to ensure they're both taken care of, and I'm glad Aziel seems to be on the same page as we wait for Silas to reach for Charlie. He curls his fingers around her waist and pulls her back against his chest, and when his hand slides down her torso, I turn back to Aziel.

He grabs and squeezes my dick, his grip firm as he forces out my arousal. A thick amount leaks from my tip, and I groan as he covers himself with it.

"When was the last time you were fucked?" Aziel asks.

I moan, my breath hitching. Is he going to fuck me? My eyes slam shut as I try to remember.

"A long time ago, maybe twenty or so years," I answer, my voice breathy.

Aziel grins, stroking himself as he plants a hand next to my head and brings his mouth to me. His kiss is soft, and I feed on everybody's lust as he runs the length of his cock along mine.

Fuck.

Aziel subtly turns toward Silas and Charlie, checking on them.

I run my hands down Aziel's back as Silas guides Charlie onto his thigh. They're facing us, and Charlie plants her hands into the mattress as she rocks against Silas's muscular leg.

Silas licks his lips and grips his cock before grabbing her hips to help guide her. His hands flex as he teaches her what to do, and a soft smile spreads over his lips as he meets my eye. Silas may prefer to sub, but that doesn't mean he can't step into other roles when the moment calls for it.

Charlie and Aziel may be new to sex, but at least Silas doesn't need coaching.

Aziel turns back to me and runs his hands down my abs,

feeling the muscle before clearing his throat and meeting my eye.

"How much prep do you need?" he asks.

I rock my hips.

"None, if you use my arousal," I say, taking hold of my cock and squeezing out some more.

My body will open easily for him, and my arousal will ensure I don't feel any pain. Aziel holds my knees and leans back as I coat his cock with more, ensuring he's nice and covered before I nod and let go.

I practically hyperventilate as I struggle to absorb all the lust in the air, not wanting any of it to go to waste. Aziel grins, his eyes soft as he stares down at me.

"You know I love you, right?" he asks, clearing his throat before looking at Silas and Charlie. "All of you. I love all of you," he clarifies.

Charlie nods, her cheeks red as Silas continues to help guide her. The sweet thing still hasn't gotten the act of riding down.

"Yes, yes, we love you too. Fuck him, please," she begs, her eyes wide as she watches us.

Silas agrees with a jerky nod, his cock leaking against his abs as Charlie bumps into it with each movement.

Aziel doesn't need any further encouragement, his attention sliding to my ass. He grabs my balls and holds them against my body so he can better see, and he sucks his bottom lip between his teeth as he lines himself up and sinks inside.

I gasp and place a hand on his chest to stop him. He pauses, giving me a moment to adjust. It feels so fucking good, but it's a lot.

Aziel is big.

He slides his fingers up my torso, tickling my skin, before tracing the vein on the underside of my cock. It jolts, and I clench around him when he does it again.

"Okay," I say, wiggling my hips as I urge him to continue.

Aziel hesitates, seemingly worried about hurting me, before continuing forward. He releases a low moan as he bottoms out, his hips flush against mine.

"I'm not going to last long," I warn, already holding back an orgasm.

The lust in this room is too much, and I squeeze my cock as I try to hold it back. Aziel doesn't look much better than me as he thrusts. He doesn't need to be nearly as gentle with me as with Charlie, but he doesn't seem to realize that as he eases himself in and out at a painfully slow pace.

I smile, proud of how well I've taught him, as I curl a hand around his neck and bring his ear to my mouth.

"I'm not going to break, baby," I whisper, licking his neck. "Fuck me."

He seems hesitant as he pulls back and stares down at me, and I drive my hips up hard to prove my point. It seems to do the trick as he curls his fingers around the front of my neck, and he shifts his weight onto that hand as he leans over me and drives his hips forward.

I choke out a moan, struggling to breathe, which only seems to spur Aziel further on.

He grunts, burying himself deep into me. "Fucking take it."

I squeeze around his cock and stroke myself as he thrusts.

Charlie cries as she watches us, her noises quiet and pretty. "P-Please," she begs.

Aziel turns and gives Silas the go-ahead, and Silas doesn't hesitate to shift Charlie and finally let her rub her clit directly against his thigh. It takes only a few rocks for her to cum, and Silas pushes her onto her belly so he can jerk himself off and cum on her ass.

I breathe it in, sinking my nails into Aziel's shoulders before grabbing his neck and yanking him down.

My eyes land on Charlie's mark before I sink my teeth into the spot below it, careful not to mess up hers. I've grown attached to her small bite, even if it's in the area I initially wanted.

Aziel moans as I claim him, his cock twitching as he also rips open my skin with his teeth. It hurts, but the pain's all I need to be pushed over the edge. My orgasm triggers Aziel's, and he convulses inside me as I cum on myself.

I let him catch his breath before moving my hips once more. Aziel seems shocked as he stares down at my still-hard length.

"Again," I beg.

Aziel nods, rocking his softening cock inside me until I tense around him and finish again. I know it hurts by the way he clenches his jaw and grunts, another orgasm forced from his body.

He looks relieved as he sees my length begin to soften, and an audible sigh slips from his lips as he pulls back and falls out of me.

He'll have to get used to that. My body is greedy after so many years of our bond being abandoned.

"So you love me, huh?" I tease, grinning.

Aziel rolls his eyes and ensures Charlie's good with Silas before collapsing on his back between her and me. She curls against his chest immediately, her head buried in his armpit.

"We sleep in here from now on," Aziel says, smiling when I hurry to grab us wet towels.

Silas has found himself captive to the tiny human by the time I return, his body relaxed as she hooks an arm around his neck and holds him against her side. My lips twitch, and I clean him up before turning and repeating the action to Charlie and Aziel.

I take care of myself last.

This is all I've ever wanted. I take a moment to look at all three of my mates before crawling into bed on the other side of

Aziel. He shifts when I press my face against his shoulder, and I prepare to pull away when he hooks his arm around my neck and pulls my head onto his chest.

I wiggle further into him.

"I never would've guessed I'd end up with two mates who enjoy shoving their faces in my armpits," Aziel says, patting my shoulder.

I ignore him. This is nice.

Chapter Thirty-Three

AZIEL

HANDS SQUEEZE MY waist, and I grunt and smack at them as they pull me from my sleep.

"That's enough, Charlie."

"I haven't done shit."

My eyes snap open as her voice echoes across the room. She's standing in front of the dresser, struggling to squeeze into one of the exercise bras Gray first bought her when she arrived. It's too small on her now, my female having filled out these past few months.

Good.

I wouldn't say I'm a big fan of her exercise bras. The tight fabric pushes down her breasts until they're flat against her chest, and I prefer the easy access I have when she's not wearing one.

Plus, it's satisfying to see proof of how much she's filled out while with us. She was much too small when we first got her.

Gray snorts, and I look down to see him kneeling at her feet. He's helping to return the clothing he and Silas removed from the dresser drawers. His lips twitch as he watches her, and I can feel the bond between us humming as he finds excitement in being able to serve her.

He sets down the clothing and stands as Charlie continues to struggle, the man eager to help.

"I think it's time we get you a bigger size," he says, unrolling the elastic and flattening it against her back.

Charlie stills and levels a glare at the poor incubus as he grins and rubs her belly. Gray only further digs his grave as he comments on how well the shifters fed her. Silas clears his throat, capturing Gray's attention so he can give a subtle shake of his head.

"Thanks, Gray," Charlie snaps, her face turning red.

Gray frowns, seemingly sensing she's upset but unsure what about. He hesitates, debating whether or not to push it, before huffing and returning to her clothing.

How long have these two been awake bickering with one another? I'm usually waking with the slightest noise, and I'm shocked I slept through it for so long. It probably has to do with the two content bonds vibrating gently in my chest. They're soothing, and I rub my sternum with a soft smile.

Is this how it could have always felt with Gray?

I turn and bring my attention to the sleepy man on my right. Silas still doesn't wear my mark, saving his first bond for Charlie, and I'm running out of patience. I trail my finger across his neck before pressing into the spot where I intend to claim him.

His black eyes blink open before narrowing, annoyed with my touch. Still, he doesn't pull away as he drops his head back on my chest. I didn't take him for a cuddler.

Gray kicked me away in the middle of the night, his bony limbs pushing into my back until I rolled over and gave him space. Charlie did something similar, the woman groaning and wiggling whenever I tried to touch her.

I understand now why they insisted on such a big bed.

"What time is it?" I ask the room, slipping my fingers through Silas's hair.

Charlie responds, but I'm sleepy and don't listen to her answer.

Silas is hard against me, but neither of us comments on it.

He doesn't have a lot of interest in being fucked, and he probably won't ask for it often. It's a shame, but I'm much more interested in watching Charlie torment him, anyway. She likes having somebody to boss around, and Silas is more than willing to be that person.

Silas smacks his lips and climbs out of bed, and I resist the urge to grab him as his hard length brushes against my thigh. *Mine.*

He may not wear my mark, but he is mine just the same.

Last night was good for us, and even though there's a lot we still need to work through, things are looking better.

My males are more comfortable around Charlie, no longer skirting around the room or subtly moving away whenever she gets too close. Silas even goes out of his way to brush against her as he heads to the bathroom, his hand sliding across the exposed skin of her lower back.

They still haven't completely forgiven her, but it's a step in the right direction.

"We're getting the portal set up today," I say, enjoying how Charlie squeaks.

There's a pep in her step as she urges us to hurry up and finish dressing. I eye her as I throw on some clothes, grudgingly following her orders.

The portal in her cabin back on the shifter lands was completed two days ago, and they should have one in our manor finished this morning.

I resist the urge to carry Charlie when her shoulder lightly hits the doorframe on her way out of our room. I know it didn't hurt, but my need to keep her and my baby safe outweighs reason. I'm excited to tell her she's pregnant.

Silas says we should wait until it's been a few weeks and the risk of miscarriage drops, but I'm growing impatient.

"You smell nice," I compliment, sniffing the back of her neck as we walk downstairs.

She swats at me, and I pull away with a quiet laugh.

Gray glances at me out of the corner of his eye, and my laughter grows as I wrap my arm around his shoulder and bury my face in his mop of curly hair.

"You smell nice, too," I whisper.

"Obviously," he mutters, pushing me away before jogging to walk next to Charlie.

Silas approaches on my right.

"It seems we've been replaced," he says.

I shrug. They keep one another entertained, and I'm too happy seeing them freely interact to feel any jealousy over their rejection of my affection. I'm sure Silas is pleased by it, too. He's been doing his best to remain patient, but I can tell Gray's been getting on his nerves recently.

Silas likes space.

Charlie's footsteps slow when she sees the Wrath demons setting up the portal, but I gently nudge her forward with a soft pat on the butt. They know better than to look at her.

It didn't take long for word to spread of the punishment the men who glared at her at the facility received. It took everything in me not to address it then and there, not wanting to embarrass Charlie, but they won't be making that mistake again.

She's their queen, and they'll do well to treat her as such.

Charlie leads us to the dining room, and we all sit at the table to eat. This normalcy feels nice, and I can tell through the bonds that Charlie and Gray feel the same way. I assume Silas is pleased by it as well.

We eat in comfortable silence, and Gray happily loads up our plates with human breakfast food.

"Where do you think you're going?" I ask when Charlie gets up to leave.

Gray snickers while Silas chews and sets down his fork. Charlie turns to me with a wide grin, her head jerking toward the hallway the Wraths are working in. She's been staring at the doorway this entire meal, the female excited for the portal to be finished.

"Is it almost done?" she whispers, her voice low.

I don't like that she feels the need to whisper in her own home, and I pretend I can't hear her until she asks the question at a normal volume.

"They should be wrapping up," I say, standing and leading her to the broom closet we had converted into the portal.

I'm not exactly pleased with the loss of another closet, and even less so that Gray and Silas voted that the supplies be put in my office this time, but there's not much to be done about it.

There are dozens of closets throughout the estate, but I've collected many things over the years and filled up each one. I don't want to get rid of anything, either, much to Gray's and Silas's annoyance.

Charlie's pulse races as she watches the Wraths work, my demons meticulous in ensuring everything's adequately configured before turning to me with a nod and disappearing. I feel Charlie's excitement grow the second they leave, and I can't help but smile as I lead her to the portal.

We had the closet door removed so she could go in and out directly from the hallway, and we put the portal close to our offices so we could monitor its activity. I don't want Charlie sneaking off again.

Silas comes over to assist when it becomes clear I don't know how to turn the portal on. I never use them, so I never bothered to learn.

"I'm going to put in permissions so you can only travel to and from the shifter lands," Silas says, moving so she can't see the code he's using to lock access to the grid.

Charlie frowns and tries to peer around him. "I'm not a child."

No, but she is carrying mine. I smell her again, humming at the potency of my baby in her. I could sense it the moment the embryo implanted, and it grows stronger each day.

My baby is strong.

"I know, but I'm not risking you accidentally ending up in a dangerous land," Silas retorts, not missing a beat.

Charlie sucks in her cheeks, preparing to argue, but pauses when the portal begins to vibrate.

It looks like nothing more than an open doorway when off, but it becomes a blue haze when active. It rings as Charlie admires it, the alarm Silas set to go off whenever somebody turns it on or comes through.

Silas steps back just as Gray walks around the corner to see what's happening.

I shouldn't be surprised that the shifters have taken it upon themselves to be the first ones to use the portal, and I run a hand down my face at the realization of what I've just done. They have no fucking boundaries.

Chev comes barreling through a second later, the man clearly inexperienced with portals as he slams full-speed into the opposite wall.

"You don't need to run through it, dumbass." I huff, watching him wince and rub a spot on his head.

He cracked my wall, but other than that, he looks relatively unharmed. Kato comes running through a second later, his body slamming into Chev, who gets flattened against the wall once more. I watch Silas as the older shifter starts to panic and coddle his son.

He hates Kato, and he has no issues letting that be known.

I'm not a fan, either, and I'm annoyed he's using the portal when I explicitly told him he wasn't allowed.

"Welcome!" Charlie laughs, her eyes darting between the two.

Gray steps forward and nudges her through the portal. They disappear into the blue haze, and immediately, I feel our bonds tighten at the distance. It's uncomfortable, and I shuffle my feet until they return with wide grins.

"It works?" Silas asks.

Charlie nods and clasps her hands together as Echo appears behind her. Kato falls silent, his bantering with Chev ending as he spins and glares at his daughter.

"Go home," he orders.

I lean against the wall as Charlie grimaces, but I move to stand between her and the shifters when it becomes clear Kato is agitated.

We are the only angry males she should be around.

"You don't own me. I have every right to be here," Echo snaps.

Chev places a hand on his father's arm and shakes his head. Kato angrily stands down, and Echo turns to look around our home with a slack jaw. The awe on her face is a bit surprising, and I feel horrible as I realize it's because she's never left the shifter lands before.

Guilt slams into me like a freight truck. I'm partially to blame for that.

Shifters have always kept their females hidden, but it's never been this bad. Before the female decline, they were allowed to explore and have lives outside their realm.

Echo's attention flickers from me to Silas. She scans the man with narrowed eyes before turning to Gray. There's a lethality in her stance that I often see Charlie trying to imitate, a slight crouch with wide legs that keeps her rooted to the floor.

I see why Charlie likes her so much. She's who my female wants to be.

Echo's arousal fills my lungs when she looks at Gray, the action earning a warning growl from both the shifter males standing next to her. I'm grateful Charlie can't smell it. She'd have trouble understanding that Echo can't control it.

Gray's an incubus, and just because Charlie's gotten used to the scent doesn't mean others aren't affected.

"Like what you see?" Gray teases, the corner of his lip twitching as Echo's face grows red.

Charlie's end of the bond yanks, the action borderline painful. My nose scrunches as I turn to her, surprised by the intense jealousy I feel. She looks between Gray and Echo with a frown, and her wide eyes grow panicked as Echo lets out a nervous giggle.

Gray would never touch the shifter, but I still feel agitated that my pregnant mate is angry. My jaw clenches as I suck in a deep breath, fighting to remain calm so I don't do something I regret.

Charlie would hate me if I killed her friend.

Gray seems to notice our reaction as he moves to stand behind Charlie. His hands land on her hips, the action a silent claim, before he rests his chin on her head.

I'm happy to see Gray taking the initiative to settle her as he used to. He's always been good at it, and I'd bet money he only spoke to Echo to see how Charlie would respond.

Gray loves it when people are jealous over him, the man very much an incubus in that sense.

"You have any leftover Ucka?" Chev asks, changing the subject.

I blink. Is he seriously looking to raid my fridge?

Chev holds my gaze, his head cocked slightly to the side until I give in and gesture toward the kitchen. He straightens with a grin and tries to knock his knuckles against my head as he passes.

I smack at his hand, sick and tired of him constantly trying to do that. I don't like it when he does it to Charlie, either, even if she seems to enjoy it.

Chev wanders off without another word, the giant man looking almost goofy as he searches for my kitchen. I summon a shadow to follow him, not wanting the shifter to have free rein in my house.

I need to get a guard on this portal.

"Great, it works. You can leave now," I inform Kato.

He says something, but I don't listen as the air to my left moves.

I step in front of Charlie and Gray just as Rock materializes into the space. He stumbles, taking a moment to get his bearings before turning to me. He's smeared in blood, the sight concerning.

Kato shoves Echo through the portal before slamming on the panel until it's turned off. I'd find the way he flung her funny if Rock weren't looking at me like he were about to shit himself.

"Valentine's taken over Lust." He gasps, holding his chest as he struggles to catch his breath.

He must have been running before he teleported.

"I'm aware," I say.

Taking the Lust Kingdom from her won't be hard. All the Lust demons care about is fucking, and becoming a part of Wrath only makes that easier for them. They fuck, Wraths protect.

We just need to get Asmod's body back from the shifters first. Having it will strengthen Gray's claim to the throne.

"You don't understand," Rock argues, shaking his head. "She's aligned herself with Mammon and the ogres. They've got an army and are planning to attack."

Charlie's hands bury into the waistband of my pants, her fear pulling at our bond.

Fuck. I can't say I saw that one coming.

Valentine's only been leading Lust for two weeks, but I shouldn't be surprised she's managed to weasel her way into my affairs in that short time. She's always been cunning.

"When?" Silas asks.

I'm not sure I want the answer.

"They're mobilizing troops now."

* * *

END OF BOOK TWO

STAY CONNECTED

SOCIAL MEDIA

Follow Invi Wright on social media to stay up to date on her newest releases, listen to her gab about romance & fantasy books, get regular book recs, and join a fun community of romance lovers!

TikTok & Instagram: @inviwright

EXCLUSIVE CONTENT & CHARACTER ART

Subscribe to **@inviwright** on Patreon for:

- Exclusive access to ongoing novellas
- Exclusive audio chapters
- SFW and NSFW character art
- Partake in polls (help decide what book she'll write next!)
- A free ebook copy of every book she publishes

COMPLETED WORKS

STANDALONES

The Nanny | A Nanny/Single Father Romance
Lord of Dread | An Arranged Marriage Historical Romance
Aine | A Dark Shifter Romance

THE FEMALE SERIES

The Female is a why choose demon romance with a dark dystopian setting, declining fertility rates, captured women, and three irresistible men.

The Female
Her Males
Their War
Chev's Mate
Queens

THE CURSED KINGDOM SERIES

The Cursed Kingdom is a slow burning, why choose romance with a mystical faerie realm, two infuriatingly attractive princes, and high conflict between the faerie and shifter kingdoms.

The Cursed Kingdom
The Shattered Kingdom

TRIGGER WARNINGS CAN BE FOUND ON:

inviwright.com

UPCOMING WORKS

STANDALONES

His Assignment | A Bodyguard Mafia Romance (Coming 2026)
The Dragon's Agreement | A Dragon Fantasy Romance (Release Date TBD)

LAND OF WOLVES DUOLOGY

Land of Wolves is a high intensity shifter romance with fated mates, government indoctrination that leads to painful betrayal, and impending war between the shifters and humans.
Land of Wolves | Part One (Coming 2026)
Land of Wolves | Part Two (Release Date TBD)

ONGOING SERIES

Fates | Book Six of *The Female* Series (Release Date TBD)
The Hidden Kingdom | Book Three of *The Cursed Kingdom* Series (Release date TBD)

Made in the USA
Monee, IL
13 August 2025

23273074R00229